# The Prod

Kal Spriggs

**Books by Kal Spriggs**

*The Shadow Space Chronicles*

*The Renegades*

Renegades: Origins
Renegades: Out of the Cold (Forthcoming)

*The Lightbringer Trilogy*
The Fallen Race
The Shattered Empire
The Prodigal Emperor

*The Eoriel Saga*

Echo of the High Kings
Wrath of the Usurper
Fate of the Tyrant (Forthcoming)

*The Star Portal Universe*

*The Rising Wolf*

Fenris Unchained
Odin's Eye (Forthcoming)

**Table of Contents**

Prologue....1
Chapter One....8
Chapter Two....33
Chapter Three....58
Chapter Four....75
Chapter Five....96
Chapter Six....118
Chapter Seven....148
Chapter Eight....174
Chapter Nine....199
Chapter Ten....216
Chapter Eleven....235
Chapter Twelve....261
Chapter Thirteen....274
Chapter Fourteen....290
Chapter Fifteen....309
Chapter Sixteen....335
Chapter Seventeen....344
Diagrams....360

## Prologue

Halcyon Colony, Garris Major System
Contested
November 20, 2403

Captain Garret Penwaithe swished the cheap liquor around his mouth for a moment, just long enough to numb his taste buds enough that he could swallow it without gagging.

"This is your idea of a date?" Ensign Abigail Gordon asked – shouted really – over the raucous music that rattled the rickety table at which they sat.

"This is not a date," Garret growled, irritated as much with himself as with her for the statement. The War Dogs were a mercenary organization, so they were quite a bit more lax on things like fraternization than the military. Even so, he was *not* about to date the little sister of his ex-girlfriend. Especially since his ex-girlfriend was now married to his older brother. *For one thing,* he thought glumly, *even if it wasn't wrong in so many ways, Jessica would kill me.*

"I mean," Abigail shouted, "the food is terrible, the setting is worse, why even come here?" She wasn't wrong. The bar was a dive, one which was overrun by mercenaries and privateers of the worst sort, brought here by the call of loot to be taken in the fight against the Colonial Republic. Few of them cared that Halycon Colony fought for freedom. Fewer still had any real loyalty to the government that had hired them. Many of them were the type of scum that followed Admiral Mannetti. Almost on cue, across the room, he saw the pirate, Stavros Heraklion, step through the door, followed by two women from his crew.

*Great,* he thought, *when this goes down, I'll need to remember to watch my back, especially with his grudge against the War Dogs.* He wished that the Commodore had told him more about *why* he and Stavros hated each other so much.

Abigail cleared her throat impatiently and Garret sighed, "You mentioned nightmares, problems sleeping? This is the best way I know to blow off some steam and get your mind level." *Well,* he thought, *not the best way, but I'm not going to tell you to go get laid.* He might give that advice to some of his other recruits, but he didn't want Abigail to take that the wrong way.

"Hey," a voice growled from behind him, "pretty girl, what you doing with this loser? Me and my friends are a lot more fun."

*Right on cue,* Garret thought. He glanced over his shoulder to see one of the privateers he had seen at the bar earlier. "Get lost," Garret said.

"Yeah, get lost," Abigail echoed. She looked back at Garret, "What do you mean by blow off some steam?" Her upturned nose and freckles made her look absurdly young.

"Heya, girly, I don't think you understand," the privateer leaned over the table and even over his unwashed stink of body odor and sweat, Garret could smell the alcohol on his breath. "That wasn't an invitation, it was a warning. This worm here is wearing a War Dogs uniform. You sit with him much longer and you might get grouped with him."

"The War Dogs are great!" Abigail said, her voice far louder than she had realized. "How about you get lost, asshole!"

Garret heard stools scrape across the floor behind him as the privateer's friends stood up. The privateer leaning over the table gave a snarl and pushed Abigial, hard, so that she and her chair fell back. She rolled to her feet and brought her hands up defensively. *Good reflexes,* Garret noted.

Garret slammed his elbow into the man's midriff and as the privateer grunted and bent over, he grabbed him by his dreadlocks and smashed his face into the table top. The flimsy table collapsed, but the privateer went down with it. Garret wiped his hands on his pants, he *hated* dreadlocks.

Garret saw the man's friends start forward out of the corner of his eye. He stood from his chair in a smooth, easy motion. His two meter tall frame rose over the other men and his black face split in a grin that showed them even, white teeth. He saw a couple of them step back in fear. *Well,* Garret thought cheerfully, *I can be one imposing son of a bitch when I want.*

Abigail came up beside him, "What's going on?" she asked.

"A good way to work some of that out is a nice bar fight," Garret said just loud enough for her to hear. He cocked his head as he recognized the purple uniforms of the privateers. "Say, you're from the *Damien Walters*, eh? Should have known a bunch of cowards who'd stand by and watch their captain gunned down wouldn't have the balls for a real fight." Garret didn't know the details, but he had heard that Stavros had gunned down their captain in a duel.

Imposing or not, they came at him. *I guess that was a sore point,* Garret thought as he caught the first man and used him as a shield against two of the others. After a moment he threw his man into another and watched them both go down.

"How is this supposed to help me?" Abigail said as she ducked under a wild swing and then smashed the bottle of cheap liquor across the man's head. Someone cut the music and the shattering glass carried clearly through the bar. Garret winced as the pungent brew stung his nose and eyes in a way that only rotgut liquor could.

Garret caught another man's swing and diverted him into the other two as they struggled to their feet. The three stayed down and Garret grunted in disgust, "Eh, not much of a fight anyway..."

He heard tables and chairs shifting behind him, then and glanced over to see a lot more of the purple uniforms come out of the crowd. "Or... I could be wrong."

Garret lost track of Abigail as a wave of purple uniforms washed over them. Garret was a brawler and though he'd some hand to hand training, which always seemed to go out the window in a fight like this. He caught up his chair and used it to fend two of his attackers away and kicked another man in the crotch as he came at him from the side.

Garret didn't see the fourth man until the blow caught him from the other side. His attacker hit him again, this time in the side of the head and Garret stumbled to the ground, his ears ringing. He grunted as someone kicked him in the ribs.

He had time to shake his head and clear it a bit, just as he saw one of the privateers draw his pistol. A few meters away, he saw two others held Abigail by her arms. The one with the pistol called out, "He's one of the War Dogs. You heard what Admiral Mannetti said, some of them dies in a bar fight and she might well cut that crew some extra shares."

Garret felt his blood go cold. Suddenly this had escalated far beyond a friendly bar brawl. *Stupid*, he thought, *I shouldn't have forgotten about the politics down here and now not just me, but Abigail will be paying the price too.*

"We can have a bit of fun with this one, first, eh?" One of Abigail's captors said as he ran a hand through her blonde hair.

She spat in his face and almost pulled her arm free.

Garret saw the man's arm go back to strike her. Before he could finish the blow, someone caught his hand and stopped it. A tall man, dressed in skin-tight, red leather pants and a white button-down shirt, open to the waist stood behind the privateer. Garret instantly recognized Captain Stavros Heraklion although he had no idea why the captain had stopped the blow. The privateer tried to free his hand, but Stavros held him with little apparent effort, "Ah, I see that striking women is something that Captain Walters trained your crew on, eh, boys?"

The tone of threat in his voice was enough to penetrate the drunkest of the bar crowd. The handful of patrons that hadn't backed away or cleared out made for the door. Behind Stavros, the two women from his crew stood, hands on weapons.

The privateer with a pistol glanced down at his weapon, as if to reassure himself. "*Stavros*," he spat the name like a curse. "This is none of your business."

"Oh, I think it is," Stavros said. He gave a nod at Garret, "Now, while I can appreciate getting the upper hand in a fight like this, well, he's been assigned to my squadron. As much as I... dislike the War Dogs, well, you put him down and it'll take his gunboats out of the fight. You do that, and it'll make *me* look bad."

He released the privateer's hand and stepped to the side. "And as for her... well, slapping around a woman is something I think it best to discourage, unless they're into that sort of thing." He leaned in towards Abigail, "I dunno, are you into that?"

Abigail flushed, "No – *no*," she stuttered.

Stavros turned back to the leader of the privateers. "Well, then, see? There's two good reasons for me to put a stop to it... plus I think any men who worked for a ball-less fuck-puppet like Damien Walters are cowards and cretins."

The man with the pistol flushed red and Garret saw his hand tremble on his pistol. Yet the easy way that Stavros's hands had come to rest on his own pair of pistols seemed to take the wind out of him. "Admiral Mannetti will hear about this."

"Oh, dear," Stavros said, his eyes wide. "Well, do give her *Commodore* Stavros's regards, eh?"

The privateers began to clear out and after a moment, Garret managed to stand, though his head still spun a bit. He gave Stavros a slow nod, "Thanks." The gratitude burned a bit, for there was no doubt that the man would brag about it at some point later. *Commodore Pierce is going to be angry about this too,* Garret thought.

"It is nothing!" Stavros said with an extravagant wave. "I just like to tweak those men in their ridiculous purple uniforms. Have they no sense of style? If I hadn't already killed Damien Walters, I would shoot him again for crimes against fashion."

Garret looked over Stavros's tight red leather pants and the oiled chest hair that showed from his open shirt and just shook his head. *Not worth saying anything,* Garret thought, *besides, he* did *just save my life.* That his life had depended upon the flighty pirate at all almost made Garret want to throw up. Stavros was a womanizer, a philanderer, and a card cheat. He was also a pirate of the worst sort and whatever self-interest had made him step in was all that prevented Garret and Abigail from dying.

Garret wasn't certain if it was possible for the night to get any worse.

Abigail looked over at Garret, her face a bit pale. "Well," she said, "as first dates go, this was pretty terrible. You really better make it up to me."

***

Halcyon Colony, Garris Major System
Contested
November 23, 2403

"While it has been delightful to train together," Captain Montago said, "I'm really getting tired of this shit. When do we get to the fighting and looting?"

"Soon enough, my friend, soon enough," Mason said in the guise of Commodore Stavros Heraklion. *It is rather disturbing how easily I've pulled off this role,* Mason thought, *and even worse that I enjoy it a bit.* He put his boots up on the table and looked around at the other commanders present. Each of them represented a ship or squadron of light ships. A couple of them, like Captain Mantago, were pirates who had signed on with Halcyon's government for a safe base of operations and a cut in the overall profits. Others, like Captain Oronkwo and Captain Garret Penwaithe, were guild mercenaries, hired by Halcyon's government from the Tannis system.

*Though I have a low opinion of mercenaries, even guild mercs,* Mason thought, *I will say that Oronkwo seems pretty solid and that Frank Pierce picked a damned good officer in Garret Penwaithe... even if I did have to save his ass in that bar fight.*

The only bad news so far was that Kandergain had left earlier in the morning. She hadn't been able to tell him where she needed to go or when she would return, but she'd warned him that he wouldn't be able to count on her presence for some time.

"President Monaghan has put special trust in my capabilities as a squadron leader... and Councilor Penwaithe as our direct representative from him has told me that our last training performance showed we're ready," Mason smirked. They had run a simulated exercise against some of Halcyon Defense Fleet. Most of them were decent enough at their technical skills, but they didn't have enough leadership or experience. His squadron had won a very one-sided victory, another embarrassment for Admiral Moore. Councilor Penwaithe's angry diatribe about building relationships and teamwork between privateers and military had been punctuated by her informing them that they were ready for active raiding.

*And since embarrassing Admiral Moore makes both Mannetti and Collae happy with me,* Mason thought, *that was two birds with one stone, so to speak.* His whole purpose here was to find out what the two rogue military commanders wanted in this tiny system. So far he had hints of some greater conspiracy and a notion that there was some recovered alien technology that the locals seemed to have tight control over and that the pair of them wanted it. Given the fact that both of them had grudges with Baron Giovanni and his United Colonies, it seemed prudent to thwart them.

While the notion of a greater conspiracy bothered him, Mason felt more concern about the alien technology. He had lived under Amalgamated Worlds and as a military officer he'd seen how the Agathan Fleet had developed from a handful of wreckage and the genius of a single man able to figure it all out. For that matter, the *Kraken* was of possible alien origin, and the real Captain Stavros had run amok across a dozen star systems with the heavy cruiser until Mason had finally put an end to the man's bloody swath of destruction.

The various commanders seemed eager at Mason's declaration, so he shook off his thoughts and put on his best Stavros leer, "We'll be leaving in a few days, our target is another Nova Corp facility. It should be a lot of fun, boys and girls. And trust me, we'll be seeing a *lot* of profit off this one."

Mason had expected the smirks and glee from the pirate and privateer ship captains. The frowns and worry on the faces of the two mercenary Captains was what Mason had really hoped for, though. He had already worked things out with Commodore Frank Pierce, the commander of the War Dogs and Captain Penwaithe's superior, but they had kept his subordinates in the dark. Captain Oronkwo had no ties to Mason, though, and he wanted Captain Oronkwo to be uneasy about all this. The mercenary was here to do a job and while Captain Oronkwo wouldn't turn up his nose at profit, he was uneasy about the pirates he had to work with.

That was good, in Mason's eyes. If both mercenaries were suspicious and on edge, when Admiral Mannetti or Admiral Collae made their plays, then Captain Oronkwo and Captain Penwaithe might very well see it coming and take appropriate action. That might just swing things in Mason's favor and prevent the two rogue Admirals from getting their way. *And that is essential*, Mason thought, *or else all of this Stavros routine is just me playing dress-up for no good reason.*

# Chapter I

Faraday System
United Colonies
December 1, 2403

Alanis used a word that the daughter of the nobility and the sister to a head of state probably shouldn't use in public. Unfortunately, it didn't have any effect on the incoming fire from the crew served weapon that had her pinned down behind a rapidly eroding structural bulkhead.

"Alpha team, this is Sigma, what is your situation?" Sigma's voice was dry and calm in her ear.

The rest of alpha team, as far as she knew, were already down, including her team leader. The ambushers had caught them when they opened up from their concealed emplacement down the corridor. She had managed to return fire and move to cover, but she was the only one. The Cy-Tek Railgun down the corridor opened up with another burst to remind her of that point.

"Sigma, this is Alpha Five," Alanis responded. "I'm pinned down and the remainder of Alpha Team is down."

There was a moment's pause and then Sigma spoke again, "Alpha Five, we need that target secured, the rest of our assault is depending on you." The assault against the station would fail if she couldn't take and hold the reactor room. Cutting power there would open the security doors and allow the rest of her company to secure the station.

She swore again as the remainder of her cover began to disintegrate. *Nothing for it,* she thought, as she vaulted out from cover and used her combat armor's thrusters to augment the armor's enhanced strength.

She – briefly – flew up along the ceiling of the corridor, the sharp arc of her trajectory momentarily throwing off the aim of her attackers as she managed to down one of them. She struck the ceiling with her back hard enough that it knocked the air out of her lungs and made her see spots despite her armor's protection. She maintained her fire, though, and saw the other gunner go down.

A moment later she bounced off the floor hard enough that she blacked out for a moment.

She pulled herself up, shook her head to clear the stars, and ran a quick functions check of her armor and weapon. That done, she spoke up over the radio, "This is Alpha Five, continuing to target."

***

"As you can see, sir," Colonel William Proscia said as they watched the feeds from the academy training exercise, "we've got a fully configurable layout for almost any design of station or ship."

Baron Lucius Giovanni nodded as his eyes ranged from the holographic display that showed the overall exercise and then to the individual monitors that showed training underway. This was, he'd been told, an evaluation exercise where a 'company' of power armored cadets assaulted a captured station, defended by three companies of infantry, albeit without powered armor. He glanced around to make certain that none of the Marine Colonel's staff was within earshot. "I can't help but notice that the current layout is a very similar design and layout to our Skydock Station in orbit."

Colonel Proscia gave a very slight nod, "Yes, sir, it is. In fact, it is based upon the latest modifications, currently underway. I figure it is best to train for the fight I expect." He gave a grim smile, "If it comes to a fight, I have units of cadets, backed by cadre, who can be airborne and ready to assault any of our key infrastructure as well as any of our ships in orbit, all of them in powered armor."

Lucius felt a chill at that, yet he couldn't argue with the Colonel's preparations. The recent revelations that there was some sort of cabal or conspiracy within the ranks of the Fleet with unknown goals and a playbook that had already included assassination had made Lucius more than a little paranoid. A heavy battalion's worth of powered armor infantry, backed by combat shuttles could destroy almost any conventional ground or security forces. In all likelihood, he wouldn't need that kind of support, but if he did, he would *really* need it. *After all,* he thought, *the enemy may well have three battalions worth of "disappeared" Marines and equipment.*

Lucius winced as he watched one of the cadets bounce sharply off the ceiling, firing at the enemy and then hammer into the floor of the corridor. "You might want to tell that one that this is just training," he said. It looked as if whoever it was had activated their jump boots, which should have been locked down in such close confines.

Colonel Proscia glanced at the cadet's biosensors and gave a slight smile, “She's within safety parameters. That was a nice bit of hacking to get around the safety lock outs and then good gunnery to hit two targets in those conditions.”

“She could have seriously injured herself,” Lucius said. “We don't need officers who are a danger to themselves and their people.”

“Well,” Colonel Proscia said, his tone light, “Perhaps you could tell her yourself, sir, she's *your* sister.”

Lucius's jaw dropped. He had known, consciously, that his sister was here at the Academy and participating in the training, but he hadn't thought of her in these types of conditions. “Well,” he heard himself say, “I suppose I should let you do your job and stop meddling.”

***

The conference room with it's landing pad sized table hadn't changed, the officers around it were mostly the same, but to Lucius, this meeting felt far different from those which had taken place there before. Part of that was the fact that they had gone to war, not just once but several times. That gave Lucius a better appreciation for the skill and measure of each of the officers in the room.

The other part, of course, was knowing that a significant number of the officers in the room belonged to a cabal whose apparent goal was to institute a coup de tat followed by a military dictatorship. The fact that they had tried to kill his good friend, Captain Anthony Doko, and and his friend's wife, Lizmadie, made him that much angrier. *If I knew who all was involved I would move on them now,* Lucius thought darkly, *yet if I miss even one or two of their key people they may still be able to take action and get too many good people killed.*

Lucius found it difficult to keep a polite face while knowing that some of the men and women here planned to have him and his friends killed. The roiling anger he felt about their petty selfishness and ambition made it that much harder to appear calm. The human race as a whole was at stake, yet these selfish bastards refused to put aside their own interests to save it.

Half of the conference room was empty, a pointed reminder that Admiral Dreyfus and a sizable portion of the Fleet remained in position at Tehran and Danar. Once again, Lucius wondered just how he would break the news of the conspiracy to the old Admiral...

and if he could fully trust the man. In part he was grateful that Admiral Dreyfus's wounds and the damage to his ships had kept him in the Tehran system. At least gave Lucius more time to consider how to go about the difficult tasks of figuring how to tell the old war hero and a bit more time to identify more of the conspirators.

"Well," Lucius said, "Let's begin. Captain Beeson, would you give us a status of forces update?"

"Yes, sir," Captain Daniel Beeson stood, his face impassive. The once beefy-young man had lost a great deal of weight since he first signed on with Lucius's forces. He had also lost his eager smile and much of his optimism, which saddened Lucius a great deal. Then again, his entire extended family, one of Faraday's oldest military families, had died under the Chxor occupation of Faraday and that would be enough to change anyone. "All of our Crusader-class ships are at ninety percent capacity or better, with Admiral Dreyfus's flagship, *Paladin*, in the worst shape after his battle at the Tehran System."

Captain Beeson paused and brought up an overlay of the fleet as a whole. Lucius winced, again, as he saw the swath of red across the lighter elements of their fleet. The most painful among those losses were the battlecruisers and heavy cruisers whose firepower and staying power had filled a vital role in their fleet. Those losses were all the worse for the fact that their shipyards were not up to replacing ships of that size yet.

"Our lighter forces, as you can see," Daniel Beeson said, "are at less than seventy percent overall strength. Twenty percent of those ships are at thirty percent combat effectiveness or less." The obvious reason for that was the bad mauling that Admiral Dreyfus's forces had received at the Tehran system. Lucius blamed himself, for it seemed as if many of the officers in command of the legacy ships of the Dreyfus Fleet still thought in terms of the era of warfare from the time of Amalgamated Worlds. They didn't understand – or didn't *want* to understand – the changes in tactical and strategic paradigms. Admiral Dreyfus's ships had closed in a close range fight against a numerically superior Chxor force at Tehran.

While the Dreyfus Fleet's ships were better, the lighter ships of his screen were also far smaller and less armored than the Chxor dreadnoughts they had engaged. They'd annihilated the Chxor fleet in the system, but only at severe losses and even his massive

Crusader-class ships had taken heavy damage.

"Admiral Dreyfus's Task Force Two remains staged at the Tehran System undergoing repairs, other than the three vessels that returned here for more serious repairs. Task Force Three retains the Danar system. Our Nova Roma allies," Daniel Beeson nodded to where Emperor Romulous IV, Admiral Mund, and Lord Admiral Balventia sat, "have finished refitting and upgrading their vessels and they are staged to assist in the defense of Faraday or to go on the offense as needed."

"That ends my status of forces estimate and I'll be followed by Captain Magnani," he said calmly. It was some measure of his self-control that he didn't let any of his antipathy for Captain Magnani to show in his expression or tone.

Captain Magnani was not his equal in that regard. "Yes, well, *thank you*, Captain Beeson." Her moue of distaste could not have been more obvious. "Unfortunately, our logistic situation has been exacerbated not only by the losses suffered by Admiral Dreyfus, but also by the large expenditures of munitions in both battles. In fact, I estimate that we will be at only sixty percent of our total munitions in any future battle."

"Sixty percent?" Lucius asked sharply. That didn't match with the estimates that he had already seen. By those estimates, they had two complete load-outs of munitions. The heavy antimatter warheads that the Dreyfus Fleet ships used were far more powerful than the equivalent fusion warheads used by both the Chxor and Nova Roma.

"Yes, sir," Captain Magnani seemed to relish the opportunity to deliver the bad news. It was a pointed reminder to Lucius that his investigation had so far implicated her involvement in the traitorous cabal. "Unfortunately, it looks like our prior estimates of warhead reserves were overly optimistic. After going back and doing a thorough inventory, it appears that almost three quarters of our stocks were actually consumed in the Third Battle of Faraday." She shrugged slightly, "It appears there was an accounting error on the part of Commander Jin Wong, who was killed in the Tehran System. I think that she had noticed the error but actively worked to cover it up in order to prevent disciplinary actions."

"What?!" Lucius asked. To level such an accusation, whatever the founding, in the middle of a brief was unacceptable. This was the kind of thing that was handled through appropriate channels, not thrown in front of the senior commander of the fleet in a casual manner.

"Baron Giovanni," Captain Wu said quickly, "I'm afraid that Captain Magnani spoke out of turn. This was something I wanted to bring up, personally, as my people were doing the investigation."

Lucius sat back and he felt a wave of cold wash over him as he caught Captain Magnani's slight nod at Captain Wu. Whatever the two of them had said, this was not something that had happened on accident. From the smooth fashion in which Captain Wu stood and her confident expression as she spoke, Lucius could tell that this was something that they had planned and possibly even rehearsed. "Ladies and gentlemen, I'm afraid that it appears that Captain Magnani's statement is correct. After she noticed certain discrepancies within logistical inventory, I ordered a full investigation. What we have uncovered so far appears to be either a deliberate cover-up of incompetence or quite possibly a conspiracy on the parts of senior officers to protect Commander Jin Wong from the consequences of her failures. My staff is continuing the investigation, but there are implications that someone of senior rank had assisted Commander Jin Wong's delinquency, possibly as a result of an improper relationship."

Her calm, matter-of-fact voice made the statement sound suitably grave. Had Lucius been unaware of the cabal, he would have had no reason to doubt her words... or to look any deeper than the evidence she had no doubt carefully arranged. *Thank you,* he thought to himself, *for showing yourself to me.* As far as he knew, Captain Beeson and Ensign Forrest Perkins had not previously had any suspicions of Captain Wu. Yet the implications of her collusion with Captain Magnani along with her own incredibly valuable position as the head of intelligence for the Dreyfus Fleet suggested that she must have a *very* high rank within the cabal. *But not the leader,* Lucius thought, *that would be whoever put them up to this... possibly to gauge my response.*

Lucius nodded slowly, "That is a serious set of allegations, yet I trust that you wouldn't bring them up without having conducted at least a preliminary investigation."

"Of course, sir," Captain Wu said. "Yet, my people have gone as far as they could without further approval. Thus, I ask for you to authorize me to follow this investigation to its conclusion."

*And there it is,* Lucius thought. A blanket approval, probably crouched in some vague terms, would give her carte blanch to "uncover" crimes and misdemeanors on the behalf of whatever officers the cabal wanted removed. It would then be a simple matter for them to have the officers that they wanted appointed to the vacated positions.

*How long,* Lucius wondered, *have they worked their way through every aspect of the Fleet, all the while unknown to Admiral Dreyfus?*

Part of Lucius wanted to blame the old Admiral, yet how could he? Lucius himself knew the trust that built up over time between officers. Admiral Dreyfus had served with many of these officers for over a century. Before their self-imposed exile, they had fought and bled together against the Provisional Colonial Republic Army, two Wrethe Incursions, and a host of other threats. These men and women had all volunteered to leave their nation behind, to abandon everything they knew, in order to be the last, hidden hope of humanity.

*And some of them,* Lucius thought darkly, *either planned to hijack that hope from the beginning or have come to want payment for their sacrifices.*

Lucius realized that he had been quiet too long when Captain Wu cleared her throat. Lucius shook his head and gave her a slight smile, "I'm sorry, Captain, the implications are disturbing, I must admit. Have your request written up and forwarded to my Flag Lieutenant. I'll look it over and authorize it as long as I don't see any legal issues."

"Thank you, sir," Captain Wu said.

"Now, then," Lucius said, "Let's continue the briefing, shall we?"

***.

Lucius paused as he stepped into his office. He wasn't certain what had made him pause, not at first. It was as if there were something wrong, subtly about the entire room. Something that felt not just wrong, but dangerous, *hostile* in such a way as to almost make him turn around and shout for help. The moment passed, though, and Lucius walked forward, his gaze searched for anything out of place. He frowned, then, when he saw a small slip of plasfilm setting square in the center of his desk.

It should not be there. His office was in one of Faraday's former government buildings that the new United Colonies government had appropriated. The building itself had extensive security from the prior government, the Chxor occupation, and then from Alicia Nix's Federal Investigation Bureau. Due to the sensitive nature of the information that went across his desk, only a handful of people had access to his offices.

Not long ago, a psychic had managed to gain access, but he had since *become* a part of the additional layer of defenses. Even if all the other precautions failed, his secretary, Cindy, should have notified him if anyone had accessed the office.

Lucius almost called her in to ask about just that, but he hesitated. There was every possibility that his security had been compromised, which itself was a threat. However, there was also a strong likelihood that whoever this was, they didn't mean him any harm.

Lucius reached out and picked up the note. He blinked as he saw that there was nothing on it, just an empty slip of plasfilm. Then, the surface rippled. *Biometric plasfilm,* he thought, as it reacted to his touch, *a message meant only for me.*

A message that could just have easily been a tailored neurotoxin, he reminded himself.

The short message contained only two things: a name and a twenty-four character ansible code. The name Lucius recognized very well. Lucretta Mannetti had twice tried to kill him and was a renegade Nova Roma military officer and a highly successful pirate. The ansible code, however, was one he hadn't seen before but he could assume that it would work.

He set the slip of plasfilm down and its text disappeared again. The message itself told him several things, one of which was that his benefactor, if he could call him that, had valid biometric data on him. That in itself was notable, as it implied a high level of access to either the Fleet's databases, Alicia Nix's files in the FIB, or possibly Nova Roma's data.

Lucius frowned over the possibilities as he picked it up again and committed the ansible code to his memory. If it was a direct connection to Admiral Lucretta Mannetti as it seemed to be, then it might be very valuable, indeed. A direct link to her would give him the opportunity to confirm several things and perhaps even to clear Anthony Doko's name. Certainly Lucius would have to approach any such contact very carefully.

He sat down as he thought about his friend, Anthony Doko. The recent attempt on his life, possibly by the same conspirators who planned to seize control of the Dreyfus Fleet, made Lucius feel both guilty and angry. The evidence against Doko, while circumstantial, was enough that Lucius had no choice but to pull him out of his position. That evidence suggested that Captain Anthony Doko had been a long time agent for Admiral Mannetti. Anthony had accepted house arrest while the investigation continued. Only quick thinking on he and his wife's parts and skilled training in self-defense had prevented their deaths.

In all likelihood, the person who had provided this information was the agent who actually worked for Admiral Mannetti. Lucius couldn't guess at the reasons that he'd provided the information. For that matter, given Lucretta Mannetti's hatred for Lucius, it was even odds that she would have ordered her agent to plant a bomb in his office as likely as it was for her to want to talk to him. *Well,* Lucius thought, *more likely that she'd have him plant a bomb under my chair so that she could see my face when I called her.*

Lucius glanced under his chair, just to be certain, before he stood. Best, he thought, to have security sweep the room... just in case. That was a call that could wait, after all.

***

Captain Daniel Beeson waited while Baron Lucius Giovanni took a seat in the small, secure briefing room. It had been difficult to arrange for this gap in his schedule, at a secure location where they could be certain that no one from the conspirators would get wind of it. Aboard ship, it was easier, but here on Faraday, it seemed that everyone wanted some of Baron Giovanni's time. Whether it was military officers with briefings, engineers briefing their infrastructure upgrades, or politicians wanting to get a feel for their commander in chief, everyone wanted some of the Baron's time.

*And I don't trust the politicians,* Daniel thought darkly, *half of them would blab it out in order to meet their own goals.* Daniel had a low opinion of politics in general, especially after his entire family had paid the price when Faraday's politicians had surrendered to the Chxor. The fact that the Chxor had executed those same politicians when they outlived their usefulness didn't make him any more inclined to forgive them.

The Baron looked a little distracted as he took a seat and Daniel wondered if that distraction was somehow related to his orders to have his offices swept. They hadn't found anything, but then again, the Baron had been very vague about what they might be searching for. Daniel really hoped that the pressure wasn't becoming too much for him. He saw the Baron take a slip of plasfilm out of his pocket and look at it, before looking up and giving him a nod, "Sorry, Daniel, you can begin the briefing."

"Thank you, sir," Daniel said. He pulled up the diagrams that showed the known conspirators. There were still far too many question-marks, unknown connections and ties, but with Captain Wu tipping her hand, he finally felt like they had a glimpse at the big picture... and possibly a way to stop them.

"As you can see, sir, we have filled in a lot more details," Daniel said. "This conspiracy has ties to the civilians and military of the Dreyfus Fleet and their goals are to hijack the Fleet for their own purposes, either to reinstate Amalgamated Worlds or to start their own empire." Either goal was one to prevent, Daniel well knew. Amalgamated Worlds had been more of a bureaucracy than a government, with tiers of faceless managers who controlled entire star systems and individual human lives were often lost in the overall balance of numbers.

"Now, when we first began the investigation, we had some confusion because it seemed like there were possibly two different factions." The Baron nodded at that, they had already seen a number of ways in which the conspirators had seemed to work against each other. "What we think is that Captain Wu's predecessor, Senior Captain Nelund, was their action commander... and that he grew more ambitious than the others could tolerate. We've seen signs of smaller cells, which seem to be acting on their own, without much outside guidance. What we think happened is that the other conspirators saw him building up a strong element within the cabal and that they had to take him out, before he made his power play." Senior Captain Nelund's death had come just after Lucius had made contact with the Dreyfus Fleet. Daniel thought that was itself a sign that the organization must have seen him as a risk.

The Baron leaned forward, his face intent, "So you think that these other actors are the remnants of his organization?"

"Yes, sir," Daniel said. He brought up the investigation report from Captain Nelund's death. "As you can see, sir, it was determined that Captain Nelund committed suicide after his son's death in a training accident." He highlighted the investigating officer's name and then several other data points. "It was Captain Honshu Wu who completed the investigation. The pistol Senior Captain Nelund used was an M17 with an integral suppressor, supposedly checked out by Senior Captain Nelund from the armory, but there was no video confirmation." He saw the Baron's eyes widen at that. There *had* to be video confirmation for when a weapon like that was checked out. The M17 was an extremely expensive design and it was famously the weapon of choice for many of Amalgamated Worlds Commandos, it was a design ideal for concealment, with a plastic and ceramic frame designed to fool sensors. It was the perfect weapon for an assassination.

"So," Baron Giovanni said, "we have a senior conspirator who was making his own power play and the others had him killed and put Captain Wu in his place." Daniel could see a bit of the same shock on the Baron's face as Daniel had first felt when he dug into the files. It shouldn't have surprised Daniel that the cabal had some internal differences and the ruthlessness to kill one of their own. Yet since he had first found out about them they had seemed a faceless, monolithic group. The more he learned about them, the less he liked what he saw, though. *And since I've hated what they've done to the Fleet from the very beginning,* he thought, *they're rapidly approaching a point at which they've no redeeming features.*

Daniel continued with the brief, "What we think is that while some of Captain Nelund's cells were absorbed into the whole, others have continued under his orders, either unaware of the overall organization or actively opposing them to meet his goals. This seems to be the root of the confusion we see in their lower ranks, some of them are working on a different playbook. The others can't or don't want to remove those cells, either because they don't know who they are or because the cell members are in vital positions and are willing to go to any lengths, including betraying the overall cabal, in order to survive... but we still haven't identified the head of that faction."

The Baron seemed surprised by that, "So there's some kind of quiet internal war ongoing?"

Daniel nodded, "We think Commander Jin Wong was one of

those casualties. She initially was classified as a moderate injury and admitted for overnight observation only because of a slight concussion. The medical report says that she died from an aneurysm caused by the blow to her head. But the initial brain scan should have shown that and it's missing, along with logs of who accessed her room that night and security footage of that medical suite." Daniel hadn't been able to find out *how* the cabal seemed to hack the shipboard security systems so effortlessly. The only bright bit was that the Nova Roma designed computer systems seemed resistant to the conspirator's infiltration techniques.

Daniel gave the Baron some time to think about that... how the cabal had murdered an officer under his command. It didn't matter that Commander Jin Wong had been a member of the conspiracy, she had sworn the oath and wore the uniform and until proven guilty and discharged or executed, she was still one of Baron Lucius Giovanni's people.

The determination that settled on the Baron's face reminded Daniel once again that *no one* hurt Baron Giovanni's people with impunity.

"How soon can we move?" The Baron asked finally.

Daniel brought up the diagram of their own network. "We're positioning people to move, after they've been fully vetted. The big issue, of course, is that they've had people in place for a long time, already. Since we want to minimize damage that they can do to the Fleet and our own casualties, we're trying to surround their known agents as much as possible. The areas we are focusing on, as much as possible, is tactical command, weapons positions, armories, and Marine units. The thing we are most worried about is where they've infiltrated senior officer ranks in multiple departments."

The Baron nodded at that. Part of the problem they faced with this kind of conspiracy was the very structure of the military. Officers gave orders and in an emergency, those orders *must* be obeyed. The conspirators would rely upon that. If they had the opportunity to move, they could command otherwise loyal units of Marines to seize key areas of ships or order ships to fire upon targets. In the confusion of that kind of mutiny, the people who knew what was happening would be the ones with power. Everyone else would be frozen, stuck reacting rather than making decisions.

"We're positioning teams to take down the key officers so that we can mobilize the rest of the Fleet to apprehend the others, but we still think that some twenty-five to thirty percent of their personnel that remain unidentified... including several of their key leadership," Daniel said. He pulled up the conspirator network and overlaid a diagram of their own response teams. "We know that officers aboard the *Paladin* are taking orders from someone, but we haven't identified who it is, either among Senior Captain Attanasio's staff or even Admiral Dreyfus's staff officers. Whoever it is, we know they have access to Admiral Dreyfus, so we believe it is essential to identify him or her to protect the Admiral."

The Baron studied the diagram for a long moment. "We've thoroughly vetted Senior Captain Attanasio?"

"Yes, sir," Daniel nodded his head. "There's no way that she could be the one. We've confirmed on two occasions when she was away from his ship that the conspirators aboard received new updates and began new propaganda missions. During one of those, she was in a secure conference room and had no way to get any messages out." That had been the death of Commander Jin Wong and Daniel wished he had more trustworthy people to work the data. Daniel thought that a significant percentage of the conspiracy's personnel on the *Patriot* were part of the late Captain Nelund's group, as well, but the way that both factions of conspirators were intermixed made it difficult to be certain. The very fact that much of the cabal leadership didn't seem certain of the loyalties of their personnel made the matter all the more difficult.

"Very well," Baron Giovanni said. "As soon as we've identified their senior man, we need someone trustworthy in position to take him down. The last thing we can afford is to lose him. No changes, I assume, to our own moles?"

Daniel shook his head. "Lieutenant Moritz and Ensign Jiang are the only two we've identified. Given Ensign Jiang's background, we think that she's their primary operative and Lieutenant Moritz is just there to give her support and cover." Daniel grimaced as he thought about the two members of the Barons' staff that were loyal to the cabal. Ensign Jiang *seemed* like a decent, hardworking woman, but he couldn't trust that. Moritz, on the other hand, was arrogant and lazy, his work was mediocre at best, and Daniel had a difficult time hiding his hatred for the man.

"I'm worried about the damage this is going to do to morale and unit trust," the Baron said. He met Daniel's eyes and Daniel was shocked to see the weariness in his commander's eyes. "We've managed to put together a strong fighting force, but this kind of thing is what tears units apart. Once it all comes to light, people won't be certain who they can trust... and you can't go to battle like that."

Daniel nodded. "Understood, sir, and we're doing what we can to find *all* of the bastards. I think that will make the difference, in the end. If we get all of them, if we try them all in fair and impartial courts martial, then our people will see that. They'll trust that it was done right, sir."

The Baron nodded. "Very well." He gave a sigh, "And I've looked over Colonel Proscia's action plans. I trust that the final option is only for emergencies?"

Daniel winced at that. Colonel Proscia had drafted a number of crisis response plans that ranged from small teams taking down the conspiracy's key leadership to a full-scale combat plan to seize all of the major ships and lock down everything in Faraday's orbit. The latter mobilized all personnel at the Academy, from instructors to cadets, and sent them to seize key positions on Faraday and in Faraday's orbit.

That kind of brute force approach would not be without casualties. They would go after their targets wearing powered armor, carrying live weapons, and carried in the belly of combat-loaded assault shuttles. If anyone got in their way, loyal or not, they would use lethal force to accomplish their mission. It was very likely that good people would pay the price.

But if they had to use that option, it meant that the conspirators would have already moved or were about to kick off their operation plan, whatever it was. At that point, Daniel didn't see any other option to prevent them from taking power and killing off anyone else in their way. He nodded confidently, "Yes, sir, that's our last resort."

***

Captain Anthony Doko yelped as his wife swatted him playfully on the backside. "Excuse me, miss, but I'm a married man," Tony said reproachfully.

Princess Lizmadie Isabella Doko gave him a sultry glance, "Well, handsome, your wife doesn't know how lucky she is..." She leaned forward and gave him a kiss. "Well, actually, she does. Very much." She tucked her head on his shoulder and sighed contentedly, "What'cha doing?"

Tony's own contented smile faded, "Research."

She recognized his tone. "About our uninvited guests?"

Tony nodded and for a moment, he remembered staring down the barrel of a pistol and the sharp sound of gunfire. Only his wife's excellent aim and well-trained reflexes had saved him. For that matter, only her paranoia and their constant rehearsals, as well as their safe-room, had prevented their deaths.

"Find anything?" Lizmadie asked.

"Nothing, yet, but I can't help but think that Alicia Nix and Lucius are both being very close-mouthed about it," Tony said. He looked back at his computer screen, "Which tells me that it's either related to us being under house arrest... or something else."

She considered that for a long moment. "You think that Admiral Mannetti's mole arranged it?"

Tony nodded, "Who else? I mean, that would be ideal, they could take us out, make it look like a murder-suicide, and then Mannetti's mole would be free and clear. But, since we survived, there's some evidence that we *aren't* working for Mannetti, so I'm certain that Lucius is working that angle." Tony couldn't help but feel frustrated that he couldn't help Lucius to find the traitor. He had spent the past few days doing as much research as he could through public databases, but he hadn't found anything else of value.

"Tell me," Lizmadie said, as she stepped back and then pulled up her chair.

Tony sighed and adjusted the holographic display. He didn't want his wife too involved in this business. If things went completely to hell, she had some protection being the sister of the Nova Roma Emperor. If something happened to Tony and the traitor thought she didn't know anything… that *might* be enough to keep her alive.

Yet he knew her skills with a computer. If he didn't show her the little bit that he had found, then she would do the same research herself, probably quicker and definitely easier than he had. "I've been looking over the public records as far as Admiral Mannetti and her raids. Right now, the news feeds have her based in the Garris Major system, she's working as a privateer for a planet called Halcyon."

Lizmadie leaned in to read the details, "That seems a little small-time for her, what kind of angle is she working?" Among the many things he loved about his wife, the speed at which she processed data was certainly one of them. She would have made one hell of an officer, he knew. It was just as well that she hadn't been allowed to join the Nova Roma military, else she would probably have died like most of the other officers that Tony had known. *Even working under Baron Giovanni,* he thought, *we lost so many good men.* Nova Roma had more than a little stigma attached to women in military service, a product of the nobility and their revival of antiquated cultural norms along with a bit of frontier pragmatism. Women who served or worked jobs were women who weren't having children to provide for the next generation.

While Nova Roma had a few female officers, women weren't allowed in the Fleet or Marine enlisted ranks. For that matter, the Army hadn't even allowed female officers. Regardless, the daughter of the Nova Roma Emperor, even an illegitimate one, would not be allowed to sign on.

She picked out the data that it had taken Tony several hours to notice. "Nova Corp was excavating alien artifacts, think someone found something *really* valuable?"

Tony nodded, "That's what I think. I passed that on to some of Alicia Nix's people, too." They had politely told him to mind his own business, but that was expected. He was supposed to be under house arrest, quietly waiting to be cleared of charges, not trying to clear his name with the help of his wife.

Lizmadie bit her lip, "Hmmm, weapon or technology, a single planet government like that might try to trade it to her, but they've *got* to know that she'd happily loot their planet as soon as she has it..."

"Yeah," Tony nodded. He brought up another article, "Which is probably why they hired the Nova Dogs. They've got a good reputation, for mercenaries. I've actually worked with some of them before, a *long* time ago." He sort of doubted that any of the men and women he remembered were still with the group.

"So... how does this help us?" Lizmadie asked.

Tony shrugged, "I can't say that it does... but it *might* tie into the mole here, I figured. Admiral Mannetti showed up there not long after she escaped from here. That means that she probably already had it lined up and it might tie into the timing of her escape. We already know that her agent arranged for uniforms and passcodes for her here. That means that she had to have communicated to him what she needed and when."

Lizmadie cocked her head. "...or it means that she took *orders* from the agent here."

Tony's eyebrows went up at that, "Orders? That would make the mole, what, her handler?" Admiral Lucretta Manetti was a rogue military officer, Tony found it hard to believe that she took orders from anything besides her own selfish interests and desires. Then again many of her people had been very loyal. He normally didn't see that kind of thing with pirates, most of whom would sell out their mothers. While her enlisted crew had mutinied on Lucius's order to surrender, they hadn't known anything and all of her senior personnel had escaped with her.

"I really wish I had access to some of her old crew," Tony said, "because that's a very interesting theory." As far as he knew, those of her lower enlisted crew who had mutinied against her upon Lucius's orders for them to surrender had been transferred to the penal colony here in the Faraday system. If Tony weren't under house arrest, it wouldn't have been hard to interview them and check what they knew against his wife's theories. *Granted,* he acknowledged, *Admiral Mannetti is a clever opponent, it wouldn't be unlike her to keep everyone outside her inner circle in the dark.*

Lizmadie shrugged. "It doesn't really matter, right now. It doesn't change much about the situation. The pertinent information is that whoever her agent is, she knew he had to get her out in time for her to rendezvous with her other ships and sign on with Halcyon's people. At the least, that means her agent had some secure communications with her and also enough free time to make contact with her." She frowned, "I really wish we had more access to the communications logs from the civilian ansible array."

Tony shrugged at that, "*Everyone* accessed the ansible, especially after the fall of Nova Roma, either searching for missing friends and family or making arrangements to try to get them here." Granted, most hadn't been so lucky, but some few among the crew had managed to make contact with family and get them to a safe place... or at least as safe as any place was any more.

"Yes," Lizmadie nodded, "but there might be a pattern. Maybe we could even back-track when a call was made to this agent who helped her to escape?" She shook her head, "Since we don't have that information, we have to work around who *might* have had contact with her, which doesn't give us any concrete data."

Tony pursed his lips, "Well, that's pretty close to Baron Giovanni's original investigation results." He ran over the list in his head. "I had access to her prison as a senior officer. Colonel William Proscia was in charge of boarding her ship and transporting her to the planet. Reese Giovanni was in communications along with Ensign Tascon, you had access to her through your brother..." he trailed off. "Your brother, the Emperor, had access to her as well."

"Trust me, I haven't discounted entirely that he might seek some alliance with her as some kind of leverage to hold over Lucius," she said, "But I think we can shelve that particular idea."

Tony shrugged at that. On the one hand, he wouldn't think Emperor Romulus would be foolish enough to trust Admiral Mannetti, but on the other Tony had seen just how desperate Lizmadie's brother had become to save the people of Nova Roma. "If we work back from the assumption that her agent was in contact with her, then we have another issue," Tony said finally. "After Baron Giovanni's withdrawal from the Second Battle of Faraday, we had a lock down on communications. Only department heads had access and even then, only for official business."

"That doesn't clear you," Lizmadie said with a tone of exasperation.

"No... but it does narrow the pool of suspects if our assumptions about communications is accurate," Tony said. "Which puts Reese at the top of our suspect list... especially given what happened between him and Alanis." He saw Lizmadie wince at that, but she didn't disagree. Reese Leone-Giovanni, once *Commander* Leone-Giovanni, had been Lucius's brother-in-law and had been a close friend to Doko as well. He was also the communications and signal officer for the *War Shrike*. He and his wife, Alannis Giovanni had some sort of argument about her joining the military which had escalated rapidly. Tony hadn't heard the details, but he *had* found that Reese was now wanted here in Faraday... and he'd also found official divorce paperwork filed by Alanis.

That in itself was a hard blow for Tony. As Lucius's Executive

Officer aboard the *War Shrike,* he had seen the growing divide between Lucius and Reese, particularly in regards to Lucius's decision to remain at Faraday when Nova Roma fell to the Chxor, rather than returning to fight them. Even Reese had to know that returning with one damaged battleship to fight an entire Chxor fleet was a fool's errand, yet Reese had seemed focused on his wife's safety. Tony could understand that, yet now he wondered if he had somehow missed an ulterior motive and how that might tie into the rogue Admiral Lucretta Mannetti.

"If it *was* Reese, then we'd have a hard time proving it," Lizmadie said. "As communications officer, he had full access to the ansible, and he definitely has the technical ability to modify the logs."

Tony nodded, "And that goes for Ensign Tascon, as well, who *also* happens to be related to Admiral Mannetti."

Lizmadie waved a hand, "While I can't entirely discount blood ties, I think the investigators overestimate it a bit in his case." She pulled up the profile that they had developed for Ensign Alberto Tascon. "He's a narcissist. His family couldn't inherit Admiral Mannetti's title and estate without her being killed or tried and found guilty of treason." Admiral Mannetti's title as Baroness Kail, in theory was very valuable. After her implication in a coup attempt, Emperor Romulus III had ordered her arrested, but as a noblewoman, he had not been legally able to try her *en absentia*, which meant she retained her rank and privileges as a noblewoman. Lizmadie knew well enough that her father had taken the House of Kail's estates and assets in custody until such time as her guilt (or innocence) was proven. "Ensign Tascon has every reason to hope she was captured, it would make his entire family wealthy overnight. I think that as the *War Shrike*'s XO, you had to work with Tascon enough to detest him, so you'd rather it be him. He was also a recent transfer to the *War Shrike* which means you would *rather* it be him as opposed to someone you served with for years."

*She's not wrong about either of those points,* Tony acknowledged, *Ensign Tascon is a self-centered, detestable little worm.* "Fine, but that doesn't clear him, just points out why I'd rather it be him."

Lizmadie nodded graciously, "Of course. Of anyone, I'd rather it be him, too. Especially after I found some of his sloppy entertainment hacks that he's trying to sell on the side. I'm ninety percent certain that he *would* be selling information on Lucius if he thought he could get away with it."

"Well," Tony said, "Besides those two, Alicia Nix had access to the ansible to control her intelligence agents and assets." He gave a glance at the hallway and his thoughts went to the men and women who worked for her and provided their security. If Alicia Nix *was* the agent, then she held their lives firmly in her hands at this point. Tony had worked with her quite a bit after her recruitment by Lucius to act as his intelligence officer. She was a native of Faraday and had worked intelligence for their military for years. She had also admitted that Admiral Mannetti *had* operated in the system for a few short months several years before Lucius's arrival. The admission had brought more trust, especially with the admission that they had bought pirated goods from her to augment their military forces. "It is possible that she used one of her assets to pass messages."

Lizmadie nodded, "And she could have accessed prison files or even had one of her agents put into position to enable the escape." Yet Tony could hear the doubt in her voice and he didn't blame her. There wasn't a *motive* to that action. As the late Lieutenant Palmer would have colorfully put it: she didn't have a dog in the fight. There was no reason for her to support Mannetti and every reason for her to support Lucius, especially after he'd liberated her homeworld from the Chxor.

"Other than her, Colonel William Proscia also had access as the Marine Commander, since he had security teams out escorting some of our retrieval teams," Tony said. He saw Lizmadie nod at that. Most of the civilians they had sent out had a team or more of Marines, both as protection and as an added layer of security to ensure that no one gave away their position when they'd been most vulnerable. Given the fact that they'd been selling precious metals to fund their efforts at the time, Colonel Proscia's teams had been essential on more than one occasion.

"I'm seeing several names coming up on our lists," Lizmadie said as she brought up the notes she had been taking. "You, Reese, Ensign Tascon, and Colonel Proscia."

Tony nodded, though he felt his stomach twist at that. Before recent events, he would have thought that left only one suspect, but after Reese's destroyed marriage, he couldn't say that he trusted his judgment enough to discount Colonel Proscia or Reese.

*For that matter,* Tony thought as he examined the files, *I'm not certain that I don't want it to be one of them, just so that I can clear my own name.*

***

"Well," Lucius said as he sipped at the wine, "this is one of your more effective ways to get me to attend a meeting, I must admit."

Kate Bueller, his Foriegn Minister sipped at her own wine and simply gave him a nod.

Lucius enjoyed the wine for a moment longer and then set his glass down with a sigh. "Very well, go ahead and give me the bad news."

Kate gave him a surprised expression, "Bad news, my Lord? Why would you assume that?"

Lucius gestured at the bottle, a vintage from his family's vineyards, one which, while not the best or most expensive, was literally irreplaceable since the Chxor had captured Nova Roma. For that matter, since Giovanni Vineyards was somewhat well-known for quality, he didn't know how she'd managed to find a bottle on the market.

Kate gave him a slight sigh in response, "I'm going to ask you a question and I need you to give me a real answer and to think about that answer." She met his gaze, her expression serious, "We are rapidly approaching a point where we can't afford for you to be both a military commander and our leader... is it essential for you to be at the front and leading the attack on Nova Roma?"

In automatic response, Lucius said, "What makes you think we're attacking Nova Roma? Surely you've seen the Chxor's threats to exterminate all human life in the system if we even try?"

She gave him a reproachful look and Lucius sighed in return. "Very well," Lucius said. He paused a moment in consideration. In theory, Admiral Dreyfus could handle most of the preparations and even command the fight of the plan that they had begun to develop. *But that doesn't take into account the conspiracy,* Lucius thought, *or my own uncertainties over his capabilities in the current strategic paradigm.*

The damage that Admiral Dreyfus had suffered at Tehran underlined that risk. Yet Lucius could admit to some measure of trepidation about trusting *anyone* with the various responsibilities upon his shoulders. *Admiral Mund, while capable, prefers a background role or a slot training new officers,* Lucius thought, *and he's a Nova Roma officer.*

Lucius regretted the growing division between the United Colonies personnel and the Nova Roma Imperial Fleet personnel. It was even worse for the fact that he felt there were many things that they could learn from each other. Even within the United Colonies Fleet, there was a sharp division between 'original' Dreyfus Fleet personnel and 'new' ones. The cabal seemed to play upon that division in order to create distrust and suspicion.

*Could someone else handle everything going on as well as commanding the battle?* Lucius had one clear answer to that. "I'm afraid that right now, I'm indispensable. There's a number of reasons, not least of which is with everything currently in motion, I'm the only one with visibility of it all." It was one reason for Lucius moving to the Tehran system to see the status of Admiral Dreyfus's task force and to look at the situation on the planet itself.

"I was afraid you'd say that..." Kate said. "Do some of these reasons tie back to an investigation of senior officers within the Dreyfus Fleet?"

Lucius felt the blood drain from his face, "That is not something that I can discuss, nor is it something that you should be involved in. It is a military matter and the less attention drawn to it the better." Lucius was very tempted to demand her source, but he wasn't certain that she would answer him if he did. That kind of breach could be devastating, he well knew, yet he didn't want to damage their working relationship by pressing her. Alicia Nix was probably her source. Captain Beeson had already begun an investigation into the conspiracy in conjunction with her as the head of the FIB. While he wouldn't have expected Alicia to pass that information on, it wasn't hard to believe.

"It's gone beyond a military matter when our Minister of War Newbauer is making promises and offering favors to ambassadors of foreign nations," Kate said. "And telling them that soon he'll be the one calling the shots."

"He's *what*?" Lucius asked. Julian Newbauer was the head of the War Party and the appointed Minister of War. He was also one of the civilians from the Dreyfus Fleet that Lucius had already heard some concerns about. If he had ties to the conspiracy, however, then it suggested that this cabal might have more support among the civilians... and possibly additional assets to worry about.

She gave him a grim smile, "I wondered if you had heard about that." She slid a data chip across the table. "I'd heard about it from the Shogun's Envoy, originally, and Alicia Nix confirmed it. For that matter, President Cassin has heard rumors herself and came to me to see what I knew. The details that we've been able to find suggest that he has ties back to personnel within the Fleet and it looks very much like they are planning a coup."

"I see," Lucius said. He took the data chip and looked at it for a long moment. "Clearly I'll need to expand our operations a bit. I trust that I don't need to remind you to keep this information close?" She merely arched an eyebrow at him and Lucius sighed, "Very well, what else?"

"I'm not entirely certain about your plans to discredit both the Centauri Confederation Ambassador and Shadow Lord Imperious's Ambassador," Kate said.

"You mean my 'fathers'?" Lucius asked. His actual father had been a traitor to Nova Roma, the illegitimate son of Emperor Romulus I, who had rebelled against Emperor Romulus II. Officially, his father had been executed only three days before Lucius's fifth birthday. Somehow, though, some forty-seven years later, not just one, but two men claiming to be his father had appeared. One was the Ambassador for the Centauri Confederation and the other was the personal envoy of Shadow Lord Imperious. Both men had credentials to back their claims and both men appeared, to the detail of fingerprints and DNA, to perfectly match every record of his father. Both of them had brought with them offers of alliance, which boiled down to varying offers to be subjects or a client nation.

It was not something that had made Lucius want to stop and consider his feelings. Lucius had built his life around being a success in the military *despite* his father's legacy. Atop the anger he felt over the sudden reappearance of his "father" had been the added rage at the blatant attempt to manipulate him. On almost every level, it didn't *matter* if one or the other actually was his father. His decision on how to deal with both of them came from that realization.

"You aren't certain about us stating that they are both liars and that their attempt to deceive us is a hostile action?" They had developed the plan with a bit more finesse than that, with the goal of putting both powers in a reactionary position. This would give the United Colonies long enough to solidify alliances with star systems and nations that would be far better allies.

She nodded, “I know you have the Iodans are working on the biology side and I don't doubt they'll find *something* we can use, but are you certain that it will prevent them from acting? I mean, neither the Centauri Confederation as a whole and President Spiridon in particular are known for being forgiving or easygoing and we're going to accuse them of lying in a diplomatic setting! That doesn't even touch on how vindictive the Shadow Lords can be!” Lucius snorted at that. The Shadow Lords were extremely powerful psychics, who controlled entire fleets and acted much like pirates and warlords. Individually their forces were on par with or even stronger than what a nation like Nova Roma might have mustered in its prime. Some of them were thought to be even more powerful than that. While Lucius had learned quite a bit more than he had ever believed possible about the five Shadow Lords, much of that was the type of nightmare fodder that made words like vindictive seem painfully inadequate.

The Centauri Confederation on the other hand was the most powerful human nation remaining, with some of the highest technology and the largest military. They were also in the midst of an ongoing civil war which had begun before Lucius's birth. President Spiridon had gradually consolidated power within the Centauri Confederation over the past seven decades, to the point where his homeworld, Elysia, was little more than a police state and many of the other worlds were controlled by state-run military and police forces. Those that weren't fell under what was commonly called the Tau Ceti Separatists, though there were a host of factions, insurrectionist movements, and constantly shifting alliances that made any look into the internals of the Centauri Confederation murky at best.

“I expect that they won't know *what* to do,” Lucius said. “President Spiridon isn't a forgiving man, but he's also not stupid. The last thing he needs right now is another war on another front, far from his borders and against a tough, well-trained and technologically equal opponent.”

Lucius sighed, “As for Shadow Lord Imperious... I'm expect him to be either unwilling or unable to directly act against us." His hopes in that regard came from Kandergain, the mother of his child, and herself a psychic as powerful as or perhaps even *more* powerful than any individual Shadow Lord. "The Shadow Lords are kept in check by one another as well as some outside forces," Lucius said, thinking again of Kandergain, "which should prevent Imperious from moving directly against us."

"I hate being the Foreign Minister and not having a good feel for what effects this will have on our foreign relations," Kate growled. As Lucius opened his mouth to explain, she waved a hand at him. "Okay, I know how much the Centauri's are hated, even by their own people. Embarrassing them will give us a nice boost of good will. I know that this isn't the kind of thing that President Spiridon should *want* to go to war over... but I don't have a good feel for it. I've dealt with Colonial Republic planet and system governments. I know how they think. I know how they're going to act, by and large. I don't have the same gut feeling for the Centauri Confederation and I'm nowhere near that when it comes to powers like the Shadow Lords."

Lucius nodded and he realized that Kate had taken on more and more responsibilities, well beyond her original scope as Minister of State. Part of that was because Lucius was focussed on fighting the war and he had done her a disservice by leaving her to shoulder those duties. "You're doing a fine job, Kate," Lucius said.

"I know *that*," she replied sharply. "What I'm concerned about is whether I'm doing a good enough job with the fate of humanity on the line."

Lucius couldn't quite find a response to that. It was, after all, his own private fear.

***

## Chapter II

Tehran System
United Colonies
December 15, 2403

Of all the worlds that had fallen under the rule of the Nova Roma Empire, Tehran was one of the few that Lucius had never visited. Part of that had come from his determination to avoid the planet. It was considered one of his father's victories from his prior loyal service in the Nova Roma Imperial Fleet. The privateers that had operated from Tehran had been a vicious threat to Nova Roma's merchant ships and Lucius's father had removed that threat, conquering the system in the process.

That was not something to endear Lucius's family name to the people of that system. The name Giovanni was tied into a painfully embarrassing defeat, where a single cruiser had destroyed or routed over a dozen privateers and commanded the surrender of an entire star system. The handful of officers and enlisted from Tehran that Lucius had encountered had viewed him as the very symbol of the Great Enemy... and they were the ones considered trustworthy enough to serve in Nova Roma's military.

That highlighted another issue with the planet and system. While the general population maintained a fairly high level of technology and education, a large fraction of their people were religious zealots of the least accepting sort. They were reactionaries who distrusted technology, distrusted outsiders, and were willing to resort to violence to get their way.

Their opposition of control by Nova Roma had ranged from intimidation and threats to armed uprising and everything in between. Under various names and organizations they had murdered hundreds of thousands of their own people and thousands of Nova Roma citizens. The sheer brutality of their actions had given the system a reputation of distaste to the point that the very name had become synonymous with untrustworthiness and savage violence.

It wasn't even that there weren't decent and good people there, Lucius felt. It was simply that the decent and good people who stepped forward to improve things were often the ones who were made examples of by the violent men who they tried to oppose.

Tehran had become a quagmire, long before the war with the Chxor was even a possibility. After the Chxor capture of the Danar system, the Nova Roma garrison had abandoned Tehran. They had evacuated all of their personnel and left defense of the system to the locals.

From what Lucius had heard, they *had* defended themselves against the Chxor. The last broadcasts from the planet, before Chxor occupation, had showed destruction of several Chxor ships in the force sent to seize the system. They had done so only after officially surrendering, which had led to a Chxor policy of engaging and destroying all possible threats rather than risking a surprise attack.

Since the Chxor had no way to really gauge or understand human religion, they simply assumed that all humans were untrustworthy and reacted accordingly.

Knowledge of how their actions had resulted in a Chxor policy that killed millions of unarmed men, women, and children had deepened the distaste with which most Nova Roma officers viewed the planet. Lucius was honest enough to admit that he was among that number.

Yet as he stared down at the green and blue surface of the planet, he never would have thought that the planet itself might be so beautiful.

"Sir," Ensign Forrest Perkins said from the doorway of the conference room, "Interim President Quzvini is here for the meeting."

Lucius restrained a slight sigh. Nevertheless, he turned and gave the Ensign a nod, "Thank you, Forrest, please send him in." It was something of an irony, he thought, that a native of Saragossa, serving under an officer born to Nova Roma, had brought the leader of Tehran for a meeting. *Even more so,* he thought morbidly, *since the Saragossans helped to conquer the system since their shipping was under as much a threat as our own.* That Nova Roma had turned upon Saragossa, decades later, made a muddled picture even worse.

Once again Lucius wondered if there was any way that his homeworld might ever regain its former position among human space. Certainly they had a long list of enemies made in their foreign policy, along with dark secrets that would further discredit them when they came to light. It made his own determination that much more solid when he considered his path with the United

Colonies. Negotiation in fair terms and abiding by treaties they established would be difficult in the short term, but in the long term those policies might well save them all.

Otherwise, to Lucius, when all the nostalgia and patriotism were stripped away, there was nothing worth saving. A people must stand for their nation.... but in return, the nation had a duty to be something worth standing for,

On that thought, Interim President Quzvini stepped into the room and Lucius had his first surprise.

The stereotype of the citizens of Tehran was the elder, bearded man, typically with a harsh, lined face and often dressed in robes. President Quzvini was a young man. Even with the use of some form of life extension treatment, there was no way to hide a certain gravitas that age brought to people. Quzvini was *young,* with a spring to his step and an eagerness to his face that almost made Lucius envious. This was a young man who saw possibilities and potential in every day.

Quzvini didn't wear a dour expression, his face was cheerful and he wore a smile like he didn't know any other expression. He also wore a simple and worn, but well-cared-for suit, old enough that Lucius would guess it was second hand or passed down, but tailored to fit, not a cast-off. Quzvini stepped forward and before Lucius even knew it, they were shaking hands. "Baron Giovanni, may I say it is a pleasure to meet you, face to face, and give you the thanks of not just my people and world, but of my own family, for saving us from the Chxor."

Lucius was completely taken aback. He had expected bluster, threats, even condemnations. He had, in fact, braced himself for a painful and unpleasant meeting, probably spent with men who didn't understand how little power they had being at the bottom of a gravity well without any way to strike at their enemies. The cheerful and yet humble thanks completely disarmed him.

Lucius realized that he had been silent too long and he shook the other man's hand as dutifully as he could manage, "It was the men and women of the Fleet who did the work, Mr President, not me."

The Interim President waved a hand at that, "Please, Baron, no need to be formal. My appointment at this time is merely a product of my positioning prior to your fortunate arrival to the system. My father, peace be upon him, would slap me across my ears if I were to insist on such a title." Quzvini gave a snort, "He being a baker, he had no patience for pompousness and less for arrogance." Quzvini gave a slight smile, "My given name is Muhameed Jubani, though most people simply call me MJ."

Lucius gave the younger man a bemused nod, "Very well... MJ, please, have a seat."

The younger man took a seat and glanced at the tea and quirked and eyebrow, "Thank you, Baron, for the tea, but I will have water, if you don't mind. I'm not quite the traditionalist that you might otherwise expect."

"So I guessed," Lucius said with a shake of his head. "Ensign Perkins, please have one of the stewards bring some water for our guest." He sat back and took a moment to study the young man across from him. Quzvini was taller than Lucius, almost taller than Forrest Perkins. He was also clean-shaven and his dark hair was neatly trimmed. His brown eyes were just as cheerful and energetic as the rest of him.

The young man seemed to read his mind. "Well," President Quzvini said, "If I don't live up to the stereotypes of my world... well, all the better, especially so that outsiders can see that we have more to offer besides unpleasant old men, yes?" The young man sipped at his water. "Have you visited Tehran before, Baron?"

"No," Lucius said. "I've not been stationed here and I had... reasons to avoid the system before my time in the military."

"Ah," Quzvini said, "Your father. Yes, it is probably to the best. He was not the most popular man in our history. Some of my people might have attacked you, sins of the father and that sort of thing." He waved a hand, "Thankfully, those times are past."

"Oh?" Lucius asked with narrowed eyes. "Forgive me if I'm doubtful, but it is my understanding that your people have very long memories."

The young Interim President gave a smile, "Yes... that is one way to say it. My grandfather told me tales about the Mongols of Old Earth and how they plundered our lands and destroyed our great cities... and he cursed their name while he told those stories. Grudges are things that we do not forget, old grievances are nursed and cherished as a way to keep warm in a long winter." Quzvini shrugged, "But my world has changed, much, since the Chxor came."

For just a moment, his expression of good cheer slipped, replaced by an expression of iron determination. "Those times were trying for my people, Baron. Trying in ways that you may not understand. Have your people told you how many of us there are, now?"

Lucius shook his head.

"By the very best efforts of my people, we guess only two hundred million," Quzvini said quietly, his smile gone. "There were nearly five hundred million of us when the Chxor came." Lucius looked away from the raw pain in the young man's face. "Three fifths of our population has died, Baron Giovanni... and that puts minor things such as mere retaliation for raids into perspective. Not even the Mongols of my ancestors times were as devastating. What is a small grudge over a minor humiliation compared to a near-extermination?"

Quzvini sighed, a sad, regretful expression, "Even the long memories of my people can set aside slight differences when the Chxor have taken so much from us. You must understand, Baron, that they killed us in numbers to the point that even they grew tired of it. They destroyed every temple, every mosque, every synagogue, and every religious school in an attempt to break us of our ways. They killed our leaders, our clerics, our teachers, and our doctors. Even, I must admit, our lawyers... though perhaps in that they did us some slight service."

"I am sorry," Lucius said softly. Yet in the pain he saw in the young man, he couldn't help but fear for the fate of his homeworld. How had Nova Roma fared with its population of billions?

"As are we all," Quzvini said. "I have buried my father, my grandfather, my mother, my sisters, and my brother." He shrugged, "Yet it is not as if we did not provoke the Chxor to still greater atrocities." His face went hard, "You have no doubt heard of the fanatical zealots among my people?"

Lucius nodded in response.

The young man's face was iron hard. "They were the ones who launched the suicide attacks that crippled many of the Chxor invasion ships. For their actions, the Chxor scorched every spaceport, every spacecraft, destroyed generations of effort in only a few hours... and that was merely the beginning." He closed his eyes in thought, "The zealots launched suicide attacks against Chxor barracks... so the Chxor would destroy a village in retaliation. Every blow they struck, the Chxor would kill ten, a hundred, even a thousand of us for every Chxor they killed. This went on for months... years... until we could take no more."

Quzvini met Lucius's eyes, his gaze solid and his face confident, "In the end, when faced with the extinction of not only our families but our very culture... we turned upon our own. It began when one of the holy fighters demanded a village provide them shelter before their planned assault on a Chxor spaceport." Quzvini shrugged, "The villagers knew that the Chxor would trace the attack back to them and that they would pay with their lives for the actions of these men. So they did what they knew they must... they killed them all." Quzvini shrugged, "You can imagine how it went from there."

Lucius winced a bit. A civil war the likes of which Quzvini had implied would be violent and vicious. Families would be split, as some chose religion over blood. This would be a fight in which they would know their enemies by name and where friendship, trust, and civility would vanish in a brutal melee in only a few seconds. On top of that, they were under the control of the Chxor, who would see *any* violence as an uprising and react accordingly.

"We lost a few more cities, but our more... reactionary members at that point were removed," Quzvini said. "Those moderates who sympathized with them resolved to restrain themselves and to the Chxor, I'm certain, it seemed as if we had done most of their work." He shrugged, "In a way, we had. But we had also learned some ways in which we could fight the Chxor without their instant retaliation."

"Oh?" Lucius asked.

Quzvini sipped at his water, "Yes. Hacking their systems and scrambling their orders and commands. Changing their shipping manifests. In some cases, sabotaging their vessel maintenance so that their cargo vessels malfunctioned and their shuttles fell out of the sky." He shrugged, "This seems to have worked, if not to remove them from our planet then to at least slow their assimilation of it. Long enough, anyway, for your fleet to arrive... which brings us here."

"So it does," Lucius said. "As you have no doubt heard, we have no intentions of claiming your world, we're merely conducting our war against the Chxor."

"Of course," Quzvini said. "Which is why I wish to offer, on behalf of my planet, a request of annexation into the United Colonies." He said the words lightly, as if he were asking for another cup of water.

"Excuse me?" Lucius said. He had expected threats, bluster, intimidation, possibly even violence and sabotage from the locals in efforts force the United Colonies out of the system. A polite request for annexation was not something he had even considered.

"A request for annexation," Quzvini said, a slight smile on his face. "Which I can see surprises you. It would have been better, I think, if I had felt out some of your people on this matter, but it is something that has come together only over the past few weeks." He sighed, "I'm sorry, Baron Giovanni, that I am not better at explaining this."

"I think it's less that you aren't doing a good job and more that this was rather unexpected," Lucius said dryly. "I suppose you have somewhat more concrete terms than 'annexation'?"

Quzvini nodded, "Of course, Baron. Our interim government has spent the past few days discussing what we would be willing to accept and I have drafted it up for you to look over."

"I'm not the final say," Lucius said in warning. "This will go before the United Colonies government, you understand. They'll have to put it to a vote." He would send copies to Kate Bueller to look over before it even went that far.

"My people understand this... yet we have seen what it is to be alone in this universe, without allies and friends. We want to avoid that in the future, to stand with those who have saved us and perhaps one day call them our friends," Quzvini said with a slight smile. "More than that, I wish, as do many of my people, to stand for those who need help as we did." His intensity and honesty shone through in every word.

Lucius was grateful for that. The hope and optimism he saw in Quzvini's eyes restored some of his faith in humanity and that was not a bad thing at all.

***

Lucius paused as he stepped into Admiral Dreyfus's quarters. He had heard that the Admiral's injuries were severe, yet he had somehow expected that after several weeks of recovery that the old man would somehow look himself.

Instead, Admiral Dreyfus sat. He was propped up in a hover-chair, his left leg still in the binding cast and his face still seamed with scar tissue. There was a pallor to his skin, too, and despite his anti-aging treatments, the Admiral looked very, very old. Even so, he managed a smile, "Baron! My apologies if I don't rise. Please, make yourself comfortable. I know we have the meeting in a few minutes, but it doesn't hurt to let the staff officers sweat a little, eh?"

Lucius didn't miss how stiffly the other man's head turned to follow him as he came to sit across from him. *The neck injury,* Lucius thought, *they mended the cracked vertebra but it hasn't healed fully yet.* Even so, Lucius could see that it wasn't his physical injuries that pained the old Admiral.

"How are you doing today, Baron?" Admiral Dreyfus asked.

"I'm doing better to see you up and about," Lucius said as he took his seat. "Though your doctor assures me that you should *not* be up and around just yet."

Admiral Dreyfus waved a hand in dismissal, "I've been hurt worse before and continued the mission then, as I will now. There are repairs and refitting that need my attention as the senior officer in the star system."

Lucius nodded, though he privately thought that there were other things that could use Admiral Dreyfus's attention. His earlier conversation with Interim President Quzvini highlighted the issue. Admiral Dreyfus seemed to have confused priorities… and issues that should have demanded his attention had fallen by the wayside. *It comes back to trust,* Lucius thought, *and how can I trust a man who let a century-long conspiracy go on under his nose?*

That thorny problem once again caused him to hold his tongue on the subject, because there was no good answer. Either he told Admiral Dreyfus now and they handled the situation together or he continued to keep him in the dark. Either choice made for some serious issues.

"Well," Lucius said, "I can't say I'm happy about the damage our people took here at Tehran, but I'm glad to see how hard they are working to repair it."

Admiral Dreyfus nodded and the shadows in his eyes suggested that the losses of men and women under his command had left other, deeper scars. "As per our earlier discussion, I will reorganize the Fleet as soon as these ships are combat capable. We'll go into a bit more detail during the staff meeting."

Admiral Dreyfus nodded, yet there was a hesitancy to that nod, almost as if he realized there was something that Lucius wasn't telling him. After a moment he activated his chair controls, "Well, we should get to that staff, meeting, eh? We wouldn't want them to think we were conspiring together in here, would we?"

"No, we wouldn't want that," Lucius said with a slight smile in return. He followed the Admiral out and then down the corridor to the briefing room.

The two staff sections as well as senior officers from many of the ships of the Dreyfus Fleet had assembled already. Lucius took his seat and glanced around the table, "Everyone ready?"

The nods that met his gaze were all confident, yet Lucius couldn't help but wonder at the confidence behind some of them. His gaze lingered on those he knew to be members of the conspiracy and he couldn't tell if they were more or less confident than their fellows around them.

"Go ahead, Captain Franks," Lucius said.

Admiral Dreyfus's Chief of Staff gave him a sharp nod, "Of course, sir," he said. "We'll begin with our best estimate of the Chxor positions in and around Nova Roma." He brought up a hologram that showed the Nova Roma system in abbreviated detail. "Captain Wu will begin the brief."

"Thank you, Captain Franks," Captain Wu said cheerfully, her face polite and attentive. Even so, her words instantly put Lucius's back up. Knowing that she was senior in the conspiracy, he distrusted almost everything she had to say. "As you can see, gentlemen, we have some limited intelligence based upon deep space scouting runs." Lucius nodded at that. The extensive Chxor sensor network did not extend much past the inner system, but the Nova Roma sensor network extended almost to the outer limit of the *outer* system… and the Chxor had full access to that with occupation. Those two sensor networks would detect the emergence of a ship from shadow space anywhere within the system and quite a distance outside. The only way around that was for a ship to emerge in deep space, well outside the system and to coast along the edges of the system with its systems on standby or to use one of the vessels equipped with stealth systems to creep through the system and back out into deep space. "We have confirmed some of what High

Commander Chxarals transmitted as well as giving us some idea of where their forces are deployed."

"The problem there," she said, "is that we have identified over seven hundred of the Chxor 5-class dreadnoughts and three thousand of their 10-class cruisers. Worse, they are operating in cohesive groups and adjusting their positions. That eliminates the prospect of jumping in on top of any one force in a surprise attack." Lucius grimaced, because that would have made an attack much easier. Normally the Chxor kept their ships at standby status until an enemy arrived in system. It was easier on their systems and it lowered maintenance costs. Most human nations, on the other hand, would maintain active drives in at least some percentage of their ships in a war situation. The adjustment by the Chxor commander was not one that Lucius approved of... he'd much rather fight an incompetent enemy. *Even a marginally competent enemy can get far too many of my people killed with seven hundred dreadnoughts at his disposal,* Lucius thought.

"While we have no way to confirm the presence of bombs or nerve gas in the habitats and stations throughout the system," Captain Wu continued, "There is little reason to suspect that they would need to lie about that in their broadcast to us."

"In all, the Chxor outgun us and have eight billion hostages which they have threatened to kill if we make a move on the system," Captain Wu said.

"Very well," Lucius said. "Now that we have that out of the way, I want everyone in this room to focus on one goal: a successful liberation of the Nova Roma system from Chxor occupation. I want every parameter investigated: infiltration, raiding, a full attack, *everything*. The end state is saving the eight billion people in the system, destabilizing Chxor control throughout the region, and assisting our Nova Roma allies in returning home."

Lucius's words met with silence. Most of the faces around the conference table were thoughtful, men and women who had already begun to work on the problem and to whom this was merely a case of openly stating what they already expected.

Some faces, however, held rather different expressions.

Senior Captain Ngo spoke up, "Baron Giovanni, I can't help but note that you have set us with an impossible task. Any battle plan we undertake will pose not only massive risk for our own forces but also inconceivable risk for the inhabitants of the star system."

"Excuse me?" Lucius asked.

"Well, Baron, we have all seen High Commander Chxarals's broadcast. The Chxor are willing to kill every man, woman, and child in the star system if even *one* of our ships enters the system. The important thing is, however, that they're willing to cease their attacks, to establish a permanent border. If that is the case, and if we can perhaps work out some sort of lasting treaty with them, then we might maintain the safety of the people in that system without risking their lives and our forces." Senior Captain Ngo said the last with a tone of eagerness, as if he had solved some problem quite handily.

Lucius stared at him for a long moment. "That is dependent upon two factors which we have no reason to believe to be true: one, that the Chxor will abide by any treaty for a longer span than they see some advantage in breaking it and two, that we would betray our word to allies who have put themselves at risk multiple times to defend us." Senior Captain Ngo opened his mouth to argue and Lucius stared the man down until he closed his mouth. "Regardless of what we do, be assured that the Chxor will kill every man, woman, and child on all the worlds they control. They will do that because they see themselves as a superior race. They have killed *hundreds* of millions here in the Tehran system with systematic violence and utter disdain for human life. They will continue to kill humans until we can either shatter their empire or force them to reevaluate their fundamental principles."

Senior Captain Ngo looked pained, "Baron, surely this is them doing just that? We have every reason to believe that they *have* changed their belief system. We've seen changes in their operating parameters and–"

Lucius cut him off, "Everything we have seen thus far is merely an extension of their current paradigm applied to the problem. Holding an entire star system hostage to our good behavior? Threatening extinction of innocent people while offering us a meaningless peace treaty that will last only until it suits them? The Chxor are merely consolidating their forces and trying to delay us long enough to give them the time they need to return to the offensive. If you believe otherwise, Captain, you are sadly mistaken."

Senior Captain Ngo flushed and he opened his mouth to reply. As he did so, alarms started to wail and a voice came over the intercom, "All personnel, battle stations, Chxor fleet inbound."

***

"Count is two hundred and thirteen Five-class dreadnoughts and six hundred and twelve Ten-class cruisers," Ensign Camilla Jiang said as Lucius stepped onto his flag bridge. She immediately brought up a holographic overlay that showed their position within the Tehran system. "So far, they haven't begun jamming and they seem to be in a cruising formation rather than battle formation."

"Possibly a convoy en route that didn't get the message?" Lieutenant Moritz asked nervously.

"No," Lucius said, even as he saw most of the rest of his staff shake their heads. "Chxor capital ships mount ansibles. They're more power intensive than Nova Roma designs but they're good enough for them to be updated the status of their systems. Any Chxor commander coming here would know who holds the system. If it were meant to be a surprise attack, they would have come in *much* closer. If this were a deliberate attack, they would have larger numbers."

He saw the others nod at that. "This is something else..." He pursed his lips and then his eyes narrowed at a sudden thought. "Have we challenged them, yet?"

Ensign Konetsky shook her head, "Not yet, sir."

Lucius took a seat at his station. "Very well, transmit this to them with standard Faraday encryption: Greetings, Captain Kral and welcome back." Faraday encryption was the code frequency sets that they had used for the Third Battle of Faraday

Konetsky stared at Lucius for a long moment, before she turned back to her console. A moment later she looked up, "Sir, they've responded with a broadcast, encrypted with one of our codes, I'm putting it up on your screen."

"Greetings, Baron, I hope you didn't take our little surprise the wrong way?" Kral the Chxor said. His expression was what passed for humorous, though only weeks of working with him had taught Lucius even that much. *I don't even want to think about how his laugh sounds,* Lucius thought. This though, was about as good as Chxor humor seemed to get and even then, it was only those handful that embraced emotion and who Lucius had liberated from the Benevolence Council that might try such a "joke" as this.

"Well, we *were* in the middle of a staff meeting, but since you nicely highlighted a point I was making at the time, I suppose I can forgive you," Lucius smiled in return. The rubbery, gray flesh of his only Chxor friend was just as repulsive as he remembered. His waxy, lumpen features and box-like head made him look a caricature of a human, like something created by someone who knew all the measurements but not *quite* how they were supposed to go together.

"Well, it is best to maintain operational readiness," Kral said perfunctorily. "Still, I have much to discuss with you and, as you can see, I've met with some measure of success in my mission."

"It certainly seems so," Lucius said. "I'll transmit orders to stand down and you can bring your ships in. We've a great deal to discuss, I expect."

"More than you realize, Baron Giovanni," Kral nodded.

***

There was obvious strain on the faces of the Marines who escorted Kral and two of his fellows to Lucius's quarters. Whether that was because they didn't trust these Chxor or simply because they didn't trust *any* Chxor, Lucius couldn't guess. That didn't stop him from dismissing them out into the hallway.

He didn't recognize the other two Chxor with his friend, but he trusted Kral. Kral might have betrayed the Chxor Empire, but he had done so only after they had murdered his sole offspring and their inept commanders had left him and his ship's crew to die. Kral had held Lucius's life and the lives of his men in his hands on more than one occasion. More than that, he was a consummate professional... he would never allow anyone into Lucius's presence unless he felt certain that they would bring no harm to him.

Besides, as a show of trust, it would go further with them than any number of words.

"Baron Lucius Giovanni," Kral said, "Allow me to introduce Fleet Commander Khron and System Commander Thxun." Lucius gave them both polite bows, which they returned. "Fleet Commander Khron is from the Garan system and System Commander Thxun controls the Ull system. They are here as representatives of a larger group of senior Chxor officers who disagree with the edicts of the Benevolence Council.”

Lucius didn't miss the fact that Kral had not used the words 'unhappy' or 'displeased' which in turn suggested that one or both of these Chxor officers were less enlightened regarding their own repressed emotions.

“I find it efficient that we undertake an effort to organize our opposition together,” System Commander Thxun said. “In particular, I think that mutual self-interest requires that we plan higher level strategy in order to synergize our efforts for maximum effectiveness.”

Lucius gave the Chxor officer a nod of agreement, “Of course. Am I correct in estimating that you would like a full brief of our capabilities prior to any strategic discussions?”

“This would be most efficient,” System Commander Thxun said.

“Good,” Lucius said as he toggled his intercom, “Ensign Jiang, System Commander Thxun and Fleet Commander Khron are ready for your briefing.”

As Camilla Jiang stepped through the open hatch, Fleet Commander Khron held up one hand politely. “I will be along in only a few *juhn*, System Commander. I must confer with Fleet Commander Kral and Baron Giovanni in regards to the dispositions of my ships.”

Thxun gave him a nod of acknowledgment before he followed Ensign Jiang out of the quarters. To Lucius's surprise, Khron gave Lucius a nod and a wink as he took a seat, “System Commander Thxun can be a bit... proper, sometimes, Baron.”

“Oh?” Lucius asked as he sat down behind his desk. He shot a glance at Kral, but his Chxor friend's face was rather impassive.

“I apologize for putting you off your guard,” Khron said, his voice far more expressive than any other Chxor that Lucius had encountered. “I believe that I caught young Klar off guard, as well, upon our first meeting.”

“And how was that?” Lucius asked.

“I arrested him and several of his crew as they tried to infiltrate the Garan system,” Khron said jauntily. “They had already carried out their infiltration in several other systems and so they were rather surprised when I apprehended them immediately after their arrival. Still, I think it was a larger surprise to Kral when I revealed *why* it was that I so easily apprehended him."

Lucius cocked an eyebrow at that, though he could admit to himself that he was more impressed by the easy way that Khron expressed himself and showed emotions than his statement. "Why was that?" Lucius asked.

"Khron is my father," Kral said softly.

Lucius froze, "I thought that Chxor offspring were raised in a separate crèche and that they never met their parents?"

"They are," Khron said. "I have, however, managed to monitor my son's progress. While I could not actively take a role in his life, until now, I have managed to shelter him from some of the consequences of growing up under the Benevolence Council."

"He saved my offspring," Kral said.

That took a long moment to register for Lucius. Kral had admitted to Lucius not long after his surrender that his offspring would be killed as a consequence of his defeat by 'inferior' species such as humans. He had, however, also stated that the lives of his crew and officers meant more than the life of just one Chxor, which is why he had surrendered. For that matter, Kral had been certain that whether or not he went down fighting, his child would still pay the price for his failure. Lucius clapped Kral on the shoulder, "Congratulations! That is excellent news, my friend."

"Thank you," Kral said. "It was something of a shock. I had not met my offspring – that is, Khrol, until after System Commander Khron captured me, but it was good to finally meet her."

"His arrival triggered some of my security protocols," Khron said. "Which allowed me to capture him and his companions quietly. After I told him *why* he could trust me, he told me about his efforts and about you, Baron," Khron said. "Which is what brings us here, as you must realize."

Lucius did the math, "You have a conspiracy of your own in place already."

Khron nodded, "We've been waiting for the opportune moment for some time, now. The strain on the Empire from the war with Nova Roma has pushed it almost to the breaking point. The addition of being able to control our own reproduction without the oversight of the Benevolence Council has given us freedom we had not expected. We believe that we can take and hold over thirty percent of our Empire's worlds, many of them supply and manufacturing hubs. Another thirty percent are recently captured human worlds which we think will be either abandoned or recaptured by human forces."

Lucius sat back at that, "Which means the Chxor Empire would cease to be a threat to humanity... if you succeed."

"And my people would no longer be locked under the rule of the Benevolence Council as they have for over ten thousand *akron*," Khron said. He looked at Kral who nodded.

"What we aim to do, Baron," Kral said, "Is to strike a joint blow, against the largest and most loyal force that the Benevolence Council has fielded in the history of the Chxor Empire. We think that if we can defeat them, the rest of the Empire will realize that the Benevolence Council is not infallible... and that there are other options."

Khron leaned forward, "We want to help you defeat High Commander Chxarals at Nova Roma." His remarkably expressive voice showed his excitement and Lucius marveled at the Chxor's self control that he had lived so long in hiding. The Chxor would exterminate any of their own kind who expressed emotions. How had Khron survived so long and risen to such a high position? Was it some measure of the power of his conspiracy or a measure of his own capabilities?

Lucius sat back as he considered their offer. "I assume that infiltration by Chxor agents will be the main method of support?"

"We are willing to lend the entire force here under Fleet Commander Kral as support as well as agents already in place and en route to the Nova Roma system," Khron said. "Through the efforts of some of our agents, Fleet Commander Kral has very authentic orders placing his force under the control of High Commander Chxarals."

"Really?" Lucius asked, surprised. "That can be *very* useful." An agent on the inside, particularly an agent with two hundred dreadnoughts, would be an asset that Lucius couldn't discount. "How large a percentage of your overall forces is that?"

"This force represents almost half of the forces that we can actively muster," Khron said. "However, we believe that a solid defeat of High Commander Chxarals will swing many System Commanders into our ranks. It is, as you humans say, a gamble. Right now we have many senior Chxor officers who are ambitious but lack true conviction to fight the Benevolence Council." He looked over to the door, "System Commander Thxun is representative of those. We believe that a solid defeat will show others that the Benevolence Council is weak and therefore, must be replaced."

"But all the same, they don't view humans as favorable allies?" Lucius asked.

Khron shrugged, "To be honest, few of my kind looks upon yours in any favorable light. Only the fact that my son speaks well of you has swayed me this far... but that we discuss this in the Tehran system shows that you *can* defeat Chxarals. The only way my people will win this is to defeat him, destroy his fleet and show that he and those he supports are inferior."

Lucius cocked his head, "And who will end up as the leader of your new nation?"

Khron gave what might pass for a knowing smile, "This is something that those such as Thxun have put much thought upon. I am certain it will shape out in a way that favors those who have put the most thought into it." His tone suggested that he would be more than willing to be the leader of that new nation... which suited Lucius just fine. In fact, Lucius didn't care if the Chxor spent the next century involved in an internal civil war, so long as they weren't a threat to humanity.

"Well, we've much to discuss, then," Lucius said with a matching smile

***

Ensign Camilla Jiang watched the hatch close behind the two Chxor officers and gave a slight sigh. The arrival of these new allies made Baron Giovanni's position on liberating Nova Roma all the stronger. In theory this should have converted those who opposed that action to his perspective or at least convinced them to quiet their arguments.

Camilla, however, had a unique perspective on just why this wasn't the case. Her position within the secret organization that ran the Fleet from behind the scenes allowed her to see far more than anyone might have guessed, including her nominal superiors within the organization.

What she saw was nervousness and fear. They had operated in the shadows for so long that recent events had made them uneasy. While Command hadn't discussed it, someone had tripped security alarms on certain files. Someone suspected... and this kind of conspiracy was something that thrived *only* in complete secrecy.

Camilla knew well enough that it had to be some of the Baron's agents, if not the Baron himself investigating. It was something she had expected, ever since his arrival. His people were far too capable, he showed far too great a presence and focus to ever be the figurehead that Command had hoped to use for their own goals.

It was, in fact, why she had orchestrated certain rumors to be passed along... not with the goal of discrediting him, as Command had directed, but with the purpose of drawing his attention. If her plan had proceeded, she would have had the opportunity to deal with the situation in her own way... in a fashion that Command would not have approved.

Yet, things had moved far too quickly. The victories against the Chxor had come too quickly. The plan to liberate Nova Roma would come soon, far sooner than even she had anticipated, and with Command already on edge over the threat of being revealed, they might just pull the trigger on Omega Protocol.

Camilla didn't want that. At best, it would leave thousands dead and create chaos. At worst, it would trigger infighting that would tear the Fleet apart and leave it a vulnerable target for their enemies. Command knew that, but they were afraid. Fearful men did stupid things, as Camilla well knew. Fear was what had put them in this position, fear and worry about a future planned out by someone else.

*It seemed so simple to them,* Camilla thought sourly, *ensure that the power to control our future lay in the hands of capable men and women, not the hands of a tyrant or populist, but the hands of officers who cared about the men and women under their command.*

Camilla had seen that go wrong from the very beginning, as secrecy and fear twisted the idealism that they had started with. Part of that came from ambition and the rest from distrust. The sheer power represented by the Fleet, combined with the fact that they had already violated their oaths, meant that for those who joined their organization, this was not an opportunity they could pass up. Men and women who could have looked forward to prestigious careers could instead become rulers of entire star systems. Why should they not, when they had given up their lives, their families, and abandoned everything to save humanity?

And since they knew that some of their fellows and that most of the crews didn't feel the same way... well, they knew they had to maintain secrecy. And that secrecy had become more and more ingrained over the past decades. At first, they had killed only to maintain that secrecy, but those times were past.

*Now their precious secrecy is at risk,* she thought, *and they're so close to their goals, but so afraid that Giovanni will lead them into a battle they can't win.* They had lived too long, she knew, lived lives where they hadn't been called to risk themselves. The fight with the Balor at the Third Battle of Faraday had been a wake-up for many of them, a reminder that in war people died. For many, especially for Command, that was a rude awakening.

Fear had made them jumpy, the reminder of their own mortality even more so, and now Baron Giovanni had a solid base with which to build a battle plan upon. *He has forced them to act, even if he doesn't realize it,* Camilla thought anxiously. Some part of her wondered if he *had* planned to force them into action, but she didn't think he was so drawn to risky gambits. She suspected that he'd become aware of the conspirators, but she didn't know for certain. For all she knew, one of his loyal officers had only begun the investigation when he had tripped the alarm. The Baron might not even begin to suspect the plotting going on in the shadows around him.

Camilla had to act. Yet, at the same time, her own cautious plans were in as much disarray as those of Command. Decades of hard work could be undone in an instant and Camilla feared that even if she took action, it might only trigger the bloodbath of Command's Omega Protocol anyway.

***

Tehran System
United Colonies
December 16, 2404

"So, Emperor Romulus," Lucius said, "What we are thinking is that we will begin to infiltrate human personnel in conjunction with our Chxor allies..." He trailed off as he saw Emperor Romulus IV scowl at Admiral Valens Balventia. "Is there a problem?"

"We've... already begun infiltrating personnel and weapons to the Nova Roma system," Admiral Balventia said as he shifted in his seat

"*What?*" Lucius demanded. Around him, he heard the conference room buzz with surprised conversation. The Chxor had threatened to kill everyone in the star system if they saw any sign of aggression. Lucius found it hard to believe that the Emperor of Nova Roma had risked the lives of his people in such a dangerous fashion.

"I requested some plans from Admiral Balventia regarding the possibility of putting people into the system," Emperor Romulus sighed. "We have something of a... hidden resource in the system. Since we weren't entirely certain that you would move against the Chxor after their ultimatum, we thought it wise to begin our own operation... just in case."

Lucius ran a hand over his face, yet after a calming breath, he just gave a nod. "Very well," he said. "What can you tell us?"

Admiral Balventia gave a suspicious glance at Kral the Chxor, "I'm not entirely certain that we should be discussing this..."

"Admiral," Lucius said in as calm and even a tone as he could manage. "Kral has risked his life numerous times, including infiltrating several Chxor worlds. He has had multiple opportunities to betray us, yet every time he has proven that he can be trusted."

"Maybe by *you*," Valens Balventia snapped.

"Enough," Emperor Romulus IV said as he glared at his Admiral. "I will tell you... and I will take responsibility if it turns out that this was a foolhardy risk." He gave a sigh, "My father was... not a particularly trusting man, particularly after the coup attempt by your – by Marius Giovanni." He pulled out his data pad and typed in several commands. "As something of a precaution, he had a secret installation built which could act as a hideaway or as a location from which to launch a counter-coup. It was code-named Theta Station. We've been slipping ships in and out of the system there and meeting clandestinely with some of the resistance groups."

Admiral Dreyfus leaned forward, "The Chxor occupation strategy is to seed the entire system with sensor arrays and buoys. How can you be certain they won't have found this station and they aren't already aware of your activities?"

Admiral Balventia sat up straighter, "We are certain that the Chxor are unaware, because Theta Station is located in the Periclum Debris Cloud."

Most of the staff looked blank, but Lucius nodded slowly. He looked around and seeing the confusion, spoke up, "Periclum was Nova Roma's weapons testing area for over fifty years, it used to be a planetoid until it was destroyed by a collision with a comet. It is one of the densest debris fields in the system and it is also where a number of radioactive hulks and older ships were towed for use as target practice. In addition to that, it has a number of still live mines, missiles, and who knows what else." Just the density of the cloud would make sensor readings difficult. Some areas of the debris had been bombarded by exotic particles or fused into superheavy or unstable isotopes that gave off extreme radiation that would make it nearly impossible for any sensors to get a good reading off the cloud.

Emperor Romulus IV nodded, "And not all of the ships sent there were used as target practice. There is a small fleet, mostly assault shuttles, fighters, and light frigates, kept at Theta Station in mothball, along with large supplies of weapons and ammunition. It is positioned in between the orbits of Nova Roma and Nova Umbria, with access to both. It is also near enough to several mining operations that mining and supply ships can link up with our vessels to transfer personnel and equipment."

"Which isn't to say it's ideal," Lucius said. "The Chxor are leaving the orbital infrastructure intact, for now, but soon they'll take more centralized control. It's only a matter of time before either you'd have to shut down those connections or risk discovery."

"I was hoping that we could move before then," the Emperor of Nova Roma said.

"We'd better," Captain Franks said, "else the Chxor will pile onto that station and then probably leave the rest of the system in ruins."

Lucius looked up at that, "You know... you may have a point there."

"What?" Captain Franks asked his eyes wide, "Certainly you can't be suggesting–"

Of everyone, it was Admiral Balventia who caught Lucius's point, "That just might work." As the gazes of the assembled officers leveled on him, he gave Lucius a small but respectful nod. "Our main issue, so far, has been to draw the Chxor away from both planets in enough size that their reserve forces could be engaged and destroyed without risking the planet. However, if the Chxor learn about a smuggling operation within the system that supplies the resistance fighters there, then they will almost certainly respond in force."

"Particularly," Lucius said with a nod, "If they learn that this base is both well-defended and stocked with bombers, fighters, and light warships. They'll want to smash that kind of force before it can become a threat, especially if they think *we* don't know about it yet."

Around the table, Lucius saw heads begin to nod.

It was Captain Daniel Beeson who spoke, "And then," he said, "we can bring our *own* fleet in and smash the bastards when they're vulnerable."

Admiral Balventia gave Lucius a slight smile, "Okay, Baron Giovanni, that sounds like a plan I like." It was the first time that Lucius could remember the Admiral using his title, a not quite sign of approval, and it made Lucius feel almost off-balance. "Well," Lucius cleared his throat, "what resources do we have in place there? Whatever we can bring online will both make the Chxor more anxious to respond in force and give us a bit more of an edge."

"We've a small team of personnel at the station," Admiral Mund said slowly. Clearly he felt uncomfortable having kept the secret, but just as clearly he felt better for being able to talk about it. "They haven't completed the full inventory, but so far it looks like just over a hundred and fifty of the old Canis-class bombers, forty-eight of the newer Regis-class interceptors, twelve of the Icon-class corvettes, and six Patrician-class frigates."

"Two wings of bombers, two squadrons of corvettes, and a squadron of frigates," Lucius mused. He sat back in his seat and then slowly gave a nod, "It's a respectable force, one that the Chxor won't be able to discount. I'm not certain it will be enough to draw all of their forces, though."

Admiral Dreyfus frowned, "I assume the plan is for us to move into position to support the defense and engage them from surprise?" Lucius gave a nod and Admiral Dreyfus's frown deepened, "We'll need to draw them close to the facility. From what I understand, Chxarals operates his forces in separate task forces, he may not send all of them."

Lucius nodded slowly, "That is my concern, as well."

"Surely," Senior Captain Gronsky said, "Some is better than none?"

Lucius gave the man a sharp look, "If even one dreadnought is positioned where we can't destroy it or at least take it under fire, then they could still kill millions with their main armaments alone. Given enough time, a squadron could volley their missiles and kill billions." He shook his head, "No, we need to lure the majority of Chxarals's forces to where they *can't* engage the planet. Which means into the vicinity of Theta Station. But we don't have anything valuable enough to do that, or at least not without Chxarals deciding to have done with it and annihilate the system."

"Me," Emperor Romulus IV said.

"What?" Lucius asked in surprise.

"Send me. I will be a target too important for him to risk letting me escape. We leak information that I'm personally on hand to lead and direct a popular uprising against the Chxor. Given my value as a figurehead as well as the strength of my forces, we can be absolutely certain that Chxarals will try to hit me with everything he's got." The young Emperor looked around at the surprised faces, "Better yet, we let them see what I have in position, my entire force. Allow one of their ships to get close enough and survive to report."

"Your Majesty," Admiral Balventia said, "You *can't* be serious. If we lose you..."

"If this effort fails, we lose Nova Roma, possibly for good. The billions of people there have no choice in how we risk their lives... the least *I* can do is put my own life on the line." Emperor Romulus IV said. He looked over at Lucius, "I'm afraid that I will have to insist. It is, after all, my resources we're using to pull this off."

Lucius gave him a slight nod, "If you insist, then I won't stop you. I agree, the combination of your forces and yourself present will be extremely tempting for the Chxor. Even if Chxarals doesn't want to move out of position, he might be overruled." The report of the Emperor's return to Nova Roma would certainly be information that would reach the Benevolence Council, Lucius figured.

"This might just work," Admiral Dreyfus said with a look at his staff. Lucius wasn't certain, but he thought he saw an expression of either distaste or disagreement on Captain Wu's face. *Is that because she doesn't like the plan,* Lucius wondered, *or because the conspirators don't want to see Nova Roma liberated?* Not for the first time, Lucius wished he had some better idea of what the conspirators wanted. Maybe, if they had come to him in the first place, they could have reached some agreement. *Then again*, he thought, *they had already killed a dozen people between the shuttle accident and a few other deaths, possibly more from some of the new evidence Captain Beeson uncovered.*

"Very well," Lucius said, "I want a working plan on how we are going to conduct the infiltration with a secondary organization, one the Chxor will locate, whose purpose is to leak the position of Theta Station and the Emperor's presence." He winced as he thought about just how *that* would go with the men and women involved.

"Criminals," Admiral Balventia said.

"Excuse me?" Admiral Dreyfus asked.

"We send in some criminals, pirates, murderers, that sort of thing. Tell them only what we want them to know. Sooner or later, they'll slip up and the ones the Chxor capture will probably offer them whatever they know to save their own skins. If they aren't captured, your Chxor, Kral, tips the authorities off and they pinch them anyway. If they do some damage to the Chxor, fine, if not, then we're out only the cost of transportation."

Lucius winced again as he thought of the cold calculation of sending men in to die, yet he under-stood it. He looked at Captain Beeson, "How many of those pirates we've captured are from Nova Roma?"

The younger man looked down at his notes, "I don't have exact figures, but I would guess about two dozen at most." The prisoners were on the icy moon in the Faraday system, where Lucius had started a pair of prison colonies to hold the Chxor and captured pirates. Sometime in the past, someone had seeded the planet with an Earth-type ecosystem, so while it was a frigid, inhospitable place, it was inhabitable, with enough oxygen to sustain life and enough wildlife to sustain a small population. Captain Beeson looked up, "There's about three hundred of them from Admiral Mannetti's crews that we captured."

"That seems fitting," Admiral Balventia said with a shrug. "Many of them are traitors and worse, anyway. Give them the option to fight for their freedom..."

Lucius sighed. In truth, many of them *were* pirate scum, some of the worst sorts, yet they had already spaced the ones that they could convict of actual crimes. For that matter, many of the ones left were men who had been captured aboard Nova Roma ships and either forced into piracy or volunteered from there. While they weren't precisely innocent, it seemed rather cold to send them into this mission knowing they were going to be captured or killed.

Yet the fates of billions were on the lines.

"Fine," Lucius said. "From here on, those prisoners will be dealt with only by Nova Roma personnel. I only want volunteers, if we force them into this it could go bad far too quickly."

Admiral Balventia shrugged, "Of course." He looked at Emperor Romulus, "If it pleases your Majesty, we can offer them some sort of bonus as well as their freedom, if they survive."

Emperor Romulus IV nodded. "Yes, and rewards to their families, if they do not."

The table went silent as everyone thought through the plan. "Right, then," Lucius said. "It seems we have something of a battle plan. Given the time frame that this infiltration will require, we need to have a plan finalized within the next few weeks and Fleet Commander Kral will need to leave, with any additional infiltrators aboard his ships, within the next month." That would leave countless details to be planned and organized and an entire invasion to organize in only thirty days. The daunting task had to be completed between two disparate organizations, one of them secretly handicapped by a conspiracy and the other short-handed and still training themselves up to standard. Lucius could see the dismay on many faces and he gave them all a smile, "I have the utmost confidence that you can get it done."

***

## Chapter III

Nova Corp Facility 223, Kied System
Centauri Confederation
December 16, 2403

"We have missiles inbound!" Lauren Kelly snapped as her fingers flashed across primary weapons control. A missile or two wouldn't be an issue given the *Kraken*'s fire control computers and array of energy weapons.

*Fifty missiles*, Mason thought, *is something else altogether.* The Nova Corporation defenses had already taken Captain Demitrovich and his crew. The pirate-turned-privateer had charged forward despite Mason's orders. Mason figured the man had hoped to capture the base on his own and benefit from a larger share of the loot as a result. He had paid the price for his arrogance, though, when the facility's automated defenses had opened up on his light cruiser with over a hundred missiles.

"Captain Penwaithe," Mason said, "Any time now..."

"We're trying, Commodore," Penwaithe's voice was distorted from interference. "They've got damned good jammers on those missile platforms, we're having difficulty picking them up at this range."

"Captain Oronkwo..." Mason said, his voice pitched to show the impatience that Stavros would feel. They had some visual scans, but at this range they couldn't tell the difference between a research platform and a missile array.

"We can't get close enough," Oronkwo's voice held a matching level of impatience. "Their sensors are too good, they're picking off every probe we send and my ships won't last long enough to get anything if we go in ourselves."

"Well, *my* ship won't last much longer under this kind of sustained fire," Mason growled. This base was supposed to be lightly guarded with just automated systems. None of Halcyon's intelligence had hinted at this level of firepower for what was supposed to be a minor research facility in a safe star system.

The wave of missiles came in, but the training Mason had put his squadron through paid off. They didn't have the fire discipline that a military crew would, but they were almost up to standards that he would have tolerated back when he had worked as a pirate in earnest.

The privateers didn't use interceptor missiles because they were expensive and hard to replace and they used up valuable cargo space. Instead, the *Kraken* maintained an outer kill radius while the other ships of the squadron operated under that umbrella. Captain Oronkwo's corvettes acted as spotters for that fire, just ahead of the formation and dispersed enough that they couldn't be taken out by an unlucky hit.

The fifty missiles died well clear of their targets, but some of Mason's ships were dangerously low on projectile ammunition. *They have to run out of missiles soon*, Mason thought, *Nova Corp is a company and no matter how important this place is, accountants always keep their eye on the bottom line.*

On that cue, Mendoza looked up, "Captain Stavros, the enemy missile platforms have gone quiet."

"It's about damned time," Mason growled. Those defenses had fired over five hundred missiles. While some were almost certainly single shot platforms, they had identified at least ten larger platforms that had to have substantial missile storage capacity. Every one of those missiles they had fired added up quickly. *They must have something pretty damned special here that they were willing to put up with that level of expense in defending it,* Mason thought.

"Jamming is still up," Captain Oronkwo said. "But we're able to focus more on their facilities without trying to track inbound. They're rotating their jamming platforms but I think we've identified three of them, coordinates coming online now."

"Captain Penwaithe, if your Hammers would engage those platforms," Mason said, his tone light. "Feel free to burn as much ammunition as you think necessary."

"Engaging," Garret Penwaithe's voice was still tight. Then again, his Hammers had sat idle for most of the fight so far, without any targets. They were big, slow gunboats designed to kill larger ships. Their missile racks could have served as interceptor fire, but the total inbound fire made that almost pointless, a drop in the bucket by comparison. He had to be feeling frustrated.

A moment later, the jamming cut off with brutal finality. Mason gave a predatory grin as sensor data began to pile up. Thankfully, Nova Corp still went by their profit margins. The company had purchased or constructed weapons platforms, but they had relied on their jamming and weight of fire as their main defense. Their defense screens were strictly civilian grade, more to prevent damage from a collision with debris than any real protection against enemy fire.

Even better, they had cut corners by building separate energy, sensor, and missile platforms. On that cue, without prompting, Captain Penwaithe took out the sensor platforms and left the weapons platforms blind. “Captain Oronkwo, if you would do the honors by verifying that their weapons are blind?”

Another flight of drones went out from Oronkwo's corvettes. Mason waited patiently, though he made certain to outwardly fidget. Stavros, after all, wasn't a patient man.

The probes swept over and around the facility and, after a few minutes, they confirmed that the platforms were blinded. “Message the facility,” Mason said. “Tell them we will graciously accept their surrender and that if they power their weapons platforms down now, we won't destroy them and cost Nova Corp still more money in a useless endeavor.”

***

Captain Garret Penwaithe growled as he looked over the cargo inventory. “What the hell is this?” he demanded as he looked up at the privateer who had delivered the manifest along with the stack of crates ready to be loaded up in the War Dogs transport ship's cargo hold.

“Don't ask me,” the woman said, “I just checked things off the list. Hell, I don't know what any of that shit is, anyway. I just hope I didn't break anything, it's all labeled with fragile and half of it is in foam cases we found the stuff with.”

“You should hope you didn't poison yourself or kill yourself from radiation,” Garret growled as he pointed at some of the markings on the cases. “Half this stuff is labeled as hazardous and toxic, the other half is radioactive.”

“What?” she asked. She looked back at the crates, “Me and my crew, we didn't know nothing about that!”

Garret bit back a pointed remark that he could see the labels and that the facility probably had similar labels on their storage lockers. “Well, you better get someone to check your people for exposure right away." He grimaced as he realized the implications. "Leave it all here, I'll get some of my crew suited up to check it all out and make certain it is secure for storage." He glanced at the manifest and saw that there was specific packing instructions on several of the items. Knowing his luck, if he signed for it now, it would be *his* people blamed if any of it was damaged in transit.

The woman had backed away already, her face worried. "Screw my crew, *I'm* getting checked out first. They can wait in line." She hurried away and her people followed her out of the hangar bay. Garret restrained a sigh and looked over at Tyrone Barrion. "Get some of our flight crew over here and have them suit up, full hazard gear. We need to go over all of this stuff and make certain it was packed right."

"Yes, sir," Tyrone said quickly.

Garret looked over to see that Abigail Gordon stood nearby, her perky face serious. "Sir," she said, "I've some experience around hazardous materials, want me to supervise?"

"Yes, Ensign, that works," Garret said with a nod. The last thing he wanted just now was to expose his ex-girlfriend's little sister to whatever was in those crates, but she probably did have more experience with it than anyone else on his crew. Her father had run the safety team at Halcyon's chemical processing plant and she had mentioned that she worked under him for a few years to pay for school. *Granted,* Garret thought, *she told me that when she interviewed for the War Dogs, so I really hope she wasn't exaggerating.*

He transferred her a copy of the manifest and then stepped back and let her take over as the flight crew arrived already suited up in their protective gear. She ran a quick inspection of their gear even as she donned her own and Garret nodded in appreciation before he turned his attention to the rest of his job.

His Hammers were gunboats designed to engage any ship up to capital size, with mass drivers sized for much bigger ships. They hadn't burned through much ammunition in this fight, but they had stressed the hulls of their gunships. Every time they fired their mass drivers it required a complete inspection and maintenance run. The Nova Corp facility had a full maintenance and servicing bay and since it was far enough out in the Kied system that they hoped no one had noticed the attack yet, Garret had ordered his Hammer crews to make the most of the free parts and the state-of-the-art tool sets.

He would have been more worried about getting the job done and leaving, but the entire squadron seemed pretty confident after taking the facility. The facility's logs confirmed that the base didn't have any kind of ansible system and that Stavros's jamming had prevented any radio message from getting out to the local garrison.

That last was the important part to Garret. Kied was officially a holding of the Centauri Confederation. The system had two inhabited worlds, one of them a life-bearing, blue-green orb that was home to over fifteen billion inhabitants and the other a mineral-rich rock with “only” a couple billion. The Centauri Confederation presence was mostly centered around those two worlds, but it was almost certain that they would have patrols to check in on the various mining colonies, fabrication plants, and other facilities throughout the system. It wasn't a military system like Delta Pavonis or Centauri itself, but the forces present would be more than capable of defeating Stavros's squadron.

The Nova Corp facility seemed fairly secretive, for that matter, Garret thought. The defense and research platforms were hidden within a small debris cloud, the remnants of a dead comet or some other bit of stellar detritus. He wondered if Nova Corp had kept the place secret from the Centauri Confederation's government in order to keep any of their research findings to themselves, rather than being forced to share them with the government-run corporations.

“Six and Seven both show signs of microfractures,” Warrant Officer Jude Derstele said as he brought the mass spectrometer data up. “I think we can weld them, neither set is at a critical point just now, but...”

“Nine is the one that we need to be worried about, yeah,” Garret said as he brought up the display. The Nova Corp facility had some *very* nice evaluation systems for their maintenance work, and Garret had already put in a request to Stavros to see if they could pack those systems up, somehow.

*Hell,* he thought, *better that than everything on that manifest.*

“I don't think we can weld those fracture points,” Garret said as he refocused on the task at hand. “And we don't have the time to machine new braces for the mount on Nine, much less to replace them here.”

Jude nodded, his face morose, “She's deadlined, then?”

"Main gun, anyway," Garret said, "emergency fire only and we need to remind Caela to go cautious on the throttle too, but I think Nine is flyable. Thank God we found those fractures," It was a good thing they had the time to do the scan, he knew, else they *wouldn't* have found them. Over time, the mass driver's fire had torn part of the weapon mount bracing, but on the inside where a physical inspection wouldn't have seen it, not without a full tear-down.

Until they replaced the bracing it would be extremely dangerous to fire Nine's mass driver. It could rip completely free and tear the gunboat in half... or worse, tear only partially free and shred the entire ship as the grav-plates went out of alignment and generated counter-force across the entire frame.

Caela was Nine's pilot and she had been with the War Dogs since long before Garret. She was an excellent pilot and gunner and Garret was damned glad that they had caught this before it went any further.

"Right," Garret said, "Once they're done inventorying that cargo, make certain our flight crews are briefed on the work and then lets get our birds buttoned up again. I want to be ready to go as soon as the rest of our squadron is finished."

He had turned away before he realized that he had referred to Stavros's squadron as "ours" and not "them." It was an odd realization, for while Stavros had saved Garret's life, he was also a murdering piece of scum, a pirate, and probably perfectly willing to kill Garret when he saw any profit in it. For that matter, most of the rest of his squadron was made up of pirates and privateers who were as bad or worse. Somehow, though, his training had made them work together, something that was entirely unexpected to Garret.

*For that matter*, Garret thought, *sometimes it's like Stavros is almost a good leader in spite of himself.* Certainly there were times that it almost seemed that his flamboyant exterior slipped and revealed a level of thought and consideration that was entirely unexpected.

Before Garret could think about it anymore than that, Abigail Gordon came up to him, "Well, sir, we've finished the inventory. Nothing broken and the seals on all the really nasty stuff are all still intact. Some of the rest was packed badly, but we got it squared away."

"Good," Garret said. He glanced at the manifest again and his eyes narrowed at the long list, most of which was merely alphanumeric tags. Why in heaven's name they had chosen that other privateer to pack it and deliver it to him he hadn't a clue. *Hell*, he thought, *there are a couple civilians from the briefing whose job this probably is, why aren't they doing it?* The pair hadn't spoken much during the brief on the facility, other than to caution against damage of any of the research labs and the valuable equipment they contained.

His eyes widened, though, as he *did* recognize something. "Hey..." he asked in as nonchalant voice as he could manage, "Some of this is alien stuff, right?"

Abigail gave him a nod, "Yes, sir, I recognized that right off, but the manifest has those items highlighted as priority. I'm not certain why, exactly, the data on the crate just has them listed as 'nonfunctional artifacts, miscellaneous' and the datapad in the crate lists them as non-hazardous."

"Right," Garret nodded. Yet what stuck out to him was the *origin* of the alien items. They came from Tybar in the Carran system, which was where one of the bigger Zarakassakaraz excavations lay. Garret had read up on what he could find on the extinct alien race after finding an article that said the alien artifacts found at Halcyon were thought to be of Zarakassakaraz origin.

From what Garret had read, the Zar – as almost everyone without multiple doctorates called them – were a humanoid alien species who had lived in the region of space which contained the Anvil, Carran, and Garris Major systems, though some of their ruins were found as far afield as Nova Roma space. They had died out in some ancient cataclysm or war almost a million years earlier... and their working artifacts were generally considered extremely valuable because their technology was generally usable or adaptable to humans.

If those parts came from Carran and *if* they were as important as he suspected, then this might just be the clue that Commodore Pierce needed to put this all together. "Well, before you load it all up, I'd like you to take some pictures of the alien stuff, just to make certain our ham-handed friends didn't break anything. It's nice to have proof that it was like that when we got it, right?"

Abigail cocked her head at him for a moment, before her eyes went wide and she gave him a nod. "Yeah, I'll get right on that, sir."

*I had better talk to her again*, Garret thought, *when we get a bit more privacy and see if she knows any more than she's told me about what they found at Brokenjaw Mountain.*

***

"Ah, this is the life," Commodore Stavros said, his feet up on his console and his black leather boots polished to a high sheen. He puffed at a cigar, taken from the facility administrator's office and blew smoke rings into the air.

Lauren Kelly just rolled her eyes as she ran down her checklist. Most of the rest of the crew had become so inured to his activities that they would take it amiss if he *didn't* act that way. For that matter, Lauren had come to compartmentalize her thoughts of Mason and Stavros. The one was a chauvinistic, self-indulgent pig and the other was the man that she could privately admit that she was coming to love. One was the public appearance and the other a persona adopted in an effort to make right after years of villainy every bit as bad as Stavros. Lauren had spent many long, wakeful hours thinking about the nature of love and redemption.

It was Mason who had cautioned that the facility's senior administrator had become entirely *too* cooperative, pointing out expensive parts and equipment that would take "only a little longer" to get loaded up. As Stavros, he couldn't express those cautions, but he had been able to exaggerate his own eagerness to stay to the point that most of the other ships captains got anxious to leave. Still, Lauren worried that it was too late. Granted most of their cargo ships were away already, but Captain Montago and his crew were still at work disassembling a replacement main battery for his ship.

Lauren privately doubted the advanced energy weapons used by Nova Corp's automated defenses would replace the antiquated main gun from Montago's elderly Independence-class light cruiser. Still, she wasn't an engineer, so she couldn't say that it wouldn't work.

"Captain," Mendoza said. "I read ten vessels that just emerged from shadow space at seventy thousand kilometers." The sensor officer's voice was tight. "They're bringing their targeting systems online!"

Stavros's feet dropped off his console with a smooth motion and his voice was relaxed despite the tension that surged through the bridge, "Orders to all ships, defense screens online and commence jamming. Transports are to move to course..." Lauren could see him do the rough calculations in his head, "Three one eight. We'll begin plotting our shadow space jump as soon as all ships are up and operational."

Lauren pursed her lips at that. If it were up to her, they would jump now and leave the pirates still too busy looting to their fates. She'd seen enough of their "skills" to know that they were no more than dead weight in a surprise fight like this.

As if to underscore that thought, Captain Montago's voice came on the net, "Commodore Stavros, we'll need as much time as you can give us. We've got the weapon off its mount but it'll take us some time to get it transferred to my ship."

Stavros leaned into his display and Lauren saw anger loom in his eyes, "Montago, get your people back to your ship and get it moving. My sensors show three battlecruisers, two heavy cruisers, and a screen of five destroyers. If your ship isn't under way in the next three minutes, we'll see if you can handle that all on your own." His threat was all the more ominous from the way he didn't even raise his voice, Lauren thought.

Three minutes was more than she would have given the pirate, but it should still give them some margin for error. At seventy thousand kilometers, the enemy ships were well within missile range, but it would take them some time to get anything like accurate sensor readings to make accurate shots with their weapons, especially with the debris that surrounded the research station and the platforms that made up the facility itself.

*Three Nagri-class battlecruisers*, Lauren thought as she looked over the data, *which matches Nova Corp's response team for this area.* That meant that something had triggered the response and that the facility administrator must have known their response time. *Mason was right*, she thought.

"Missile launch!" Mendoza called out.

Lauren brought up the sensor feed on the missiles. Behind her she heard Stavros give orders on targeting envelopes for different ships. Before he even said anything she had uploaded the parameters into the computer. Her display updated as the missiles swept closer. Montago would have his three minutes, but only just. If they'd had Kandergain with them for this run, the psychic could have plotted a course quickly enough to escape to shadow space before the missiles arrived. Instead, they had to do things with a navigation computer.

"I'm not picking up active sensors, yet," Mendoza said as he tapped at his controls. "Not even from probes." He frowned. "Those ships *can't* have missile lock at that range on passive sensors!"

"I need better data on those missiles," Lauren said. The missiles weren't transmitting active sensors either, which made them very hard to see and shoot, especially at long range.

"They're not taking any kind of sensor feed from their ships," Mendoza said as his hands raced across his controls. "Dammit, it's like they're on passive sensors but they *can't* be that accurate at this range."

Lauren bit her lip. As the missiles swept in, she began to engage them. The *Kraken*'s main batteries were designed to engage capital ships, but they still had enough accuracy to engage the lighter missiles. Even so, targeting the small, barely radiating missiles was easier said than done. She felt sweat bead her brow as the eighteen missiles swept through her engagement area... and she only stopped five. Each of those detonated with sharp bursts of radiation when destroyed, a certain sign that they carried antimatter warheads.

"They'll *have* to go active on final approach," Mendoza said, his voice frantic.

"Captain Penwaithe, engage with interceptor missiles," Stavros snapped, "those birds are hot: one good hit is all it will take." That wasn't an underestimation, Lauren knew. The estimated payload on one of those would hammer even the *Kraken*'s defense screen flat and probably destroy the entire ship as well.

Azure Squadron volleyed a flight of interceptor missiles and more of the inbound fire died. The War Dogs carried some of the best missiles that money could buy, and their wickedly fast and agile interceptors swept into the formation, yet they didn't stop them all.

"Final protective fire, evasive maneuvers," Stavros said and turned the various ship captains free to maneuver and engage on their own. Lauren knew that a military unit would maintain overlapping, cohesive fire, but the various ship commanders lacked that level of discipline and trust.

Lauren's fingers roved over the controls and she overlay a mesh of fire at the missiles that came close. The two missiles she saw were damnably hard to see, even at this range and it took far too many shots for her to bring them both down. *They never went active,* she thought as the blazing flashes of antimatter and matter signaled their deaths.

She widened her sensor repeater just as the last pair of missiles broke through the squadron's defensive fire and swept past, both colliding with a pair of the transports formed up to jump away.

The three hundred megaton detonations erased both light cargo ships as if they had never been.

"Their target priority is the transports," Stavros said. "Close up formation to protect the loot."

Lauren looked over at Mendoza, a sudden thought bothering her, "They *never* went active, right?"

He nodded, his face pale as he realized how close they had come to death. Mendoza had never struck her as a particularly brave individual. "Check all radio frequencies for anything out of the ordinary." The missiles should not have been able to pick out the transports on passive sensors, not with the warships radiating much more powerfully and certainly not with the research facility platforms and debris cluttering up space.

"There's, there's nothing!" he protested a moment later. "I've got just the civilian transponders from the base and some background radiation."

*Background radiation...* she thought, *the cargo manifests listed radioactive hazards for some of the cargo.* "Scan the cargo ships for any radioactive components that stand out," she snapped.

Mendoza looked back at Stavros, "Sir, they're launching again, what's your priority?"

"Do as she says," Stavros snapped.

Mendoza worked quickly and a moment later, he looked up, "I'm picking up matching radiation signatures from the *Trangor*, the *Wolf Mother*, and the War Dog's transport. It's got to be some kind of radioactive isotope."

"They tagged the cargo," Stavros snapped. "Damn them. Open me a channel to them." A moment later, his voice was harsh, "*Trangor*, *Wolf Mother*, and *Star Dog*, the enemy has tagged your cargoes, you need to jettison them, *now*."

***

"...the enemy has tagged your cargoes, you need to jettison them, *now.*" Stavros's voice was angry, as well he should be, Garret knew. The loss of those cargoes would basically mean they had wasted their time here.

Worse was that they *couldn't* jettison the cargo off of the Hammer's carrier. It was secured in a supply locker deep inside the *Star Dog*. It would take at least thirty minutes to access it in the ship's tight corridors.

*And we've got inbound missiles in thirty seconds*, he thought. He keyed his radio to Stavros's channel, "Commodore," he said, "that's a negative on jettisoning our cargo, we haven't the time."

"And we're not dumping ours either," Captain Jack of the *Wolf Mother* snarled. "That's fifteen million per box in rare isotopes."

"*Wolf Mother*, you'll dump your cargo or I'll shoot you down myself," Stavros snarled. "Captain Penwaithe, we'll provide as much support as we can, but the navigation computer will take another ten minutes, at least."

"Acknowledged," Garret said. While the destruction of the *Star Dog* would leave his two squadrons of Hammers intact, it would also strand them in the system. Given the fuel requirements of his ships, they'd be sitting ducks within six hours, even if the enemy didn't want to use the missiles to kill them quickly.

*For that matter,* he thought, *the bastards might just sic the system security on us.*

They could evacuate the *Star Dog*, ditch their Hammers, and get picked up by one of the other ships in the privateer squadron. But that would be a deathblow to the War Dogs participation with Halcyon. Replacing twelve of the Hammers, even as surplus, would cost more than Commodore Pierce could afford. It would save Garret's pilots and support crew, but it would leave his homeworld at the mercy of pirates like Lucretta Mannetti, without any allies they could trust.

"Azure Flight," Garret said, "Let's disrupt the enemy a bit." The range was *very* long for their main guns. Even with the smart rounds for their mass drivers, the enemy's maneuvers would likely take them out of pocket for their rounds. "We'll fire brackets, on my mark." he said. The eleven Hammers would fire in boxes around the enemy ships in a pattern designed to allow at least a few of the rounds an eligible target despite the maneuvers. He brought the nose of his Hammer into line with his target and spoke as soon as his board flashed green to show the rest of his flight was ready, "Engage." The gut-shaking hammer of the mass driver's fire slammed him into his seat restraints. That comforting feeling hit him four more times before his magazine went dry. *Even one or two hits might distract them enough to make a difference*, he thought.

It would have to be a big difference, though. Even with his Hammers blasting active sensors, those missiles were damnably hard to see. Combined with the fact that they were probably the best missiles that money could buy and that they didn't need to go active to find their targets, and that made them *very* hard to see.

*There has to be some way to save the ships*, he thought. He positioned his squadron to screen their transport and then positioned Caela in Nine with its damaged weapon mount near the rear of their formation. He pondered the problem as he listened to Heller's pounding music blasting through her earbuds. "You got any ideas, Heller?"

"Doesn't make sense," she said.

"What doesn't make sense?" Garret asked, even as he monitored the inbound flight of missiles.

"Radiation homing, at that range," Heller said. "Radiation sensors, they are good, yes, but not that good. They would need a repeater at close range."

"We took out all of the sensor platforms here at the station," Garret said.

"Combat, yes, but research sensors?" she asked. "Those can be calibrated, yes? Transmit data to the enemy?"

Garret swore, "Check the civilian platforms, see if any of them are broadcasting."

"They have their transponders up," Heller said. "I'm not seeing any data transmission."

Garret brought up her data on his own display. He stared at it, even as he watched the count-down timer out of the corner of his eye. He had arranged his gunboats to interdict as much of the inbound missiles as he could and, if possible, to physically block direct flight paths to the *Star Dog* with their own defense screens. It was a tactic that worked well enough for the Chxor, so it might do the trick here. Even if it cost him several of his Hammers, it might save the rest of them if they could get out on their carrier craft.

The empty bunks at the end of the day would haunt him, but he would face that if it meant he could save most of them.

He didn't see anything that Heller hadn't. The civilian transponders were all as they should be, even on the platforms that had taken light damage during the initial attack. He had to hand it to the repair mechanics at the base, they had even managed to keep the transponder from the energy weapon platform online despite the looting done by Captain Montago's crew. He saw that transponder flicker again, pulsing on and off.

"Son of a bitch!" he said. A moment later he noticed a flicker from a different platform, there and gone again so fast that the computer barely noted it. "Commodore Stavros, the enemy is using their civilian transponders to provide targeting data to the enemy ships. I'm forwarding you my sensor data now, but I recommend we take out any unoccupied platforms."

"We'll take out *all* of them," Stavros snarled in reply. "And the rest of their damned facility too. Let them explain *that* to their penny-pinching accountants."

Garret opened his mouth to protest, but there wasn't time. He knew that most of the civilians on the station *hadn't* played any part in the betrayal, but their boss had. Stavros wasn't the type to take that kind of thing well. Garret would have argued, but the second flight of missiles was almost upon them.

Over the net, he heard Stavros's voice, "Attention all Nova Corp personnel. Your administrator has violated the terms of our agreement and is transmitting targeting data using your station transponders. Therefore, I've just given orders for my squadron to engage all civilian platforms here at the research station. You have thirty seconds before their fire shifts from unmanned to manned platforms. I suggest you use that time to evacuate."

Garret's eyes widened in surprise at the warning. It was a surprisingly decent thing to do, especially from a pirate with as... colorful a history as Stavros. *Then again,* Garret thought, *maybe he just wants to watch them all scurry around in panic.*

He maintained his Hammer's position, the laser targeting still lighting up the battlecruiser at seventy thousand kilometers. The flight time of his rounds would be less than that of the missiles, so any moment now he should see something...

Heller gave a snarl as the rounds from Azure Flight went active. Their corrective drives blasted them on course to track in on the laser designators projected by Azure Flight. Right off, he could see that almost three quarters of the rounds were out of range, their short drives burned out before they could correct them onto their targets.

Of the fifty-five rounds fired, only fifteen were 'in pocket' and able to adjust their flight paths for intercepts. The battlecruisers had only a few seconds to realize that the kinetic rounds were correcting their courses before the rounds impacted. The mass drivers of the hammers launched their projectiles at a significant fraction of the speed of light, so when the heavy tungsten tipped rounds struck the defense screens of the battlecruisers, they bled off some energy, but they weren't significantly deflected.

Three struck the battlecruiser at the lead and Heller gave a whoop behind Garret as detonations exploded around the bow of the battlecruiser.

"I'm reading three hits on Battlecruiser One, one on Two, and one on Three," Heller said with a purr of pleasure. Her sharp accent on the words punctuated the pinpricks of light and damage icons that suddenly haloed the three big ships.

"Looks like a solid hit on Three," Garret said. He noticed a shift in the inbound missiles, almost half of the inbound flight shifted erratically, as if they had lost telemetry. They shifted back, though, quickly enough that it was clear that the redundant systems aboard those battlecruisers had taken over.

"Thirty seconds," Heller said, her accented voice tight.

"Counter fire," Garret said, even as he launched his remaining interceptor missiles. His, like the others, took telemetry data from the rest of the squadron, part of Stavros's overlapping defense they had trained on. Right now, Garret just hoped it would be enough.

*If we had the rest of my wing online,* he thought, *maybe.* Azure Flight, when the rest of it reached full strength, would be six squadrons of twelve Hammers. Commodore Pierce, commander of the War Dogs, hadn't yet selected the last of the flight crews and personnel yet. For that matter, Garret didn't know if they had the money to get that many of the old gunboats operational.

As the interceptor missiles shot out and inbound missiles began to die, Garret bit his lip. His squadron's fate was at the mercy of the rest of Stavros's squadron, at this point. If they could stop enough of those missiles...

*They can't,* he thought as he watched the missiles sweep through the defensive fire, *there were fifty missiles targeting five ships and two got through, now there's fifty of them coming at just* one.

This would be Stavros's perfect chance to make his grudge good against the War Dogs, yet Garret somehow knew that the flamboyant pirate wouldn't do so.

"Azure Command, this is Seven," Abigail's voice spoke over Azure's net, "I'm intercepting some tight-band radio traffic from Platform Gamma. I think that it is the one transferring data to the others." A glance at his display showed that Azure Seven hung near that platform, possibly near enough that she could pick up some scatter from a tight beam transmission

*Fifteen seconds*, Garret thought, *not enough time to get Stavros to make that platform the priority target.* They had seen it too late for someone else to take action, and Azure Flight had expended all of their Hammer rounds on the enemy ships and their missile loads on the inbound missiles.

*All but Nine*, he thought, just as Caela spoke up on the net.

"Command, Nine, I'm engaging Platform Gamma," Caela's voice was calm, almost bored.

"Dammit, Nine," Garret snapped, "That's a negative, your bird has structural issues..."

He trailed off though, because he could see that she had already begun to fire. Three rounds went out and at the close range, Platform Gamma disintegrated before the third round even struck. But Nine's icon flashed yellow and then crimson. Hanging in formation, he was too distant to see Nine disintegrate with the naked eye, but Heller had brought it up on his display.

It was immediately clear that Nine's weapon mount had failed mid-shot. The recoil had ripped the mass driver free, starting to cut the vessel in half, but the round itself had then tumbled and shed it's kinetic energy through the hull of the gunboat. Nine's hammer had come apart like a party favor and debris, most of it smaller than the palm of Garret's hand, rocketed outwards in a cascade of shredded metal and composites.

"Azure," Stavros said, "Whatever you did, good job. Those inbound missiles lost telemetry at the last minute. They're launching another flight, but we'll be jumping to shadow space before they can hit us."

Garret's hands clenched hard enough that he heard his knuckles pop. He let out a ragged breath, but then just keyed his microphone, "Acknowledged." He took a deep breath, "Azure Flight, initiate docking procedure. We're leaving."

He knew there wasn't time to conduct search and rescue... but that didn't matter. Caela and her targeting officer, Clint, were both dead, probably shredded into pieces before they even realized what had happened. They had died because they saw what needed to be done and they'd done it... even knowing that it would probably kill them.

Garret was furious with them for doing it... but only because he wished they hadn't had to do it. If only he had been smarter, faster, or more capable, he might have saved them all.

***

## Chapter IV

Halcyon Colony, Garris Major System
Contested
January 5th, 2404

"I nearly lost all of my ships and *did* lose a good portion of the valuable loot from this raid," Mason said with some of Stavros's hyperbole, "and we still have no idea just how Nova Corporation knew to target that cargo?"

Counselor Jessica Penwaithe's expression was pained. Admiral Duncan Moore, on the other hand, just gave a wave of his hand. "We think that they merely stumbled into a lucky tactic. We know that our raiding of their facilities has had an impact upon their profits. It was only a matter of time before they took action to mitigate that impact."

"They didn't have transponders on any of the rest of it," Mason said. "Just on the radioactive isotopes that we were specifically instructed to remove. So either they *know* that you need them for something or they have someone inside your organization that *told* them about the raid."

Counselor Penwaithe's eyes narrowed and she looked as if she were about to speak, but Admiral Moore just waved his hand again, "Nonsense," he said, "all of our people aware of that raid had every reason to want to see it succeed. I would merely assume that Nova Corp knows the value of those generated isotopes and therefore took action to label them to prevent unauthorized use or theft. Clearly, if they had expected you to attack they would have had their ships in position to intercept you."

Mason wanted to push the point, but Stavros wouldn't have reason, at least, not that the Halcyon Defense Fleet's senior officer would know. *Mannetti would expect me to ask a few more questions, since she's hinted at some of what is going on here,* he thought, *but Counselor Penwaithe and Admiral Moore still think I'm a happy, little privateer.*

"Fine," Mason said with a broad gesture of dismissal, "If that is what happened, then who am I to argue. Still, I was surprised at the bonus for completing the assignment. Only the War Dogs managed to retain their cargo."

“Yes, well,” Counselor Penwaithe said, “In light of the other resources your squadron obtained and the fact that they did manage to bring back some of the isotopes, we felt a full bonus was in order.” She smiled slightly, “The fact that the isotopes you couldn't bring back were destroyed also increased the market value of the ones that you *did* collect. Lastly, of course, the artifacts that your squadron retrieved may be of some value to collectors and such.”

She said the last bit perfunctorily, as if she didn't think Stavros would think much of it. Yet Mason knew that collectors of alien artifacts normally targeted specific artifacts for acquisition, not bulk lots. Some part of him wondered whether the entire purpose of the raid had been to acquire those artifacts and the rest of him was certain that they played some essential role in whatever plan the people of Halcyon had developed with Admiral Mannetti and Admiral Collae.

*Well,* Mason thought, *not the people, the government.* That was an important difference, he knew. If the people of the planet had made that deal, he wouldn't have sympathized with them. In fact, he didn't even think that Councilor Penwaithe had signed off on that decision. Someone higher had made that call and Counselor Jessica Penwaithe wanted to make the best of a bad situation.

*Unfortunately,* Mason thought, *I have the feeling that her father-in-law was somehow involved.* Mason still didn't know how Spencer Penwaithe fit in. By everything Mason had seen, he was only a minor politician on the planet... and a disgraced one to boot. Yet somehow he treated Admiral Collae as if he were a servant and had pulled strings within Halcyon's government with little apparent effort.

Admiral Collae was a powerful renegade military commander within the Colonial Republic Army Navy, itself a radical paramilitary wing of the Colonial Republic. Collae could command an entire fleet and call upon substantial support across the Colonial Republic. At least a half dozen warlords would come at his call and yet he answered to a man who Mason had never even heard of until only a few months earlier.

“Now,” Admiral Moore said, “President Monaghan has made a special request of the Halcyon Defense Fleet, acquiring essential munitions and supplies to maintain our war efforts. Your next mission ties into that. It should be a nice, easy run for you after that last fight."

"Oh?" Mason asked.

"Yes," Counselor Penwaithe said. "Your squadron will travel to the Anvil system. Admiral Mannetti has graciously set us up with a meeting with an arms dealer who has agreed to supply us with munitions and spare parts for many of our ships. It will be a non-combat mission, ideal for you to undertake while training additions and replacements to your squadron."

"Excellent!" Mason said, even as he felt his stomach sink. Mannetti must have arranged this assignment, which meant this wouldn't be the easy run that these two expected.

"Well," Counselor Penwaithe said, "Thank you for your time, Commodore. Please contact me if you have any additional issues." There was an edge to her voice, a mix of exhaustion, anxiety, and even a little despair. *She's tired,* Mason realized, *tired of worrying about the safety of her planet and tired of dealing with pirate scum like Stavros.*

For just a moment, Mason very nearly asked her directly what the agreement with Mannetti involved. He felt that the openness and honesty might well provoke a similar response. Telling her that she had allies might well swing things around.

Yet, Admiral Duncan Moore's presence was anything but reassuring. Mason had little respect for the man's competence and his position suggested that *someone* wanted him where he was. That, in turn, suggested to Mason that he was involved, possibly as a cut-out for when something went wrong, but also possibly as an inside man to make certain that things went according to plan. *And whose inside man he might be is a very interesting question,* Mason thought.

"Right," Mason nodded, "I'll call my Captains together and we'll get right on it."

***

"Good work on that last run," Commodore Frank Pierce said as Garret took a seat in the mercenary commander's tiny office. Like everything aboard the *Warwagon*, the room was cramped, the fittings were positively spartan, and space was at a premium. For someone who was over two meters in height, it was not a comfortable room, but then again, neither was the cockpit of a

Hammer.

Garret was used to confined spaces. He was less used to failures. "I lost Caela and Clint."

The Commodore gave a nod, "You did." His tone was stern, "But you could have lost eleven more Hammers and their carrier along with all the people aboard them, which would have been far worse. Caela knew the risks... hell, she's been with the War Dogs almost since we began." He shrugged, "She came in like a firecracker, full of piss and vinegar... a lot like your young ensign, Gordon's her name, right?"

Garret nodded.

"She wasn't ever as cute, though, else I might have been tempted to take her up on a couple of her offers." The Commodore shook his head, "Caela was, if nothing else, quite eager to sleep around. Not big on relationships, but..." he shrugged. "Speaking of which, I understand that you have provided some mentoring for Ensign Gordon."

"We are just friends," Garret said, back straight and his voice kept level only by sheer will.

"That's a nice thought to have," Commodore Pierce said with a slight smile, "but she clearly doesn't think so. You had better either break free of her entirely or just give in, boy. She seems like the type who knows what she wants."

Garret shook his head, "Christ, Commodore, I dated her older sister, I'm ten years older than her, at least!"

"Yeah and unless I misread our Company Charter, the War Dogs provide all personnel who sign on with complementary life extension treatment. So while that might matter at your age, in fifty years or so, it won't bother either of you very much."

Garret just shook his head, "Well, it's fraternization. Besides, like I said, she's the kid sister of an old girlfriend, I just don't think of her that way." He could admit to himself that she was attractive, smart, and capable, but it wasn't as if she were really his type. She wasn't anything like Jessica, in most ways. Outspoken, yes, but cheerful and friendly, where Jessica could come across as confrontational. *I mean,* he thought, *I can't really say that I have a type... there hasn't really been anyone since Jessica and while I feel some attraction to Abigail, it's just that. After all, it would be wrong if I let it become anything more.*

He felt his stomach drop as he realized just what that meant. It wasn't that he was disinterested in her... it was that he was afraid to express that interest.

The Commodore seemed to read his expression, “It's important to be honest with yourself and to seize the opportunities you can in life.”

Garret shook his head. He felt suddenly punch drunk, “Sir, you aren't suggesting that I sleep with someone under my command, are you?”

Commodore Pierce sighed, “Garret, we aren't military, we're mercenaries. Yes, in our charter I've got a section on fraternization... but I wrote that section with a note that professional behavior is the essential factor. If I thought you *couldn't* behave in a professional matter about this, I wouldn't bring it up.”

Garret looked away, uncertain how he should take that.

“You may not know this, but Caela and I served together long before I founded the War Dogs,” Commodore Pierce said. “I knew her very well and considered her a friend. She and I had lost more comrades than you really want to know. I saw her change, saw her resort to alcohol and trivial, one night stands as a way to keep everyone at a distance. When she died, she died protecting the only family she ever had: the War Dogs.”

“Are you saying that's a bad thing?” Garret asked.

“I'm saying, don't miss your chance at something a little more meaningful,” Commodore Pierce said. “Like I said, we're mercenaries. When it comes down to it, we fight and die for money. Caela died protecting her family, but she was in that situation because of money.”

Garret looked away, he couldn't really argue with that. He thought back to his conversation with Jessica and his brother, Harris. They had made him an offer, a chance at a life outside of a career as a mercenary. “Sir, Halcyon made me an offer, commander of their Defense Fleet.”

Commodore Pierce nodded, “I know.”

Garret's mouth dropped, “You *know*?”

The Commodore smirked, “Well, they told me, but I expected it anyway. I knew about your family connections, Penwaithe being a relatively uncommon name, after all, and I figured that was half of why they hired us in the first place.” He gave a shrug, “Honestly, I think you could handle the job, though it wouldn't hurt for you to get a bit more experience under your belt."

Garret shook his head again, "I'm not really certain what to think. I like serving with the War Dogs, sir. Partly because there isn't the pressure, the responsibility that I'd have if I took their offer... but part of it is that I've felt more at home here than I ever did on Halcyon."

The Commodore just gave him a nod, "I appreciate that... but remember, your life is what you make of it. I'd be glad to keep you, you're a damned fine officer. Like I said, though, don't pass up a chance at something a little more meaningful." He stared at Garret for a long moment and whatever he saw on his face seemed to satisfy him. "Now, personal issues aside, I've got a final roster for flight crews and support personnel for your full strength wing. We've also got all of those Hammers operational. So, starting tomorrow I'd like you to begin full operations with them, and they'll be going with you on your next mission..."

***

Reese Leone sighed as he stepped up next to Admiral Mannetti in the cramped compartment. "Are you certain I need to be here for this?" He hated the whining tone to his voice, but he lived at the woman's mercy. Really, he just wanted to get back to his other work at the base. After his work restoring the computer coding in the base mainframe she had appointed him as overall head of base repairs. He liked that he didn't have any responsibility over personnel, he just managed repairs and tackled individual projects. Other people directed the actual work, he could spend hours working on a problem by himself, without people around to distract him.

"Yes," Admiral Mannetti said. "Everyone needs to watch this." Her voice was a weird mix of anticipatory and reverent.

The volunteer stood near the pod, her face tight. Reese remembered her from one of the training sessions where he went over how to handle the alien coding. *Well, I hope it helps,* Reese thought, *but I doubt it.*

"You've made this all possible, after all," Admiral Mannetti turned to him and there was an odd light to her eyes, almost as if she were in the midst of some emotional or physical rapture. "Without the coding you adapted from Stavros's ship, we could never have gone this far."

"I know," Reese said. He didn't bother to hide his unhappiness with that fact. In the end, he didn't care much what happened to Lucretta Mannetti's people... but he knew he wouldn't be able to sleep tonight after what was about to happen.

She ignored his tone and gave a nod to her head engineer, "Begin."

The engineer went through the activation sequence. They had already done all their calibrations, Reese knew. For that matter, they had a mass of sensors and equipment designed to monitor the entire process in order to better calibrate their systems. In only a few minutes, they would see whether it worked... or whether Admiral Mannetti would have to ask for another volunteer.

The pod opened to reveal a mesh of wiring and conduits. The volunteer climbed inside and the pod slid closed on its own.

Reese waited impatiently. He couldn't think of the volunteer as human, he told himself, or else he wouldn't be able to sleep for weeks.

Circuits around the pod went live and a whir of machinery signaled the start of the process.

*Maybe,* he thought, *they got it right this time.*

That was when the screaming began. The muffled screams came from inside the pod and they went on far longer than Reese thought any person *could* scream. There were no coherent words, just screams of terror and agony that gradually grew... wet.

The machinery whirred louder as the screams finally trailed off. Then, with a soft whine, the pod rotated and opened.

Reese stepped back with the others as a wave of red washed over the sides of the pod and then splashed across the floor. He restrained a sigh as bits of the volunteer streamed across the floor of the compartment.

"Failure," Admiral Mannetti said with a moue of distaste. She didn't even seem to notice that she stood in the remains of the volunteer. "Another failure." She shook her head and looked at Reese. "We need the rest of the base files examined, there must be *some* way to succeed. The secret *must* be there."

"Of course," he nodded, "I'll get right on it." Yet as he turned away and sloshed through the remains of what had once been a human woman, he wondered if maybe it wasn't better that a woman like Admiral Mannetti didn't succeed.

***

"Stavros, darling," Admiral Mannetti said as she walked in the door, "You don't call, you don't write, you don't give me any gifts, I'm starting to think you don't love me after all." She strutted across the private conference room, her skin-tight black uniform augmenting her display.

Mason stood up slowly from his chair, "Well, you know, you *did* tell me to keep things quiet."

She halted a few steps away and Mason saw her shift bodyweight. He could have caught the blow, but not without giving away his own speed. The slap caught him across the side of the face hard enough to snap his head around. "Stavros, if you think sulking will draw my attention, well..." Lucretta Mannetti trailed off and her hand came back to stroke Mason's cheek suggestively, "Well, you might be right about that."

"I am entirely at your disposal," Mason said, putting some of Stavros's leer into his words.

She grabbed him by the hair and pulled him down for a kiss. Again, the predator within him responded to her. Lucretta Mannetti was a violent sociopath, but she was also extremely capable, devious, and without a doubt one of the most dangerous women he had ever met.

She broke off the rough kiss, apparently satisfied, "I've had a rough day, Stavros, but somehow that made me feel so much better. So... Stavros, are you ready to prove your loyalty to me?" Her hand stroked down his chest and then down lower.

"Of course," Mason said, even as he wondered if he was prepared to go as far as she'd implied. As much desire as he felt for her, he was equally repulsed by the woman. She was utterly despicable, untrustworthy, and appeared to be driven entirely by self-interest. If that weren't enough, Mason felt more than a little confused with his developing relationship with Lauren Kelly.

"Good," Mannetti said and turned away. Mason gave a silent sigh of relief as she took a seat across from him. "Because the time has come to show me your dedication." She smiled sweetly, "And, you can get a bit of payback to Commodore Pierce in the process."

Mason gave his patented Stavros smirk, "Oh?"

“It would be a tragic shame if something were to happen to the War Dogs' Hammers on this latest mission of yours,” she said. “Pierce just brought his “wing” of them up to full strength, but their pilots have to be inexperienced.

“What do you have planned?” Mason asked with a broader smile. *If she already has something in the works, I may not be able to stop it,* he thought, *not unless she gives me more to go on.*

“You're a clever fellow, *you* think of something,” Mannetti growled. “I've got enough on my plate here on Halcyon. Deal with Azure Wing, prove to me that you're worth bringing into my organization... and then maybe we can indulge ourselves a bit.” She arched her back as she stood, giving him an ample display of what that indulgence would involve. Lucretta Mannetti turned to leave, swaying her hips suggestively. She paused at the door, “Oh, and Stavros, who was it who did your ship's programing? I'm in need of a good programmer, myself.”

*Ah,* Mason thought, *there's the point of that display.* “Programmer?” Mason licked his lips, “Oh, for the *Kraken*, right. It was a woman... uh, Kallee, Kylee, something like that.”

Mannetti paused at the door, her gaze intent, “Would you be a darling and put me in contact with her?”

Mason gave a sigh and a shrug, “I'm afraid that's impossible. She died, very tragic.”

Mannetti's eyes narrowed. “That's... inconvenient.” She gave him a last nod and swept out of the room. Mason sat back down and rubbed at his face. Things were getting very complicated. It was time to have another talk with Commodore Pierce.

***

“So,” Commodore Frank Pierce said, “I've confirmed that the alien artifacts we collected as well as the radioactive isotopes were both shipped to Brokenjaw Mountain.”

“Thanks, Frankie,” Mason said as he took a seat across from him. Both of them were dressed like locals and the change of clothes made Mason feel far more like himself. The roleplaying of Stavros had almost become too involving and sometimes Mason caught himself wondering if he was losing some of himself. It was good to leave the role behind, if only for a few minutes. “Admiral Mannetti was asking about the *Kraken*'s programmer. She wanted me to arrange contact with her."

Frank's lips formed a flat line. "That'll be a little hard. What did you tell her?"

"The truth, sort of," Mason said. "I made it vague enough that she may not realize that it was Stavros who killed her." He sighed, "I *am* sorry that you didn't get a chance to finish the bastard."

Frank Pierce looked away, "Just as well. She never did think much of revenge." He looked back at Mason, "Mannetti wanted to meet with Kaycee... that almost certainly tells us functional alien technology."

"Possibly the same technology as the *Kraken*," Mason said.

"So... you think it's related, somehow?" Frank Pierce asked.

"I wish I knew," Mason growled. "I don't know squat about alien tech. I mostly just avoid the damned stuff, especially after what happened with Stavros and Kaycee." In his life as a pirate, he had come across some of it, but he had always left the handling of it to those who *did* know its dangers and values. Now was not the time for anyone to notice "Stavros" reading up on alien technology.

Frank nodded, "I picked up quite a bit of general knowledge, but anything beyond knowing warning signs and picking out the more valuable trinkets is beyond me. We need an expert for this sort of thing."

"Well, while we try to find one of those, we've got bigger problems," Mason said. He let out a deep breath. "Mannetti is planning a move against you," Mason met Frank's gaze, "She plans to use Stavros to do it."

"Well," Pierce said with a sigh, "that's a relief."

"A relief?" Mason asked. "She wants me – well, Stavros, but to her there's no difference – to make certain you lose Azure Wing on its first mission."

Frank Pierce gave a nod, "Of course. Makes sense, too. She wants to hit me when my people are most vulnerable." His gaze went distant, "It would be harder to counter if it were someone else. Her last little 'warning' cost my people badly enough. Truthfully... well, I want to get my people out of danger. This isn't their fight, they're in it for the money and the profit margin is pretty slim on this, just now."

"You're going to pull out?" Mason's jaw dropped. He had never known Frankie Pierce to back down from *anything*.

"If I do it now, I *might* save a lot of my people," Frank Pierce said softly. "And we both have way too damned many ghosts in our pasts for you not to understand that."

Mason nodded. He *did* understand... but he also knew there were too many lives riding on this. Baron Giovanni was trying to hold off the Chxor. Whatever Admiral Mannetti's long term goals were, he would bet that they would involve the destruction of the United Colonies, which in turn would leave the Chxor free to expand across human space. Lucretta Mannetti *might* try to stop them, but it was just as likely that she would only defend those worlds she found to be of value.

"I need you to stay a little longer," Mason said. "We'll think of something as far as this next mission, but this is too big, there's entire star systems riding on this now."

Frank gave him a slow nod. "I'll stay," he said, "but my people had better not pay the price."

***

Garret paused outside Abigail Gordon's quarters, hand raised to knock. *This is stupid,* he thought, *I shouldn't be here.*

It had taken him most of the past few days to work up the courage to do this. He had timed it so that he knew Abigail's two roommates would be away, one on shore leave on Halcyon and the other conducting training. He had thought carefully about what he wanted to say, yet as he stood in the corridor, he found the words and courage both slipping away.

Finally, he lowered his hand. *Tomorrow,* he thought, *I'll just try again tomorrow.*

In that instant, the hatch opened. Abigail stood there, her red hair still damp from a shower, wearing a simple sun dress. "Oh," she said, "Sorry, Captain, is there something you need?"

Garret forced himself to give her a pleasant smile, "Uh, not really, I was just passing by. Going out?"

She gave him a sunny smile, "I was. Jessica commed me. She and the munchkins will be at the park and I thought I'd go down and see them all. It might be my last chance before our next mission." She cocked her head as she noticed he was in civilian clothing and a sudden twinkle came to her eye, "Say, would you like to come?"

Garret hid a wince. The last place he wanted to go with Abigail was to see his ex-girlfriend, now sister-in-law, and her kids. "I don't know," he said, "I do have some paperwork to catch up on..."

At that moment, Heller stuck her head out into the hall a few hatches down. "He's lying, he'd love to go." Her voice was pitched loud and Garret could hear the music in her earbuds even several meters away.

Garret turned a glare in her direction. *Seriously*, he thought, *how did she know I was even out here?* Heller just gave him a smirk and closed her hatch.

"Great!" Abigail said. "I'll comm her to tell her you're coming too!"

Garret stood in the hallway for a long moment. It was good, he thought, that he had picked up so many languages. It gave him a much broader vocabulary of curse words.

*Jessica is going to kill me,* he thought.

***

"Bridge is cleared," Lauren said as she set down a sensor wand. "And I checked the systems. No signs of any surprises left by Mendoza. We should be secure."

Mason nodded and ran a hand over his face, "Good." Though he still wore Stavros's clothing a marked change had come over him. She couldn't say *how* but the man that stood there was entirely Mason McGann, who just happened to be dressed in tight leather pants and a lime green shirt open to the waist.

"So what is this about?" Lauren asked as she came to stand near him. Privately, she hoped they would have time for more than conversation, but she didn't know how long the rest of the crew would buy the "Angry Stavros in Temper Tantrum Mode" routine, even with the pre-recorded diatribe set to play at the hatch for the bridge.

He sighed, "Things are moving quickly now. I'm not sure *what* is going to happen over the next few weeks. Mannetti wants Stavros to move on the War Dogs and I'm still not entirely certain how that's going to fall out. Admiral Collae and Spencer Penwaithe seem willing to bide their time, but I don't know what their endgame is either. I wanted to take some precautions."

"Oh?" Lauren asked.

"The *Kraken*'s automation systems are set to identify biometrics and respond to commands from authorized users. We already authorized you, but there's an added level of security that I can allow you to access. From there you can override everything, including any standing commands in the system," Mason tapped in the commands on the captain's console and a moment later, a pedestal raised from the deck. "This level of security actually predates Stavros, by the way, so no one would expect you or I of being able to do this."

Lauren's eyes went narrow. "Why are you doing this?" She asked. She could think of any number of reasons why giving her greater access to the ship would be good. Unfortunately, most of them would mean that Mason was either dead or incapacitated.

"Just a bit of insurance," Mason said, his voice calm. His dark eyes, however, held more than caution. *He's worried,* Lauren realized, *worried that this is going to go very wrong.* "Just put your hand on the scanner. You'll feel, well, it's kind of hard to describe..."

She put her hand onto the scanner. For just a moment nothing happened and she thought Mason must be playing some kind of joke. Just before she pulled back, though, she felt her entire arm tingle. A heartbeat later, she felt intense heat, but as she tried to pull her hand back, she found it was stuck, held in place as if it were clamped in a vise. The tingling sensation mounted, almost like an electric current, yet it didn't spread any further than her shoulder.

The green light of the scanner flashed to purple and it released her hand so quickly that Lauren stumbled back.

A bright light strobed and part of the deck folded back. Lauren gasped as she saw the cocoon-like structure that lay revealed. It was part nest and part acceleration couch, but run through with wires and circuitry. "What is *that?*"

Mason came up next to her, "That is the primary controls for the ship. At least, I think it is."

"What?" Lauren asked.

"The scientists who discovered her, they thought that the ship was designed to be operated by a single pilot, wired into the ship's systems and melded into her computer systems with a direct neural interface. A pilot like that would be able to react far faster than any normal crew and they could utilize the ship's computers to multitask all of the *Kraken*'s systems with no issue." Mason said it all quite matter-of-factly, as if it were of little note.

"Wait, has anyone tried that?" Lauren asked. Maybe it was just her, but plugging ones brain into alien technology sounded a little dangerous.

"Oh, no," Mason said. "No one has been that desperate. For that matter, Stavros stole the damned thing and killed most of the scientists who brought the whole thing online, so it's not as if anyone else had the chance to research their findings."

"Great..." Lauren said with a shiver. She stared at the cocoon with a mix of fascination and dread, "How do I make it go away?"

Mason pointed out the controls. "You can bring it back out from the captain's console at any time, the same way. Not that there's any real need, you understand, but it does make a fancy parlor trick, wouldn't you say?"

He took a seat at his console and Lauren felt a twinge of worry as she saw just how tired he looked. She knew the strain that playing this role had put upon him. She'd seen the regret that he felt in going back to many of his old ways, even if only in farce.

She moved up next to him and her hand found his, "We'll get through this."

He seemed surprised at her touch and she thought he might even try to pull away, but instead he just gave her a nod and squeezed her hand, "I know. I just worry about how many good people are going to die in the process."

"Less than would die if we weren't here," Lauren said confidently. They still didn't know exactly why Admiral Mannetti was here, but Lauren had little doubt that the bitch planned to hit the United Colonies in revenge for her earlier defeat there. What she would do to Halcyon, after she got her way, wouldn't be any better.

"I hate that I'm so good at this and no good at anything else," Mason said as he dropped his head into his hands. He gave a ragged breath and Lauren felt her chest ache at the agony in his voice. "I've tried so hard to put this life behind me, but I feel it all coming back... and damn me, but I've never felt as alive as when I command a ship in battle."

"That's not so bad," Lauren said.

"Not bad?" Mason looked up, his eyes two pits into hell. "I've killed more people than I can even count at this point. Sure, now we're fighting corporate security goons, but most of them are just there for a job. Hell, the Colonial Republic ships we've destroyed so far I'd say the majority of their crews are just ordinary people, many of whom signed up just to defend their worlds."

Lauren caught his hands, "Yes. But they're the enemy right now. They would kill us without hesitation. And those worlds they're protecting? More than half of them are ruled by despots and military councils. The other half are corrupt oligarchies whose common people probably *wish* they had the kinds of opportunities to be found in a military dictatorship. What we're doing is protecting the United Colonies and the freedom and future they represent."

She pulled him close into a tight hug, "That's a future for *both* of us." She could feel him go tense at her touch, yet after a moment he relaxed and his arms clenched around her.

Mason gave a sigh, "What would I do without you?"

"Probably sleep with that skank-whore Admiral Mannetti," Lauren said. She tilted her head back and a moment later, his lips met hers. She felt her whole body tingle as she clutched at him, "You know," she said as she finally broke away, "We probably have at *least* another hour before the crew gets curious..."

His response was to reach for the zipper on her jacket. *Take that Admiral Mannetti,* she thought as she reached for his belt.

***

Anvil System
Colonial Republic Space
January 28, 2404

Garret yawned slightly as he brought his Hammer's systems online. Behind him, he heard Heller snort, "Girlfriend keep you up all night?"

Garret scowled, but he didn't comment. In truth, he *had* stayed up late with Abigail, but they'd been talking about Halcyon and some of the changes they'd seen. It was odd, to him, how easy he found it to confide in her about things. Part of that was just her personality, he knew, but the rest was that she somehow made him feel comfortable. That feeling had only been reinforced by their "date" in the park and the dinner they'd shared afterward. While it was true that Jessica's attitude had been, at best, disapproving, Garret had still had a good time with Abigail and, to his surprise, with young Garth and Henry as well.

And at this point, it was pointless to argue about the relationship anyway, he could admit. He didn't know if he would classify her as his girlfriend, but they *were* in a relationship. Half of the War Dogs had already assumed that, apparently, and the other half didn't care one way or another.

Still, Heller needed some kind of response or else she would assume the worst, "Did you ever isolate those odd readings we had on our sensors after that last exercise?"

He could sense Heller's scowl from here. "Nein," she said, her accent harsh. A moment later, she grudgingly spoke, "I *think* it is a software glitch, but I haven't isolated it yet."

It wasn't often that Heller found herself unable to fix a problem and when it did happen, she tended to take it personally, probably because she was a damned good weapons officer. "Well," Garret said with a smile, "That's unfortunate." Humor aside, the odd sensor ghosts they'd seen in their last simulation could be a problem, particularly if they showed up during actual combat. Still, he was inclined to agree with Heller in that it was a software glitch from the exercise simulation. The various ships in Stavros's squadron had a variety of technology and equipment and the past few exercises had been rife with software incompatibility issues.

Which wasn't to say that Garret disagreed with the idea of the exercises. He had appreciated the extra training time for his flight of Hammers. Controlling thirty-six of the big gunboats was far more complicated than a single squadron. It also represented a sizable quantity of firepower, albeit a fragile element of it. A single squadron of interceptors could potentially destroy his entire flight, if they got inside his formation. Managing their ammunition and munitions over the course of a battle was something of a nightmare, because once a Hammer expended it's missiles and five rounds for its mass driver, it was effectively useless for any offensive role.

Thankfully, though, this mission didn't look to require that level of finesse. A nice, easy shopping trip, with a show of force to keep everyone honest. His pilots and crews could use that experience, he knew, because although they were combat-ready, they still had plenty of rough edges.

"All squadrons," Garret said, "thirty seconds until we emerge from shadow space. Squadron leaders, give me your update status."

A moment later, all squadrons reported in and Garret opened a channel to Stavros's net, "Azure Flight, standing by." A curt response from the privateer was the only acknowledgment. *Odd fellow,* Garret thought, *sometimes he can be impressive and a damned skilled fighter and he's a likeable bastard, even charismatic, but he's about as despicable a human being as they come.*

The last few seconds ticked away and Garret brought his Hammer to full readiness and checked to see that all of his flight had done so as well. Even though he knew that this was supposed to be a supply run, that didn't mean that things couldn't go horribly wrong.

On that very thought, the gray nothingness of shadow space vanished, replaced by the star-lit blackness of space. Ahead of him, close enough to set off alerts on his sensors, hung a tangle of still-sparking debris and clouds of ionized gas. *The convoy*, he thought, *someone hit it... and they're probably still here.*

"Incoming!" Heller snapped. That was bad. His Hammers were immobile targets while attached to their carrier craft, which were themselves little better than converted civilian transports.

"Azure Flight, emergency detach, now!" Garret barked.

On his screen he saw his squadrons begin to break away from their carrier craft, but too slow.

The *Sky Dog* and the *Hot Dog* vanished in a series of detonations.

Garret heard confused chatter in the background as almost half of his flight died before they even saw what had killed them. He detached from the *Star Dog* and spun his Hammer away. The remainder of his flight had begun to form up as the second wave of missiles struck their carriers. The *Star Dog*, *Space Dog*, and *Big Dog* all died as the missiles ripped the unarmored transports to pieces.

"Form on me," Garret snapped. On his display, he saw that his weren't the only people taking hits. Captain Montago's *Saber* took at least three solid hits, his cruiser going into a sharp spin as the engine pods on the starboard side erupted into a chain of explosions. "Dammit, Heller, get me a target!"

"I am *trying*," Heller snapped. "Whoever it is, they are too far out, the squadron can't even see them!"

The problem was, a swarm of fighter craft was within close range. The light, swift craft swarmed over the squadron, firing off bursts of energy weapons and salvos of light missiles at point blank range. *This isn't a battle, this is a massacre,* Garret thought, even as another of the privateer ships erupted in explosions.

"Azure Flight," Stavros's voice was harsh over the net, "Targeting data coming online now, engage those bastards with everything you've got!"

Garret didn't need to be told twice. With the loss of his carriers, his Hammers were as good as dead if Stavros was forced to withdraw. For all he knew, the pirate commander had already set his navigational computer to plot an escape route and Garret couldn't blame him. He sent out the target priorities to his surviving squadrons even as he brought his Hammer around onto target. They had brought a mix of heavy and light missiles along with full loads for their mass driver cannons. As his systems locked onto the enemy ships, he gave a grim smile. "Azure Flight, engage."

Heller had bracketed the largest of the enemy ships for him and Garret fired off his rounds in quick, body-jarring succession. A moment later, he switched over to his missiles and toggled them onto the secondary targets and cut those loose as well. The twenty four remaining Hammers volleyed one hundred and twenty mass driver rounds, a hundred and forty-four fission-tipped *Hunter*-class medium missiles, and two hundred and eighty-eight of the lighter *Jackrabbit* interceptor missiles. The fifteen enemy ships that were their targets were at long range, but the targeting data grew more refined as Stavros continued to feed Garret data on their attackers.

*Three battlecruisers,* Garret realized with shock, *and what looks like some converted merchant ships for missile platforms and carriers, and a mix of destroyers and frigates in escort.*

It was very similar to the Nova Corporation response force they had faced at the Kied system. *No,* he realized, *not* similar, *it* is *the force from the Kied system... only they're here, waiting for us, with a few extra friends.* And they seemed to have solid data on his systems, because the enemy ships went into evasive maneuvers even as their inbound missiles shifted from paths aimed at the rest of the squadron and onto paths aimed at Azure Wing.

His Hammers couldn't transfer control of their missiles off to one of the other ships. Nor could they fire their main guns at this range without using their laser designators, which would require a stable flight path to guide the smart rounds into their targets.

The enemy clearly had that information and they knew that if they killed his Hammers, they would have a much easier time of weathering the inbound flight of missiles and projectile rounds. At best, the missiles they'd brought would go into active homing mode and be easier to target, at worst, they would lose track of their targets entirely and be no threat at all.

"Stavros," Garret said, "It looks like they've shifted targeting priority to my Wing, I need some help here."

"I'll get you what I can," Stavros said, "But their damned fighters are right in among us. I lost my squadron on launch and they've already torn apart our formation." Even as he spoke, Garret saw another of the pirate frigates stagger out of formation, engulfed in a wreath of debris and venting gasses. "We're plotting a shadow space jump, but I don't want to leave anyone behind."

Garret's gaze went to his monitors. By his estimates, there were over a hundred inbound missiles, almost all of them targeted on his squadron. With the enemy fighters already within Stavros's formation, none of the other ships would be able to provide cover fire against the inbound missiles without making themselves more vulnerable as a result. His Hammers were already trapped, against a numerically superior opponent who had the advantage of surprise. Stavros couldn't win this fight, Garret knew. He could either escape or stay and die. "Negative," Garret said, "go get clear, Stavros, there's nothing you can do for us."

The pirate didn't answer for a long moment. When he did, his voice was solemn, "Kill as many as you can, Garret."

Garret switched back over to his wing's net, "Listen up, boys and girls, I've got some good and bad news. The bad news is, we are their number one priority and we have no way to escape. The worse news is that Stavros and the other ships are able to withdraw and they're about to leave us behind."

"Fuck me," someone said over the net.

"Yes, but the good news is that our rounds will be arriving five seconds before the inbound enemy missiles. So if we hit them hard enough, we'll live long enough to guide our own missiles in on those bastards." Their only other option was to ditch their Hammers now and hope that the enemy would pick them up. Given the damage they'd done to Nova Corp, he doubted they would be so neighborly. "Now, I'm uploading evasion patterns for right after our rounds go on target, follow those patterns and we should be able to see our missiles in, fifteen seconds later."

For a long moment, everyone was silent. Just when he thought that they had decided he was crazy, he heard Abigail's cheerful voice, "Sounds like a good plan, Azure Actual, let's do it."

He felt tears prick his eyes at her words. At least he wouldn't have to face Jessica after this. Somehow, that didn't make him feel any better. "Azure Wing, maintain your targets and let's kill some of these bastards."

Heller spoke up, "Fighters have shifted priority, half have focused on wounded ships and other half are on us," her voice was clipped, her accent harsher than normal. *That makes sense,* Garret thought. The fighters could probably detect the shadow space drives charging. They were trying to take down as many as they could before they escaped while some of them focused on knocking his Hammers out of the fight.

Garret knew that they were painfully vulnerable. His Hammers flew straight and level as they guided their rounds in, and the enemy fighters focused their fire to bring down one after the other. His people didn't flinch or evade, either, he saw. They flew straight on, guiding their rounds into their targets.

At last, however, their turn came. The smart rounds drives kicked in and despite the evasion patterns of the enemy ships, at least thirty of the rounds were within range. One of the enemy destroyers vanished as three rounds impacted it while another staggered from a hit on it's bow. Two of the enemy carriers vomited gas and debris as multiple rounds impacted. The lead battlecruiser took at least two hits and the big ship lost power.

Garret gave a whoop at the damage even as he spun his Hammer up and away. The big, slow craft had heavy armor and good defense screens for its size, but the individual enemy missiles were more than capable of a kill, particularly given the size of their warheads.

*One one thousand*, he thought, as his sensors showed the squadron's shadow space drives spinning up. *Two one thousand,* he saw two more of his Hammers die as the enemy fighters swept in among them. *Three one thousand,* the rest of the squadron leapt away to shadow space and safety. *Four one thousand,* an enemy fighter collided with Jude's Hammer and the two ships ripped each other apart. *Five one thous–*

A hundred enemy missiles detonated across the formation and Garret's world went black.

***

## Chapter V

Nova Roma
Chxor Empire
January 30, 2404

Demetrius knelt in the shadows a few meters away from the door. His eyes searched for any sign that the Chxor had learned of this meeting and awaited him. The long months of Chxor occupation had taught him a great deal of patience and caution, which was one reason he was still alive while so many others who oppose the Chxor were not.

At last, though, he slipped out of the shadows and moved to the back door. After a moment he opened the trick lock, without setting off the explosive charge tied to it and then took the stairs down into the dimly lit basement.

"Demetrius?" a low, familiar voice asked.

"Hello Paulos," he replied. Yet he hesitated as he saw several figures behind his long term contact. "I thought I told you it was too risky to bring in people?" The Chxor required identity cards for anyone trying to move through the city. Those lacking a card were arrested, most of them went to a work camp while some considered too dangerous for that were simply executed. Besides, they didn't need more fighting men, they needed more weapons and equipment. He knew that the weapons came from the new Emperor, but that didn't mean he wanted to deal with him any more than necessary.

"We have valid papers," a man said as he stepped forward into the light, "so we'll be able to slip around freely. We've been sent to help prepare and train you."

Demetrius scowled, "Who says we need anything you can give us?" He didn't like strangers with offers. The government had already failed to defend them, the military too.

"Because of what we can give you," the other figure said and stepped forward. Demetrius had his pistol out and aimed even before he saw the gray skin and lumpen features of the Chxor. The Chxor made no hostile move, though, and Demetrius hesitated to fire. If the alien wasn't here alone, the shot might bring others. He looked at Paulos, who held his hands up in a conciliatory gesture.

"You need to hear what he has to say, friend."

Demetrius jerked his head, "Fine, then."

The man spoke, "I am Captain Ramos, Emperor Romulous IV sent us–"

Demetrius spat, "A pox on Emperor Romulus, and a pox on you. We don't need his help and if he's a filthy Chxor collaborator now..."

"I am not working for Emperor Romulus," the Chxor said. "I am Kral, and I am allied with Baron Giovanni, who is helping the Nova Roma Emperor."

"You could be working with the Virgin Mary and I still wouldn't..." Demetrius trailed off. "Wait, did you say Baron Lucius Giovanni?" It seemed impossible to believe, why would the Baron work with a Chxor?

"Yes, he captured me at Faraday over a year ago," the Chxor said. Demetrius could have been wrong, but he heard the slightest inflection in the Chxor's voice. "He offered me a position on the crew of his ship, the *War Shrike*. Since then I have worked with him to fight the Chxor Empire."

Demetrius's mind raced. If that was true, if Baron Giovanni still lived... *This changes everything,* he realized, *not only is the Baron alive, but he has allies among the Chxor...*

He realized that he had lowered his pistol. "How do I know you're speaking the truth?"

The Chxor shrugged, "Because of what I can offer you. Passes to secure areas, weapons, and information on patrols and raids that the Chxor will conduct."

"How do you have that level of access?" Demetrius demanded. They had bagged a couple of lower-level Chxor officers, but they rarely knew more than general information and they were almost painfully helpful. It almost bothered him that they had to kill them after questioning... until he thought about how many friends and family he had lost in the occupation so far.

"I am ranked as a Fleet Commander here in the system, so I have access to everything except what Supreme Commander Chxarals keeps to himself," Kral said.

Demetrius began to smile, "That's good, that's very good, we can use that..." He trailed off. "Wait, why exactly did the Baron send you if you have an entire *fleet* at your access?"

"Because we're coming back," Captain Ramos said. "We're

coming back with an entire fleet of our own and we're going to kick the Chxor Empire's asses right out of the system."

Demetrius's smile grew broad, "You know, I like the sound of that."

***

Faraday Colony
United Colonies
January 30, 2404

Emilee Stark yawned a bit and glanced up as she heard her daughter wimper in her sleep. She smiled slightly as her daughter simply rolled to the side and snuggled up to her stuffed frog. A look over at Baron Giovanni's daughter showed that she, too, was fast asleep.

That was fortunate, for it had seemed that over the past week the two of them had tag teamed her to the point of exhaustion. While she didn't mind the work as wet nurse and nanny for Baron Giovanni, she wouldn't have minded another set of hands as well. Her smile faded a bit as she thought of her husband, then. Matt had died in the Chxor occupation and a part of her ached that he had never seen his daughter.

*The Baron is taking payment on that from those alien bastards*, Emilee thought with dark satis-faction.

She sighed as she glanced at the time. It would be best if she got some sleep herself, yet the free moment had given her the urge to refresh her knowledge of current events. The new government fascinated her, not least for the fact that she actually had a vote now, unlike under the old government. She wasn't entirely certain about the news from Tehran, about them wanting to sign on with the United Colonies. Her husband had mentioned something to her about them being religious fanatics and that his uncle had been aboard a merchant ship and was killed by pirates from there.

Still, people could change, she knew. Her life had changed dramatically over the past few months, perhaps the people of Tehran had changed as well. *Doesn't hurt to give people a chance,* she thought.

A sound in the outer room of the apartment made her look up. She glanced again at the clock, it was nearly midnight, far too late for the apartment's maid service. "Hello?" she asked. She stood and went to the door, "Is there anyone there?"

She opened the door, the dark room beyond silent. *Probably just hearing things,* she thought, *I definitely need to get some sleep.* She turned away.

A heartbeat later she felt a pair of strong hands grab her, one hand across her throat and the other around her waist. She tried to scream, but the hand clamped tight around her throat. She struggled and fought, her hands reached back to rake at her attacker's eyes. She heard him grunt and swear, but the hands on her only held tighter.

Emilee felt her vision begin to fade. She fought more desperately now, not just to escape, but to breathe. Her eyes locked on the two cribs, only a few feet away. *My baby,* she thought, *I have to save my baby...* She suddenly remembered what her husband had told her, about being attacked from behind.

She elbowed her attacker in the sternum and his hands loosened. Emilee tore herself free and stumbled away. "*Help!*" She screamed at the top of her voice, yet she knew that most of the apartments nearby were empty, the officers gone to the Fleet.

She reached the cribs and spun, her hand picked up a lamp to swing or throw. Behind her, she saw two other figures had joined her attacker. "This is taking too long," one of the new ones said, with a glance at her first attacker. "Finish it and lets go."

Emilee braced herself, readying to throw the lamp, but her attacker didn't advance. He drew a pistol and before she could do anything, he fired once.

The shot seemed muffled and Emilee hoped that it had misfired or broken. She threw her lamp. It went true and struck one of the attackers, who seemed surprised enough that he didn't dodge. Emilee felt satisfaction as she saw it shatter on his head and he swayed at the impact.

Yet she felt an odd coldness spread across her chest. She felt all of her exhaustion catch up to her at once, yet she felt satisfaction. Surely someone had heard. Surely her fighting back had dissuaded her attackers. She was so tired, she would just sit down and sleep. Only for a moment.

She smiled a bit as she leaned back against her daughter's crib. Her husband would be coming for her soon.

***

Tehran System
United Colonies
January 31, 2404

Lucius looked over the last set of orders one last time before he authorized it and hit send. That done, he had finalized the attack on the Nova Roma system. Weeks earlier, they had started to send the first people. Kral's forces had already arrived at the system and should have begun to make contact with the existing rebel cells, and he carried with him personnel and weapons to seize the key defense stations and platforms. The Emperor had begun to ready his forces and best of all, Reginald, Lucius's psychic associate had informed him earlier in the week that the Shadow Lords and their fleets had withdrawn from their positions near Faraday. That meant that Lucius didn't need the Emperor's fleet to protect Faraday... he could release him to a more active role.

The withdrawal of the Shadow Lords renewed Lucius's hopes. While one of them, at least, seemed inclined to leave Lucius be, the other four seemed determined to either absorb the United Colonies or destroy them. They had lingered in shadow space, waiting for the opportunity to pounce for months, held by their secret peace accord with Emperor Romulus I that prevented them from attacking any Nova Roma forces unprovoked. By Lucius's best estimates, they must have run their supplies and fuel to the thinnest of margins to stay as long as they did. Given the embarrassment of being foiled by their own agreements, Lucius couldn't discount the possibility that they would return, but he also knew that they would need weeks, if not longer, to fully restock.

Lucius would use that window of opportunity to strike the Chxor and hopefully win the war. If he was successful, he could reposition the United Colonies fleet and hold strong against any potential attacks by the Shadow Lords, the Chxor, or whoever else might attack. *Emperor Romulus IV will be in position within six weeks,* Lucius thought, *the Chxor will move on him within a couple weeks after that.* All he needed was two months and he could win the war.

For the first time in decades, Lucius felt that there was finally a solid chance at not just winning this war, but a lasting peace.

His comm chimed and he frowned as he glanced at the time.

What could have happened, he wondered as he answered it, "Yes?"

"Baron," Ensign Konetsky's voice was nervous. "I have a priority message for you from Faraday. It's from the head of the Federal Investigation Bureau. She sent it encrypted, but I've got it decoded for you."

Lucius arched an eyebrow, "Well? What is it?"

"One moment, sir," She said.

A moment later, Alicia Nix's face appeared. She looked haggard and tired, "Baron Giovanni, I..." she trailed off, "I'm afraid to report that someone has kidnapped your daughter. I'm sending this message right before I go to find out details, but at this time, it looks like they killed your nanny, Emilee Stark and that they took both your daughter and hers."

Her eyes locked on the screen, determination shone through, "I promise you, Baron, I will put every effort into locating your daughter and bringing the men who kidnapped her to justice... but I think you need to be here." She sighed, "Hopefully, by the time you're back we'll have some more information for you."

The transmission ended and Lucius stared at the screen, his eyes wide. He felt something ugly roil through his stomach. Kidnappings back on Nova Roma weren't uncommon, particularly for the nobility. Whether for political or monetary reasons, kidnappers both professional and amateur were common enough that Lucius had actually coordinated with several such investigations as a military officer, more often than not preventing ships from leaving the star system without a thorough search.

That was why he knew just how poor the chances were that the kidnappers would be found if they hadn't been discovered immediately. *I should have had better security,* he thought, *I put my daughter at risk and for my own arrogance.*

Emilee Stark had already paid the price for that arrogance. Lucius felt an iron hard determination form. His jaw clenched as he thought of just what he would do to the men in question if he caught them. Faraday had a death penalty for murder, but he was quite certain that they wouldn't have the opportunity for even a trial.

Lucius switched his display back to Ensign Konetsky. "Thank you, Ensign. Please inform Captain Beeson that I'll be heading back to Faraday with the next courier vessel. Please have him make the preparations." He closed off the connection before she could respond.

Lucius's mind was already racing. He wanted to call Alicia Nix directly, but he knew better than to jog her elbow as she worked. She would locate the kidnappers, she did not need him looking over her shoulder, not just now.

Later, he would have time for self-recrimination. Right now he had to think, he had to focus, because his daughter's life was on the line.

And if the worst had already happened, then he would have to think about what to do to the men responsible... and just how painful he would make their deaths.

***

Faraday Colony
United Colonies
February 3, 2404

"I *hate* being in the dark," Anthony Doko said as he stared at his datapad.

"Oh come, now, you have to admit there is some fun in ferreting out the truth from the tiny hints here and there," Lizmadie said cheerfully.

Tony just leveled a glare in her direction. That glare lacked any real force, less because she was right and more because he knew she was just trying to distract him from his worry.

And he had plenty of reason to worry. Earlier in the week, Alicia Nix had pulled all but two of her agents off of his protection detail. Given the fact that they were there to prevent another assassination attempt, that meant that something else had taken priority. The team of Nova Roma Marines, set in place by Lizmadie's brother, the Emperor, meant that he didn't feel entirely exposed, yet the sudden change had alerted Tony and his wife to the other signs.

The news feeds had all been suspiciously quiet, yet Faraday's online forums and unofficial news outlets had reported odd goings-on. Military style checkpoints and searches were the most obvious, most of them centered in the area around the military and government apartments. Less obvious was the increase in police traffic stops and patrols all across Faraday. Even less obvious was the "temporary" space traffic freeze put in place. *That* one should have set off a number of alarms for people, but Faraday's traffic control had said it was tied to a new set of panels being transported and installed on the solar array.

*They are searching for someone or something*, Tony knew, *and they want to keep it quiet for some reason.* There were any number of things they could be searching for, but Tony suspected it was somehow tied to his own private investigation into who had framed him.

"We're going to have to hack FIB," Tony said.

Lizmadie quirked an eyebrow at him but didn't look up from her own datapad. "That's hardly the way to prove our innocence, you know. Hacking into a government database and accessing secure data is a felony." Her tone, however, was more than a little gleeful. For a princess, she was quite the anarchist at times. "Well, even assuming that we were to do that, and assuming that we found out who they are looking for, what then?"

"Who, or what," Tony corrected automatically. They didn't yet know if the FIB hunted for someone or something that had been stolen. He thought it likely enough that someone had stolen information of some kind, which might just be how it all tied back into his own investigation. "We figure out how it ties into the traitor who framed me for freeing Admiral Mannetti," Tony said.

"That's assuming that there *is* a connection," Lizmadie looked up. "And assuming that once you find out what this is about that you can stay out of it." She sighed, "You do realize that one reason Lucius has closed you out of the loop is to protect you, right? So you wouldn't go digging around into something that would only put you in more trouble?"

Tony froze and looked up from his datapad. Lizmadie sounded downright protective, which he appreciated, being her husband and all. Still, that meant she knew something. "Tell me."

She sighed again, but a moment later, Tony's datapad pinged. It was an official memorandum, dated for three days previously. It had a picture of a young baby, with dark hair and blue eyes. "Missing: Kaylee Giovanni, taken at twelve forty five..." Tony looked up, "Someone kidnapped Lucius's *daughter*?" His face paled as he thought about the potential consequences.

"Yeah," Lizmadie said. "There's a bit more in their files, but most of the details are on the memorandum there. That's what the manhunt is about. Apparently they found a ransom note at the scene, but it's not in the system, so I suspect the contents are either extremely sensitive or dangerous or both. This is a big mess and I don't think it involves us."

Tony just shook his head, "Those *idiots.*"

"Who, the FIB or whoever was on Lucius's protection detail?" Lizmadie asked.

"No," Tony said, "the kidnappers." He winced as he thought about the one time someone had tried to hold some of Lucius's crew hostage. "They have no idea what they've brought on themselves... and if they hurt his daughter..." He shook his head. "I mean, you were kidnapped yourself, think about what he did to rescue you, even not knowing that you were related to the Emperor at the time. He just thought you were some innocent girl in the wrong place at the wrong time." He saw his wife nod at the reminder. Since it was also how they had first met, Tony felt oddly grateful that she *had* been in those circumstances, but no one involved would forget just how Lucius Giovanni had resolved the situation. Even for a stranger he had never met. He would move worlds to save his own daughter. "There's no way that anyone close to Lucius thought this one up; they would know just how he would react."

"Or maybe, *overreact...*" Lizmadie said in an intent voice. She leaned over her datapad and brought up more information. "Listen to this: The crime scene gave all the signs of amateur criminals. They took the nanny's daughter, either because they didn't know which baby was which or some other reason. They disabled the security camera systems in the building through force. One of them was injured by the nanny, they left the bullet casing from killing the nanny... There are a dozen other details here, but then there's this: the pistol used to kill the nanny and the guards at the front door was a Centauri P7K with a suppressor."

"That's military hardware," Tony said. He frowned as he considered that. Faraday had once had an embargo on imported weapons. During the Chxor occupation, Lucius had shipped in a supply of arms for the rebels to use against the Chxor planetary defense bases, but Tony didn't think that had included any Centauri weapons and the emphasis had been on rifles and submachine guns, not pistols. "It could have been something from a private collection that someone picked up in the looting, I suppose..."

"Or it could be something that our spy slipped them, while he convinced them to kidnap her," Lizmadie said, her voice flat with anger. "Think about it, how to best put Lucius off his game? He's got to be in the middle of organizing the attack on Nova Roma, if not about to give the final go-ahead. If the person who framed you wanted to distract Luicus at the last minute, this would be the perfect way."

Tony couldn't argue with that. Even isolated as he was, he knew that preparations were underway for an attack of some kind. The Nova Roma officers and enlisted had all but vanished from the streets and Lizmadie's brother, Emperor Romulus IV, had been particularly busy of late. Given Lucius's stated goal of liberating Nova Roma, Tony knew that meant the attack would be underway soon.

And Lizmadie's assumption that this kidnapping's real purpose was to distract Lucius made all to much sense in that light. It *would* be the perfect way to derail the attack plans… but to what goal, Tony didn't know. He could guess that Admiral Mannetti might want to delay or distract Lucius for some reason and whatever it was, it wouldn't be good. "Okay," Tony said as he pursed his lips, "So, someone slipped these amateurs, probably local criminals, a suppressed pistol and maybe some advice or even the location of Lucius's daughter."

"Almost certainly the location," Lizmadie nodded, "that wasn't publicly available, so either it had to be someone in the military or someone who hacked their files." She looked the data over and Tony felt a rush of warmth as he watched her work. He had married an amazing woman. "Listen to this, the FIB found traces of a hack into the military housing network. They're assuming it ties back to these apes, but I'm not so certain." She worked for a moment longer, "Right, here it is: The hacking software used isn't commercially available. It looks like Nova Roma coding, maybe military in origin."

"Which sounds more and more like our spy," Tony nodded. He brought up the display of their suspect pool. "So, our spy has or had access to Nova Roma systems as well as a military grade suppressed pistol of Centauri manufacture," he said.

"Given what we already knew," he frowned, "and since that eliminates Reese since he's left the system..."

Two names remained. Ensign Alberto Tascon and Colonel William Proscia. Either of them had access to military coding, but only Colonel Proscia should have had ready access to a military grade suppressed pistol. Lizmadie seemed to have mirrored his thoughts, "Does Colonel Proscia have any background or experience in hacking or computer software?"

Tony's hands shook a bit as he pulled up the Marine's full file. How could the Colonel have betrayed them? Lucius had saved the man's life and that of his men at Danar when he had returned against orders to pick them up. He had served with them for years... and then again, so had almost everyone else on the short list of possible traitors.

Part of him desperately wished that he wouldn't find a last bit of evidence against the man. William Proscia was not only a solid and capable officer and Marine, he was someone that Tony had considered a comrade and friend.

At the very bottom of his file, Tony found the last bit of damning evidence. "His first assignment as a Lieutenant was the signals officer for his battalion. He completed a full communications, database management, and decryption course, and up until recently he maintained those qualifications in good standing."

He looked up and he felt some part of him suddenly aghast. He had begun this investigation hoping to prove his innocence, but some part of him had never really believed that anyone *could* betray his friend and mentor, especially not one of the better officers that Tony had served with. Yet the evidence was there, the motive made sense... and that meant that Tony and his wife had found the traitor. He met Lizmadie's eyes and spoke the words aloud, "Colonel William Proscia is the mole."

***

Lucius stepped down off the shuttle ramp and paused as he saw the assembled men and women awaiting him. He had expected Alicia Nix as the head of the FIB and Kate Bueller, his Foreign Minister had commed him to let him know that she would also be present, in part to speak for President Sara Cassin. Lucius had not expected Colonel William Prosica along with a squad of Marines in tow. Nor, in any reasonable expectation, had he thought that Ensign Alberto Tascon would be present. The self-centered young man had been last assigned to one of the Fleet's supply ships, as Lucius vaguely remembered.

Alicia hadn't missed his look at Ensign Tascon. "Baron," Alicia Nix said, "If we can get you into a more secure location, I can provide you with a full update." Her voice was brusque, but Lucius didn't miss the distress in her voice. Lucius could only hope that wasn't because the worst had happened. *Please, God,* he thought, *not my daughter.*

He followed them off of the private landing pad and into the government building behind. This was the first time he had used the pad and he was glad for the distraction of looking at the building to keep his mind from spiraling into despair or anger. The past ten days had been a living hell, trapped aboard a ship without an ansible, with his mind alternating between wondering about what had happened and thinking through what he wanted to do to those responsible.

The building was to be the new military annex, he knew, with meeting rooms and offices for managing the entire Fleet, not just as it was now, but as it further expanded. The building had four private shuttle pads, designed to allow officers quick access to the building without having to drive across town to the space port. *That will be most convenient,* Lucius thought, *if I have a sudden need to get to orbit to direct ship fire on the people who kidnapped my daughter.*

He suppressed that thought as he followed Alicia into a briefing room. "Well?" Lucius asked, too impatient to wait even for the others to finish filing in behind him. He didn't miss how Colonel Proscia's Marines formed up protectively outside the door, while a pair of them stood inside.

"Your daughter is still alive, Baron," Alicia said quickly.

Lucius took a seat at the table and he felt like a puppet whose strings had been cut. "Thank God," he said.

Alicia brought up the display, "Baron, before I start, I'd like to offer you my full resignation. This happened on my watch and it is entirely my fault. I should have had a protective detail placed on you..."

Lucius waved a hand dismissively, "It wasn't your fault, it was mine. I should have taken precautions and I shouldn't have dismissed yours and Colonel Proscia's earlier warnings about my safety. I'm not going to fire you for my failures. Now get on with the briefing."

"Yes, sir," Alicia said, her eyes suddenly bright with tears. "As far as we can tell, this looks to be a local, amateur group that is politically and economically motivated." She brought up a pair of images, both men were light complexioned, "We've identified the DNA from two of the kidnappers. The first man is Tyler Stuts, he's the son of Gregory Stuts, who was a prominent member of the Conservative Party under Faraday's old constitution. The other man is Randal Schultz IV, he's the son of Randal Schultz III, who was the former head of Schultz Enterprises." Lucius grimaced at the revelation. Schultz Enterprises had tried to squash his manufacturing plant when he first came to Faraday. Since that plant was producing fighters to defend the system, Lucius had not taken it well. During the Chxor occupation, Schultz had been a firm collaborator with the Chxor, including selling out a number of rebels to the Chxor and using slave labor on his mining vessels. He had been tried and executed for crimes against humanity and Lucius hadn't even been aware that the man had any children.

"So it's partially motivated by revenge as well," Lucius said. That was bad. Amateur kidnappers were the most dangerous in general. They were likely to lose their heads and panic as they realized just how serious things had become. People who were afraid were likely to do unthinkable things to try to salvage the situation. Given that Lucius was at least indirectly responsible for the death of one of the kidnapper's fathers... the situation was rather dire.

"They left a ransom note," Kate Bueller said, "Which is basically a laundry list of everything that the Conservative Party would have wanted: reinstatement of the original Faraday Charter, full deportation of all non-native people, restoration of the old currency, and about a half dozen other nitpicky things that only a privileged idiot would care about, before it gets to a demand for three hundred million Colonial Republic Solari." His Minister of State wore a sour expression, as if the sheer distaste she felt for relaying their demands.

Lucius nodded slowly, "Their terms are probably utterly ridiculous if not entirely impossible." Just the effort involved in moving several million people off of the planet was preposterous. That they wanted a return to how things had been made sense... most kidnappers were caught up in their own fantasy world until reality came knocking. "But at least a couple of them are practical if they're asking for that much money... foreign currency too." With Colonial Republic Solari, they could go almost anywhere in human space. The currency had less value in places like the Centauri Confederation, but they could still exchange it. "What else?"

Alicia Nix's gaze went to Ensign Tascon. "The Ensign here has an offer for us."

Lucius's dark eyes focused on the young man in question.

Ensign Tascon licked his lips nervously, "Well, you see, I was the one who located the hack they used to locate your apartment."

"You were?" Lucius asked. "Why would a communications officer aboard a military supply ship be the one to find that out?" There wasn't a legitimate reason, Lucius knew. Which meant that either Ensign Tascon was involved somehow... or that he had another reason.

"He was hacking the planetary network, already," Alicia Nix said. "And when we were sifting through the network for clues, we caught him."

Ensign Tascon looked at Alicia Nix and flushed, "Still, I was able to backtrack the hack, I can give you an address and I identified the source of the code. I can give you a great deal of other information including criminal contacts that they have. I pulled a lot of information off of their drives."

"So you say..." Lucius cocked an eyebrow at Alicia.

She shrugged, "My own programmers aren't certain about that. Unfortunately, Tascon's hack muddled everything quite a bit... possibly because *he* wanted it to be that way."

Lucius turned a basilisk glare on the Ensign, but Alberto Tascon stood straight. "I can give you all that information... and all I want in return is a small payment for my services, exoneration for any laws I broke, and a release from the military."

Lucius gazed at him for a long moment. In reality, what Tascon asked wasn't terrible. He wasn't much different from a private investigator or someone with a tip coming forward. Yet some part of Lucius felt a burning rage that this man wanted to extort him for information that could save his daughter's life. He bottled that emotion away, however as he gazed at Tascon. "Fine."

"Could I get something in writing?" Alberto Tascon asked as he looked between them.

"You have my word," Lucius said. "I will release you from your oath as an officer, I will recompense you for your efforts, and you will not face prosecution for any crimes which you may have committed or will commit in the rescue of my daughter." His voice was stern, but something of his anger must have shown in his face because Tascon cringed back.

"Well," Tascon said as he pulled out a data chip. "This has all the information and contacts along with a bill for my finder's fee." Alicia took it away from him and plugged it into her data pad. "Now if that's all, I'd like the money transferred to my account..."

"Not so fast," Colonel Proscia said. "The Baron said you could go free, but only in exchange for good information. You come with us."

"Us?" Lucius asked.

"Colonel Proscia has activated a tactical team from his cadre at the Academy," Alicia said absently as she browsed through the data. "He and I agreed that due to the..." she trailed off and gave a suspicious glance at Tascon, "...various threats, you should have a protective detail of well-armed Marines on hand."

"It'll be headed by Sergeant Timorsky and Lance Corporal Namori, sir, if that is agreeable," Colonel Prosica said. "They picked out the rest of their team, and I've hand selected another team for retrieving your daughter, as well."

Lucius nodded. It went without saying that the Colonel would have selected men for their capabilities and loyalty. He looked back at Alicia, "Well?"

"Apparently Ensign Tascon has a very... colorful array of business ventures, including freelance hacking, illicit sales of copied entertainment modules, and illegal collection of demographics data," Alicia said slowly. "However, he appears to have isolated the location and computer from which the hack occurred and he inserted some sort of worm that gave him access to that computer."

She rotated the datapad, "He also had captured images of the people in vicinity to the computer, two of whom match our known suspects." On the screen, Lucius could see Randal Schultz IV and Gregory Stuts, along with the faces of three other men. "We have positive identification of suspects as well as an address and reasonable suspicion.

"So..." Lucius said, "What are we waiting for?"

“I'll ready my assault team, sir,” Colonel Proscia said.

“I'd like to have my personnel establish a perimeter, Baron,” Alicia said. She typed in commands to her datapad. “And all respect to Colonel Proscia, but my people have more recent training for hostage rescue.”

Lucius frowned, “Get both teams ready. I'm coming along as well.” He pondered the information, “I want Colonel Proscia's team on lead, they have quite a bit of experience and I've seen him handle hostage rescue before.” Granted, that had been years ago, but Lucius didn't know Alicia's personnel and right now, he wanted to go with someone he trusted. This was, after all, his daughter's life on the line. He looked around at the serious faces in the room. “Let me know as soon as you are ready.”

***

“Baron,” Reginald said as Lucius stepped into the office, “I want to offer you my unqualified apologies and should you want it, my resignation, as I completely understand if you want me to be replaced. I should have spent additional time watching over your daughter...”

Lucius waved a hand, “Reginald, you're only one man. It isn't your fault. If anything, it's my fault for not having a proper escort like these two,” Lucius said as he hiked a thumb at Sergeant Timorsky and Lance Namori who had followed him into the office.

“Still, Baron,” Reginald said, standing straighter, “I feel responsible. I ask that you allow me to accompany the strike team when they go to retrieve your daughter.”

“Have you ever been in a firefight?” Lucius asked with a raised eyebrow.

“Yes,” Reginald nodded. “More times than I like to remember. It is not my strong point, but perhaps I can help your team to find your daughter safely. It is the least that I can do.” In his eighteenth century British Military garb, he should have looked ridiculous. Somehow, though, the psychic looked confident.

Lucius took a seat behind the desk as he thought about it. On the one hand, Reginald was a precious resource, the only telepath that Lucius had to rely upon. He was also Lucius's only connection to Kandergain and Lucius feared what might happen if something should befall him. Then again, having a telepath present to pull the thoughts out of the minds of the kidnappers would be handy for Colonel Proscia's team.

"Very well," Lucius said, "Tell Colonel Proscia I've authorized you to join his team. I want you at the back, where it is safe, though. No heroics, leave that to his Marines, understood?"

"Of course, my Lord," Reginald gave a low bow. "Thank you for this opportunity." He turned and left. Lucius gave a look at his escort. "I'd like a moment alone, please."

The two gave each other uncomfortable looks, but they nodded and stepped out. It was a reminder to Lucius of how much his life had changed. *I never wanted to be the ruler of a nation*, he thought. If anything, the failed ambitions of his father had made the very idea repugnant. Marius Giovanni's failed coup against Emperor Romulus III had left such a stain upon Lucius's childhood that such ambitions were expunged as a matter of survival.

Yet now he had that position and authority… and the fact that he had *not* embraced it had put his child at risk. People had died because Lucius had not taken the proper precautions in protecting himself.

That would have to change, he knew. Colonel Proscia's protective detail was a step in the right direction, but Lucius knew that it was only a step. If his infant daughter was a target, then so was his sister and her son. For that matter, the simple apartment he'd lived in would not do from a security standpoint. While he didn't want anything as ostentatious as a "palace" he would almost certainly have to have a private house of some kind, probably with areas for meetings for his staff, politicians, and for foreign dignitaries as well.

*And defenses*, Lucius thought, *my new home will have considerable defenses to keep my family safe.* Thinking about that would give him something to keep him occupied until the time came to move.

Lucius looked up as the door to the office chimed. "Enter," he said, even with a look at the clock. Colonel Proscia had said he wanted to wait for Alicia's people to establish a perimeter before he moved his team up. That shouldn't have happened just yet. The FIB was trying to move in quietly without alarming the kidnappers.

Lucius felt his mouth drop in surprise as Admiral Valens Balventia stepped through the hatch, followed by Sergeant Timorsky and Lance Namori, both of whom had suspicious expressions on their faces. Then again, the rivalry between Lucius and Valens was something that had become common knowledge long before the fall of Nova Roma.

Admiral Valens Balventia stopped a couple meters away. His expression was hard to read and Lucius wondered if he had been sent by Emperor Romulus or if he was here to gloat. *Probably to gloat*, Lucius thought darkly, *the bastard would never miss an opportunity to rub it in.* Lucius suddenly regretted the fact that he had notified Emperor Romulus IV of the kidnapping.

"Baron Lucius Giovanni," Valens Balventia said, his voice oddly formal. Lucius blinked a bit, since he couldn't remember the other man *ever* using his full name and title. Normally he called him by his rank, a way to remind Lucius that he was below him. Lucius's rival paused and seemed almost at a loss for words.

"Lord Admiral Balventia," Lucius nodded in return. If the other man wanted to be formal, so much the better. While he could be just as caustic in that fashion, at least he was somewhat restrained. He glanced at the clock, "Is there something important that brings you here? I am under something of a time constraint, just now." The understatement was clearly a bit too much for the other man, who coughed slightly at the rebuke.

"Baron," Valens said, "I heard about your daughter's kidnapping... and I wanted to express my sincere condolences." Lucius felt his jaw drop in surprise. The last thing he would have ever expected was to hear *anything* like what Valens Balventia had just said. The Admiral gave him an uncomfortable nod as if almost as surprised to hear the words himself. "You may not know this, but a couple of years before I attended the Nova Roma Military Academy, my younger brother was kidnapped." He cleared his throat a bit, "Tibus and I were very close. So I know what you are going through and I hope that your daughter is safely returned to you."

Lucius met the other man's gaze. Apparently this shared experience was something that transcended their hereditary feud. Lucius could recognize the olive branch for what it was... however temporary it may be. "Thank you," Lucius said, "That means quite a bit to me."

Valens Balventia turned away without a word and headed to the door, the brief civility apparently too much effort to continue.

"What happened to your brother?" Lucius asked. He knew that

Valens' sister had become a prominent businesswoman, but he didn't remember hearing about the man's brother.

Valens paused in the doorway. "The kidnappers panicked and killed him," He said without turning around. "I hope that what happens with your daughter has a happier outcome." A moment later, he was gone.

***

Anthony Doko gnawed at his lip as he watched the clock. He glanced over at Lizmadie, but her face was as serene and composed as ever. He knew that under that outward appearance she had to be just as worried as he was, but he still envied her composure.

Military bearing in battle was one thing, but this was a betrayal of serious scope. It was all that Tony could do to avoid storming out of the door and shouting it to the rooftops. He *hated* this kind of intrigue.

At last, though, the door chimed. A moment later, one of the two FIB agents brought their visitor. "Alanis, thank you for coming," Lizmadie said as she rose. "I understand that your time is limited..."

Alanis Giovanni snorted, "Try nonexistent." She shook her head and Tony saw how tired she looked. Her attendance at the Faraday Military Academy was no doubt stressful. Tony had heard that they worked cadets eighteen hours a day. "I'm on leave now, but that's because I'm *supposed* to be standing by the incubator for my son's birth. You made it sound pretty important that I be here, so, I'm here." Tony could be wrong, but he heard the slightest note of relief in her voice. Once again, he wondered about what had happened between her and Reese. She had pressed charges against him despite the fact that they were expecting a child. It almost seemed as if Alanis was somewhat eager to avoid the birth of her son.

"We are certain we've identified Admiral Mannetti's agent," Tony said as he stood. He couldn't help but fidget as he thought about just how much danger Lucius must be in. "And we need you to pass the word."

Alanis frowned, "Now is not the best time." She glanced over her shoulder at the door. "Look, I shouldn't be telling you this, I only know because Lucius commed me. He's here on planet, now, but he's trying to keep it quiet."

He and Lizmadie looked at each other and Tony saw realization in his wife's eyes. “Look, that's how we figured this out. We're certain that the traitor is involved, probably setting the whole thing in motion, all in order to distract us or sow chaos.”

Alannis shook her head, “Well, if that's the case, they couldn't have picked a better way.” She pursed her lips, “Someone has kidnapped Lucius's daughter, Kaylee.”

“We know that already,” Tony said. “We have to act now, before the traitor accomplishes whatever his goal is. He's exposed himself and this is our opportunity to nab him. Lizmadie and I hacked the FIB database–”

“What?” Alanis said, “Aren't you both supposed to be under house arrest?”

“Trust me, this is important,” Tony answered. He took a deep breath, “We know that the kidnappers are a local group, but we think they were set in motion by the traitor, so we backtracked what was out of character for them. The hack that gave them Lucius's apartment was done with old Nova Roma military coding, something that pegged it as having to be from the traitor. They used a Centauri P7K, with an integral suppressor. Going off our list of suspects, there's only one person who could have access to that kind of hardware to give it to them.”

Tony waited as Alanis thought that through, “But...” she frowned. “The only person who should have that kind of equipment would have been...” She went pale, “You can't seriously be accusing Colonel Proscia.”

“It fits,” Lizmadie said with a calm voice. She brought up some of their other evidence, dates and times that showed that he would have been able to slip out to help the kidnappers... and also a blank space of time when he could have helped Admiral Mannetti in her escape almost a year previously.

Alanis shook her head, “You do know he's the Commandant of the Faraday Military Academy, where I'm a cadet, right? I'd look pretty damned silly trying to arrest him. I assume you want to pass that information on to my brother?”

“Yes,” Tony said. He looked at his wife, “You're the only one we can trust. After we realized that Colonel Proscia was behind this, neither of us want to risk anything by trusting anyone else. You are the only person who we know for certain isn't involved.” He turned to pace, suddenly unable to contain his nervous energy, “I mean, we don't even know he's doing it on his own volition. He might have been coerced, blackmailed, or even mind controlled by a psychic, who knows? But we're certain it's him."

"Well, then," Alanis said as she pulled out her datapad, "We have a big problem, because right now, my brother has Colonel Proscia in charge of retrieving his daughter from the kidnappers... and he just left with him to go do just that."

***

Lucius sat back in his seat as Lance Corporal Namori drove the sleek black car through Faraday's streets. It was about as inconspicuous an armored vehicle as Lucius could ask for, but it still made him nervous that someone would see them coming.

That was the reason that about a dozen other unmarked vehicles had set out for the Old Town district. Faraday's capital wasn't a megalopolis, not like the major cities of Nova Roma much less Elysium in the Centauri System, but it was still a sprawling town with enough traffic to hide their movement, or so Lucius had hoped.

"Not long now, sir," Sergeant Timorsky said.

Lucius gave the sergeant a level look. "Am I that obviously nervous?"

"Your daughter's been kidnapped, sir," he responded. "If you didn't look at least a little nervous, I'd say there was probably something wrong with you."

"Thanks... I think," Lucius shook his head. "Did Colonel Proscia pick you because of your sense of humor?"

The Marine didn't respond, his gaze went out the window, his attention utterly focused.

"Is something wrong?" Lucius asked as he followed the other man's gaze. He saw they had stopped at a traffic intersection the other street's traffic had begun to slow as the light changed.

*Why is that truck still coming?* Lucius had time for that thought, even as he heard Sergeant Timorsky shout, "Contact right! Incoming vehicle!"

Everything seemed to happen in slow motion. Lucius saw Lance Corporal Namori had already started to accelerate as the signal changed. He heard the warning a fraction of a second too late and the vehicle had already started to pull into the intersection. He seemed to realize that and Lucius saw him shift, as if he were trying to reverse their movement.

The heavy truck struck the side of their vehicle at that instant. The front end of the car whipped around and Lance Namori disappeared into cocooning foam as the protective panels blew out in the front.

The impact wasn't enough to do the same in the back of the vehicle and the seat restraints bit painfully into Lucius's shoulders as the vehicle spun away from the impact. Sergeant Timorsky fumbled with his weapon, which was tangled in his seat straps, even as he wiped blood out of his eyes from where his head had struck the car's frame. "Sir, we need to get out of here–"

He broke off as he saw something, and Lucius looked over to see someone just outside his door. At first he thought it was someone trying to help, but a moment later the entire door shuddered and then ripped out of the frame.

The Sergeant brought his weapon up, but Lucius heard a sharp crack and the sudden smell of ozone stung his nose. Someone had hit him with a stunner. Lucius reached for the Sergeant's pistol, but then the figure in the doorway shifted over and Lucius finally saw his attacker's face. "I don't believe this," he said… and then his betrayer fired.

***

## Chapter VI

Faraday Colony
United Colonies
February 7, 2404

"Do we know any more?" Colonel Proscia asked.

He thought he heard tears in Alicia Nix's voice, but he wasn't certain. "Not yet. I've interviewed your team, but both your men on the scene were incapacitated. I think we should have risked being noticed and had a full team with the Baron."

Colonel Proscia grimaced at that, because it had been his idea. "The Baron should have stayed in a secure location. I should have spoken up about it, but we were operating as if this was just the kidnapping. I think it's now likely that the conspirators are involved."

"Are you certain?" Alicia's voice was troubled.

"You said it yourself," Colonel Proscia said, even as he watched his team gear up. "Someone hacked your traffic network and your people just now noticed that someone *else* hacked your database and knows that the Baron's daughter was kidnapped. It looks like his kidnappers tracked his communications unit. I think we need to resort to our precautions."

"That's a big assumption," Alicia said, her voice hard. "We don't know if this is all connected, and if we pull that trigger, there's no putting the genie back in the bottle."

"If we don't pull the trigger on our response teams, the conspirators might take the initiative," Colonel Proscia said calmly. Everything depended on her agreement. If he didn't get that, then almost certainly the whole thing would fall apart. *I knew that Baron Giovanni was the key,* he thought, *but I never would have believed that people would fall apart this much without him.*

"Sir, you need to see this," Captain Perez said and passed over his datapad. It was a news feed, one that showed video footage of Lucius Giovanni being dragged out of his vehicle by two masked figures. *Well,* he thought, *that's unfortunate.* There would be no keeping anything quiet now.

"Are you seeing this?" Colonel Prosica asked.

"Unfortunately, yes," Alicia responded. "It's hitting all the news feeds."

Colonel Proscia shook his head, "Alright. I'm going to move on the kidnappers, hopefully before they see that and decide that their hostage isn't worth risking their lives over. In the meantime, *you* need to enact the protocols we discussed. If the conspirators are behind this, they *will* make decapitation strikes. You, President Cassin, Minister Bueller, and many others are without a doubt priority targets. At least take *some* precautions."

He could almost hear her thoughts. Although, this was something they had discussed and prepared for, talking about sending out police and military units to detain men and women in high military and government positions was very different from actually doing it. If they were wrong about who was behind this, they would be crippling their government *and* military at a time when they might be under some other threat.

*Please,* he thought, *make the right decision.*

"I'll go to phase one," she said finally.

He grimaced at that. Phase one was a half-measure, where the key members of the counter-conspiracy would move to secure undisclosed locations. It was a safety measure, a defense. That wasn't what needed to happen. "Fine," he said, "but look at phase two."

"I will. Rescue the Baron's daughter and then get back here," Alicia said.

"That's the Baron's plan," Colonel Proscia said as he gazed out the window and across the street. He just hoped things went according to *his* plan. "Be sure you keep that bastard Tascon close, I don't trust him," Colonel Proscia said as he cut the connection.

***

"Well," Alanis said cheerfully, "That went better than I thought it would."

"Says the one who didn't get stunned," Lucius grimaced and rubbed at his chest. He *hated* stunners. A pair of lasers ionized the air for a high voltage discharge designed to convulse a targets muscles and overwhelm their nervous system. It typically also left a mild but painful burn and left Lucius feeling like he had been in a car crash. Then again, he *had* been in a car crash.

"So..." Lucius said as he looked over at where Tony Doko and his wife, Princess Lizmadie, sat in the other seats. Tony drove while Lizmadie seemed to be working on her datapad. "Why exactly did you feel it necessary to attack me and drag me away unconscious?"

"It's a long story," Tony said as he wove through traffic. "But the short version is that we think that Colonel Proscia is Admiral Mannetti's spy and that he was behind the kidnapping of your daughter."

"What?" Lucius shook his head, "That's absurd." Colonel Proscia had multiple occasions where he could have betrayed him before. It didn't make any sense that he would do so... or at least no more than anyone else from his original crew betraying him.

"They have pretty good evidence," Alanis said. "And if it is true, then letting him have you and your daughter in a volatile situation like a hostage rescue is dangerous."

Lucius's blood ran cold at that. The implication was that Colonel Proscia would kill both Lucius and his daughter, or possibly just take them *both* hostage. Since he had control of both the protective detail *and* the hostage rescue team, Colonel Proscia would be perfectly positioned to take advantage of the situation. "Fine, explain it to me, but you had better be convincing."

They laid out their information, Tony and Lizmadie taking turns to speak as they alternated between driving and whatever systems infiltration the Princess was doing. He bit his lip as he realized just how much work that Anthony and his wife had put into clearing his name. Once again, Lucius felt a wave of guilt for the fact that he had allowed Dreyfus's people to convince him to pull Anthony out of his position. Lucius had known all along that Anthony was innocent, he just didn't know how to prove it to everyone else.

He frowned as they finished. The data about the old Nova Roma military coding and the pistol *did* appear to point to Colonel Proscia. At the same time, he couldn't discount the possibility that someone else hadn't managed to access the pistol or that the weapon hadn't been here all along, possibly a trophy kept by one of Faraday's elite... which was who the kidnappers came from, after all.

"Okay, there's a reasonable suspicion, I'll agree," Lucius said. "But the situation is a bit more complicated than any of you realize." He sighed, "Even if Colonel Proscia is the spy, there's a whole other aspect that none of you are aware of."

“Do tell,” Princess Lizmadie said with an arched eyebrow.

Lucius hesitated a bit, conflicted between the need to tell his trusted friends and the equal desire to keep them ignorant and safe. In the end, his wisdom won out. They would make the best decisions if they knew everything. “I've uncovered evidence of a conspiracy or conspiracies whose goal seem to be to take charge of the Fleet.”

Doko craned his head around, “What!?”

A horn blared and he looked back in time to swerve back into his lane. He pulled over, parking half on the sidewalk and turned around in his seat, “You *can't* be serious.”

“Unfortunately, I am,” Lucius said. “I didn't want to believe it myself, but there have been incidents, rumors, and even sabotage and murder. Between Captain Daniel Beeson and Ensign Perkins and some others, we've put together the clues that show a massive conspiracy with roots going back to before Admiral Dreyfus led his fleet out here. They have solid control over Fleet Intelligence, Logistics, and several of the combat ships.”

“Shit,” Anthony said. “Sir... what can we do?”

Lucius gave a tight smile, “I've been taking some actions of my own. It looks as if they are waiting for something before they move. It seems as if they're currently doing their best to delay or prevent the invasion of Nova Roma. I'm not certain why or what their end goals are. But I *am* almost entirely certain that they plan to oust myself, to remove Admiral Dreyfus, and probably to institute some kind of martial law here on Faraday. They also seem to want to conquer other star systems.”

“That bastard Julian Newbauer, eh?” Princess Lizmadie asked.

“You know about him?” Lucius asked.

“His War Party is almost always broadcasting some message about how other worlds should 'share in the burden' and 'help to support their defense.' A lot of it is designed to hit someone in their feelings, stir up fear and anger in equal doses and then put the blame on whoever a good target is,” Lizmadie said. “It's pretty similar, actually, to some of the propaganda my father signed off on during Nova Roma's expansion.”

Lucius nodded, he couldn't say he was surprised. “In any case, we've uncovered a lot, but we still don't know all the key players and I didn't want to move until I'd identified them.” He saw Lizmadie and Anthony nod in reply. It would almost be worse in a way, to remove only part of the cancer. It might just give the surviving conspirators enough leeway to hide deeper and to rebuild their network to strike another day.

"My main fear is that either they are behind this or they'll take advantage of the situation," Lucius said. If that was the case, then his sister and friends had done the worst thing they could possibly do, they'd taken Lucius out of the picture and given the conspirators freedom to act in the confusion. "They would have access to weapons such as the Centauri P7K and they've taken actions like this before."

He saw Anthony pale, "The attack on Lizmadie and I... that was them, wasn't it?"

Lucius nodded, "We're almost entirely certain. I'm fairly convinced that some of the evidence against you was manufactured by them."

"But that still doesn't discount the possibility of a traitor," Lizmadie said. "Whoever accessed the prison and freed Mannetti did it *before* we made contact with the Dreyfus Fleet. And Tony and I have checked the transfer dates for the money that went to his account. They went through only a few days after her escape. For that matter, it doesn't explain the Nova Roma military coding."

"It doesn't, but if your assumptions are right, then we've got even bigger problems," Lucius said. He took a deep breath, "Colonel Proscia was central to our plan to take down the conspirators. He helped to organize our plans to isolate and secure the conspirators in sensitive positions as well as to defend our own key personnel. More than that, I know that he has activated at least a company's worth of Marines as response to this kidnapping."

Anthony went pale as he made the connections, "He's in perfect position to execute a complete coup, take down *everyone*. He could give Mannetti the entire system on an open platter if he wanted."

Lucius gave a grim nod, "Exactly. Which is why I hope you're wrong."

***

Captain Daniel Beeson rubbed tiredly at his face as he looked over his reports one last time. The position of Chief of Staff for an Admiral was one that came with a great deal of responsibility.

While Daniel had a credible amount of combat experience, he had a very accelerated career serving under the rapid expansion of Baron Giovanni's initial fleet. He knew very well how to execute combat maneuvers and fight a battle.

He had little experience with the staff and planning aspects. The Baron had been very patient as he got his feet under him, but Daniel still wasn't certain that he would ever be a *good* staff officer, much less a good Chief of Staff. So much of his job was to anticipate what Baron Lucius Giovanni would want or expect and to direct the various staff sections in those duties.

*As if anyone can really foresee what the Baron will do next,* he thought as he closed out the last of the reports. The most recent order, to move the entire Fleet with all speed to Faraday, had come as a surprise, but Daniel had grown used to such surprises. Much of Daniel's respect for the Baron came from the very nature of his superior's devious mindset. It was his foresight and careful planning that had liberated Faraday from the Chxor and now they seemed poised to do the same for Nova Roma.

*Not that the conspirators are making that easy*, he thought with a sour grimace. To be fair, one reason Daniel had so many issues getting his feet under him as a Chief of Staff was that he spent a large portion of his time investigating the conspiracy that ate away at the Fleet's heart like a cancer. He and Ensign Perkins had put together their own network, one that had uncovered all the dirty little secrets that the conspirators had to hide.

And some of them were very dirty, he thought. Tipped off by Commander Jin Wong's death, they had delved into some of the other "accidental" deaths throughout the Fleet. Some of them, particularly a few among the civilian dependents, had formed a very ugly pattern. It looked as if the conspirators had eliminated *anyone* who was positioned to move counter to their agenda. Other "deaths" seemed to be orchestrated only to remove people from the public eye so that they could act more freely in the shadows.

In all, the conspirators had killed almost a thousand people by his estimation. Nearly a third of those had been innocent civilians, some of whom they had killed in whole lots. The worst was the fire aboard the passenger carrier *Hongbo*, which had killed almost three hundred men, women, and children. Forrest Perkins had requested time off after they traced that back to the conspiracy. Daniel had seen that Forrest felt so sickened and disgusted that he wouldn't be able to work around the two spies on the Baron's staff without giving the whole thing away.

*Not that I can blame him*, Daniel thought. His anger and disgust with Lieutenant Moritz was hard to hide. Ensign Camilla Jiang seemed to be cut from different cloth, but there was no doubting that she had deep ties to the conspiracy.

Speak of the devil, he thought as his door chimed and he saw Ensign Jiang in the hallway on his monitor. "One moment," Daniel said. He reached into his desk drawer and checked his pistol and then shifted it to his lap. Daniel had killed Chxor at close range in the liberation of Faraday. He didn't know if taking a human life would feel any different, but he doubted he would hesitate if it became necessary. "Come in," he said as he keyed the outer door open with his other hand. *Thanks dad,* he thought, *for teaching me to handle a pistol with either hand.*

"Captain Beeson," the Ensign said, "I have those reports you asked for earlier, the ones about Chxor sensor platforms." Her face was calm and pleasant, but there was something in her dark eyes, almost a warning.

Daniel frowned, he hadn't asked for any reports. "Uh, thanks, come in and close the door." His hand tightened on his pistol's grip. *A thousand people,* Daniel thought even as he wondered if Ensign Camilla Jiang had personally killed any of them.

Ensign Jiang passed over a data card, "You'll find the report on there, I think it best you look it over so I can answer any questions now."

Daniel slowly extended his hand and took the card. Everything about the Ensign's behavior was wrong. Telling an officer to look a card over would be acceptable from a superior or even an equal, from a junior officer like her, it was borderline insubordinate.

*She's trying to tell me something*, he realized. Of course, whether he could trust anything she had to say was far more problematic. Before she was an Ensign, she'd been a Warrant Officer for forty years, which was hard to remember with her youthful face. Senior Captain Ngo had signed off on her commissioning packet, and since he was thought to be a central member of the conspiracy, that had identified her as a threat early on in Daniel's investigation. While an Ensign technically outranked a Warrant Officer, it was in reality a big step down. Warrants held a great deal of respect and authority, while Ensigns had little of either. Daniel still wasn't certain *why* she had taken such a big step down.

He put the data card into his reader, all the while keeping most of his attention on Ensign Jiang. "Can't wait, huh?"

"Very time sensitive," she said. Her face was polite and attentive, but her body was tense. Daniel wished he knew whether that meant she was about to attack him or something else. *I wish I'd swept the room for bugs recently,* he thought, *but that would have been suspicious behavior.*

Her data card held only one file. On it was a short, terse message:

*Baron Giovanni did not order us to return to Faraday. There is a coup in progress, you are in danger. We need to meet in the secure conference room and I will tell you more.*

"Well," Daniel said as he glanced up, "This does look like it will require a bit more intensive discussion than I had realized. How about you go prep the secure conference room? I'll have Ensign Perkins meet us there, since he knows the Baron's mind a bit better."

"Of course," she said as she stood up.

Behind her, he saw motion on the monitor. A moment later, the door opened and Lieutenant Moritz stood there, pistol leveled at Ensign Jiang. Daniel fired before the other man could, his pistol barking from under his desk. The Lieutenant stumbled back, an expression of shock on his face.

To give the Ensign credit, she didn't flinch at the gunfire and went into a defensive crouch, her hand diving for where she must have a concealed weapon of her own.

"Don't move," Daniel said, "Since it would appear that things are in motion, let me just tell you that I am aware of your ties to certain people, including the late Lieutenant Moritz. I think it best that you place whatever concealed weapons you have on the floor and step back while I initiate some of my own precautions, understood?"

She gave him a nod and slowly drew out a small pistol and set it on the floor.

"Good," Daniel said. He kept his pistol trained on her as he sent out a draft message. It appeared to be a normal message, a reminder of a staff meeting to review their training schedule. In reality, it contained a code phrase that should put the Baron's immediate staff on war footing and notify their security teams to prepare for an attack. Daniel really hoped that the latter wouldn't be necessary... but the fact that Lieutenant Moritz had tried to kill Ensign Jiang in front of him was a bad sign.

A moment later, Ensign Forrest Perkins arrived at the hatch, a snub-nosed riot gun held ready in one hand. He had it leveled at Ensign Camilla Jiang as he stepped over Lieutenant Moritz's corpse. "You called?"

"We have a situation," Daniel said. "The Ensign here has some crucial information. We need to get to the secure room. Make certain the rest of our people meet us there." The secure room was supposed to be their rally point anyway, since it was a defensible position and should be clear of any bugs.

"Yes, sir," Forrest said, he turned and scanned the hallway, "Looks clear, let's move."

Daniel gestured at Ensign Jiang to lead the way.

They moved through the corridors quickly. The staff section was almost empty, right up until they reached the secure conference room near the flag bridge.

"Room is secure," Ensign Michele Konetsky said from the hatch, where she stood waiting. She gave a nod at Camilla Jiang, "She try something?"

"She came to me with a warning and Lieutenant Moritz tried to kill her," Daniel said as he gestured for Ensign Jiang to lead the way into the conference room. "So I'm inclined to hear what she has to say."

Once they had retreated into the secure room, Ensign Konetsky locked the room down. "We're good. Sensors shouldn't be able to pick us up and I've wiped the records of us coming here. That should keep anyone from finding us for a few minutes at least."

All gazes went to Ensign Camilla Jiang. She cleared her throat, "You may not be aware of this, but there's a cabal–"

"We know," Ensign Konetsky sneered. "And if that's all you're bringing..."

Daniel waved a hand to quiet her down. Michele Konetsky had lost her husband and daughter to the Chxor and she had originally received the news of the conspiracy against Baron Giovanni with anger and disgust, especially when it seemed as if the conspirators undermined the war effort. "We know some of the key players: Senior Captain Ngo, Captain Wu, Captain Magnani, and Senior

Captain Gronsky. We also know that you're trying to undermine Baron Giovanni and Admiral Dreyfus and that your people have killed before."

The Ensign didn't look away, "Well, then, you know quite a bit, although you have some details wrong." Her guarded expression didn't give anything away and Daniel worried that this was some fishing expedition. If the conspirators knew about the investigation, how better to find out more than to send in a false informant?

Ensign Jiang gave a sigh, "This conspiracy, you have to understand, it didn't start out as anything like what it has become. Most of the junior officers and enlisted simply wanted to be certain that their sacrifices, that leaving everything they knew behind, wouldn't be thrown away. It is the people at the top that have manipulated it. We call them Command, it's a group of four officers, who keep their identities secret. Everyone else started in this because they wanted some accountability from their leaders."

"Accountability?" Michele Konetsky demanded. "So you operate from the shadows, lead rumor campaigns, and kill off people when they're in the way like Commander Jin Wong?"

Ensign Jiang looked away. "Commander Jin Wong was one of my people."

"*Your* people?" Daniel asked.

She nodded, "I've operated an organization within the overall cabal. My group's purpose, whether you want to believe it or not, was to diffuse the entire situation. We were organized by Senior Captain Nelund after he realized just how much Command had misled us. He was part of the secondary officers, you've named a couple of them: Senior Captain Ngo and Senior Captain Gronsky. Captain Wu took Senior Captain Nelund's position after the cabal had him killed."

"We suspected that," Daniel said as he took a seat, "But we thought that this secondary group was at the head of the organization. You're saying they're not?"

Ensign Jiang shook her head, "No, they're just the cut out, in case things go badly wrong. Most of the cabal isn't aware of Command's existence. It's the last failsafe, established since the very beginning, and I only know more because I was Senior Captain Nelund's most trusted agent." She gave a nod at Michele, "Yes, I've cultivated a patronage relationship with Senior Captain Ngo, but the purpose of that relationship was to get closer and be able to operate from a position of trust within the cabal's ranks. I've managed to twist some of their efforts and policies and sabotage their rumor campaign."

"The rumors about the Baron," Daniel said with narrow eyes, "You're saying you did that to draw attention?"

"Exactly," Ensign Jiang said. "Look, like I said, most of the people in the lower ranks aren't bad. They're normal men and women who just wanted to feel like they had some say in things. You have to understand what growing up under Amalgamated Worlds was like. The elite made all the decisions. We fought and bled and died in star systems that were only spots on a map to those people... and we saw far too many of our friends die because some nameless, faceless bureaucrat didn't want to upset the system and lose some face. We've an inherent distrust of senior authority, something of a survival mechanism. Because all too often, the people making the decisions about where we went did so from personal interest rather than any coherent strategy or foresight."

"That doesn't excuse suborning military authority in a time of war," Michele Konetsky snapped.

"It doesn't," Ensign Jiang said, "But you have to understand, to many of the officers of this fleet, it's hard to wrap our heads around the fact that the Chxor are that much of a threat. For the junior officers, it seems preposterous. The Chxor had only one star system and were only beginning to understand the capabilities of the shadow space drive when we left. To think that in that time they've spread across a hundred or more star systems, even reading the intelligence reports... it is difficult to even begin to understand. And the Balor... well, they seem more like some weird boogeyman. Those officers saw the Third Battle of Faraday as the culmination of a war, rather than the opening shots. We've fought before, but in squadrons against numerically and technologically inferior opponents. We've never fought anything on this scale."

"So?" Daniel asked.

"So my goal was to generate enough of a risk of being revealed that would make most of the junior members of the cabal think seriously about giving it up. Senior Captain Nelund's plan was basically to remove that power base of personnel and leave Command with little option but to either act publically or give up their own plans."

"I'm assuming, by the fact that you're here, that hasn't worked," Forrest said dryly.

She shook her head, "Things are moving too fast. The senior members, including Command, are scared. You don't realize it, but you set off some alarms when you delved into some of the old sealed documents. They know that *someone* is investigating things. Worse is the invasion plan for Nova Roma. It's a risky plan–"

"No riskier than some," Michele Konetsky said, "and at least we're hitting the Chxor."

"Well, to them, you're putting the entire Fleet at risk, when they feel a more moderate approach might accomplish the same goals," Ensign Jiang answered. "And to the senior members of the Cabal, the fearful part is their own lives will be at risk. They've lived for well over a century and the last eighty years or so, they were safely cocooned away. They aren't used to danger and the Third Battle of Faraday was a wake-up call that they might well die in Baron Giovanni's campaign to liberate humanity."

Daniel shook his head, "You're saying they're that selfish?"

"I'm saying they're old, and tired, and afraid," Ensign Camilla said. "Hell, *I'm* old. I just hold to my oaths. Age changes things. I'm older than everyone in this room combined. I've lived that entire span in uniform, first under Amalgamated Worlds, then in Admiral Dreyfus's Fleet, and now under the United Colonies. You have to understand, that many years takes a toll. Some of these Lieutenants and Commanders have been at their ranks for decades, many of them at the same job, day after day. Even for the ones who aren't tired, the routine puts you into a sense of complacency, like nothing will ever change."

Forrest Perkins shook his head, "So... they're planning a coup because they're tired?"

She shook her head, "The junior members, most of them don't even realize it will go that far. They think they'll quietly support the right officers and they'll take the senior people aside and explain the situation. Yes, this is the fate of humanity... but who says humanity needs to be a vast empire? Surely a few systems is enough, right?" She shook her head, "They don't know about weapons being set aside, about combat teams being secretly positioned. They don't know what will happen if Command pulls the trigger on Omega Protocol."

"Wait, what's Omega Protocol?" Daniel asked.

"It's the final option from Command," Ensign Jiang said. "I don't have anything near the full details, but I know they have around three battalion's worth of combat strength, a mix of Amalgamated Worlds Commandos and Marines, along with enough equipment to outfit them with powered armor and mechanized support. I think they've positioned many of them ground-side, but I know that at least a few teams of them are hidden aboard several ships and even aboard the civilian station."

Daniel bit back a curse. They had found signs of that group, 'ghosts' in the system, men and women who had disappeared from the files, one or two at a time over decades. They suspected that the group had been behind the attempted assassination of Captain Anthony Doko and his wife Lizmadie. He had hoped that they would be able to locate them and deal with them, but it was one of the main reasons that they hadn't been able to move yet. "Okay, so Omega Protocol triggers them seizing the Fleet, to what purpose? They can't force everyone to do what they say at gunpoint."

"They won't," Ensign Jiang shook her head. "These teams are trained to operate in secret. They're skilled killers and most of them are either fanatically loyal to Command or motivated from ambition. They'll eliminate their targets and then stand down. At that point, the cabal's officers will step in to restore order. It will look like there was an attempted mutiny and it was suppressed, but not without casualties. They'll kill off any senior officer and public officials they don't need and detain the ones that might be useful."

"Jesus," Forrest Perkins said. "That's... that's bloodthirsty."

"It wasn't their optimal plan, but they're running scared," Ensign Jiang said. "Keep in mind, the last thing they want to do is put their own lives at risk and if they try to do this against a readied opponent, it could all backfire."

"Yeah," Daniel said, "You bet your ass it would. We've already got teams in place of our own."

"I don't know if *they* know that, but I've discovered a few," Ensign Jiang said. "Which is why I came to you." She sighed, "They need two things to trigger Omega Protocol: they need Baron Giovanni out of action and they need the majority of the Fleet in position at Faraday."

Daniel blanched, "Oh God... you can't mean they're behind the

Baron's daughter's kidnapping?"

Ensign Jiang blinked in surprise, "Is *that* what happened?" She shook her head, "As far as I know, no, they aren't. I'm seeing too much scrambling and panic, Lieutenant Moritz is a perfect example. He's here as an informant and a second set of eyes, not a trigger man. They know that the Baron is distracted, so they took advantage of the situation. They had one of their people put together a fake set of orders to move the Fleet to Faraday, in the Baron's name."

Daniel swore. "I should have looked more closely at it. It didn't make any sense at the time, but I thought it was tied to some plan of the Baron's." He looked around at the others, "We're going to have to go with Plan Delta." Plan Delta was the Baron's equivalent of the cabal's Omega Protocol.

"Whatever you're going to do, you have to do it soon," Ensign Jiang said. "Because Command is going to hit everyone with Omega Protocol as soon as we get to Faraday, if they haven't already kicked it off." She pointed at the clock on the wall, "We've got less than two hours at this point, so I suggest you be ready to move."

Daniel frowned, "This is really going to be tight. We still haven't identified a significant portion of the conspiracy. I'll need names, especially for those in senior positions... and I need to know who runs this whole show." Her earlier information that someone else called the shots made all too much sense, especially the apparent rivalry between Senior Captain Ngo and Senior Captain Gronsky. If someone else had maintained their own secrecy and controlled everything from behind the scenes, then it bespoke a dangerous level of competence.

For the first time, Ensign Jiang hesitated. She looked down at her lap and gave a sigh, "I've always referred to them as Command. The only things I know for absolute certainty are what Senior Captain Nelund told me, just before they had him killed." She looked up and met Daniel's eyes, "There are four of them... and Admiral Dreyfus is one of them."

***

Lucius looked up as his sister stepped into the room. The tiny apartment that she had procured for them as a temporary safe house wasn't much to speak of, but at least it had a decent connection to the planetary network. Lucius had managed to access some of his private communications lines and what he saw there left him with a bleak feeling.

Alanis read his expression, "That bad?"

"Alicia Nix and Colonel Proscia have initiated phase one of our worst case scenario," Lucius said. "Either because Colonel Proscia plans to execute a coup or because he and Alicia think that the conspirators already have begun."

"Well," Alanis said, "It could be worse, you could be in the dark."

"I *am* still in the dark," Lucius said. He felt as if he had swallowed a lemon. "Only I have vague impressions to go on which are almost more hindrance than help." Despite his words, he still felt he could resolve the situation... it just involved a great deal of personal risk.

He sighed, "Apparently Alicia picked up on *your* disappearance as well and her messages to her agents are that you might be a kidnap victim as well. Her words on Anthony Doko and Princess Lizmadie are somewhat less generous."

"We didn't kill either of her agents," Princess Lizmadie said graciously.

"You stunned them both and then ordered your Nova Roma Marine escort to keep them secured," Lucius said as he shook his head. "Right now, if nothing else, it makes it look as if you were involved, somehow."

"We are involved," Anthony Doko said, "Just now we are taking a more active role rather than sitting on the sidelines watching." He seemed more than a little irritated, but Lucius couldn't blame him. It had eaten at him to keep his longtime friend in the dark about the conspiracy, particularly when it had become clear that the conspirators had targeted him and his wife for abduction or execution. "So, fearless leader," Anthony said, "what's your plan?"

Lucius took a deep breath, "The way I see it, we have two options. The first is to go public. If you are right, most of Colonel Proscia's people are still loyal, they'll side with us. The problem is that it will gut our response to the conspirators at what might end up being a critical time." He held up one hand as if weighing the option, "And if you're wrong, we'll not only destroy Colonel Proscia's career but we will also cripple our response to the conspirators when they may be the ones behind this crisis."

No one spoke. It was the less than ideal approach, Lucius knew.

"My other option is to confront Colonel Proscia directly in order to provoke a response. If he is the traitor, he'll react and we can take him down. If he isn't, then we still have his network intact and we can do apologies all around and focus on the threat of the conspirators."

"That second approach sounds more risky to you," Anthony Doko said. "If he planned to kidnap or kill you, then he'll have at least one team of people willing to kill or take you hostage. They won't be far away."

"That's where you three would come in," Lucius said. "He still doesn't know of your involvement.

"Everyone is missing one particularly scary possibility," Princess Lizmadie spoke up. She took a deep breath, her face strained, "What if our traitor and these conspirators are working together?"

Lucius felt his stomach roil, "You mean that Colonel Proscia has worked with the conspirators, that all of our plans are known to our enemies and that they're working in collusion?" He closed his eyes as he thought that one through for a long moment. "No... that is being a little *too* paranoid, I think. For one thing, without the Fleet here, they can't take full advantage of the situation for a military coup. For another, they wouldn't need to go through this charade with my daughter's kidnapping... they could just move on us at their leisure without a false crisis." He shook his head, "This whole thing is too much of a mess for it to be entirely orchestrated. One side or the other is behind my daughter's kidnapping, not both."

"Or maybe even a third party," Alanis said. "We've plenty of external enemies. The Shadow Lords are known for assassination, blackmail, and kidnapping. For that matter, the Centauri Confederation is too." Her face went bleak as she said that, reminding Lucius that the Centauri Ambassador claimed to be Marius Giovanni. Would their own father be capable of kidnapping his granddaughter? *Quite possible,* he thought, *and it* was *a Centauri pistol the kidnappers used.*

"Regardless," Anthony said, "I don't think you should put yourself at risk directly confronting him, sir."

"I don't really have much of a choice," Lucius said. "He's just reported to Alicia that they took down the kidnappers and that he's moving to link up with her at the primary safehouse. It's a bunker that the Chxor built for their senior officers, complete with an underground shuttle hangar for them to escape. We've repurposed it as a safe house in case the conspirators attack, tied it into the planetary network, upgraded the communications systems, and swapped out the Chxor shuttles for some spare combat shuttles. The problem is, if Colonel Proscia is the traitor, then he'll have half of the government as well as several key officers present." He sighed, "It will require my access codes to get inside that bunker. More than that, I don't think anyone else will be able to provoke him into revealing himself. He could simply have you two arrested... and as for my sister," he nodded at Alanis, "he can discredit what she has to say based on her position as a cadet and outside the decision making process."

"So your plan is that you will just walk in there and confront Colonel Proscia, accuse him of treason and a host of other crimes?" Alanis asked. "What do we do, stand by with guns ready to shoot him if he tries something?

"That pretty much sums it up," Lucius said.

***

Lieutenant Commander Chuck Mathis blinked as Senior Captain Ngo stepped onto the *Saladin*'s bridge. As far as he knew, the Senior Captain was supposed to be off duty for another six hours while he and the rest of the third watch had the shift. Then again, it wasn't uncommon for the Senior Captain to do inspections at random times, from what Chuck had seen since his arrival to the *Saladin*.

What *was* uncommon was that the Executive Officer, Commander Argyle also arrived at the bridge, followed by half of first watch. Since Chuck Mathis was assigned primarily as part of the Baron's contingency against the conspiracy and since Chuck knew that the Senior Captain and his XO were both a part of that conspiracy, the sudden change of routine was very alarming.

"Lieutenant Commander," Senior Captain Ngo said, "I have the bridge, you stand relieved."

"Sir?" Chuck asked, even as he looked around the bridge. He knew that Captain Beeson hadn't had an opportunity to send him any backup, yet. If this were something related to the conspiracy, if they were making their move, he had to do *something* to stop them.

"Admiral Dreyfus wants to run a standard readiness drill, I'll be taking over," Senior Captain Ngo said as he walked towards his command chair.

Chuck stepped forward to intercept him and as he did, he saw several of the first watch crew's hands jerk towards what could only be concealed weapons. Chuck's blood ran cold. As officer of the watch, he had his sidearm, but most of the bridge crew weren't armed at all. This could quickly become a bloodbath... yet if he didn't take some action, the conspirators might have free reign. Chuck smiled as ingratiatingly as possible, "Sir, could I give you a status update, first?"

Irritation formed over Ngo's face and Chuck saw the twitchy men behind him relax. No doubt they had suspected him as an outsider. He had just come across as an overzealous busybody, rather than an actual threat.

"No need," Ngo said. "There will be time after the drill." He looked around the bridge, "All personnel should report to their battle stations."

Chuck feigned confusion, "But sir, since I'm the officer of the watch, shouldn't my post be here?" He shifted a bit closer to the Senior Captain. *A few more meters,* he thought, *and maybe I can use him as cover and they won't shoot.*

Just then Ngo's comm unit pinged and he looked down at it. Chuck took another step closer but he kept his hand away from his pistol as he saw Commander Argyle's hand settle on his.

When Senior Captain Ngo looked up, all pretense was gone from his face. "Omega Protocol," he said, his voice flat. "No witnesses."

Chuck went for his pistol. Before he could get it all the way out, Commander Argyle drew and fired. Chuck stumbled back. Around him, he heard gunfire echo and the third watch died, many of them still strapped in at their stations, caught by surprise as their own shipmates turned on them.

Chuck felt his legs give out and he sat and then fell back. He slumped back against the command chair's base.

Senior Captain Ngo stepped forward. He lightly pushed Chuck out of his way and stepped over his prone form. Chuck heard his voice from a distance as he felt cold wash over his body. "Clear the bodies out of the way," Ngo said. "Then bring us online."

Chuck's eyes locked on the pistol that still lay in his hand, only a few centimeters away from Ngo's right foot. Chuck put everything he could behind a last surge of strength. As his world went black, he heard a final gunshot and a shrill scream from Senior Captain Ngo as Chuck shot him in the foot.

***

Staff Sergeant Tam Chen, United Colonies Marine Corps, read the alert message with wide eyes. To all appearances, it was merely a message from the Baron, reminding all Fleet personnel to verify their pay was in order from the transition to the new currency.

In actuality, it was a coded message for Captain Beeson's counter-conspirators. Staff Sergeant Chen recognized the message for the worst of the lot: the conspirators were about to move and that it was now his job to stop them.

Luckily, he happened to be on duty in the *Templar*'s forward armory. The first thing he did was to lock down the access hatch and then to move over to where his powered armor awaited. The *Templar* had the contingent for an entire battalion of Marines. Staff Sergant Chen's primary task was to secure the forward armory and equip other of the Baron's teams to take down the conspirators. Since they knew that Brigidier General Morris was one of them, along with Colonel Trout and Senior Captain Gronsky, Staff Sergeant Chen had felt that there would likely be a larger scale response if things went violent. Chen didn't know all the details, but he knew that corrupt officers wouldn't hesitate to turn to violence.

*And when that's the case,* Chen thought as he backed into his powered armor, *violence is called for to prevent evil men from winning.* He knew well enough the cost for staying quiet. His brother's entire family had been taken away by the Centauri Confederation's secret police. He'd later learned that his parents had stood by and allowed it to happen, despite the fact that his father could have warned his brother in time to let him flee.

Tam hadn't had the opportunity to save his brother or his brother's family, but he had one now to stop the same type of men from doing what they wanted. As his powered armor clamped down around his chest, he gave a grim smile. He would avenge his brother's spirit.

That smile turned to a look of surprise as the armory hatch swung open. Someone had overridden his lockdown. In his armor, he saw a countdown until the startup finished. *Twenty seconds,* he thought, *that's way too long.*

Yet he could do nothing. His armor held him as securely as any prison.

"Bridge, this is Response Force Three," the leader spoke. Staff Sergeant Chen recognized Captain Ducherne, Brigadier General Morris's aide, "we've accessed the armory. Did one of your apes lock it down? I thought the plan was that you'd leave it open. I had to call the boss to get his override codes."

*Override codes,* Tam thought, *of course, Brigadier General Morris could override the lockdown.* He glanced at his timer and saw he had another fifteen seconds. As long as they didn't notice him...

"Captain," one of the others said, "no sign of the guard in the outer room, what if he's in the armory proper?"

"Kill him," Captain Ducherne said absently. "Omega Protocol, we don't know who knows about us, and we don't want any witnesses, just like on the bridge. We killed all of them up there, we do the same for here. After you do that, suit up in powered armor, Command says to take down our other targets." Tam gritted his teeth as Ducherne calmly talked about murdering his fellow shipmates.

"Yes, sir," the voice said as he stepped through the inner hatch. He was followed by five other Marines and Tam grimaced as he recognized them. They were from Brigadier General Morris's personal detail, which shouldn't have surprised him. They were all Force Recon and they had stuck to themselves to a degree that had bothered Tam even before he knew about the conspiracy.

It made a bit more sense to him now, seeing as they had to be prepared to kill anyone who wasn't part of their leader's plans. It wouldn't do to allow any emotional attachment to people you might have to murder in cold-blood. *Seven seconds,* Tam Chen thought, even as he saw two of them walk in his direction. His armor would be vulnerable even to small arms fire if he was stationary. For that matter, they could just disconnect the power cables and leave it immobile if they got to him before it started up. Without power, the suit would either dump him out or, if he overrode it, he could suffocate as the internal environmental systems shut down for lack of power.

"Hey, Captain Ducherne, this suit is powering up."

"What?" Captain Ducherne turned around from where he had just opened up his own suit of armor. "Is there someone inside?"

*Three seconds,* Staff Sergeant Chen thought.

One of the mutineers stepped forward and peered at the equipment display. "It might just be a diagnostic..." he trailed off and looked up, his face pale, "Sir, it's–"

"*Too late,*" Staff Sergeant Chen's voice boomed over the suit's speakers. He lurched forward off of the armor rack and swung with all of the suit's enhanced power. The blow crushed the nearest man and sent his body tumbling into the man next to him. Down the armory, Tam saw men scramble for weapons or cover. Tam just smiled behind his visor. "Judgment day, you bastards." He brought up his Talyn Mark V assault cannon. The barrels spun up after only a second and Tam swept fire down the tight corridors of the armory. It took only six seconds, by his suit counter, from when his suit came online to when he ceased fire. The dozen mutineers lay dead, ripped apart by the fully automatic chain gun.

All but one. Down at the end, the suit's sensors heard panicked breathing. Tam stalked down the corridor and he paused in front of Captain Ducherne's powered armor. Behind it, the traitorous officer gasped into his comm unit, "Bridge, it was an ambush, there's–"

Tam Chen reached out a calm hand in his powered gauntlet and caught the officer by the throat. His servos augmented his strength as he crushed the bastard's throat.

He threw the coward away and turned back to the door, just as the rest of his team arrived. "Suit up, boys and girls," Tam said, "we have traitors to kill."

***

Lucius led the others through the outer and inner security perimeters with no issue. Part of that was because Lucius had made certain that he knew about the various secure access points. The rest was because he had made certain that his access codes could not only bypass that security, but override any alarms. *Paranoia is a survival trait,* he thought absently as he paused before the last door.

Lucius looked over at his sister and then at Captain Anthony Doko and Princess Lizmadie. All three of them wore body armor and carried slung rifles. Lucius hoped that they wouldn't have need for them. They had managed to arrive within a few minutes of when Lucius expected Colonel Proscia to arrive, and Lucius said a silent prayer for the safety of his daughter.

He felt an icy calmness wash over him as he opened the last door and stepped into the room.

"...absolutely certain?" Alicia Nix asked with a look of dismay. The head of the FIB stood only a few meters away. Next to her were a pair of her agents as well as Ensign Tascon. Apparently she hadn't let him out of her sight. While Lucius approved of her diligence, he somewhat regretted the man's presence for what was certain to be a sensitive discussion.

"We verified it before we left," Colonel Proscia said. "My men swept the entire site three times, there was..." He trailed off as he registered Lucius's arrival. He and three of his men were present. One of them carried a wrapped bundle that made gentle baby noises. Behind them and to the side stood Reginald.

"Baron Giovanni!" Colonel Proscia said, his face blank with shock, "You're alive! We expected the worst after the attack..." He trailed off as he registered the presence of Lucius's companions. Their silent, threatening demeanor seemed to confuse him.

"Alicia," Lucius nodded at the director of the FIB. "I'd like to apologize for my absence. Captain Doko felt it necessary to reach me personally in regards to the traitor in our ranks." He put emphasis on that and the others in the room went still. Only the baby made any noise and her soft noises seemed out of place in the somber chamber.

Lucius gave a cold smile and continued to speak.

***

Ensign Alberto Tascon felt his blood run cold as Baron Giovanni spoke. *Traitor in our ranks,* he thought, *he knows something... but what, how can he know?* The Baron's next words might as well have been gibberish as Alberto's mind went into overdrive.

Instantly he thought about everything he had done wrong, things that he hadn't dared to put on the data card he gave up earlier. Certainly he'd needed to give them some dirt so they wouldn't look too deep, but he hadn't dared to mention the secrets he'd sold or the information he had passed along, all of it for far more money than the simple software hacks and copyright infringement he had owned up to.

And of course, none of those matched up to the real reason he had come forward to help.

It had seemed such a simple thing at the time. One of his long-time contacts in the upper ranks of Faraday's society had asked for military grade software for hacking. Alberto had assumed it was some rich kid wanting to clear out his traffic tickets or something similarly stupid. He'd done the same thing before, multiple times, and he had just assumed that this contact wanted the thrill of doing it himself.

What was a little bit of old Nova Roma military coding worth, after all? It was advanced for a network like Faraday, but it wasn't like it was good enough to get into a truly secure network. If worst came to worse and they got caught, it was old enough that Alberto knew the authorities would assume it was stolen or taken long before Baron Giovanni ever came to Faraday.

He had never imagined that the idiots he sold it to had planned to kidnap Baron Giovanni's daughter. Only the fact that he'd planted a Trojan in the coding meant that he'd realized where they used it... and then managed to connect the dots.

*There's no way that he's connected it to me,* Alberto thought, even as his hand went to the concealed pistol tucked away in his belt. Despite their precautions, no one had thought to search him when he first came forward. If all else failed, he figured he could at least threaten or bluster his way out of the situation. *They can't know...*

"...what swings the whole thing, though," Baron Giovanni said, his voice cold and his face solemn, "is that the hack utilized an old set of Nova Roma military coding. I find it extremely unlikely that they just happened to stumble upon that."

"No!" Tascon gasped. He hadn't realized he had spoken aloud until he saw everyone's gazes lock on him. *He knows,* Alberto thought, *how did he know?* His hand grasped the pistol, seemingly of its own volition and he brought it up, aimed roughly at Baron Giovanni. "Listen, I don't want to hurt anyone, but I'm going, and I'm going now!"

There was a sharp crack and Alberto felt an impact, like someone had punched him in the sternum. He spun to face Captain Doko and his eyes went wide as the officer fired again. This time, Alberto felt not only the impact, but a wash of pain. His pistol fell and Alberto stumbled back. "It wasn't supposed to be this way..." he gasped. "I'm rich... I have money... I..."

He coughed and stumbled to his knees, his legs suddenly too weak to hold him. His gaze met that of his killer and Alberto felt his eyes go wide in fear. “I don't want to die.”

The last thing he saw, as the world went black, was Anthony Doko's cold, pitiless gaze.

***

“Well, that was unexpected,” Lucius said as he looked down at Alberto Tascon's body.

He looked up at Colonel Proscia who still had a confused expression. “I'm sorry I accused you, Colonel. I'd hoped it wasn't you... and I guess we smoked out the actual traitor on accident.”

Colonel Proscia just shook his head, “I suppose so.”

Lucius stepped forward to where a Marine stood with the baby, “Thank you, Colonel, for retrieving my daughter.”

Alicia stepped forward to cut him off, “Baron...”

Lucius stopped, “What is it?”

“That's not your daughter, sir,” Reginald said, his voice tight.

“What?” Lucius demanded.

“This is Patricia, Emilee Stark's daughter,” Colonel Proscia said, his own voice tired. “We searched the kidnapper’s area three times, there was no sign of your daughter. The one prisoner we took alive said that they only brought the one baby back to their safehouse.”

Lucius felt as if he'd been punched in the gut. He stumbled back from the Marine with the baby and took a seat just before his knees gave out. “What... what did they do with my daughter?”

“We're still trying to figure that out,” Alicia said, her face solemn. “Colonel Proscia's prisoner is being interrogated now, but he wasn't one of the brains of the operation. The three primary kidnappers all went down fighting.”

Lucius felt his hands tremble. *My daughter,* he thought with despair, *what did they do to my daughter?*

“We think they may have had some other supporter,” Colonel Proscia said. “They had a number of military grade weapons and some of them showed signs of recent training when we stormed their safehouse. I think it likely that if Ensign Tascon was involved, then there may be other involvement as well. Possibly some wealthy or powerful backer who made a deal with them and convinced them to ransom Patricia Stark in place of your daughter.”

Lucius shook his head, “They would have to know that we'd

confirm her identity." Anyone who had the resources to back the kidnappers would also know how easy it would be to check her biometrics against her medical records.

"Yes," Alicia said, "but the kidnappers might not have realized that."

Lucius looked up, "So they just wanted the kidnappers as a front, possibly as a way to distract us while they took my child." He felt a cold anger kindle in his heart. Whoever was responsible, Lucius would turn over every rock on every inhabited world to find his daughter.

"That's what we think," Alicia said. "Furthermore–"

She broke off as one of her aides rushed in. A moment later her eyes went wide in shock. "Baron, our data feed from the Defense Center... the Fleet has returned, they've been in orbit for almost thirty minutes, my people just now were notified."

Lucius frowned, "What? Why? They should be preparing for the attack on Nova Roma..."

He broke off as he realized why the entire fleet would come back to Faraday, while he would be distracted by his daughter's kidnapping. "The cabal."

Alicia brought up the data feed on the display. Lucius's eyes went narrow as a broadcast icon lit up. "They're broadcasting on all channels, an emergency override."

A moment later, Admiral Dreyfus's face appeared on the screen. "Citizens of the United Colonies. I regret to inform you that it has come to my attention that a plot is underway against us all."

Lucius felt hope blossom. Admiral Dreyfus must have become aware of the conspiracy, he thought, and now he was taking action to put it down.

"This plot has been perpetrated by mutineers and ambitious men and women in the Fleet and in your government. Even now, they are fighting aboard the ships of the Fleet and I have word that they are storming government centers as well. I am not yet aware of their goals or their reasons, but one thing I am certain of: these men and women have killed Baron Giovanni and they mean to seize power for themselves."

Lucius's eyes went wide at that. "What?" He looked around the room, surely he had heard the Admiral incorrectly.

"Right now we have identified the forces of the Federal

Investigation Bureau as being involved, as well as certain elements of the Foreign Ministry. Minister Bueller and Mrs Nix are still at large and are considered to be extremely dangerous. As of this time, I am instituting martial law on Faraday until this crisis is resolved. I ask all civilians to get indoors and remain there until we have brought these criminals and their supporters to justice. In the interim, Minster of War Newbauer will be the acting head of state until a proper quorum can be established."

"People of the United Colonies, we stand in the midst of a crisis just as terrible as the invasions of the Balor and the Chxor. I ask you now to trust in the authorities and the loyal men and women of the Fleet to protect you," Admiral Dreyfus said the last in a solemn, sanctimonious tone that set Lucius's teeth on edge. "Admiral Dreyfus out."

The signal went to a holding pattern and Lucius felt the gazes of everyone in the room.

He felt as if his entire world had shifted under his feet. Some part of him wanted to believe that the Admiral was mistaken, that he'd been deceived by the conspirators who had taken over his staff, yet that didn't fit with what Admiral Dreyfus had said. He had instituted martial law and he had claimed that Lucius was dead. Furthermore, he had declared Alicia Nix and Kate Bueller to be the masterminds of his death.

He had moved far too quickly for it to be mere confusion or deceit. This was the action of a well-thought-out plan. That could mean only one thing: Admiral Dreyfus was part of the conspiracy.

It made no sense to Lucius, but at this point: he had only one option: he must adjust to the new circumstances and move on. He looked up and his gaze swept the room. "Very well, we're in phase one already. We've lost the initiative, but I want to execute Plan Delta," he said, referring to their final plan. It was their last, most desperate move, he knew. As soon as the order went out, their teams aboard ships and here on the planet would go into action. Men and women throughout the Fleet would try to take down the known conspirators and their supporters.

Since Admiral Dreyfus was the front for the conspiracy, it was all too likely that many otherwise loyal people would support him, unknowingly aiding the conspiracy. There was really only one way to counter that, Lucius knew. "Can we get any broadcast out?"

Alicia shook her head, "They're using the Fleet's jamming and transmission systems. We don't have anything on the planet to match that."

Lucius sat back as his mind raced. "I need to get up there."

Colonel Proscia had begun to snap commands into his communications unit. He looked up, "Baron, my people will be ready to go within an hour, but I strongly advise against you going up with the first wave, the casualties are going to be rather severe."

Lucius shook his head, "No, I need to be up there *now*. Not an hour from now. There's going to be confusion and chaos aboard those ships and down here and whoever gets their message out is going to be the ones who get active and passive support from the people who don't know all the details." He took a deep breath, "With Admiral Dreyfus backing the cabal, the *only* person who can override him is me... and because he has already declared me dead, then I guarantee putting me on the air will discredit him."

"Since he's declared you dead, sir," Alicia said, "he's almost certainly going to act to make that true. If you try to get aboard any of the ships in the Fleet, he'll have you shot down."

Lucius pursed his lips. "Search all the frequencies, see if there's *anything* they missed. A navigation buoy, a weather satellite, anything." He scanned across the network himself, but most of the planetary network was down or just held the emergency holding image. Clearly the cabal had already moved on much of the network.

Colonel Proscia spoke up, "Military communications are down outside of short range line of sight comms and encrypted frequency-hop transceivers like I've equipped my teams with," he tapped the transceiver on his hip. "I've got a hard-line connection back to the Academy, but they don't have the broadcasting power to overcome the jamming and even if they boosted what they have, the cabal can take them out with a single shot from orbit."

Lucius looked up at a burst of static and a flicker of imagery from where Doko worked. "What was that?"

Anthony Doko shook his head, "I thought I had something, it's on one of the research connections to the ansible network." He moved to the main display and adjusted the input carefully, "It was just about... there."

"Terrance, are you there? Dammit, Feliks, I *told* you we needed to boost the signal more," an irate voice said. "What is it with this interference, anyway? Terrence, is that you?"

"Can he see us?" Lucius asked.

"Of *course* I can see you, and hear you too," Rory said. Lucius recognized the alien technology engineer through the static, though more for his arrogant tone than by sight. "Baron, you have to understand that Feliks and I are in the middle of a very delicate procedure and whatever military exercise is going on, it's interfering with our work."

"Sorry, Doctor," Lucius said with a roll of his eyes, "There's a coup underway and we're trying to resolve it as quickly as we can."

"Oh, good," Rory said with a distracted tone, "Well, then if you'll just let me know when... did you say a coup?"

"Yes," Lucius said. "Admiral Dreyfus has seized control of the Fleet and is jamming on all frequencies. Which begs the question of not only how you are getting a signal out, but how you're receiving *our* signal."

"Tell him about the fighter," Feliks said in the background.

"I don't think I should tell him that right now," Rory said.

"He's going to find out anyway, you should just tell him," Feliks said.

"I don't *want* to tell him..." Rory trailed off.

"If you don't want to tell him, then don't tell him," Feliks said, "but I think you should tell him."

"Excuse me," Lucius said, his patience at an end. "What about the fighter? Are you broadcasting using its systems?" It seemed absurd that a fighter's transmission systems could get through the jamming from the entire Fleet.

"Oh, no," Rory shook his head, "that would be ridiculous. The interference is far too strong for the fighter's systems to compensate. No, we've hooked its power systems into the Balor destroyer we've been working on. It's really quite amazing how..."

"You're punching through an entire fleet's worth of ships jamming with a destroyer's systems powered from the fighter?" Lucius asked incredulously.

"Well, yes, I suppose," Rory said. "You see, I had a bet with Terrence that we could get a number of the secondary systems online just from the fighter's reactor while we waited on the go-ahead from you to fire things up. I was just discussing with him about how innovative the Balor communications system is. You see, not only does it allow you to push increasing power through it, but it also has this amazing ability to fine tune your receiver. Terrence was pretty impressed, and he was just about to admit that *I* won the bet, but then we were disconnected." Rory frowned, "Wait, did you say coup?"

Lucius looked over at Colonel Proscia. "Colonel, I need my security team and some personnel to operate combat systems on a ship." Lucius brought up his datapad, "If you can get into contact with Captain Beeson, tell them that I'm shifting my command to the Balor destroyer. He frowned, "Rory, fire up that destroyer."

"Wait, what about it being too dangerous?" Rory asked. "I mean, I give it a ninety percent–"

"Mmm, fifty percent at most," Feliks muttered in the background.

"Eighty percent chance of success," Rory said, "But I thought you wanted to take precautions..."

"I do," Lucius said, "But I also want to head off a military coup which is already underway. Your ship out there has the systems to broadcast through the jamming, which means I need to be aboard. Get that ship operational, Rory. I'll be there in fifteen minutes." Lucius cut the signal. He had to hope that with everything else going on, that their enemies hadn't picked up the open broadcast.

"Fifteen minutes?" Alicia Nix demanded. "How the hell are you supposed to get up there at all much less within fifteen minutes?"

"Have you still got a tap into traffic control's network?" Lucius asked.

"Yes..." she said after a moment. "I'm seeing a lot of traffic between ships in the Fleet, reinforcements I'd guess. I'm also seeing some traffic between there and groundside. From the communications feed, they have control of Skydock Station and they've locked down all other traffic."

"Fine," Lucius nodded. "All you need to do is take over the network and order all ships on Faraday to lift off."

"What?" Alicia said. "But they've threatened to shoot down..." she paused and cocked her head. "They can't shoot all of them down, can they?" Most of those ships would be civilian freighters, but some would also contain foreign dignitaries and even some military escort ships. No matter how hell-bent Admiral Dreyfus was on taking over, he wouldn't want to make that many enemies.

Lucius nodded, "Make it a bomb threat. Colonel Proscia can

probably set a few bombs off to get people moving more quickly. Just get it done. Also, have your people prep the combat shuttles here in the bunker. We stored them ready to go, but they might need some attention." He looked back at Colonel Proscia, "You should probably launch your people at the same time. Whatever people you can spare for me, get them downstairs... and make certain I have a qualified pilot."

Colonel Proscia didn't look up, "Your sister is qualified."

Lucius looked over at Alanis, "You up for this?"

She frowned, "You know, I think my son is supposed to be born in an hour or so. I'd really meant to be there for that." She looked up, "But even more than that, I'd like to make certain that he doesn't have to grow up under some totalitarian dictatorship. Let's do this."

***

## Chapter VII

Faraday Colony
United Colonies
February 8, 2404

Lord Admiral Valens Balventia grimaced as Minister of War Julian Newbauer finally appeared on his display. "I've been kept waiting for nearly thirty minutes. What is the meaning of this?"

"I'm sorry, Admiral," Newbauer said with a snide smile that put lie to his statement. "Things are just a bit chaotic down here at the moment. Admiral Dreyfus and I had to have a discussion about some of the practicalities before I could talk with you."

Valens gritted his teeth. While he personally despised Lucius Giovanni, it was clear to him that the men conducting a coup against him were far worse. At least Giovanni had some personal honor and spoke his mind. Newbauer was a snake. While Valens had viewed Admiral Dreyfus with a great deal of respect, the fact that he had backed a man like Julian Newbauer did not bode well for the future. "I asked a simple question, may I be cleared to retrieve Emperor Romulus from the surface of Faraday?"

"Well, that's something of an issue, Admiral," Julian Newbauer said easily. "Things are just so chaotic and dangerous down here that we don't want to add foreign military elements into the mix." His broad smile suggested he didn't care how Valens took the lie. "To reassure you, however, we've detached a company of United Colonies Marines to provide an additional layer of security for the Emperor... and Admiral Dreyfus assures me that his ships can provide aerial support if the company should prove inadequate."

Valens' face flushed. The threat was clear enough. If Valens did anything that Admiral Dreyfus or Julian Newbauer disapproved of, they would kill the Emperor. A company would be enough to overwhelm the platoon that Emperor Romulus had with him at the moment. Aerial support from fighters would be there to prevent Valens from reinforcing him or trying to evacuate him.

"I understand," Valens snarled, too angry to pretend to be polite. "I will await further contact."

He broke the connection off before Newbauer could further irritate him. Valens looked up and saw the tight expressions of his staff. "The Emperor is alive," he said, and many of the faces eased their tension. He nodded at his sensor's officer, "What can you tell me about what's going on in their Fleet?"

The officer gave a nod, "My Lord," he said, "I'm still seeing signs of fighting aboard many of the ships. Many of their lighter ships have gone dark, clearly someone has cut power in order to prevent their use." Valens nodded at that. The lighter ships would be more useful in this kind of large-scale mutiny or coup. They could pull alongside larger ships and transport troops as well as provide targeted support, blasting compartments containing the enemy into space.

"What about their bigger ships?" Valens asked.

"*Paladin* shows no signs of combat, but also has not had any transports moving from it," the sensor officer said. "Their super-capital ships all show some signs of combat, venting gas, some sections without power. Clearly they don't have things in hand as well as they would like."

Valens nodded. Part of him wished those who opposed the coup the best of luck, but with Giovanni dead, he suspected that they fought a losing battle. *Funny,* Valens thought, *as much as I've always hated him, he's been a constant throughout my life, a rival to judge my own success against.* Now that Giovanni was dead, Valens could admit that he had at least respected the man's capabilities.

*What a waste*, he thought. If nothing else, he doubted that Newbauer or Admiral Dreyfus would support the Emperor's efforts to liberate Nova Roma nearly so much.

He wondered how Lucius had died. He had seen the video of the kidnapping, of his rival being dragged limply from his smashed vehicle. *I wager he didn't give in,* Valens thought, *not him, he was too stubborn to die easily.* He hoped that the man had at least had the opportunity to take some of his assassins down with him.

"Very well," Valens said. "For now, I want all ships at full combat readiness... and I want all Marine units standing by at their shuttles with full combat load out." He saw them look up in surprise at that. "If we need to get down there to save the Emperor, I want them ready to go at a moment's notice." He knew that three battalions worth of Nova Roma Marines would be excessive. Still, better to have them standing by... just in case.

***

*Well, this sucks,* Captain Daniel Beeson thought as a figure in powered armor cut through the bulkhead only a few meters away.

He brought his pistol up and fired into the faceplate of the armored figure even as he shouted, “Contact, rear!” In the chaos of the fighting aboard the ship, there wasn't really any way to tell friend from foe until they opened fire. Even then, Daniel knew that good people were killing each other in the confusion. Generally, however, only the enemy had powered armor and given this particular form of entry, he was certain to be an enemy.

The armored attacker stumbled back from the impacts of bullets against his viewport, despite the ineffectual nature of the attack. That gave Warrant Officer Ngomi long enough to turn and aim her plasma rifle. “Clear!” She shouted.

Daniel dove for cover. Even with the moment's warning, the heat bloom from the superheated plasma round as it passed down the corridor dried out his sweaty back instantly. The audible hiss of the plasma's passage through the air ended in a sharp crack and then a roar as metal and flesh oxidized.

What that meant to Daniel was that he shouted in pain and slapped at the molten hot embers of his attacker as they spattered across the back of his legs.

A glance back showed a pair of armored legs that spewed fire and smoke like truncated roman candles. Yet Daniel saw motion behind them. “Incoming!”

Warrant Officer Ngomi fired into the breach twice more and fire and debris vomited out as her shots hit something. Yet a moment later a solid stream of tracers lanced back down the corridor to cut Ngomi and the bulkhead she sheltered behind in half. A moment later another bulky powered armored figure strode through the breached bulkhead, his armor scorched but intact. Again Daniel brought up his pistol, but his enemy didn't so much as shift as the bullets struck the faceplate, he merely leveled his Talyn Mark V chain gun in Daniel's direction and the barrels began to spin.

“Grenade!” Forrest Perkins shouted and an object landed at the armored figure's feet.

That got his attention and he spun away from Daniel to find cover of his own. Daniel rolled away, again trying to find cover, even though he knew at this range it must be futile.

Yet there was no sharp detonation, no wrench of awful pain and darkness. Instead, a moment later, Daniel heard another pair of shots from the plasma rifle and then the dull roar of the rounds impacting. Daniel cocked his head around to see the armored figure downed, and Ensign Perkins with a goofy grin on his face. "Take that!" Forrest shouted. He paused to pick up the empty magazine he had thrown before he ran up to the edge of the breach and fired through the opening, "Yeehaw!"

Daniel climbed slowly to his feet. He fished around through his pouches for a fresh magazine for his pistol, then gave it up and tossed the empty one away and stooped to pick up a submachine gun from the limp hands of one of the dead. "Forrest," he said, his voice pitched to carry over the not-so-distant sounds of combat. "Aren't you from Saragossa?" He had split off the rest of Lucius's staff to link up with the other response teams and secure docking locations for the help that he hoped would arrive. That help would only come if Colonel Proscia had enough time to get his response plan initiated and wasn't captured or dead. Given the fact that most of the people who had come after them so far wore either black tactical armor or unmarked powered armor, he figured they were the enemy.

If that was the case, then Daniel was determined to hold out as long as he could and take down as many of the bastards with him as he could, until help arrived or ammunition ran out.

"What?" Forrest asked as he squinted around the jagged edge of the breach, "Yeah, born and raised." He brought the plasma rifle up and fired, a moment later there was a hissing shriek as the superheated gas ate through armor plating and boiled the flesh beneath. "Take that!" Forrest shouted. "You don't like that, do you, you mutinous traitors?!"

Daniel spun as he heard movement in the corridor behind him. He turned in time to see a pair of men in body armor as they came around the bend, weapons raised. Daniel cut off two quick bursts. The FMN-3 ripped off two bursts of six rounds. The first man tumbled back, his face a bloody ruin while the second stumbled as the rounds cut his legs out from under him. Daniel finished that man off and then ejected the empty magazine and loaded another. *Say what you want about these bastards,* he thought, *but at least they have good choice in weapons.* "I thought all you Sarogossan's had an accent and came from the same background, you know," he adopted an admittedly poor accent, "My name is Armand, I come from a long, distinguished family."

Forrest didn't say anything for a long moment, "Well, actually, my wife Catharine, did come from one of the better families. Most of Sarogossa was settled by colonists from Spain." There was an odd note to his voice and Daniel suddenly kicked himself for reminding the other man about his past and his losses. Daniel knew well enough that Forrest had lost his wife and child in the Nova Roma attack that left the colony devastated. *Now is not the time to reopen that kind of wound,* Daniel reminded himself harshly. "But my family, we didn't come from the upper class or senior families. My father's family name was Salazar. He was an abusive asshole and thankfully drank himself to death. My stepfather was the one who raised me. He was a retired merchant spacer from New Texas, who fell in love with my mother, which is why I followed his footsteps and why I took his family name."

"Oh," Daniel said. "Sorry to pry."

"No worries, sir," Forrest said. He fired the plasma rifle again, followed by another inhuman shriek as the plasma round cut down another armor clad figure. "Plasma rifle therapy is apparently wonderful for anger management."

***

Alanis absently wondered what her brother, Baron Lucius Giovanni, thought about the fact that his little sister was behind the controls of the first assault shuttle going into the crucible.

She breathed calmly as her fingers danced across the console in front of her. Unlike civilian ships or the holovids, the combat shuttle didn't have a control yoke, it had a slew of reconfigurable holo-panels that she interacted with as much with gestures and the motion of her eyes as she did by actually tapping at them.

The combat shuttle was amazingly responsive, which was good, because otherwise she would have eaten some of the inbound fire. She could vaguely feel sweat beading her brow as another pulse laser flashed past close enough that the drive field on that side fluctuated from the pulse of energy.

She fought the spin caused by that and brought the nose of the shuttle back around on the evasive maneuver that flipped her under the belly of the destroyer that had opened fire on them. A moment later, the destroyer's fire shifted, too late, to a combat shuttle on an intercepting course.

That shuttle slammed home and Alanis whispered a prayer for the pilot. High velocity intercepts like that were extremely dangerous. The armored prows of the combat shuttles were designed for it, but that design only went so far.

Still, it wasn't as if they had much choice. The civilian launch had screened the launches from the Academy and the bunker, but only until they broke atmosphere. At that point, the combat shuttles had no choice but to break orbit and head directly for their targets. Alanis's flight path wasn't really anywhere near the Fleet, but the lone destroyer had come out to intercept ships headed for Skydock Station, and it had killed two shuttles in the process.

The enemy jamming had somewhat eased, either because they needed to communicate themselves or the fighting aboard their ships had grown too heavy for them to maintain uniform jamming. She didn't know which, but she hoped it was the latter. With the destroyer gone, Alanis headed in a straight line for the platform.

She only began braking maneuvers a few thousand kilometers out and as the combat shuttle slammed against the docking collar, she was pretty certain she damaged the structure enough that they wouldn't be able to undock, at least, not any time soon.

"We're here," she said over her net. A moment later she unstrapped and headed into the passenger compartment.

Her brother waited patiently as his security team swarmed through the docking collar. He waited for the all clear before following them. She still wasn't certain why they were here or who the men he'd talked to were. For that matter, she didn't really care beyond the fact that he thought it important enough to come.

The handful of Fleet officers and enlisted followed her brother and she gave a shrug and followed them.

The station on the other side had a very temporary feel to it. Prebuilt structures had been welded together and piping and conduits ran through cuts in the bulkheads. Two civilians stood at the far end of what looked like a workshop or laboratory.

"Is the ship online?" Lucius asked.

"Ah," the first man said. Alanis thought she had heard Lucius call him Rory. "Baron Giovanni, well, it wasn't quite as simple as just hooking things up and hitting a switch." He was short and overweight, with thinning brown hair.

"It is very, very complicated," the second man said. In contrast to his companion, he was tall and thin, with a hunched, almost bird-like demeanor.

"Why aren't you working on it now?" Lucius asked. Alanis recognized his tone and she winced. People were dying while these two were explaining and Lucius wasn't wrong to be angry.

"It's not like hotwiring a ground car," Rory said. "We're trying to jumpstart an alien power plant that was never meant to be operated by a crew who wasn't psychically attuned to the ship. If we do this wrong, there's going to be a *really* big bang and then we're all dead!"

Lucius stalked forward, "Right now, there are hundreds of men and women fighting and dying. Some of them killing each other don't even know *why* they're fighting. If you don't get that ship operational, then I can't put a stop to that, do you understand?"

"Tell him about the control module," Feliks said.

"Thanks, Feliks," Rory said in a sarcastic tone. He straightened up, "I understand all of that, trust me, I do. I've been in combat before. The problem is... well, Feliks and I cobbled together a control module for the fighter, but we weren't planning on bringing the destroyer online yet. We don't know if the destroyer's reactor will stay stable in the long term... or even at all."

"Will it work?" Lucius asked.

Rory ran a hand through his thinning hair. "I'm not sure."

"For almost a year now you've been saying that you had all the answers," Lucius snapped. "I've given you time, resources, almost everything you've asked for... and now, when we really need this ship's systems, you admit that you can't deliver?"

"No!" Rory said.

"Well, sort of," Feliks muttered.

"Look," Rory said after giving his companion a glare, "I know we can bring the destroyer online. I know you'll have time to use the transceiver. I just don't know if the reactor will stay stable enough that we'll have time to get clear if something goes wrong with the control module."

"At best," Feliks spoke up, "we would have twenty, maybe thirty seconds to try to escape."

Lucius looked back at Alanis, "Is that long enough for you to get us out of here?"

She shook her head as she thought about the docking collar. Worse case scenario, she could probably rip the shuttle free. "To pull away, maybe. To get everyone aboard and get to a safe distance, I seriously doubt it." She felt suddenly aware that she was a mere cadet and she had just told a number of officers that she couldn't do something.

They didn't seem to notice.

"If we have time to transmit," Lucius said, "then that will have to be enough." He looked at Rory, "Do it."

Rory and Feliks hurried over to a console. "We've directly attached the fighter to the hull of the destroyer. The hull's material can be configured as a superconductor to aide in power transmission, so we *should* be able to dump the energy straight into the reactor. Feliks will monitor the power discharge here while I'll be at the reactor to control its output."

Lucius looked around, "You set up the transceiver already?"

Rory nodded, "Yeah, it's on the destroyer's bridge. We've already fitted an entire control system, based off standard human designs and ripped out most of the Balor control systems." He opened a hatch and Alanis saw it led to another docking collar, this one connected to an odd, gray metal corridor.

"We've put lighting in the primary corridors," Rory said as he led the way. "The fighter's reactor isn't enough to power gravity or environmental systems, but we've put a few emergency oxygen units aboard, which should be good for at least ten hours of use with this many people."

"Longer if you don't talk too much," Feliks called.

"Did I mention I hate him?" Rory asked as he paused at a branching corridor. The corridor split in an odd fashion, at an angle that made Alanis's head hurt. The walls and corridors were rounded and smooth, almost organic in appearance. "That way leads to the bridge. You can't miss it," he pointed. "I'll be down this way, and I've got my comm unit tied into the ship so if you need to reach me, there shouldn't be any problem."

He scurried away. Alanis followed the others down the hall. Here and there, other corridors branched off, many unlit. The entire ship gave her chills. She had known that they had captured a number of Balor hulks after the Third Battle of Faraday, but she had just assumed that those ships had been either melted for scrap or maybe taken apart. She had not imagined that they had repaired one.

The corridor ended at an open hatch, which led onto a circular room. Boxy control consoles had been welded or bolted to the deck and rough cut holes and patches showed where other equipment had been removed.

Lucius moved straight to the only panel that showed signs of life. Alanis trailed after him,while the handful of other Fleet personnel moved about, some trying to bring displays online and others inspecting the work. Alanis saw him bring up the communications controls, "Rory, I'm ready."

"Okay, so are we," Rory said. "Feliks, fire it up."

"Here goes nothing," Feliks said in a morose tone.

For a long moment, there was nothing. Then as Alanis looked at Lucius the entire world exploded with noise and light.

***

"Any War Shrike elements, this is Peregrine One Three, over," the crackling voice barely came through the jamming on the comms.

Still, Daniel jerked up straight as he heard that callsign. "Peregrine One Three," Daniel said, "this is Warshrike Five, I read you, over." Colonel Prosica had selected the War Shrike and Peregrine callsigns for easy identification. Most of the loyalist teams they had put together in the Fleet had served aboard the War Shrike at one time or another. The Peregrine, her sister ship, then followed as the ideal back-up. Serving aboard the old Nova Roma swift battleship was not something that anyone on the crew would forget, even in the heat of combat.

Daniel didn't miss the tone of relief in the pilot's voice, "Warshrike Five, I have a full cargo, we're moving in on your position. Is the LZ hot?"

"Yeehaw!" Forrest shouted as he fired the plasma rifle over and over again down the breach area. The containment coils on the forward end of the barrel had begun to glow white hot.

"Yes," Daniel said in as calm a tone as he could manage. "Landing Zone is hot." He switched his carbine over to full automatic and laid suppressive fire down the corridor in quick, staccato bursts. *Not long now,* he thought, *just a few more seconds.*

An enemy grenade bounced off the hatch combing only a meter away. "Grenade!" Daniel shouted, even as he tried to slam the hatch. He half succeeded and the partially closed hatch swung back into him like a giant flyswatter. The blow sent him tumbling backwards.

Forrest broke his fall and the two of them sprawled out in a tangle of weapons and gear. Daniel let out another shout as he felt the white hot barrel of the plasma rifle melt its way through his left sleeve and into his flesh.

He jerked his arm away and tumbled onto his back. He looked up, straight into the barrel of a readied plasma rifle.

Before he could do more than flinch, the rifle came up and fired at something behind him. The passage of the bolt dried out his skin and scorched his eyebrows off. Behind him, he heard the impact. That was when he realized that the new armored attackers wore the United Colonies symbol emblazoned across their chest plates. *Reinforcements,* Daniel thought, *at last.*

The platoon disembarked from their shuttle and their section leader paused before Daniel, "Sir," she said, "Senior Cadet Wilkenson, reporting for duty."

"Senior *Cadet*?" Forrest asked as he stood next to Daniel. Daniel cradled his burned arm. He had heard that in the worst case Colonel Proscia planned to launch over a battalion's worth of powered armor into the fight. Where he got the bodies to fill those suits should not have surprised him. "Secure the vicinity," Daniel said, "Do you have comms with other teams?"

"I do, sir," She said. "Peregrine One Two has already linked up with Ensign Konetsky and they report minimal enemy activity. We think that they were centered on you as the target and were unaware of our response."

"Okay," Daniel said. "Well, then, let's link up with them and then expand our area of control." He didn't think that the cabal could have many of their inner circle combatants aboard the *Patriot.* He hoped that they had accounted for most of them at this point.

"We'll push out from here," Daniel said. "What's the overall plan?"

"I was hoping you would know more, sir," Wilkenson said. "All I know is that Colonel Proscia ordered us to link up with you and await further orders from Barion Giovanni."

"The Baron's alive?" Daniel asked. He stumbled a bit, overcome by relief.

“Yes, sir,” she responded. “I heard he came up with the first shuttles.”

“He's up *here*?” Daniel asked. As much as he respected the man's ability to lead from the front, he thought the worst place for him to be was in the melee of the shipboard fighting.

“I don't know where, sir,” Wilkenson said. “Colonel Proscia just said it had to do with communications.”

“Right,” Daniel said and nodded, even though he had no idea what she meant. The cabal had taken over the Fleet's jamming and communications systems. Without capturing most of the ships, there was no way to ensure communications. Still, best to look confident, he thought, “Let's move.”

*I hope the Baron made it, where ever he went,* Daniel thought, *and I hope whatever plan he has works, or else this is going to only get worse.*

***

“What was *that*?” Lucius demanded as he shook his head. The dazzling light display and roar of noise had almost overwhelmed him. A look around showed almost all of the crew he had brought aboard were affected, some stunned or even prone on the deck while the others looked around in confusion.

“Oh,” Rory said over the comms, “Sorry, I had to wait until power up to deactivate some of the Balor's alarm system. It broadcasts on a psychic level, anyone who isn't completely mind-blind like me would have felt something.”

Lucius looked over to where several people were unconscious, including his sister, “Some people felt more than something.”

“It would have had a slight debilitating effect on those who have some latent psychic abilities,” Rory said. “Confusion, disorientation, maybe even unconsciousness.”

Felix spoke up, “Rory, tell him about the control–”

“Yes, Felix, I know,” Rory snapped, “My god, why I even put up with you...” He trailed off, “Baron, I suggest you make whatever broadcast you plan to make. I don't have a good picture on how long this patched control module will hold and we may have to evacuate.”

“Right,” Lucius said. He switched the communications console over to broad spectrum and took a deep breath before he hit transmit. His eyebrows raised a bit, in spite of himself as he saw the emitter power throughput shoot well past any sane rating.

"Attention people of the United Colonies," Lucius said as the transmitter light went green, "I'm afraid that I must inform you that treason of the worst sort is currently taking place." Lucius put every bit of his sincerity into his voice and he prayed that his message would reach those who needed to hear it the most. Even now, he knew that Colonel Proscia's assault teams would be boarding ships of the Fleet. The natural response of those crews would be to oppose such boardings.

"I've suspected for several months that there was a conspiracy among not only some senior officers of the Fleet but also elected government officials. These ambitious men and women sought to breed fear and confusion in a desire to seize power over the United Colonies and to establish their own regime. While I still remain uncertain of their true goals, I do know that they have killed and plan to kill again. They have betrayed you, first by stating that I was dead and then by attempting to seize control over Faraday by force. Even now, they are killing those who seek to uphold their oaths to our constitution."

Lucius locked his gaze on the camera. "I will not stand by while they kill good men and women. I will not stand down and allow them to tear down what we have built together. I will stand against them... and I ask you all to do so as well. The conspiracy's leaders will try to get you to fire on loyal shuttles and ships. I have sent those men and women to board your ships and arrest the guilty, do not oppose them. I promise you this now," Lucius said, "there will be no witch hunts, there will be no show trials. For those who have conspired against the freedom and liberty of our people and murdered their fellow men and women in arms, there will be a proper trial and they will face justice. For those of you who have been deceived, you will not be punished for their crimes. I merely ask that you lay down your arms and allow us to resolve this."

Lucius stood straight, "This is Baron Lucius Giovanni, out." He cut the transmission and stepped back. He hoped that had been enough.

"Sir," an Ensign said from near the sensor display. "I'm detecting targeting sensors from the *Saladin*." His nametag read Miller and he vaguely recognized the officer from when Lucius had commanded the *Peregrine* at the Battle of Melcer.

Lucius looked over. Sure enough, the Crusader class ship's sensors had gone active and Lucius could recognize the signs of weapons powering up. It was equally clear that the enemy didn't have full control of the ship, however. *Senior Captain Ngo has hostage several thousand innocent crew against retaliation,* Lucius thought. "Rory, can we power up the defenses?"

"What?" Rory asked. "Yes, I suppose. I mean, I don't see any reason why not."

"How?" Lucius asked as he moved over to what he thought was the defenses console. In truth, he guessed that all the consoles were reconfigurable, but this one, at least, had some controls he recognized as jamming.

"Uh..." Rory said. "I'm not certain we should do this, just now. I mean, this control module is only barely functioning and maybe we should evacuate?"

Lucius looked over to where his sister still lay comatose. "Our shuttle pilot is still down from whatever that alarm was, so unless you feel like flying a shuttle through interceptor fire..."

"No, no," Rory said quickly, "I think we had better work on defenses. Feliks!" Rory called imperiously, "Come take over here, I need to get to the bridge."

"Of course," Feliks said over the net. "Don't ask me to activate the defenses..."

"Feliks, we both know perfectly well that you *could* activate the defenses," Rory puffed as he hurried down the corridor, hopefully on his way to the bridge. "But *I* could do it better than you."

Lucius ignored the muttered imprecations from Feliks as he brought up a diagnostics and then slowly began to feed power to the systems. He had almost finished as Rory hurried onto the bridge. "What are you doing?" He demanded.

"Just getting things online," Lucius said as he monitored the power flow carefully. *Just a bit more,* he thought as he tweaked the throughput a bit more.

"Don't be absurd!" Rory said, "This is a very complicated alien system that you know almost nothing about. To make things even more complex, we are docked with a space station. You would have to angle the ship's shields to either avoid or encompass..."

Rory trailed off as the defense console's display shifted. A moment later, it showed a rapidly expanding bubble that encompassed the ship and station.

"...and as I was saying," Rory said, "Clearly, I made the entire control system easy to understand and figure out so that you wouldn't be *entirely* dependent upon me."

"Right," Lucius said with a smirk. In truth, he *had* relied heavily upon the intuitive nature of the controls, but he thought the arrogant engineer could use a little bit of an upset. Lucius looked around the bridge, "We have defenses, sensors, and communications all online, what about engines and weapons?"

"You know, you're asking for an awful lot," Rory ran a hand through his thinning hair and his plump face looked strained. "We haven't tested *any* of these systems. The power system is barely holding, half of the conduits are untested and the other half are still damaged. We're working with technology that we barely comprehend–"

"Enemy weapons are coming online!" Ensign Miller said.

"Now is the perfect time for a live test!" Rory all but shouted. He rushed over to another console. "I'll bring the engines online. The main weapons are over there," he waved generally at another console.

Lucius nodded at another officer who came over to take his place. On his way to the weapon's console, he helped Alanis to her feet, "You okay?"

She shook her head, "I have a throbbing headache. What was that?"

"Some kind of psychic alarm system," Lucius said as he helped her to a seat and then moved to join the officer at the weapons console. The weapons display showed power available to the primary and secondary weapons systems. Lucius nodded at Lieutenant Shaw, "Bring those online, let me know when you're ready to fire."

He looked over at Ensign Miller, "You know the layout of the *Saladin*?"

"Yes, sir," the officer said.

"Get on those sensors, get me the tightest target you can for her command section." It was deeply buried, Lucius knew, and heavily armored against such a shot. Yet the big ship was an unmoving target, her defense screens were offline, and the jamming was completely focused on communications rather than targeting. Given the demonstrated power of the Balor weapons, the shot might be possible. Taking out the *Saladin*'s command bridge would put them out of the fight. It might take the fight out of the cabal as well and convince those who hadn't yet decided to pick the right side.

Ensign Miller gave him a nervous nod and Lucius moved over to where Rory had brought the engines online. "We're still attached to the station," Rory said. "We don't have much of an airlock in place..."

"*Saladin*'s weapons power levels spiking," Ensign Miller said. "They're about to fire!"

"Engines online!" Rory shouted. "Feliks, close the airlock!"

There was a distant chuff, cut off a moment later as they broke away from the station. Lucius brought up visual and saw a trail of debris spew from the station as it spun. Rory winced, "That was my stuff..."

He trailed off as the *Saladin* fired. At this distance, Lucius could *see* the ionized gas of the directed fusion beam. The platform didn't explode, it turned into a cloud of ionized metallic gasses that spread in a huge, multicolored cloud that slammed the destroyer hard enough to send it into a spin. Lucius stumbled back and his grasping fingers barely caught the edge of his console as the ship spun madly. *This is getting a little out of hand,* he thought.

***

"Admiral Balventia," a gruff voice spoke from the display.

"Ah," Valens smiled politely, "to what do I owe the pleasure, Admiral Dreyfus." He didn't bother to hide his pleasure at the frazzled look to the other man's face. While he couldn't say he was *fond* of Lucius Giovanni, he could admit to some relief to the man's survival.

That relief was matched by a bit of glee to see how he had upset the man who conspired to hold the Emperor hostage to Valens' good behavior.

"I'm afraid that I can no longer afford to have you sit this out," Admiral Dreyfus said. "I need you to move your fleet forward, engage the Balor destroyer, and launch your Marines to support my people."

"What?" Valens asked. On the one hand, the fact that Admiral Dreyfus needed the Nova Roma ships to engage Giovanni's vessel suggested that the Admiral had lost control of his ships and the demand to send his Marines to support them only emphasized that.

On the other, clearly, he knew that Valens *had* prepared his Marines to launch or else he wouldn't have requested it.

"Launch your Marines," Admiral Dreyfus said. "I've uploaded target coordinates and priorities. Please don't force me to be so crass as to state what I can do to your Emperor if you refuse my orders. We still maintain a company in position."

Valens saw the *Saladin* fire at the destroyer, a near miss that still knocked the tiny vessel about. Yet the fact that he *had* missed at such close range told Valens that even aboard the one ship he trusted to fight, the Admiral didn't have everything his way.

Admiral Dreyfus leaned close, "Valens Balventia, this is your opportunity, you realize this, don't you?" His voice was low and intent, "You can prove yourself the better man, purge the stain upon your family placed there by the Giovanni family. I've been informed that not only is Lucius aboard that ship, but so is his sister. Two birds with one stone and then you would be positioned as not only the Emperor's protector... but also his only heir."

Valens met the Admiral's gaze. The offer would be insulting, but for the man who made it. Admiral Dreyfus was a hero to Nova Roma. He had defended the system from the Wrethe Incursion. He had won numerous battles against the Provisional Colonial Republic Army, back when Nova Roma had supported Amalgamated Worlds. He had exterminated the Tersal Pirate clans.

If Valens had his support, he could return to Nova Roma not only as a hero, but as their new Emperor, acclaimed not only for his successes but also by a hero of legend.

All he needed to do was to reach out and exterminate his rival.

Valens gave Admiral Dreyfus a nod. "Understood." He brought up the generic combat orders for his combat shuttles and quickly adjusted their priorities, before he authorized them... in the name of the Emperor.

"Orders to all Fleet Elements," Valens said, his voice cold. Despite the risks he took, he felt remarkably calm. Treason, it seemed, was easier than he had ever imagined. "Advance and prepare to receive targeting orders."

***

"They're going to kill us!" Rory shouted. Despite the obvious panic in his voice, he still worked frantically at his console.

"They're the enemy, that's what they do. Luckily, their aim was a bit off," Lucius said. "and they are not engaging with more than one of the weapons," he brought up a closer image of the turret that had fired. "I'd guess they only have control of the one turret and probably only the manpower to operate one of the weapons."

He worked on his console for a moment, "Alanis, take the helm, I've plotted an evasive course that takes us out of their firing arc." The bulk of the *Saladin* should protect them from additional fire at close range... so long as the conspirators didn't get other turrets online. "Shawn?" Lucius asked.

Ensign Miller looked up. "I think I've got a shot lined up, sir," he said. "There's a lot of armor on the underside, so I plotted it through the side. It's a longer distance through the ship, but the shot goes through the aft hangar decks and should actually cause less damage."

Lucius frowned, "What about any antimatter warheads in storage?" The hangar deck would have storage bays for the fighters and if Lucius remembered right, they would have ready munitions aboard those same fighters. Unlike conventional fusion warheads, antimatter ones had a tendency to detonate when damaged.

A chain reaction of antimatter warheads would rip the *Saladin* apart, killing the entire crew along with the handful of conspirators.

"I've angled it through the aft hangar bay because it's the shuttle bay and we should be clear, sir," Ensign Miller said. "It's either that or we risk hitting one of the reactors on the bottom."

Lucius gave the Ensign a nod, "Very well." He hoped that Shawn Miller was right. He wished that he had a good engineer who knew those ships. Rory was focused entirely on his work on another panel, "What's our weapons status?" Lucius asked.

"Primary weapons are online," Lieutenant Shaw said. "I'm getting some kind of error message with the secondary weapons."

"*Don't* fire the secondary weapons," Rory said. "The power conduits for those are still iffy, you might well vaporize half the ship if you try to fire them. The primary weapon should be fully operational, I'd give it a ninety-five–"

"Seventy," Feliks interjected.

"Ninety-*nine* percent chance of fully functioning," Rory snapped

Lucius laid the target on his display and adjusted the evasion vector he'd given Alanis. "Ideal shot in twenty seconds," he said. He took a moment to marvel at the light ship's acceleration and maneuverability. They had closed three quarters of the distance between them and the *Saladin* in under a minute, even while conducting extreme evasive maneuvers.

Even as he thought that, the *Saladin* fired again, this time the directed fusion explosion passed close enough to flare against the destroyer's shields. Lucius winced as he saw the energy output, yet the shields held. On his visual sensors he could see them fluoresce as they bled excess energy.

"We can not take another near miss like that," Rory snapped from his console. "We just had a hiccup in the control module when the shields dumped energy back into the control system."

"They won't have time for another shot," Lucius said with far more confidence than he felt. They were firing an untested, possibly damaged, alien weapon at one of their own ships. The attack that would probably kill hundreds even if they made the shot perfectly. If Ensign Miller was wrong or if Lieutenant Shaw didn't get the shot just right, they might destroy the *Saladin* and kill thousands.

Yet, as they came up on the engagement point, Lucius didn't let any of his worry reach his voice. "Engage," he said.

Lieutenant Shaw fired. The destroyer's energy weapon lanced into the hangar bay doors and for a moment, Lucius thought they had missed. He saw no sudden outburst of debris or gas. He brought up visual sensors and only then, under magnification, could he see the small, precise hole drilled through the armored hatch. *They were depressurized,* he realized, *so our shot shouldn't have done much damage there.* He wasn't certain if the enemy had depressurized the bay to prevent loyalists from accessing the shuttles or if it were the other way around.

After a moment, Lucius saw a slow stream of debris. "Damage estimate?" Lucius asked.

"We're not being hit by targeting sensors anymore," Ensign Miller said. "I'm not showing any of their other systems coming online, either."

Lucius brought up the communications controls on his console, "Attention all United Colonies Fleet vessels, this is Lucius Giovanni. As you can see, I am in possession of a fully operational Balor destroyer. I have engaged and destroyed the *Saladin*'s command bridge and I am prepared to do the same to any vessel which does not immediately power down their systems and surrender."

"Sir," Ensign Miller said, "I'm showing that the Nova Roma Fleet ships just launched combat shuttles and a fighter screen. They're also closing the range."

Lucius bit back a curse. It didn't take a genius to guess that Admiral Dreyfus must have offered them something. He wondered if it was Emperor Romulus IV who had accepted or if Valens had simply jumped at the opportunity to finally end their families' feud.

"I'm picking up a broadcast from the *Emperor Romulus*," Ensign Miller said.

"Show me," Lucius said.

Admiral Balventia's face filled the screen. "Attention all United Colonies Fleet personnel," he said, "I am Lord Admiral Valens Balventia of the Nova Roma Imperial Fleet. Believe me when I say to you that I take no pleasure in what I am about to say."

He took a long moment, almost as if he had to force himself to speak. "Admiral Dreyfus is a traitor and a coward. He has threatened the life of my Emperor, my sworn liege, to blackmail me into firing on Lucius Giovanni. Furthermore, he has offered me his support in supplanting the Emperor should I follow his orders."

He looked as if he had swallowed a frog. "He has insulted my honor and the honor of all those who wear a uniform. So I say to you all: those who fight Lucius Giovanni's forces will also fight *my* forces. Those who fight the United Colonies Marines will also fight the Emperor's Marines... and any vessel that does not power down and await boarding will face the entire might of the Nova Roma Imperial Fleet."

Lucius felt his jaw drop in surprise.

"Admiral Valens Balventia, out."

***

Lucius stepped around the twin hulking figures of Nova Roma and United Colonies Marines in powered armor and through the hatch they guarded.

The room inside showed signs of the conflict as did much of the rest of the *Crusader*. The smashed furniture, in a way, seemed far more dramatic and the military memorabilia that had been ripped or blasted from the walls gave Lucius a stark feeling, a symbol of sorts to the destroyed lives and betrayed trust.

Admiral Dreyfus reclined against the far bulkhead while a corpsman worked to save his life. Colonel Prosica stood over him, carbine held at the low ready. The Marine Colonel somehow managed to direct further combat actions while watching the fallen Admiral with a hawk's eye.

Lucius came forward until he finally stopped a meter or so away. For a long moment, he struggled to find words, but his eloquence failed him. Finally, he asked, "Why?"

Admiral Dreyfus just gave a gasping chuckle. "You know, you Giovanni's are like cockroaches. Almost impossible to exterminate."

Lucius blanched at the vitriol in the other man's voice. "I thought we were friends," Lucius said as he shook his head. "My God, you were a mentor to me. For heaven's sake, I even *offered* you command of everything from the very beginning. There was no need for any of this!"

Admiral Dreyfus spat phlegm and blood on the deck at Lucius's feet. "You offered it, yes, but I knew I couldn't have it. Hell, I didn't want it anyway, but I knew that no matter what happened that *you* would be the one to have it... unless I took it from you." He shuddered and the corpsman gave Lucius a shake of his head as he struggled to seal the wounds enough to make the old Admiral stable for transport.

"Do you think the people of Faraday would ever trust someone besides you to lead them, even with your assurances?" Dreyfus shook his head. "Do you think that Emperor Romulus IV would listen to me? Do you think that your homeworld would honor *me*?"

"You're a legend," Lucius said, "You're a god-damned *hero*, why?"

"Because I saw the truth," Admiral Dreyfus snarled and struggled upright. He shook off the medic's attempt to restrain him and leaned forward. His bloodshot eyes were intent. "I saw the future, Giovanni." He all but spat the name. "My wife was a telepath, which is how John Mira convinced me to abandon Amalgamated Worlds to save the human race... he convinced her and she showed me what he had seen... but she showed me more than he realized."

Dreyfus sat back, his energy suddenly spent. His gaze went distant, "I've seen things, Lucius. Battles where casualties are in the millions, where victory is accounted by being able to muster *any* ships to fight another day. War and death on a scale that beggars the imagination." He dropped his head, "Billions dead, Lucius... and this is the *hope* that John Mira and Kandergain preach about. This is their candle in the darkness. You will lead us into that future, Lucius, and damn me, I would have followed you blindly, sending men and ships to their deaths to haunt my dreams forever."

"I'm sorry," Lucius whispered.

"You're *sorry?*" Admiral Dreyfus's head came up. "You can't begin to understand what I've done. I killed my own *wife*, Lucius, because I knew she would never support this course of action. She was a telepath. She would have known if I planned to kill her..."

Lucius felt his blood run cold. "The call from Senior Captain Gronsky, that was you."

"I orchestrated it so that I didn't know," Admiral Dreyfus said. "And I moved on from there. I worked so that when the time came, I could *take* power from you, turn humanity on the right course. We have no need to be the bright and shining future built upon the blood of billions. With the right leadership, we didn't need to sacrifice so much."

Lucius spoke, "Admiral..."

"Don't patronize me with ignorant statements," Admiral Dreyfus groaned. "I've *seen* the future. In nine out of ten results, even with help from Shaden and Kandergain... we still lose. We lose so damned many good men and women and all of it for *nothing.* Do you understand, Lucius, we fight, tooth and claw and nail and we're just not good enough and we *lose*!"

Lucius didn't know what to say.

"But not this path," Admiral Dreyfus gasped. "John Mira never saw me coming... I would master my future. I wouldn't have the blood of billions on my hands... I would succeed where you failed."

Lucius looked away from the terrible madness he saw in his mentor's eyes. He saw that the corpsman had stopped his work and shook his head.

"I tried to stop it, but some things are unstoppable..." Dreyfus shook his head. "And other things happened out of order or not at all and I don't know what I changed. And you're hell bent on returning to Nova Roma, their prodigal child..." Admiral Dreyfus trailed off and shook his head.

Lucius leaned forward, "Admiral, you're dying. Make things

right. Tell me how to dismantle your organization, surely you have files."

Dreyfus chuckled, "Oh, yes, repent!" He glared at Lucius, "I regret nothing. I repent nothing. I am the master of my future... and if I couldn't save those billions, Lucius, at least I saved my soul from torment in the trying." He leaned forward, blood frothing his lips. "I am but the first of many who will haunt your dreams, Giovanni..." he gasped "...and when the Balor... finally send you to hell, I'll await you."

***

"As you can see, Mr. Ambassador, I think that we can offer you an excellent compromise..." Julian Newbauer trailed off as the doors to his office slammed open and a team swarmed inside. "What is the meaning of this?"

Lucius treasured the look of shock on the man's face as he stepped into the room behind his security team. In reality, he had no cause to confront the politician face to face. If nothing else, the events of the coup attempt had shown him that he *was* essential to the survival of the United Colonies... however much he might wish it otherwise.

Still, seeing the look on Julian Newbauer's face was something that he hadn't wanted to miss.

"Minister Newbauer," Lucius said, his voice calm and cold. For while he felt some amusement at the traitor's expression, he felt none at all for the man's actions. "You are hereby arrested on charges of high treason against the United Colonies."

While Newbauer's expression was one to treasure, that of his guest was one for consideration. The Centauri Confederation Ambassador claimed to be none other than Marius Giovanni... Lucius's father. The fact that he was one of two envoys to the United Colonies who claimed that position would have been disturbing enough.

The slight smile on the Ambassador's face disturbed Lucius even more.

"What?" Julian demanded. "I insist that I have done nothing wrong! I merely operated off of the information provided to me by Admiral Dreyfus..."

"The specifics of your involvement with the Dreyfus Coup are too numerous and sensitive to go into just now," Lucius said with a nod at the Ambassador. "But I will state that they include conspiracy to commit murder, conspiracy to overthrow the constitution, false statements to the public, kidnapping and holding a foreign head of state hostage," Lucius gave silent thanks that Emperor Romulus IV had survived unharmed, "and lastly, unauthorized negotiations with a foreign ambassador."

"Ah," Marius Giovanni shook his head, "That's quite the list, Julian. Perhaps you should straighten this all out and we can revisit our discussions?"

"No..." Julian said, "Please, give me asylum..."

"That's not how this works," Marius said with a slight smile. "You know that well enough." He stood silent as the guards dragged Julian from the room. "That was quite the play, son."

Lucius cocked his head at the Ambassador. He refused to think of him as his father. "I'm afraid that due to some of the local unrest, I'm going to have to ask you to return to your ship, Ambassador." He didn't bother to ask the man if he even cared about Kaylee's kidnapping… or to tell him that he had adopted young Patricia Stark after her mother died to protect Lucius' daughter.

"Of course," Marius said. "I'll go there directly."

Lucius turned away, flanked by his escort.

"Oh, and Lucius?"

Lucius turned and the smirk on Marius's face showed something akin to smug satisfaction.

"I just wanted to say that my earlier offer still stands. Think about it, full access to the Centauri Confederation's technology base, scientists, ships, and Fleets. You could end their civil war in a matter of months and then spread peace and civilization throughout human space."

The offer was all the more bitter for the fact that the Dreyfus Fleet lay in shambles. The damage and destruction weren't crippling, nor was the loss of human life. What had ripped the Fleet apart was the violations of trust. Crews had turned on their officers, shipmates had killed one another, all for a conspiracy that seemed to have its roots in the ambition of a few men. Admiral Dreyfus had gone from a hero to a villain of the worst sort and in the process, no one really trusted anyone else.

Right now, Lucius didn't know if it would be possible to launch the assault on Nova Roma... which was all the worse for the fact that his people and their Chxor allies were already too engaged to pull out. If he did so now, it would be a betrayal of the worst sort and he knew that not only would they never get this opportunity again, but the people of Nova Roma wouldn't trust them. Yet if he didn't pull the plug on the operation then they would almost certainly lose.

Marius's offer from the Confederation would give him ships and manpower to pull it all off... at a cost of their autonomy and freedom. Almost certainly it would be as much a betrayal as leaving them to the Chxor, for Nova Roma would be occupied by President Spiridon's people as soon as the Chxor were defeated. Worse, the Centauri forces would disarm any rebels as they relieved them... and no doubt take down names in case of troubles later on. Even if he trusted them to really support him in that operation, he couldn't allow them to seize Nova Roma.

Luicus just shook his head and turned away.

***

Faraday System
United Colonies
February 8, 2404

"Congratulations, you have a healthy son," the doctor said.

Alanis gave him a smile, though as she cradled her newborn baby, she felt more than a flutter of unease. Part of that, she knew, came from the manner of his birth. Incubators were used for a number of reasons, from life-saving necessity to ease of living for the wealthy. That they created a divide between mother and child was why almost all doctors and midwives cautioned against them.

While Alanis hadn't had much choice about the matter if she wanted to pursue her military career, she could admit that part of her eagerness to use it had been a desire to distance herself from the pregnancy. She had hoped that it would allow her to disassociate Reese from the baby.

Instead, as she held the tiny, newborn boy, all she could see of him seemed to come from Reese.

"He has a healthy set of lungs," Lucius said from nearby. She looked up and saw that he had a mix of pleasure and pain on his face. His own daughter was still missing and at this point it was almost certain that she was dead. Why else, after all, would no one have attempted to use her as leverage? How much did it cost him, she wondered, to be here and support her when he feared for his own daughter?

Alanis gave him a nod, "You'd think we were trying to kill him, eh?" The boy sucked fiercely at the bottle in his mouth with an expression of utter concentration.

"Well," Lucius said, "Unfortunately, I have to go. How long until you go back to the Academy?" His voice was level, but she could hear the concern in it. That concern was well founded. The cadets had served as the lead elements of the boarding parties sent by Colonel Proscia and they had taken heavy casualties. At least a dozen people she had known, trained with, and even considered friends were dead. On top of that, the instructors and cadre had also participated and around thirty of them had also died in the fighting. Many of her fellow cadets had sought counseling. A handful had even resigned, traumatized by what they had seen and lost.

Unlike most of her fellow cadets, though, Alanis had already suffered plenty in her life. She'd been orphaned almost from birth, been rejected by society as the daughter of a traitor, and in her escape from Nova Roma she had seen many, many people die. "I'm going back tomorrow, actually," Alanis said. "I want to take my first year tests and I'll need to study for them."

"So soon?" Lucius asked, surprise clear on his face. "I'm sure if you needed more time with your son–"

"No," Alanis interrupted, "I'm fine." She forced herself to smile, "You know how it is, duty calls." Lucius gave her a level look and she could tell she hadn't convinced him. "I'll have plenty of time after the end of this trimester of classes," Alanis said. In truth, spending time with the boy was the last thing she wanted to do. The blonde shock of hair was only the beginning. She could see subtle features of Reese in every aspect of him from his chin to his dimples, and she felt anguish as she thought about that.

"Have you decided on a name, yet?" Lucius asked.

Alanis felt a momentary disorientation. A name. She had thought of one... yet now it didn't seem right. She opened her mouth, "Anthony William," she said impulsively. The one name for Anthony Doko, who had saved Lucius's life and the other for the man she had thought was a traitor, yet who had saved the United Colonies.

Lucius smiled, "A good name. I'll see you later." He left and for just a moment, she wanted to call him back, to open up about how she felt about her son. Yet the moment passed and she cradled the boy to her. "Anthony William," she murmured to herself. It was a good name. Anthony Doko was a close friend and Colonel William Prosica had character aplenty. The boy would grow into those names and hopefully leave any of his father's heritage behind.

As the boy fell asleep in her arms, for just a moment she felt the connection that she had hoped she would feel. At exactly that moment, the nurse came back into the room. "Sorry, ma'am, we'll need to take him for his examination..."

Alanis gave the woman a tight smile, "Of course." She passed Anthony over and felt a sense of relief as she did so. Later there would be time to bond with him. After she finished her classes there would be time for the boy.

Even as she turned away, she knew that there would be many things to occupy her time for many years to come... and she was shamefully grateful for that fact.

***

## Chapter IIX

Halcyon Colony
Contested
March 15, 2404

Counselor Jessica Penwaithe sat patiently through Admiral Moore's briefing. Like most of his, it was merely a regurgitated form of what he had been given and Jessica had found that his daily briefings to the President were the best time she had to think. Time wasn't something she had a great deal of, so she appreciated his droning tone that allowed her to tune him out and think.

Of course, her thoughts were anything from positive. Stavros had returned only a month ago, but the effects of the ambush at Anvil were still being felt. The military disaster had cost them five of their more loyal privateers as well as the entire War Dogs contingent. Commodore Pierce had pulled the remainder of his mercenaries out of the system, almost without a word. The immediate response from most of the population had been one of shock. Stavros's outlandish behavior and generous demeanor had made him something of a hero and though Garret hadn't known it, there had been a popular opinion of the local kid coming back to do right by his homeworld. The simultaneous loss of Garret and defeat of Stavros had crushed morale.

Public support for the war effort in general had continued to go down when Admiral Mannetti brought in her Helot-class Carrier. While she said it was to help defend the planet, no one believed that, especially not when she had parked it in high orbit over the planet.

Surprisingly, Stavros had donated money to the families of killed pilots recruited from Halcyon. Jessica still wasn't certain where that moment of generosity had come from, though she wasn't prepared to discount that it was some effort to sleep with grieving widows.

To make matters worse, Admiral Collae had arrived with a battalion of his ground troops to provide "additional security." At least they kept mostly to themselves, unlike some of Mannetti's people who had already been accused of a variety of crimes ranging from rapes to murders.

Things had rapidly spun out of control, Jessica knew, yet she didn't know how. *Garret is dead and so is my sister,* she thought, *and all I can think about is how it has ruined our plans.*

"Excuse me, Mr President," one of the aides spoke up. "I've just heard that there's an announcement from Spencer Penwaithe."

President Monaghan leaned forward, "What?"

"I haven't heard any more than that, sir," the aide said as he brought up a video feed.

Jessica's lips pursed as Spencer Penwaithe's image appeared. Just like every other time she had ever seen him, he wore an impeccably tailored suit and his neatly trimmed mustache and beard made him look very different from his two sons.

Spencer Penwaithe spoke, his deep voice calm and measured, "My fellow citizens of Halcyon. I speak to you now as a fellow concerned citizen. We have all heard of the tragedies which have befallen our defenders. Some of you, like me, have lost close family to this expeditionary blunder. Some of you have lost jobs due to the disrupted economy. All of you have expressed your concerns... concerns that have not been addressed by President Monaghan."

"Because of the questions he has not addressed and the numerous failures of his administration, I have felt it necessary to leave retirement and I am formally announcing my intention to seek impeachment of President Monaghan and selection of an interim President until such time as a full and proper election can take place."

Jessica leaned back and she felt her stomach roil. It had taken a powerful alliance to force Spencer Penwaithe out of politics. Spencer knew where too many of the bodies were buried. Monaghan had managed to pull together enough grassroots support on top of the various special interests to challenge Spencer, but even combined with her husband renouncing his own father and the fact that Garret had left, Spencer had retained enough support that it nearly hadn't worked. With this disaster, it was quite possible that the public would support *him*.

Jessica looked around the conference room and she saw shock and appreciation for the scope of the issue on every face. President Monaghan, of them all, had the most to lose. Unlike the others, he had been one of Spencer's close associates, a pawn, but a well-positioned one. His determination to found his own administration had given him the confidence to reject Spencer Penwaithe and stand on his own.

*Since the old bastard isn't known for taking kindly to rejection,* Jessica thought, *it's likely that he'll bury Monaghan if we let him back into power.* Right now President Monaghan needed to seize the initiative, he needed to step forward and lead. With the right approach and enough energy, they could turn this around, Jessica felt.

Yet a single look at Monaghan robbed her of that hope. His face had gone gray and he sagged back like a deflated balloon. There was no energy or drive in his eyes, it was like looking into the gaze of a condemned man.

Jessica opened her mouth, but before she could, he rose, "I think that we all need some time to recover from this. Mark, clear my schedule for the afternoon."

Jessica rose, "Mister President, don't you think that we should have some kind of response? Something to show that we *are* fixing these issues?" To allow Spencer free rein to spread whatever lies he wanted, without even refuting them, would be tantamount to giving him the Presidency.

"I think it best that we don't give him more ammunition," President Monaghan said, though his tone sounded more defensive than anything else. "We would just play into his hands if we took an aggressive approach."

Jessica stared at him in shock. It was almost as if he had given up and merely wanted some excuse to escape.

"Very well, sir," Mark Strombos said, "I'll be certain to follow your guidance in regards to media inquiries." He subtly positioned himself between the President and the rest of his staff. Jessica caught the motion and she wondered if Mark's purpose were to actually shield the man or if he simply wanted to enable President Monaghan's escape... in order to better position himself to sign on with Spencer Penwaithe.

*Harris is at the economic summit,* Jessica thought, *he'll have seen all of this as well.* Some part of her wondered at how her husband would react. With Garret, Jessica knew that some emotional outburst would have occurred first, followed by a head-on collision with his father. Harris would be more restrained, yet she couldn't help but wonder if her husband would side with his father. To be certain, he viewed the man's ethics with distaste, but he also agreed with his end goals. She knew that her husband had a full share of his father's ambition, as well, and his father might well make some appeal to that, if he hadn't already. Her husband's caution and intelligence made him a hard man to read and Jessica worried that she wouldn't know which way he would go until he moved.

She didn't miss the irony that she understood Garret far better than the man she had lived with for the past decade. *Hilarious,* she thought with a scowl, *and all the more so for the fact that Garret is dead and my little sister with him... damn this war and damn the toll it has taken from me.*

And damn her for never telling Garret the truth while he still lived.

***

Nova Roma
Chxor Empire
March 15, 2404

Demetrius grimaced as the Chxor foot patrol wound its way through the alleyways of the lower city. In other times, they would not have dared to come so far without far more firepower. Yet the plan called for them to lull their enemies into a false sense of security, so the patrols went unmolested and Demetrius's people let them past.

He knew it wasn't the same all over the planet. The violent rabble that Emperor Romulus's people had slipped into the system had a very different game plan. They posed as rebels and seemed to want to provoke a general uprising against the Chxor. The plan wasn't bad... except for the fact that the Chxor would massacre anyone who followed their lead.

Demetrius worried that they drew too much attention and that they would provoke a Chxor response too soon. Certainly his people weren't ready yet. The skirmishing, kidnapping, and assassinations they had conducted were nothing near the scale of what they would need to accomplish. Even just working together and coordinating their attacks was something that they had to rehearse... and only Kral's notifications of when they could conduct those attacks made them remotely possible.

Captain Ramos seemed a bit taken aback by how people had related to the Chxor officer better than his people. Some part of

Demetrius wanted to gloat over that, but mostly he felt bad for Ramos. Ramos had spent the last years of the war with the Chxor as a prisoner. His rescue from the Melcer penal station had given him a far different perspective from that of the average Nova Roma citizen. He had missed the decline, the grinding anxiety as the previous Emperor grew increasingly unstable and those who supported him became more desperate.

Demetrius, however, had a front row seat to those events. Imperial Security's reach had grown and grown, especially after the Imperial Security Act. Too many men and women had disappeared in the night into unmarked vehicles, collected merely on the suspicion of sedition. Demetrius had to grit his teeth as he thought of just how much terror the last Emperor had inflicted upon his own population.

Only the heroes of those last days had given anyone hope. While Emperor Romulus III and his advisers had heavily censored even the victories, they couldn't stop word of mouth, especially in regards to the handful of heroes. Baron Lucius Giovanni was one of those heroes. Even Demetrius, cynical as he was, felt some awe in the Barons survival. He had led his battleship in battle after battle with the Chxor. Against the scale of the war they were mere skirmishes, Demetrius knew, but the small victories had brought hope to the population... right up until the final defeat of the Nova Roma Imperial Fleet and Emperor Romulus III's surrender.

Demetrius had watched that last battle from the surface. The pinprick flashes of light that had signaled the deaths of their last hopes... and the announcement from Emperor Romulus III had punctuated the end of hope. He could admit to himself that his own ongoing war with the Chxor had been more of a bitter refusal to give in than any real expectation of victory.

Yet Kral's presence and those of his officers and the handful of humans that Baron Giovanni had sent finally brought real victory within their grasp. That was why Demetrius's people worked so well with Kral. Kral brought with him a connection to Baron Giovanni. He had been defeated by the Baron, then convinced to fight against his own people, and finally sent here on a mission as a trusted companion. His story, backed by the humans who had come with his Fleet, was one that resonated with the freedom fighters that Demetrius led. Lucius Giovanni hadn't merely survived like some other officer. No, he had led a successful campaign that had liberated several worlds from the Chxor, including the Danar system. His fleet prepared only a few days away, ready to liberate his homeworld.

Demetrius had made damned certain that those who supported him knew all of that. From there, the message had spread like wildfire. Baron Giovanni was coming to save them. No longer did humans walk with bowed heads and fearful gazes... and soon they would no longer need to worry about the Chxor Empire at all.

Demetrius gave a cold smile as the last of the Chxor foot patrol rounded the corner and went out of sight. *Let them enjoy their minor victory*, he thought, *soon it will be our turn to win the war.*

***

Halcyon Colony
Contested Space
March 20, 2404

Mason gave a broad smile as the long, sleek aircar settled next to his shuttle on the landing pad. That was normally illegal on just about any world he had visited. Traffic control hated to have space craft and air vehicles operating in the same airspace, much less landing in the same zones. If even a shuttle took a collision and crashed into a populated area, thousands could die. Some of the larger bulk freighters lacked the maneuverability of a shuttle and came with the ability to kill millions if one fell out of the sky in just the wrong place.

Yet when Spencer Penwaithe had invited him down to the planet, he had specified that he would have him picked up at the landing pad. His assumption had been that he would have sent a ground vehicle. As the driver climbed out and opened the door, Mason knew that he was wrong... and just how perilous the situation had become. A glance at Lauren Kelly showed that she fully appreciated the danger as well.

*If he can flout laws as important as air space control,* Mason thought, *then he doesn't care about little things like rule of law either.* Given the fact that Spencer Penwaithe was Garret Penwaithe's father, Mason felt a little unnerved about what might happen should he get in that air car.

Yet both Spencer and Collae had put him in the position where he had little choice over how to play the game. They knew that Mannetti would be after the War Dogs... and they knew that Mason would have to do what he could to survive.

*That I'm trying to play both sides against the middle just adds a bit more excitement to the job,* he thought. He gave the driver a nod as he stepped forward and then stooped to enter the vehicle. It was surprisingly cramped on the inside, a product no doubt of heavy chassis armor.

"This thing could take a direct hit from a tactical nuke," Lauren muttered as she climbed in behind him.

"Not quite," Admiral Collae said from near the front. "But it *is* rated for close proximity." He cocked his head as he looked between Lauren and Mason. "The invitation specified that you come alone, Mr. King."

Mason couldn't help an eye twitch at the name. It had been years since anyone called him Tommy King, years spent in recreating himself from the infamous pirate he had become. Mason had gone by McGann or simply Mason for most of that time, a name taken from one of his oldest friends... and a man who had died at his own hand.

*Besides,* Mason thought, *no one has called me "Mr King" since my seventh grade English teacher.*

"She's here because she's my backup, Admiral," Mason said as he met the man's eyes. "If this is some assignment or mission, I'll have to brief her anyway, so this saves us both that time."

As always, Admiral Collae's pitted face showed so little expression that it could have been carved from stone. "Point," he said, his gruff voice measured. He settled back into his seat as the driver closed the door. "It's a short flight, Mr King, but I'd recommend you catch up on the news."

"I've been watching closely," Mason said. President Monaghan had gone into seclusion and from what Mason had seen, that would be followed shortly by either a quiet resignation or a "suicide." Given the way Spencer Penwaithe seemed to play, Mason wouldn't put even money on Monaghan's long term survival.

"You probably don't want to miss this," Admiral Collae said as he sat back and closed his eyes, "There's going to be an announcement soon."

Lauren brought up a news feed. Her eyes went wide, "There's just been a vote in Halcyon's Congress, to immediately suspend the current administration and instate Spencer Penwaithe as interim President."

Mason looked over at Collae. The rogue military commander didn't express any sign of pleasure. It almost seemed as if he were somewhat irritated by the announcement, as if he thought the sideshow were a waste of time. He still didn't know what Spencer Penwaithe had over Admiral Collae. Despite the power Penwaithe seemed to wield here on Halcyon, he shouldn't have anything on the Colonial Republic Army Navy Admiral. Halcyon was technically at war with the Colonial Republic, or at least the Garris Major faction of it. As byzantine as the politics of the Colonial Republic could be, a declaration of independence from it was generally something guaranteed to draw hostile attention from all military forces, if only to prevent other worlds from following suit.

Granted, the Colonial Republic Army Navy was an outlier as far as military organizations went. A cross between a paramilitary organization and what other nations considered special operations, it had grown up from the original terrorist cells of the Provisional Colonial Republic Army. The Colonial Republic Army Navy operated a surprisingly large force of ships and personnel, enough that Collae was far from the only "Admiral" in their ranks. Many of their commanders, like Collae, operated outside of the normal factions. Mason knew that Admiral Collae operated independently, with no supervision. On many Colonial Republic worlds he was considered a revolutionary and on others he was denounced as a pirate.

His goal seemed to be to defend humanity from the Balor, but his tactics had ranged from using civilians as bait to launching hit and run raids against other Colonial Republic forces to keep his own men supplied. More than that, he and Baron Giovanni had come into conflict once already and Collae had come off the worse for it.

"That was quick," Mason said.

Admiral Collae just shrugged, "I understand that the preparations had already taken place."

Mason's eyes narrowed. He had suspected that things moved far too smoothly since his return from the Anvil system. "You knew about the ambush?"

Admiral Collae shrugged again, "We did."

"You could have warned me," Mason said. "A lot of people lost their lives."

Admiral Collae didn't open his eyes, "Mr. King, you have proven remarkably resourceful in your long and tarnished career. Even if I had been allowed to tell you, I see little reason that I should have done so. If you were so incompetent as to fail, then we would only have lost an imperfect tool. You survived and in the process, you have earned Admiral Mannetti's trust. I think this worked out as well as could be expected."

Mason didn't miss the fact that Collae hadn't suggested that he *liked* the plan… only that it worked out as well as could be expected. *Am I mistaken*, Mason thought, *or do I detect a bit of conflict within the ranks?* How that tied into the mysterious Spencer Penwaithe, he wondered, and how the man pulled so many strings with so little apparent effort.

The aircar landed at the back of Halcyon's Capitol Building. Mason started to sit up, but Admiral Collae opened his eyes and held up a hand. "Your weapons."

Mason grimaced, but he unbuckled his belt and set them aside. A moment later, Lauren followed suit. The driver opened the door and Mason slid out of the vehicle. They had landed at a private pad and a team of men in security uniform escorted them into the building a moment later.

*Clearly I'm not considered a VIP... or else they just don't want anyone seeing me meeting with the new President,* Mason thought as they worked their way through service corridors until they finally came to a more public area. The security team led him into a secure conference room.

"Ah, the infamous Tommy King, who would ever suspect that we might set together here?" Spencer Penwaithe said from his spot at the end of the table. His impeccable suit and precisely trimmed beard, along with his height, made him look every bit the distinguished statesman. For a moment, Mason was surprised at just how similar he looked to his son Garret in height, build, and every aspect, really, from his dark skin to his facial structure.

Mason cocked his head, "My condolences."

"Condolences?" Spencer asked, "What are you talking about?

Everything is going to plan."

"Your son was killed under my command," Mason said. "I regret..."

Penwaithe waved a dismissive hand. "Nonsense, he is replaceable. Political upheavals such as this are opportunities to be capitalized upon, and if I am down an heir, at least it is in a fashion from which I profited."

Mason felt his blood go cold at the man's words. Combined with the fact that Collae as much as said that Spencer Penwaithe had ordered him not to tell Mason about the ambush, it suggested a level of callousness that shocked even him.

"Very well," Mason said, "to what do I owe the pleasure of this audience?"

Spencer waved at Admiral Collae, who stepped past Mason. "We fully expect Admiral Mannetti to bring Stavros fully into her confidence soon. Given the removal of all obstacles to her goals, it won't be long until she is ordered to move against us."

"Ordered?" Mason asked with some surprise. Lucretta Mannetti had struck him as self-centered and narcissistic to an enormous degree. He could not imagine her taking orders from *anyone*, not in the long term and certainly not without good reason.

"That is of no consequence," Spencer Penwaithe said with a flat look at Admiral Collae. The Admiral's lack of expression didn't give anything away, but Mason felt that the word had not been a slip. Admiral Collae had given him the information... though for what purpose Mason couldn't guess.

"Now that she has brought the majority of her forces into the system," Admiral Collae continued, "She can meet Halcyon's forces on more than even grounds. Without a significant investment of forces, we would not be able to swing any kind of battle against her." Mason's eyes narrowed at that. Collae hadn't said that they *didn't* have those forces, just that it would take many of them. "Therefore, we want you in position to find out her plan and either sabotage it or simply remove her from the equation."

Mason frowned, "You want me to assassinate her?"

Spencer Penwaithe smirked, "Please, tell me you aren't feeling moral qualms about this? I understand you've killed many men and women. I can assure you that Lucretta Mannetti is far more deserving than some."

Mason's gaze went to the man, "I've killed before. I've even conducted assassinations, I just want to be clear on what is being asked of me."

"Nothing is being *asked*," Spencer Penwaithe said, his voice flat. "We are *far* beyond the point of asking. Whatever value you think you might have, understand that you can be replaced." Given the man had just commented that his own son could be replaced, Mason didn't doubt him.

*Which isn't to say I'll go along quietly*, Mason thought.

"So, infiltrate her operation and either sabotage her plan or neutralize her," Mason said. "Anything else?"

"See to it that she doesn't have the opportunity to realize you work for us," Spencer Penwaithe said. "If she does, be certain she doesn't relay that information to anyone. That would be... unfortunate."

"Understood," Mason said. "So... how are you settling in to your new duties?"

Spencer Penwaithe gave him a level look. "I had thought you had merely adopted the appearance of a buffoon, not that you had allowed yourself to become one. Do not assume that the presidency of this backwater world is the sum of my aspirations... or that it is even a tiny measure of my total resources. This is merely one more move among many... and if you want to remain a valuable piece, then do not try my patience any further."

He waved his hand, "You may go."

***

Admiral Collae dropped them off outside the spaceport. Mason transitioned back into full Stavros mode, complete with swagger and attitude. It was just as well, because Lauren passed him his communications unit a moment later. "Mannetti."

"This is Commodore Stavros," Mason said as he put the earpiece on.

"Stavros, darling..." Lucretta Mannetti purred, "Now that things are a bit more settled here on Halcyon, I finally have some time to give you my full attention."

"Is that so?" Mason said with some of Stavros's leer. Inwardly he shuddered a bit. While he couldn't deny that some part of him found her manipulative and deadly natures attractive, he was also repulsed by those same qualities.

"Yes," she said. "I notice you're at the spaceport, did you just arrive?"

*Is it my paranoia,* he thought, *or do I sense a note of suspicion?* "No," he said, "I came down to see if there was any chance of loot to be had, but this new President seems to have less balls than the last one. No raids going out, scared as sheep, the lot of them." He figured she couldn't have had eyes on him, so that meant she probably had tracked his comm unit. Since he had left that in the vehicle with his belt, that meant she shouldn't have any idea of who he had met.

Admiral Mannetti gave a laugh, "You don't know how true that is, Stavros." Mason wasn't certain if she was being deliberately obtuse or merely snide. "Well, I'll have a car sent over. I look forward to seeing you again."

She cut the connection before Mason could respond. He glanced at Lauren, "It seems Admiral Mannetti wants to meet with me."

Lauren's expression was guarded. "Do you want me to go back to the ship?"

Mason hesitated. On the one hand, he wouldn't mind the backup in person, on the other, if things went wrong then having her in position to utilize the *Kraken* to support him would be far more valuable than any amount of personal firepower. In the end, he decided that he felt better having her close. "No... you should come along."

Mannetti's air car showed up after only a few minutes. This time there were a pair of armed guards that opened the door and the pilot took them out of the city almost immediately. Mason glanced over at Lauren who had a concentrated look on her face. *She's trying to fix landmarks so that she can pilot back,* he thought. The rugged terrain of Halcyon's only continent all looked the same to him: mountains and more mountains.

That perspective changed, though, as they rose over a pass. A colossal series of peaks rose over the valley below, a sharp, jagged up thrust ridge of black rock that rose around an almost tabletop flat plain. The ridge looked very much like the jagged lower jaw of some massive, primeval beast. The emptiness of the broad valley was broken up by only a few slight rises and clusters of scrub trees.

The air car settled quickly towards an industrial installation of some kind on the shoulder of the ridge. No sooner had the vehicle landed than the guards had the doors open.

Mason swaggered out, “Where's the Admiral?” he asked as he looked around. The location had many similar features to mining sites. Heavy machinery trundled back and forth, some of it heavily loaded with black rock and others crushing it into gravel or digging at the sparse soil and the rock beneath.

“Admiral Mannetti is inside the facility,” one of the guards said. “She will meet you there. Follow me, please.”

Mason didn't miss how the other one moved to the rear or how the external guards monitored their movement. It wasn't just remote cameras, he saw foot patrols around the perimeter and at least one team in a vehicle that watched them as they moved towards the central building.

*A very well armed and alert group for any kind of mine site,* he thought, *at last we get to the point of all of this.* For months he had worked his way into Mannetti's confidences. Now that he finally had an opportunity to find out why she and Admiral Collae valued Halcyon so much, he almost felt trepidation. Secrets like this were dangerous enough that just knowing them changed someone's life. He knew that well enough from his experience with the Dreyfus Fleet... and his own past for that matter.

The guard led them through the outer area of the building and down to an elevator. It was a simple platform, but the control had a biometric lock. An added layer of security on a place already blanketed with it.

The guard unlocked the control panel and then set the elevator to descend. It began to drop fast enough that Mason's ears popped at the pressure change and then again as they continued downward. As the naked rock flashed past, Mason began to feel anxious. What if this were some kind of trap, he wondered, and Mannetti just planned to use some random mine as the ambush point?

His hands dropped to the butts of his pistols. Mason felt some of his fears ease at the comforting feel of the twin grips. If worse came to worse, he could fight his way out, especially with Lauren at his side.

The lift finally came to a halt and Mason frowned at the hatch in front of them. It was big and made from some kind of bronze-like alloy. It seemed oddly familiar for some reason.

The hatch slid open and they followed the corridor beyond.

Mason's curiosity grew as the long corridor continued straight for over a hundred meters. Just how big *was* this installation?

The corridor ended in another hatch. This one slid open soon enough and Mason stepped into the large room beyond.

The first thing he noticed was how busy it was. Dozens of people hurried about, many of them carrying equipment or engaged in hooking it up. While a handful wore Admiral Mannetti's black uniforms, most were civilians. They were working in and around alien-looking consoles, some of which were live while others showed signs of damage or and still others sat dormant and dark. The floor and ceiling were the same bronze-like alloy as the hatch, with heavy reinforcing.

The next thing he noticed was that despite their long descent, the room seemed to be perched up high, with balconies that looked down into open space. Each balcony had an armored bulwark or railing that hid what lay below, but the ceilings of those massive spaces looked even more heavily reinforced than the one in this room. Mason counted twenty four balconies in all, each at an angle with this room as the central hub. He started towards the nearest, but then heard a voice to his side.

"Stavros, darling, so glad you could make it," Admiral Mannetti said as she sashayed over. She held up her hands, "What do you think of the place?"

Mason looked around, "I was thinking we would meet someplace a bit more private, personally."

She gave a chuckle as she continued forward, right into his personal space. "Oh," she said in a soft tone, "that is for later." She circled around him, "Your assistance has made all of this possible, so I wanted to share it with you."

"What is it?" Mason asked.

Admiral Mannetti smirked "It is a precursor installation... over a million years old. The locals found part of the exterior, but they didn't have the resources or expertise to even get inside. Better yet, they had no idea the value of what they had found." She started to walk towards the nearest balcony and her hips swayed suggestively.

"Oh?" Mason asked as he followed her.

"Did you ever think it odd, Stavros, how quickly they jumped at hiring you?"

The odd question startled him and he paused, a few meters away from the balcony. "What do you mean by that?" Mason asked in an aggressive tone, more to buy time than anything else.

Admiral Mannetti leaned back against the railing of the balcony and she chuckled. "Oh, please, Stavros, I wasn't trying to be insulting. I merely acknowledge the fact that you are a wolf. The sheep of this planet could not have felt easy at hiring a man like you, am I right?"

Mason gave a shrug, "I hadn't really thought about it." In truth, he had assumed that the possibility of using him as a disposable asset had appealed to them as much as anything else.

"Your ship, your marvelous ship, of course," Admiral Mannetti said. "Advanced jamming and electronic warfare, automated systems, and incredible firepower." She shook her head, "The *Kraken* is so amazing, so unique, don't you think?"

Mason stepped forward, eyes narrowed at her gloating tone. "My ship is excellent, yes."

As he came up beside Admiral Mannetti and looked down, he felt his jaw drop in surprise.

Admiral Mannetti continued, "Tell me, Stavros, what do you think I could accomplish with an entire *fleet* of Krakens?"

***

Reese swore a bit as he realized that he was late. He still didn't understand the importance of this meeting or why Mannetti had pulled him away from his work. *Yes, I can admit that winning over the only experienced captain of a Zar ship is important,* he thought, *but it's not as if Stavros uses anything near the full capabilities.*

Besides that, what he had heard of "Commodore" Stavros Heraklion turned his stomach. Not only was he an unrepentant pirate, but he was also a womanizing drunk. From what Admiral Mannetti said, he was a clever but self-absorbed man. She didn't need the pirate's help, not really, especially not when she already had people in place who could seize his ship.

Still, she had said she wanted Reese to go over some of their plans for the ships in the Brokenjaw Mountain facility. Some part of Reese wondered if she just wanted to embarrass him by forcing him to admit that they still didn't have even one of their ships operational, while a man like Stavros had managed to somehow do that without their resources.

*I still think the ships were trapped,* Reese thought, *but she refuses to listen.* They had lost another pilot just a day earlier and Reese wondered how long before Admiral Mannetti would stop asking for volunteers and start shoving conscripts inside.

While that might be wrong, Reese could admit that it would streamline the procedure a bit.

On that thought Reese finally came into the control room. As usual, the place was a mad house, with technicians scrambling about trying to get the alien base's secondary systems operational. Reese ignored most of them, many were natives and quite a few others were conscripted by Admiral Mannetti. They did the scut work as far as wiring in human systems and repairing what they could of the alien systems, other than that they were inconsequential. Luckily, the Zarakassakaraz technology was very similar to human tech, only more refined and advanced, so the technicians could make some inroads to repairing it. While some xenothropologists might refer to the Zarakassakaraz, most of the research that Reese had seen abandoned the lengthy name and shortened it to Zar.

A glance around showed that Admiral Mannetti stood at the Hangar Twelve Overlook. That was her favorite, with the largest of the Zar ships being there. Reese knew well enough that once they did have neural interface systems operational, Admiral Mannetti planned to make that ship her own, a Zar battlecruiser to lead her armada.

*More power to her,* Reese thought dismissively. He had no desire to interface with the ships himself, even discounting the dangers they had seen thus far. Captaining a ship had never been something that appealed to him. The power of a warship like that gave him no rush. It was nothing, after all, compared to the power of being close to the people who controlled the *use* of those warships.

That was, after all, the reason that working for *Marius* Giovanni appealed to him. The fact that he controlled Admiral Mannetti as only one of his tactics suggested layers of plans and a network of influence far more powerful than anyone could suspect, even if they knew he still lived. *And since no one knows he is still alive,* Reese thought, *that is truly impressive.*

Reese closed the last few meters to where Mannetti stood and for a moment, as he watched her flirt shamelessly with her guest, he felt a spike of rage. She looked enough like Alanis that they could have been sisters or cousins and the reminder of how his wife had rejected him burned like acid. *I will have her back,* Reese thought, *and she will come to realize that everything I've done was for us.*

He turned his gaze and attention to Admiral Mannetti's guest. Stavros stood with his back to the room, his gaze fixed over the balcony. Reese couldn't help a grimace as he took in the man's skin-tight black leather pants, garish red vest, and white shirt with billowing sleeves. If anything it seemed that people had understated his terrible taste in clothing.

Nearby, Reese saw Stavros's aide, her attention similarly fixed on the contents of Hangar Twelve. "Ah, Stavros, this is Reese, he's taken over as the base manager here," Admiral Mannetti said. "Thanks to his diligent work we have many of the base primary systems operational and more and more secondary systems coming online."

Stavros turned and Reese finally saw his face and missed a step. Reese's gaze went to his companion and he nearly choked. *How did they know I would be here,* Reese thought, even as he immediately realized that Lucius had sent them. They had acted as his agents before and it only followed that they were here on his orders again.

Recognition flashed across both their faces, but so did surprise. Reese saw that Admiral Mannetti's gaze still lingered on her ship, so she clearly hadn't noticed. *They're not here for me...* Reese thought, *they're here because of her.*

His instant thought was to denounce them, yet he had seen them both in combat. When they had stormed the Chxor Planetary Defense Base, the pair of them had slaughtered their way through an entire company of Chxor. They were sent there by Lucius, as he had no doubt sent them here. They could only be here to sabotage the mission, yet "Stavros" had been on the planet longer than Reese... which told him that they might not know how it was he had come to be here.

*They won't know for certain why I'm here,* he thought, *and if we can get them someplace secure Admiral Mannetti can deal with them quietly.* Reese gave them both friendly nods and tried to act as naturally as he could. "Good to meet you both. As you can see, the facility is quite large. We have yet to fully explore some of the lower levels."

"How is it that it came to be here?" Lauren asked. There was an edge to her voice, almost as if she suspected him.

"We think that the Zar built this base as a hidden facility in their war against he Illuari," Reese said, resorting to technical details in order to distract her. Once Mannetti knew who they were, they would both be dead anyway, so it wasn't as if giving them information would really matter. He felt a bit bad for them, but if they realized he worked for Admiral Mannetti now, they wouldn't hesitate to kill him, he imagined. "We think that they evacuated after the volcano erupted overhead. The Zar all but abandoned the base, but they couldn't pull out their ships. The hangar bays had already been buried."

"Sometime after that the Illuari took the system. They overran the base and killed the caretaker force," Admiral Mannetti said. "Not that it matters much, their war was over before we even learned how to make bronze. The important thing is that they left behind twenty-four vessels, ready for us to take charge of them."

"Are they fully operational?" Stavros asked. Reese wondered what the man's real name was. He had pretended to be a smuggler before, but his military training and killer instinct had shone through that cover when they fought the Chxor.

"Not yet," Reese said. He didn't miss how Admiral Mannetti's face clouded. She felt embarrassed about that, which no doubt would build into one of her tirades if he didn't head it off. "Unlike your vessel, these ships were never designed with a manual crew interface. We think that these ships were their newest models, just judging from subtle design changes we've noticed."

"Oh?" Stavros asked.

"The only way to crew these ships is to do a direct neural link," Admiral Mannetti said. "Which is why they're still in their hangars. I have my best people working on that even as we speak. I'm certain they're making progress." Her tone suggested that if they weren't, she would be putting one of them in the pod to motivate them. *Not necessarily a bad idea,* Reese thought, *as long as she doesn't mean me*.

"Well," Stavros said, "That's very intriguing and I suddenly understand some of your interest in my own vessel. Clearly you'll want some of my own experience to help train any potential crew." He said the last with such arrogance that Reese gritted his teeth in response, even knowing that it was an act.

"Yes," Admiral Mannetti said. "Now, I think you and I should have that moment alone to discuss strategy–"

"Ma'am," Reese interrupted, "I think I need to review those personnel files with you, as soon as possible."

Lucretta Mannetti's eyes narrowed in anger at the interruption, but her natural intelligence took over a moment later. She knew he wouldn't have interrupted her without reason. Furthermore, he had no responsibilities with personnel. She slowly nodded her head, "Very well. Stavros, I'll have one of my people lead you to my conference room while I review those files."

"Thank you," Stavros bent over her hand and kissed it, but there was something in his dark eyes, almost as if he already suspected that it was a trap.

*Suspect all you want,* Reese thought, *you'll be dead within a few hours, unless Mannetti wants to keep you alive for questioning.* He would recommend against it, assuming she asked him.

They headed away and Admiral Mannetti stepped close, "What was that about, Reese? I've been waiting *months* to get that man alone."

"Better for you then, ma'am," Reese said. He gave a nod in their direction, "The woman there is one of Lucius Giovanni's intelligence agents and 'Stavros' is another. I encountered them both back on Faraday. The woman's name is Lauren Kelly, I don't remember the man's name. I fought the Chxor with them, Lucius Giovanni sent them in to smuggle weapons to the rebels and to organize and lead the attack on the planetary defense centers."

To give her credit, she didn't take long to assimilate the information. "You are certain?"

"I fought side by side with them," Reese said. "Lauren doesn't look a bit different and the only thing different about 'Stavros' is his clothing and slicked back hair."

"Comrades in arms and you betray them so easily?" Lucretta Mannetti chuckled, "Reese, I think you were born for this life."

Reese just shrugged. It was him or them, and the last thing he wanted Lucius to know was that he now worked for his enemies.

"Very well..." she nodded, "I'll have a team sent down there." She pouted, "I just had the conference room remodeled… it will be a shame to ruin the new carpets. Ah, well."

***

As they came into an empty corridor, Lauren slipped up behind the officer, cupped her hand over his mouth and then tagged him with her stunner. He jerked once and went limp and Mason helped her to catch him.

"So, you think we're blown too?" he asked as he frisked the officer for anything that might help. Unfortunately the man was too short for Mason to take his uniform and Lauren would be a poor fit as well.

"I don't know why he's here, but Reese was pretty senior in Baron Giovanni's ranks. There would be no reason to send him here." Lauren shook her head, "And while I shouldn't be talking about this here, I helped with the investigation on Mannetti's escape, I know that there was someone senior who had to have been involved."

Mason nodded at a shadowed alcove and they stuffed the officer away. "Likely, enough, I suppose. Reese helped her escape and then when they came close to pinning it on him, he slipped away himself." Mason pursed his lips, "What bothered me was that he recognized us, but that he didn't try to make contact." In his early life he had operated undercover for a number of operations. There was a feel for a situation, more instinct than anything else, and Mason had felt in his gut that this mission was blown as soon as Reese arrived.

"Yeah," Lauren said. She looked around, "Where to?"

Mason held up the datapad he had pulled off the officer. He pointed down the hallway and they walked briskly as he brought up a schematic of the base. He shook his head, "This place is huge. I don't know how many people they have here, but if we can get into some of the lower corridors, it will take them a while to search for us."

Lauren adjusted her weapons. Mason regretted telling her earlier that day to leave behind the majority of her arsenal. She only had a pair of pistols, the hand stunner, and an assortment of knives. "That doesn't help us in the long run," she said. "Is there only the one entrance?"

Mason shook his head, "I don't think so. That one seems to be newer, a direct access point to the command center. This shows several secondary access points for air shafts, spots that they had to dig down to open those up... and yeah, the original mine off to the south. That seems to be where they bring the heavy equipment in, might be our best bet to escape." He had already checked his comm unit and they didn't have any signal this deep underground.

He showed her the long tunnel that led out into the valley. It would be far less dangerous than trying to slip out through a guarded elevator, plus that site would have transportation of some kind that they could access.

"What's the plan?" Lauren asked.

"Head that way as quickly as we can, acquire uniforms or alternate clothing, take a vehicle and get back to the ship," he said. Kandergain still hadn't returned from whatever mission had called her away. That meant he would probably have to rely on Admiral Collae, since Frank Pierce's War Dogs had left.

"Right," Lauren said and she looked again at the schematics. He could see her concentrate as she tried to memorize the path. "Let's do this."

***

Mason had finally found someone his size and switched over to a far less obtrusive outfit when the alarm sounded. "Attention, there has been a security breach. Report all unauthorized access immediately. All personnel are to report to their supervisors and check in."

Mason grimaced as he tugged on the work book. The worker Lauren had stunned snored peacefully, but they were in a more crowded part of the base. They didn't have a better spot to hide him than this small closet. Mason had tucked him away as best as he could, but it wouldn't be long before someone found him.

To make matters worse, the outfit wasn't the best disguise. Workmen didn't carry around weapons. While Lauren had traded up for a Marine's uniform, body armor, and weapons, Mason would still draw too much attention, he knew. He glanced at his leather boots that he had thrown on top of his clothing, yet he just shook his head. He had liked those boots quite a bit, it seemed a shame to throw them away for a disguise that wouldn't hold up to even minor scrutiny.

He stepped into the corridor and Lauren tossed him a pair of handcuffs, "New plan, pass me your weapons."

Mason grimaced, but he did as he was told. A prisoner being

escorted would draw less attention than a worker wondering around with a Marine.

They hurried along and a moment later Mason heard Lauren's stolen radio squawk, "Ferranti, report in."

Lauren grimaced, "Yes, sir, all clear."

"Ferranti, you are supposed to be in the blue sector, but I'm showing you all the way over near orange, what's going on?" The voice held suspicion aplenty, Mason could tell.

"Sorry, sir, I got turned around, I'm headed there now,"

"Ferranti: Oscar Bravo Tango Five."

"Say again, sir?" Lauren asked.

There was silence for a long moment. "All security elements, go to secondary channel," the voice said, "primary is compromised."

Mason shook his head. They knew where they were now.

Lauren and Mason moved to the side of the corridor as a maintenance cart trundled past, pushed by a pair of workers. Lauren unclipped the stolen and now trackable comm unit and slipped it into a slot on the side of the cart.

Mason pulled her with him as they hurried to a jog. Orange Sector was the area where the vehicles accessed the facility, so they didn't have far to go... but it was almost certain that Admiral Mannetti's people would realize that as well.

They rounded a corner and Mason saw a half dozen guards at the far end of the corridor. Before the other group could react, he had shed the handcuffs and he and Lauren opened fire. Three of the men went down instantly as Mason instinctively worked the left side while Lauren started on the right. Only the man in the middle even had time to bring his weapon up before Mason's fourth shot struck him in the head as Lauren's third shot caught him in the chest.

At that moment, though, alarms began to go off. "Intruders in the orange sector, shots fired!" Mason heard shouted over the intercom.

"Security camera," Mason said and pointed at a spot above the checkpoint.

Lauren bit off a curse, but they were out of time. They hurried forward, just as a hatch behind them opened. Mason looked back to see a squad of Marines sweep out in a tactical formation. He turned and fired even as he shoved Lauren a doorway. His shot took down their point man and Mason dove for cover. He heard a rattle of return fire, but none of it came close.

Lauren leaned over and sawed off a burst from her carbine. The Freedom Arms M-11 carbine had a ridiculous rate of fire and Mason couldn't hear the individual shots. He pawed at the door control behind him, but the light stayed red and the door didn't open. If he remembered right, they had three hundred meters of corridors to go. They couldn't allow this group to pin them down. As he thought that, Lauren pulled a grenade out of her pouch and threw it down the corridor at their attackers. "Move!" she shouted.

He was already in motion. Behind him he could hear the enemy squad scramble for cover as he ticked off the seconds in his mind. One of their attackers, either suicidally brave or just unobservant, continued to fire at them and Mason heard Lauren grunt as a bullet struck her. Mason dove around the corner, half dragging Lauren just as the plasma grenade detonated. The sharp concussion was nothing compared to the massive wave of heat. At this distance, Mason saw the paint blister in the corridor. Closer to the detonation, flesh, plastics, and even metal would begin to burn.

Mason went to pat Lauren down, but she pushed him away. "I'm fine," Lauren said, "the body armor caught the round. We have to move."

Fire alarms joined the chorus of wailing. Mason and Lauren hurried through the corridors and a moment later they were surrounded by fleeing civilians. Lauren caught him and they paused before another door. Down the corridor, he saw another squad of Marines had set up a checkpoint. The crowd of civilians flowed around and through it, but there was no way that the Marines would miss him and Lauren.

"We have to split up," Lauren said.

"What?" Mason shook his head, "don't be absurd." Yet, he understood her meaning. They couldn't fight their way through many more checkpoints like this. The crowd gave them some concealment, but once the enemy opened fire, it would be a bloodbath.

"An armed worker and a Marine together will draw attention. A worker on his own won't," she said. Just then, Mason saw a guard step out of a room only a meter behind Lauren. He froze as he saw them and Mason stepped forward and pistol stroked him across the face. The man dropped limply to the ground.

"What are you saying?" Mason asked as he turned back. She

pulled him forward into a kiss and Mason felt his body respond. The rush of adrenaline and the danger, combined with the touch of her lips, felt like a live wire had been applied to his body. It was far more of a rush than anything he'd ever experienced.

Lauren pushed him away and, as he shook his head to clear it, he saw her activate the door. "I'll distract them, you get out of here." She had taken his belt off him when they kissed, he realized as he pawed for his absent weapons. Just before the hatch slid shut, he saw her pick up the unconscious guard and start to throw him over her shoulder. The pad to the side darkened to show that she had locked it from the other side.

Mason stared at the closed hatch and, for just a second, it was all he could do not to scream in frustration. Every bit of him wanted to pound on the hatch. It was unlikely that Admiral Mannetti's people would try to take her prisoner. Far more likely, they would shoot her on sight. She wouldn't be able to move fast, not dragging along a decoy so it wouldn't take long for them to pin her down.

And then Lauren Kelly would be dead.

"Not like this, not saving *me*," Mason muttered to himself, yet he understood what had to happen. If he stayed, her sacrifice would be in vain. He turned away and stumbled into the crowd, head down. The crowd became his only defense and he kept to the center of it as they passed that checkpoint and then three others. The crowd grew more and more, until they finally boiled out of a broad set of doors and into an open space.

Mason looked around and saw that the doors came out of rock, yet the area looked to have been covered by some ancient lava flow. Off to the side, a long, poorly lit tunnel led away. Clusters of trucks stood running and guards loaded up civilians in the backs of them.

"...squad One Three is combat ineffective," Mason heard as he passed one of the Marines at the doors. "We've got them isolated in the Orange Sector pump room."

Part of him wanted to lunge for the Marine's weapon, but he knew how foolish that would be. Since Mannetti thought she had both of them pinned down, she would allow the civilians to evacuate. That was his ticket out. Only if he got out could he come back and save or avenge Lauren.

*Please,* he thought, *please don't kill her.* Yet he knew that Admiral Mannetti had no reason to allow her to live. Mason had nothing with which to bargain. She already had people aboard his ship. Admiral Mannetti had the position of strength for now and Mason couldn't even threaten her without giving away his position.

He felt anguish and no little bit of fear at that realization. Lauren had awoken him from his life as a drifter, awoken the predator part of him, somehow without bringing back the worst part of him. If she died, he feared that he would descend to the man he had been... or become something even worse.

He followed the crowd and ended up in the back of a cargo truck with a couple dozen others. As the truck began its drive down the long tunnel, Mason's gaze locked on the lights of the base, where the only person he had ever loved would soon die... and part of him died with her.

***

## Chapter IX

Nova Roma
Chxor Empire
April 3, 2404

Jacabo Urbani gave as slick a smile as he could manage as the Chxor at the checkpoint scanned his papers. He knew the papers should hold up, since he'd taken them off a Chxor collaborator he had killed. If they didn't he had a pistol tucked under his shirt.

The Chxor cocked his head, "Trustee Martinez, you are supposed to be in Sector Three Seven Five. Why are you here?"

Jacabo's smile grew a bit strained. "My vehicle broke down, so I'm here to get it repaired." In truth, he was here to pick up explosives and weapons from the supply cache, but he wasn't going to tell them that. He wished that their group had more time to reposition their equipment since the last drop off, but things had been difficult over the past few weeks. While Jacabo had jumped at the chance to get off of the damned prison colony, he hadn't realized just how dangerous this mission was going to be until he arrived on Nova Roma.

"Do you have a permit stamp for your vehicle repairs?" The Chxor officer asked as he looked at his data pad.

"Of course," he said, "Page three." Jacabo barely repressed a sneer at the bulky and clumsy looking device. The Chxor electronics were nothing compared to what someone could access even in the Colonial Republic. Jacabo knew that well enough since after a dust up with a conscription squad here on Nova Roma he had spent years in the Colonial Republic.

He hadn't missed the irony when he had eventually signed on with Admiral Mannetti. He'd left his home and everything he knew behind because he didn't want to risk his life, only to later sign on with a Nova Roma pirate in the hopes of making enough money to return home. And now he knew that he had come full circle, drafted to help liberate the planet from the Chxor by the Nova Roma Emperor himself.

Some part of that amused him, he reflected, but he had become hardened and cynical enough that he mostly didn't care who he worked for. Pirate, freedom fighter, or whatever, as long as he was well paid, he didn't care. Getting to come home was merely a perk of the job. *Not that it's a pleasant homecoming,* he thought.

"I will have to look your permit number up," the Chxor said.

"Fine, fine," Jacabo said. The work permit was the whole reason he had killed the trustee and taken his papers. Jacabo and his companions had seen far less direct support than he had expected since his arrival. At first they had found some help, but as the Chxor punished the civilians for their attacks, the general population had seemed less and less eager to provide them with even food and shelter. Jacabo could admit that some of that came from how some of the others behaved, but still, it felt ungrateful of them.

*Yeah,* he thought, *Bentucci shouldn't have raped that girl, but it wasn't as if she weren't asking for it.* It wasn't as if the girl's family had given the others any options either. After the father had stabbed Bentucci and then got himself shot, Marco had to kill the mother and daughters to shut them up. It was an unfortunate event, but it wasn't as bad as it could have been.

Jacabo knew that Marco had paid off the relatives, which should have been the end of it. Even so, it didn't seem as if that was enough, for whatever reason. Things had gone steadily downhill ever since, which was one reason that they hadn't transferred weapons to the civilians yet. Marco didn't trust that they wouldn't use them on his people.

"The work permit is not in the system," the Chxor officer said.

"What?" Jacabo asked. He couldn't believe that the stick in the mud he'd killed to get it had a counterfeit work permit stamp. *Or maybe I just killed him before he registered it,* Jacabo thought. "Well, I'm sorry, I'll just head back to–"

"We will have to detain you until this can be investigated," the Chxor said. Jacabo saw two others start towards him.

"The hell you will," Jacabo snarled and went for his pistol. He had it out and fired twice. The loud shots echoed in the street and both Chxor fell. Jacabo spun towards the Chxor officer, but before he could fire, the Chxor tackled him.

Jacabo's head struck the pavement and his world went white. As he shook his head to recover, he felt strong arms pinion him to the ground. He tried to fight, but his body wouldn't respond. Another pair of arms joined the first and he felt his hands wrenched painfully behind him and then cold metal as handcuffs were applied.

His blood ran cold when he heard the Chxor officer speak into his comm unit. "Sector Command, this is Officer Ghxul, I have captured a rebel. Please send a retrieval team."

***

Port Klast System
Port Klast
April 4, 2404

"I still can't believe you did that to me," Garret Penwaithe said as Commodore Pierce stepped into the room. "Having that bastard Stavros..."

He trailed off as several others followed the Commodore into the room. The first pair were his brother and Jessica. "My god, Garret, you're *alive*?" Jessica said, her face white with shock.

Garret snorted, "The Commodore here set me up, set up the whole convoy. There was a virus uploaded to our systems. The 'enemy' we fought was just a simulation and some of the Commodore's friends waylaid Mannetti's friends and then captured us when our ships powered down." He saw that his explanation, if anything made their expressions sink still further. "What happened?" He asked.

The final man through the door answered, "Admiral Mannetti made her play. She controls Halcyon... and it'll take quite a bit of effort to oust her."

"What about..." he trailed off, question unasked as he realized that this man seemed familiar somehow. He was tall, with brown hair and dark eyes. Though he had an expressive face, there was nothing but anger and despair in his eyes. He wore a black silk shirt and black slacks, with a pistol belt around his waist and a pistol on each hip. It was the shape of his jaw and his eyes that finally clicked and Garret blurted, "*Stavros?*"

"Tommy King," the man corrected automatically.

Garret stared at him. On the surface it was an absurd statement. But he said it with such confidence and aplomb that Garret felt in his gut that he told the truth. The man Garret had known as Stavros Heraklion, a pirate of ill repute, was instead none other than Tommy King.

A single nod from Commodore Pierce sealed the statement.

"Why are you involved?" Garret asked.

"He's got a letter of marque," Harris said, "from the United Colonies. He knew that we'd attacked them and says that Admiral Mannetti is their enemy."

Garret looked at the Commodore, "Are we good to speak?"

"It's time to share everything we know," Tommy King said. "And the only person who should be overhearing us is our host... who should be arriving shortly."

"Host?" Garret asked.

"Thomas Kaid," a voice said from the doorway. "You may not realize it, but you've been my guest since your arrival."

"Prisoner seems like a better term," Garret growled, yet he still nodded respectfully at the man. Thomas Kaid was every bit as infamous as Tommy King. The two men were polar opposites from background. Thomas Kaid had been one of the founders of the Provisional Colonial Republic Army and the driving force behind the revolt against Amalgamated Worlds, right up until the Colonial Republic signed a treaty with Amalgamated Worlds and in the process sold him out. He had fled out beyond human space, pursued by old enemies and former allies both. He was simultaneously honored as a patriot and freedom fighter and reviled as a terrorist and pirate.

Tommy King, on the other hand, was by all accounts a renegade Amalgamated Worlds officer who went pirate sometime after the fall of Earth. He had ravaged his way across much of Colonial Republic space and at one time even raided the Garris Major system, where he looted Eldorado. On multiple occasions he had marshaled entire pirate fleets in his raids. Half the famous pirates and no few number of mercenaries had run under his flag.

"Mister King has struck a bargain with me," Thomas Kaid said. "An offer that I couldn't pass up... even if it wasn't what I'd originally asked of him." He took a seat, "Now that we are present, I think it best for you to explain."

Tommy King took a seat himself, feet crossed and lounging back in a relaxed pose, yet there was nothing relaxed about his eyes. They were the fierce, hungry eyes of a predator... one which barely clung to anything resembling civility. "Admiral Collae and your father," he nodded at Garret, "tried to use me to get close enough to Mannetti to kill her and thus prevent *her* superior from seizing Halcyon and taking it themselves." He pointed at Garret's brother and sister-in-law, “It seems that your brother and Councilor Penwaithe hoped to use Collae and Mannetti against each other to prevent one or another from taking over.” He gave a little shrug, “Admiral Mannetti is working for persons unknown, with the goal of seizing Halcyon.”

“But why?” Garret asked. The planet was his home, but he knew his father wasn't sentimental about it in the slightest. His wealth lay mostly off-world, anyway, tied into various schemes and enterprises. “Some alien tech shouldn't be *that* valuable.”

“No, but an entire fleet of alien warships is,” Tommy King said, his voice cold. “These two, along with the late President Monaghan thought they could play the various groups against each other and somehow come out on top. That is, until everything came apart.”

“It wouldn't have if you hadn't betrayed us to Mannetti!” Jessica snapped. “With the disaster suffered at the Anvil system, Pierce pulled out and...” she trailed off as she realized that Commodore Pierce stood there and that he hadn't abandoned them... yet he also hadn't stayed at Halcyon.

“Admiral Mannetti had a force in the Anvil System to ambush you,” Commodore Pierce said to Garret. “Thanks to Thomas Kaid, we were able to destroy that force before you arrived. But we knew if the War Dogs remained at Halcyon, Mannetti would escalate until she moved openly. We wanted her to be fat and happy until *we* could move against her. More than that, we found out later that Admiral Collae already knew about it, so did your father, Spencer, though I hadn't thought he would be that callous about his own flesh and blood.”

“More than you know,” Harris said softly. As everyone's gazes turned to him, he seemed to shrink on himself. “You all may have noticed that Garret and I both very closely resemble our father. What isn't common knowledge is that our 'mother' was merely the surrogate. Garret and I are both clones.”

Garret winced at that. It wasn't something he was proud of. Cloning was legal in most systems, as was reproduction through that method, but it was generally seen as narcissism of the worst sort. It was, in fact, part of why their father had originally rejected Garret’s relationship with Jessica.

Commodore Pierce looked troubled, “That explains his willingness to sacrifice either or both of you, I suppose.” He cleared his throat, "What it doesn't explain is how it was that he is the one pulling the strings on Admiral Collae... and not the other way around."

"That I have no idea," Garret said. "I knew he had off world contacts, but not to that extent."

Harris looked down, "Before I broke away from him politically, he had me sit in on a few odd meetings with enior representatives from a number of systems, both in the Colonial Republic and the Centauri Confederation. It might have something to do with that."

"Spencer Penwaithe is involved at very senior levels of the Colonial Republic," Thomas Kaid said after a long moment. "I am not the least bit surprised to hear the Admiral Collae works for him, directly or indirectly."

"How exactly do you know that?" Garret asked.

Thomas Kaid gave him a level look. "I'm an information broker. I know a little bit of everything, the more secretive, the juicier, and the more valuable it is for me to know." He gave a shrug, "Besides that, Spencer Penwaithe was the brains behind the Centauri Treaty, which created the Colonial Republic and divided the Amalgamated Worlds."

"What?" Garret demanded. That made little sense. If it was true, then why would his father, who seemed to crave power and benefits, live in relative seclusion on Halcyon?

"He helped me to found the Provisional Colonial Republic Army," Thomas Kaid said as he sipped at his wine. "As I focused on the conduct of the war, he became entrenched in the politics and economics of it. He was the main money man for the entire movement at one point and he used the political power from that to forge quite an alliance. He easily won over enough support to have several other prominent leaders of the revolution sold out to Amalgamated Worlds in order to gain political power and a strong hold over what became the Colonial Republic." His smile was tight, "It is fortunate, I suppose, that you are estranged from him. Otherwise, I might have you two killed to hurt him." His eyes were cold, dead, the eyes of a shark as he casually contemplated Garret's murder.

"Now we know his connection to Collae," Tommy King said. "Of course, right now he's something of an ally. After my cover was blown on Halcyon, I managed to convince Admiral Collae to help me slip off world with his forces as they withdrew."

"Collae withdrew?" Garret asked in surprise. "Without a fight?"

"I traded him data that told him how worthless the prize was, so he and his forces pulled out. I gather that Spencer Penwaithe evacuated as soon as the word got out that Admiral Mannetti was still alive," Tommy King said. "I took a datapad that had information about the ships, they're not operational and they may never be... Admiral Mannetti hasn't been able to activate them."

"Wait, the fleet is worthless?" Garret asked and he turned angry eyes on Harris, "Damn you! You put our entire world at risk for a fleet of ships that no one can use?"

Harris held up hands in protest, "We didn't know. Hell, we didn't know *what* we had found, not until Admiral Mannetti was already there. She brought scientists, engineers, technicians, support we couldn't have got from anyone else..." Harris trailed off at Garret's furious expression.

"We did our best," Jessica said, her voice entreating. "If not for Admiral Mannetti, then it would have been Nova Corp, and our world would still be part of the Colonial Republic."

"How is that working out for you?" Garret asked angrily. Yet the hurt in her face showed he had gone too far. They had lost everything. He didn't even know if they'd managed to slip out with their sons or if they had to leave them behind. *At least they were there,* he thought, *I spent the last ten years doing everything I could to stay away.*

"In any case," Tommy King said, "Admiral Mannetti has the planet. She doesn't have the fleet online, but she does have a large force of her own and many privateers and pirates have signed on with her. She's brought in her Helot-class carrier and a number of other ships. It's a fight that the War Dogs cannot win, not on their own."

"What do you propose?" Garret asked with narrow eyes. Tommy King, while something of a folk hero for his victories against a number of totalitarian system governments, was still every bit as much a pirate as Admiral Mannetti.

"You need allies," Tommy King said as he looked around the room. "You need a fleet that is capable of taking on Admiral Mannetti, one which won't need to be bribed or bought to do so. More than that, once word gets out what you have there on Halcyon, you'll need a fleet to defend it. You will want men and women who fight for a cause rather than money."

Garret nodded, but he couldn't think of a nation that would support them. The Colonial Republic was rampant with corruption and cronyism. The Centauri Confederation was rife with civil war and police states. Nova Roma was fallen and even at their height they had betrayed far too many allies for there to be any security in an alliance or partnership with them.

"You are suggesting the United Colonies, then?" Commodore Pierce asked.

Tommy King nodded, "Baron Giovanni is a tough, capable leader. More than that, he'll deal with you fair, whether you ask for an alliance or membership." He shrugged, "I've no dog in the fight, but I would suggest annexation and membership. I almost guarantee there will be a dozen or more systems as members within another year and getting in early means you'll have more control over how everything is shaped later on."

"But we attacked them," Jessica said, her voice quiet.

Tommy King shrugged, "Tell them the truth, that it was Admiral Mannetti's idea and that she betrayed you too. You have that in common, after all."

"Fine, so we go to this Baron Giovanni, then what?" Harris said. "What if he can't or won't help?"

"You'll have the War Dogs," Commodore Pierce said.

"More than that," Tommy King said, "You'll have my fleet."

Garret cocked an eyebrow at that, "You haven't been pirating for what, at least a decade? What kind of fleet can you muster?"

Tommy King looked over at Thomas Kaid, "Lauren told me that you agreed to my earlier offer?"

Thomas Kaid gave a slight smile, "I did. I put out your message and your people have been arriving over the past few months. It's been quite entertaining keeping their arrivals hidden and their training secret, especially with so many of Admiral Mannetti's people moving through the system."

"Good," Tommy King said. "If they've trained up already then it will save us some time. I've a score to settle with Lucretta Mannetti. I'd hate to keep her waiting longer than necessary." His smile was polite and urbane, yet the look in his eyes was enough to make Garret shiver.

"Lady and Gentlemen," Commodore Pierce said, "Down with Admiral Mannetti!"

Thomas Kaid raised his glass of wine, "I believe I can drink to that."

***

Nova Roma
Chxor Empire
April 4, 2404

Armand grimaced as he looked at the clock one last time. Jacobo was well overdue. Marco had covered for his absence, no doubt thinking that his henchman had found some woman to screw or something equally asinine. It had taken three hours before Marco admitted that he didn't know Jacobo's location.

Armand figured that the Chxor had him. Either Marco's depredations had caused the locals to turn him in or the idiot had slipped up. Either way, Armand figured that it was time to go.

"Start packing up," he said.

"Boss," Marco said, "We can't leave, without Jacobo he doesn't know the location of our fallback site."

"Which is the way it should be," Armand snapped. He shook his head, "You *do* understand the purpose of secrecy, don't you?"

Marco straightened, "Jacobo would *never...*"

"He'd do whatever he could to save his neck," Armand snapped. "And even if they don't give him the opportunity, are you certain he's cleared his comm of messages? I know you've passed information to him that way, the Chxor could trace it to *your* comm and then track us back here." Armand shook his head, "Dump your comm, pack our gear, let's get out of here."

The damp and gloomy warehouse had never been an ideal base site, but it was all that they'd been able to establish. The gutter scum with him had managed to piss off the local population to the point that even Armand didn't dare go out unarmed.

*I hope that the Emperor planned for this,* Armand thought darkly, *because we're probably about to be wiped out.* Even if the Chxor hadn't already found them, it wouldn't be hard to notice such a large group moving at once. Yet he had no other choice, their smaller safe-houses weren't safe, not with how Marco's people had burned bridges. *Damn him,* Armand thought, *and damn me for thinking I could keep them in check.*

He still didn't know if this mission was in earnest or if it was some kind of decoy operation. Certainly he wouldn't have sent pirates and thugs like these men to liberate a world. Yet he didn't see the angle in sending them. He wished he remembered more of his training from the Academy, but that had been decades ago... and Armand could admit that he had never been the best student.

Armand went back into the warehouse office and picked up his go-bag. He was already packed, ready to move with all his essentials. As he turned around, though, he heard a shout.

A cloud of smoke filled the space. *Gas,* he thought, *either to kill or incapacitate.* He donned his gas mask quickly, even as he hoped that it wasn't a contact agent, else the mask would do him little good.

He heard shouts and screams in the warehouse as men rushed around trying to get their masks. Most of Marco's people wouldn't have their masks on hand, not like Armand.

He shook his head as the shouts and screams dropped off. *Pathetic,* he thought, *that I must die among men so incompetent, I wish I hadn't screwed up and been thrown out of the Marines.* At least then he could have died among brave men.

A moment later he saw movement as a team of Chxor moved through the group. He saw one of them pick up Marco by the arms and drag him out. The others seemed to be comparing the downed pirates to something on their datapads. *Pictures,* he thought, *either they have information on us from the locals or maybe that idiot Jacobo was carrying his datapad when they captured him.*

They would be after him, then. Armand glanced behind him, but he knew the back wall of the warehouse was solid, there was no escape.

That didn't mean he couldn't accomplish one last thing. They had Marco, but some of Marco's men knew details that might help the Chxor. Together they might be able to put together the fact that their group was a decoy or distraction.

He wouldn't go to his death dragged in chains or on his knees. Armand knew he had sins aplenty to atone for, but at least he could go to God as a free man. Armand smiled as he pulled a large explosive charge out of his bag. Tied into it were seven plasma cylinders, the same as would be used in a plasma rifle. He stood up and stepped out of the office. "Friends, I have important information for you!"

The Chxor spun and they leveled their weapons at him, yet he saw them hesitate at his tone. They thought he was going to bargain with them.

"The rebel leader is still at large, I know where he is," Armand stepped forward a couple more meters. The Chxor looked between each other, clearly confused.

"Where is he?" One of the Chxor officers asked.

"Right here you bastards," Armand said as he activated the explosive charge.

***

Captain Tommy King stepped up to the sensor display, "Not long now." He hadn't thought of himself as Mason since he left the base at Brokenjaw Mountain. In many ways, his life as Mason McGann had ended in the corridors of that base just as surely as if Admiral Mannetti's people had gunned him down.

"Are you sure about this?" Kandergain asked. The psychic had finally met up with him just before he left Port Klast, without a word as to her absence in the past months.

He quirked an eyebrow at her. "Of everyone involved on this venture, I would think you would be able to read my certainty the clearest." For the first time in years he felt confident in his every action. It felt good to have eased the bindings on himself, to slip back into the old role, if only to an extent. The predator had goals... rescue and, if necessary, revenge.

"I try to restrain myself from reading other people unless I have to," Kandergain said without looking up from the ship controls. "Besides, it isn't as if I could divine your real purpose from your surface thoughts or emotions. I know you feel this is necessary, but I have to wonder how much thought you put into it."

"In truth?" Tommy asked. He considered it for a moment, "This feels like the worst choice that I could make. I'm unleashing all the things that I spent the past decade repressing. In the process, I've called together an assembly of rogues and scoundrels who had happily parted ways and I am about to unleash a fleet that has sacked worlds." He shrugged, "The only binding thing I have is affection for a woman who is probably dead and a letter of marque from the

United Colonies."

Kandergain's eyes went wide at that. "Lucius gave *you* a letter of marque?"

Tommy shrugged, "He gave it to Lauren, who left it back on Port Klast so it wouldn't be found by someone aboard the *Kraken*. Just as well, since Mannetti's spies seized the ship." At least he didn't have to worry about fighting that ship. He had locked it down before he went planet-side and he felt confident that it would take them at least a month to get through the multiple layers of security, even then they might have to dump the data core and start over from scratch, especially with some of the security protocols he'd had added after capturing the ship.

Kandergain still seemed taken aback, so Tommy smiled, "Look, right now Halcyon's happy representatives will be arriving at Faraday with escort from the War Dogs. Lucius should be able to send a sizable portion of the Dreyfus Fleet to squash Admiral Mannetti using the secret shadow space route that Mannetti had plotted. So even if I go mad pirate and start looting and raping everything in sight, Lucius should be along soon to put things right."

"Don't forget the burning," Kandergain said with a sigh.

"I didn't," Tommy smirked, "The maxim goes: Pillage, *then* burn. Got to get the good stuff before I have my fun."

"If you think that quoting twenty first century cartoonists will put my mind at ease, you're mistaken," Kandergain said and looked up at him from the ship's controls. "Don't forget, I've seen you at your worst."

Tommy met her gaze. He knew full well how dangerous she could be... and the once-chained predator in him wanted to back down from the challenge it saw there. The man in him, however, refused to back down. *I am more than an animal,* he thought defiantly, *I have mastered my nature, not been mastered by it.* "Don't worry, Kandergain, that's behind me." His gaze went to the screen, where a pinprick point of light had appeared. "This is a new Tommy King... one the universe hasn't yet met."

He put a hand down to her shoulder, "You'll want to stop here and tell the other ships to stay back until I say."

She did as he said. That in itself meant less than nothing, of course. She knew well enough that he would have some traps in place.

At this range, the silent fleet seemed inactive. The ships drifted, engines and weapons powered down. It looked like a graveyard or a ghost fleet, far on the edge of the Epsilon Pacifica system, so remote that no one should have stumbled upon it. However, a glance at the sensors showed some faint clusters of ionized gas, the remains of those who had intruded on the graveyard.

Most of those, he knew, were those of his old crewmen who had sought to take the fleet for their own. One or two might be the remains of some treasure hunters with less caution than they should have had. Tommy didn't mourn the former at all and felt only passing pity for the latter. There were warnings aplenty, he had seen to that.

An automated voice broadcast on all channels, right on cue. "Attention inbound craft. You have entered a restricted area. Withdraw or you will be fired upon."

Tommy held down the transmit button and made certain his face was visible, "Furry Bunny Slippers."

The voice seemed to hiccup, "I repeat you..." the voice trailed off... "withdraw or face immediate repercussions."

"Fuzzy Navel," Tommy said with a slight smile, "Kittens."

"Access granted," the voice said. "Welcome back, Captain."

"What kind of password is that?" Kandergain said.

Tommy didn't answer. In truth, they weren't passwords. It wasn't what he had said, it was how he said them. The analysis software had cost him a fortune, but it was designed to read his emotional and mental status on top of identifying his biometrics, all from his broadcast.

If someone had somehow captured and coerced him, either through drugs or torture into showing the location of his fleet, then the ships would have opened fire as soon as he attempted to get them to stand down. It also would have fired on him if he had some kind of nervous breakdown and actually gone mad dog pirate.

"Tell everyone to come ahead," Tommy said even as he adjusted his pistols in his holsters. He waggled his fingers a bit to loosen them up even as he monitored the progress of the other ships. It seemed that those who had come to his call were above board. Then again, they had little reason not to be. The return of Tommy King was the sort of thing that even the most depraved of them would want to be a part of. Only the Shadow Lords had engendered greater fear across human space... and then only because they rarely left any survivors.

*Survivors are useful,* Tommy thought, *they eventually rebuild so that they can be robbed again.*

They drew close to his flagship and Tommy began to whistle.

"Can you stop that?" Kandergain snapped. "You know that's the same tune you whistled while you killed a few of my friends back when you worked for ESPSec."

Tommy winced at the reminder. That had been a darker bit of his past, when he had sought revenge for the deaths of his squad back when he was an Amalgamated Worlds Commando. "Sorry."

She shook her head, "If you do anything like that again, you'll be far more than sorry."

He just nodded at the reminder. Tommy had no intention of reverting to that man. He hadn't lied, he thought of himself as a new man. His years of scraping out a living as Mason McGann had changed him, as had the years at Lan's Monastery. More than that, the past months spent with Lauren had wrought a more profound change. He trusted his instincts now and he felt as if some of Lauren's ideology had imprinted itself upon him.

Kandergain brought the ship alongside. Tommy moved to the airlock and he nodded at the handful of crew who stood waiting. He could sense their eagerness, an animal tension, part pheromone and part body language. They reacted to his presence, as if they could sense the wolf behind his eyes... which they probably could, he thought.

Tommy took a moment to deactivate the traps on the airlock. This one had five, while most of the others on the ship had ten or more, several of which could kill the vessel. Kandergain followed him out a moment later. "You know," she said, "I confess to a bit of curiosity about your ship."

He held up a cautionary hand to forestall her. Tommy swept his gaze across the hand-picked crew. This dozen was the first to board his ship and he had already told them where he wanted them. They weren't disciplined military, but they were far from the rabble he had hired in the guise of Stavros. Most of them had served under him before, many had served as mercenaries or pirates in the years since, and all of them were men and women that he trusted to do as instructed... but that didn't mean he trusted them implicitly. "You know what I want done. Go do it."

They moved out, their faces set and eager as they reacted to his tone. He didn't know how he did it, it wasn't a psychic ability, he knew, it was just that people reacted to his voice and attitude in a primal, animal way. It was something tied to the predator within him, he knew.

He turned back to Kandergain, "You were saying?"

"Your ship, the *Revenge*," Kandergain said. "I've never seen it, its basic profile is similar to an Amalgamated Worlds National-class battlecruiser... but it is heavily modified. Given the timing of when you started pirating, I have to say I'm curious how you obtained it."

Tommy shrugged, "It's a long story. Most of it doesn't apply to what we're doing, and some of the details are already known by some of your organization."

Kandergain's eyes narrowed as she thought about who in her organization had associated with Tommy King. Clearly she didn't know who might know. Tommy felt a bit of amusement at that, it tickled him to tweak the all-knowing psychic. "Most of the modifications were done at Tanis. They were just getting started as an independent shipyard, so they didn't ask many questions about the work or where I got her."

When he didn't say more about where he had picked up the ship, Kandergain glowered at him. "Modifications?"

"She still has her original armament," Tommy said easily as they stepped aboard the ship. The corridors were cold, the environmental systems had brought the oxygen level up from the pure nitrogen atmosphere that had preserved the vessel, but the ship was barely above freezing. "She's got a full defense screen and has been retrofitted with what was a prototype stealth system but is now relatively available, with some upgrades over the years."

"And the other ships?" Kandergain asked. "I saw a wide assortment."

"Some are converted merchant ships," Tommy shrugged. He stepped around the corner and paused at the lift. He'd ordered the crew to avoid the lifts, with good reason. It took him a few minutes to deactivate the security measures that he had tied into them. Not that he had thought that anyone would get this far, but paranoia ran deep in him at the best of times.

As the lift doors opened, he continued where he had left off,

"Others are warships I picked up after the fall of Amalgamated Worlds. A few are captured Colonial Republic ships, though most of those are merely carriers for fighters or bombers."

"How are you for munitions?" Kandergain asked.

"I dumped the antimatter warheads before I stashed the fleet here," Tommy said. "The fission warheads weren't disassembled, so they'll probably have issues. The fusion warheads, though, should be fine. The bombers were fitted for the lighter fission warheads, but Thomas Kaid sent along a shipment to replace those. The rest of my ships can just use fusion warheads."

"He's being awful generous," Kandergain said.

"I offered him something he has wanted for a very long time," Tommy said and his gaze went distant. "It wasn't something I ever thought I would give... but it turns out that sometimes your priorities change."

They came out on the bridge and Tommy felt a tingle run down his spine as he stepped out of the lift. In many ways, it was like a homecoming. Most of his adult life had been spent on this bridge. His greatest triumphs had taken place in the command chair. Looking back, he realized that for all his anger and hunger as a pirate, it had all really come down to the challenge. Tommy had wanted to prove himself... and in only a few encounters had he *ever* met his match.

He remembered the Trinity system and the three weeks that he had maneuvered his fleet against Captain Lucius Giovanni's forces. At any one time the *War Shrike* could have destroyed much of his forces. The Baron, indeed, *had* destroyed several of his allies in that cat and mouse game. At the time Tommy had felt frustrated and stressed, he had hated his opponent and longed to destroy him.

Yet now as he looked back, it was one of his fondest memories. Giovanni had challenged him, had caught him when he was overconfident and made him pay for his errors. Though he hadn't realized it then, that had been the beginning of when Tommy King had started to look beyond himself.

That had been the first step in his redemption.

Now it was time to pay the good Baron back for what he had unknowingly done.

Tommy's left hand caressed the black leather acceleration seat and his right hand deactivated the last of the traps, this one tied to the command console. After that he took a seat and began to bring the ship's systems online.

"So Tommy King is back, then?" Kandergain asked.

"Tommy King is back and better than ever," he answered with a wolf's smile, "and it is time to make Admiral Mannetti aware of that."

***

## Chapter X

Faraday System
United Colonies
April 15, 2404

Lucius stood as Lord Admiral Valens Balventia stepped into his office, flanked by Sergeant Timorsky and Lance Corporal Namori. Their presence was less because of a lack of trust and more because they followed Lucius everywhere at this point, and they had the support of an entire platoon. Lucius hadn't had a chance to meet with the others, yet, but he would not be surprised to learn that the number of his bodyguards would grow even more in the near future.

For now they were Marines, but Lucius felt it best that they have their own chain of command, both to prevent the chance of their corruption by any remnants of the cabal and to allow them autonomy to conduct their duties. Their organization would likely include a senior officer as well as some shuttles, fighter support, and even possibly a couple of fast ships, so that he wouldn't have to pull Fleet assets to jaunt him around.

"Admiral," Lucius nodded politely. He still felt more than a little shock as he contemplated Admiral Balventia's actions during the coup attempt. Part of him wondered if the other man had simply been too stubborn to yield under Admiral Dreyfus's threats. He had seen the appointment earlier and he assumed this had something to do with the Emperor's preparations to leave for Nova Roma. "I want to thank you for what you did. You saved many of my people by forcing the cabal to stand down. I appreciate that more than I can properly express."

To Lucius's surprise, Valens Balventia shook his head, "Baron... *Lucius*, you've no need to thank me." Using Lucius's name almost seemed to cause him physical pain, but he straightened, "In fact, I have come here to apologize."

"Apologize?" Lucius asked in shock.

Valens seemed to draw some strength from Lucius's surprise. "I have." He sighed, "For decades now, we have both been rivals. I'm ashamed to admit that I've used my influence before to block your promotion and that of officers loyal to you. At the time, I told myself that surely you had motives tied to your ambitions, that despite your service record, you merely boded your time to strike, as your father had."

Lucius took a step back and leaned on his desk. The last thing he would have ever imagined from Valens Balventia was an apology.

"When I first came here to Faraday, I thought that you had finally struck your blow. I thought that you had coerced my new Emperor into going along with your delusions. When I found out that you had recovered the Dreyfus Fleet, I felt certain that it was some sort of trick or trap, even when I met the man face to face, I could not admit that you were not the man I thought you were," Valens said. He shook his head, "In truth, I clung to our rivalry because it was the only thing I had left." He straightened, "When they kidnapped your daughter, it was the first time that I viewed you as a real person, the first time I considered the stresses you were under. To my shame, I realized that while you had concerned yourself with saving humanity... I had concerned myself with a feud whose roots bring as much shame to my family as my recent actions do today."

Valens Balventia sighed, "Lucius, when I was faced with the possibility of supporting Admiral Dreyfus and protecting my Emperor against supporting you and putting him at risk, I chose the *right* decision, if not the one that my oath required of me. In that instant, I committed treason, even if Emperor Romulus IV has absolved me of it. I did so because for too long I have been your enemy. Had you my support from the beginning, perhaps we could have headed off this conspiracy. Perhaps the Fleet would be intact and we would have so much greater a chance at victory against the Chxor."

Valens knelt, "Baron Lucius Giovanni, I express my deepest and most sincere apologies for the many wrongs that my family and I have done to you and yours over the past decades."

Lucius stared at the man in shock for a long moment. Finally he spoke, "Admiral... Valens, get off the floor." He helped his former rival to his feet. "There is nothing further to discuss." Lucius couldn't quite put decades of hatred behind him, but he could at least respect the other man for the gesture. It was a fragile peace offer, one which could blow up in either of their faces, Lucius knew, but it was an honest one.

Valens cleared his throat, "Well, then. I wondered if we might discuss some of the tactics you have used to much success in your recent battles with the Chxor. In the lead up to our battle at Nova Roma, I thought that we might make good use of them."

Lucius gave the other man a smile, "Valens, I think I like that idea." He took a breath, "You see, Nova Roma military doctrine has many ties back to that of Amalgamated Worlds. Fighters in close escort of their capital ships, used to support rather than strike. I think those tactics work well enough against a numerically superior but technologically inferior opponent such as the Colonial Republic or the Wrethe. With the Chxor, however, I think a far more fluid approach is necessary, utilizing fighter squadrons in concert to flank the enemy..."

***

Captain Anthony stepped into the Baron's office and froze in shock. Baron Lucius Giovanni was caught up in fierce discussion with none other than Lord Admiral Valens Balventia. The two had the holographic display active and Tony watched as they pointed out maneuvers and vectors of ships in a paused simulation. He was certain that there might be a more impossible sight than the two rivals engaged in a friendly discussion over the merits of doctrine, but he couldn't think of one off hand.

"...so you see," Baron Giovanni continued, "once you break apart the Chxor formation, you can strike for their core. The cruisers are immaterial."

"I see," Valens said. "I've managed the same thing with screening destroyers, but generally at a high cost, they're far easier targets for the enemy dreadnoughts."

"Ah, Tony, welcome," the Baron said. "Thank you for joining us on such short notice."

Admiral Balventia's was much more reserved, "Captain," he nodded. Tony didn't miss the respect in his voice, however, or the absence of the hate and spite that Admiral Balventia had showed in their last encounter. Something dramatic had changed and Tony had no idea just what.

"I called you here," the Baron said, "because I wanted to tell you ahead of time... and because Admiral Balventia asked to be present for this as well, when he heard of it." Baron Giovanni went to his desk and pulled out a small case. He gestured for Tony to come up and then set it in his hands. "It will be official within the next few hours and we'll have a formal ceremony, but congratulations."

Tony felt the world spin a bit as he opened the case and saw a pair of stars. "Admiral?" Tony asked incredulously.

Baron Giovanni nodded. "You've earned it... and in case you haven't noticed, the United Colonies Fleet has some senior officer vacancies just now."

Tony just shook his head. In the Nova Roma Imperial Fleet, he had never dreamed of rising higher than Commander. He didn't have the family connections from the start, but on top of that, he had bound his career to that of Lucius Giovanni, who had very senior enemies.

"It is well deserved," Admiral Balventia said. "In truth, if the universe were more just, you would have received that promotion years ago. From what Lucius tells me, you have been the organizing influence behind many of his successes." Tony shook his head, too shocked by the promotion to feel surprise at Admiral Balventia's statement. "Of course, I have good news of my own to deliver," Admiral Balventia said. He pulled a small case out of his own pocket, "Emperor Romulus had already heard of your promotion. Since he knew I was coming here, he asked me to deliver this in person and to inform you that there will be a more formal ceremony later."

Tony felt too disoriented to feel surprise as he opened the case and found another set of Admiral stars. "The Emperor felt that it was shameful that your official rank in the Nova Roma Imperial Fleet was lower than your rank in that of our allies whom you are on loan to. Therefore, he has officially promoted you to the rank which he, and I, feel you deserve."

Tony just shook his head, too bewildered to speak.

"Now, then," Admiral Balventia looked over at the Baron, "While I would like to continue our discussion, I'm afraid I'll have an early morning tomorrow. Thank you for the discussion, Lucius, and I plan to work some of your doctrine into our training as soon as we get underway. If all goes well, we'll have around a month to put it all into effect."

"I appreciate that, Valens," Baron Giovanni replied. "And I promise you that we'll be there come the final battle for our homeworld."

"I quite look forward to it," Admiral Balventia said with a smile that promised repayment in plenty for the Chxor who would face them.

***

"Well," Lucius said as he took a seat. "Tell me what you've got for me."

The Iodan representative, as always, was indistinguishable from others of his species. A mass of writhing tentacles, he looked like nothing so much as a thing from nightmare. His translator unit, as advanced as it was, still spoke in a monotone and not for the first time, Lucius wondered if that was by design or simply because the Iodans were too alien for something as human as emotion. He knew that the translator unit divined the motion of the Iodan's limbs to produce a verbal component, but he had no idea if that involved any nuances such as emotion or emphasis.

"We have completed a complete genetic analysis of the two men who claim to be your father," the Iodan said. "Both the Marius Giovanni who works for Shadow Lord Imperious and the Marius Giovanni who serves as ambassador for the Centauri Confederation."

Lucius waved a hand. When he realized how ridiculous that was, he spoke, "We know that already, go on." The entire idea had been to find some way to discredit both emissaries, in such a way as to put them on the defensive rather than to give them an excuse to attack. Now that the various Shadow Lords had withdrawn, it seemed unlikely that Imperious would attack without provocation. President Spiridon of the Centauri Confederation was a bit more of a conundrum. On the one hand, he was already involved in a multiway civil war in which even his closest allies might turn against him at any perceived weakness, such as starting a new war on a new front. On the other, the man was known for holding grudges and for his diabolical machinations. It wasn't unlikely that he might maneuver someone else into attacking or to try to hurt Lucius some other way.

"After thorough analysis, we have confirmed that both men are indeed genetic matches to your father, both down to the genetic level as well as fingerprint, retinal, and even deep tissue scanning. In essence, they are both perfect copies, not only of one another, but of your actual father."

President Sara Cassin grimaced, “Well, that's no help then...”

Lucius frowned, though, “Wait, you said *actual* father?”

The Iodan's voice showed no excitement, but its tentacles seemed to quiver a bit faster, “Indeed. Through atomic analysis, we have determined that neither one is your actual father. If they had been, their molecular make-up would be tied to your world of birth. Even after living for half a century off of Nova Roma, their bone and fatty tissues would still retain a majority of isotope similarity to that of other inhabitants of Nova Roma, such as yourself. Instead, key isotopes are missing while others are present.” The Iodan activated the holographic projector and brought up a star map. “These two copies, and the others we think were made, came from material in the Altara star system. We have narrowed this down to almost exact certainty, given the slight changes in both samples isotope spectrum from the time of creation, which we project as approximately thirty Earth years ago.”

“Could you be mistaken?” Alicia Nix asked.

“This is possible, but extremely unlikely. Every star system has its own, unique spectrum, a mix of isotopes found in greater or lesser quantities. This acts as an almost infallible fingerprint and is in fact a key aspect to how Iodans organize our biometric data.” The Iodan seemed to consider that for a long moment. “The atomic makeup of any being's body is formed from what they consume with no exceptions. Lucius Giovanni has a pattern entirely consistant with someone who was raised on Nova Roma and has traveled to many worlds. He ate food grown and produced on Nova Roma which matches not only the planet but the system's isotope spectrum. It is possible that Marius Giovanni ate food entirely produced and grown in the Altara system, but this is unlikely, especially given the presence of two of him. Thus, the assumption that the two duplicates were made in the Altara system.”

Kate Bueller spoke up, “Did you say made? Don't you mean cloned?”

The Iodan spoke before Lucius could, “Cloning would not produce a subject as identical as these two specimens. Environmental factors have a significant effect upon maturation characteristics and would require extreme surgeries and attention to produce even basically similar characteristics. So too, nanoreconstruction would leave telltale signs at the deep tissue and bone layers. In essence, it would fool a careful look, but not a scientific evaluation. These two specimens are, to all intents and purposes, flawless to someone who did not take the time to do a full isotope analysis, which took us these past few months."

There was silence in response and the Iodan added, "In essence, these two specimens were constructed, entirely exact in every detail that matters. We are very interested in this because it is a process that we have never before encountered."

Lucius nodded. The question then, of course, was who had the technology to do that... and why they had done it with his father. *For that matter,* he thought, *who else they have done it with.* "You mentioned others?" Lucius asked.

"Indeed," the Iodan said, "One of the things we found at the atomic level was a slight variance with the presence of sulfur isotopes. It was a tiny thing, but one that stood out when we checked ratios, it is a simple binary code, built into both specimens at a level of detail which would be almost impossible for anyone to spot, outside their original manufacturer. The Marius Giovanni working for Shadow Lord Imperius is labeled two and the emissary for the Centauri Confederation is labeled five."

Lucius sat back. "So there could be as many as *five* of these... duplicates running around, along with the possibility that my actual father is still out there somewhere. Do we have any idea why?"

"Indeed," the Iodan said. "Additionally, judging by the samples, we believe that the brain chemistry of both specimens has been altered, perhaps to enable them to think in certain ways so as to achieve certain goals. These changes are so slight as to be minute but might make one duplicate inclined to take an action that another might not consider."

"Right," Lucius said. "So, now we know." He looked at Kate Bueller, "How do we want to handle this?"

She looked troubled, but after a moment she composed herself, "That depends on whether you want to change our plans in light of recent events or move ahead." At Lucius's level look, she quirked a smile, "I thought not. Most of those who are willing to step out of line and forge either alliances or even sign on to the United Colonies are ready. There's a handful of holdouts, who either want to get a better deal or are uncertain how things will shake down after the Dreyfus Coup."

Lucius winced at the name. He had tried to shift the public's attention to some of the other conspirators, but they had latched onto Admiral Dreyfus's betrayal the strongest. He wasn't certain who had used the title for the cabal's actions first, but it had been stamped into the public's mind. While Lucius couldn't argue with the root of the conspiracy, he still felt that the man behind it shouldn't be reviled after all the good he had accomplished in his life. *I just wish I could have won him over,* Lucius thought, *and whatever visions he had of the future, I refuse to live in fear because of them.*

"Very well," Lucius said after a moment. "We'll go with the original plan, then. Denounce them both, give a condensed version of the Iodan's research as proof, and then announce our new alliances."

"Do we want to try to get more out of our allies?" Kate asked. "Some kind of auxiliaries to support our attack on Nova Roma?"

Lucius frowned as he considered her question. In truth, that was his major concern. At the moment they *could* utilize most of the Dreyfus Fleet, yet he had no question that it would be a disaster. Several of the ship captains had dumped their computer cores, wiping out not just records of the cabal but also the entire ships' data network and coding necessary not only to operate the weapons, but also the reactors, the engines, and the navigational systems. They had brought some of that back online, but only the *Patriot* was fully operational of the six massive fortress ships. The *Crusader* and her sister ships were all completely inoperable without weeks or months of programming work. Many of the other ships, including almost all of their battlecrusers and over half of their cruisers and destroyers were in the same situation.

Even if their data networks were functional, their crews were not. The destruction of trust had almost shattered the Fleet. Even officers who had been loyal were looked on with suspicion from crews... even though they had uncovered the vast majority of the cabal's members, everyone knew that they had missed some. Of the four members of Command, they knew Admiral Dreyfus's name for certain. Alicia Nix suspected that Minister of War Newbauer was another member. The third and fourth leaders remained unknown, and all of the senior leaders below them had either died in the fighting or committed suicide shortly afterward.

That they had possibly missed one or more of the senior leaders of the conspiracy meant that they still weren't certain if they had removed all of their supporters. That uncertainty could be felt at all levels. How could a crew trust their officers when they knew that some of them might well have supported the coup, if only passively?

Also, a small but still sizable minority of the 'lost' crew and Marines still remained at large. Lucius hoped that as they continued to identify remains, more of them would be found among the dead, but he couldn't discount the possibility that the conspirators had some kind of backup plan.

All of which came back to the fact that well over ninety percent of the Fleet wasn't fit to fight.

Lucius realized that he had been quiet too long. “What will it cost us?” he finally asked. “Because while I'm willing to work trade concessions and technology transfers, what it comes down to is the quality of the forces we would be buying.”

She nodded, “Understood. In truth, I don't think we would get much in the way of quality support. Most of the systems that would give it for cheap are already in need of whatever *we* can give them and they're basically willing to sign on just for the opportunity to be protected. Others...” she shrugged, “we're already giving them damned good options and they are either too far away to help, like the Shogunate, or they have problems close to home, like Wenceslaus.”

Lucius nodded. The attack at the Wenceslaus Colonial Republic Fleet Base had been a shocking raid, conducted by allies of Admiral Mannetti. Fortunately for the United Colonies, just after the raiders withdrew, Enjeer Stangaard of the planet Schwartzkrieg had seized the base and those ships that the raiders hadn't taken. His emissary, in fact, had wanted to sign on with the United Colonies right away. The problem, of course, was that the nearer Colonial Republic worlds had immediately sent forces to put down his uprising. Stangaard had managed to hold out so far, but Lucius knew he wouldn't have forces to spare.

“Very well,” Lucius said, “We'll go with the original plan, then. Those signing on with the United Colonies will have to hold their own until we liberate the Nova Roma system, at which point we'll retask forces for security of systems that have signed on and then our allies.” Even if the Fleet were at full strength that would stretch them very thin. On the other hand, it would also give them some strategic depth. While there was nothing to stop an enemy from launching a direct attack on Faraday, given the limited shadow space routes to the system, it would take them some time to reach there, possibly enough time that their allies could get them warning.

Besides, all or nothing attacks like that were dangerous. Too many would-be warlords had found their own systems conquered by their erstwhile allies while their fleets were away.

"In that case," Lucius said, "I think we'll go ahead with the original plan and denounce the duplicity of certain envoys and our new alliances." He smiled a bit at that. While he only vaguely remembered his real father, the two men who had introduced themselves as Marius Giovanni had both rubbed him the wrong way from the start. Both of them had tried to manipulate him through either false affection or family duty to agreeing with their positions. Lucius quite looked forward to the opportunity to pull off their masks and reveal them as mere copies.

***

Lucius sat down as the envoys from Halcyon stepped into the conference room. He had already heard the summary of what they had to say. In many ways, he didn't feel much sympathy for them. For their people, to be certain, but not for the leaders who had been forced to flee.

The first man into the room, however, wasn't one of their envoys. Lucius nodded respectfully, "Commodore." Lucius had never personally met the man, but he knew of him by reputation. The fact that he had signed on with Halcyon was a mark in their favor. The fact that he had stood by them even after Admiral Mannetti sent them running was another mark in their favor.

"Baron Giovanni," Commodore Pierce said with a nod of his own. A moment later, he was followed by a tall, blonde woman and an even taller black man. "This is Jessica and Harris Penwaithe, of Halcyon."

Lucius gestured at them to sit. "Tell me what you think I can do for you."

The woman, Jessica, looked defensive. "We haven't come empty handed."

"No," Lucius agreed with narrowed eyes, "you haven't. But you *have* admitted that you were involved in an unprovoked attack designed to cripple this nation. You have offered in trade what Admiral Mannetti currently possesses and what I would have to spend lives and resources to reclaim."

Her answer was at least sincere, "Admiral Mannetti misled us. We thought that we could control her, but she and Admiral Collae worked together to outmaneuver us... and then Admiral Collae withdrew." The bitterness in her voice showed that she hadn't taken well to the failure.

Lucius grimaced. He had heard that it was even more complicated a situation than she had just described. A message from Mason McGann had accompanied them and he said that Lauren Kelly and he had attempted to infiltrate and sabotage Admiral Mannetti. Lauren was probably dead and Mason had said that he was going to make use of the letter of marque that Lucius had given her.

To top it off, he had said that Lucius's former brother-in-law, Reese, had blown their cover and that he was somehow involved in Mannetti's efforts there on Halcyon. It strained Lucius's credibility to think that Reese had infiltrated himself into her trust so quickly, so it was likely that he had betrayed Lucius long before.

"I understand your position," Lucius said in a more diplomatic tone. "However, that doesn't change my own. We are about to begin a large military operation..."

"What if we offered you more than a portion of the alien fleet?" Harris asked.

"I'm not in this for the power," Lucius cautioned, "and from what I gather, that fleet is either crippled or sabotaged. Either way, it is of little use to me."

"How about a new member for your United Colonies?" Harris said. "A full member, one that brings a fleet of warships, right now. Admiral Mannetti interned our warships and crews at Heinlein Base. If you free them, you'll add a sizable force to your side." He frowned, "More importantly, my people believe in your stated cause: freedom for mankind from tyranny."

Lucius cocked his head, "You think your people would sign on? I'm not a warlord, I could care less what your politicians would say. I want to know if your people would readily sign on to the constitution."

"We've tried to go it alone," Jessica said in a subdued voice. "Fighting for independence from the Colonial Republic and Nova

Corporation didn't go well. We tried to use mercenaries and privateers to do our work for us, but that just created the problem we have now. Mannetti will use our people for her own ends and then discard them." She shook her head, "Some part of me hopes that you are different, but the cynical side of me says that you don't get in your position without a healthy dose of ambition."

"You might be surprised," Lucius said as he thought back through the various twists and turns that had made him the leader of a nation. "If you are asking to join the United Colonies, that's a very different proposal from what you've told my people so far." In truth, it had originally sounded like they wanted to hire them like mercenaries. Fighting to liberate a world, however, was something that his people could get behind. Even more so, he knew, after the events of the coup. The damage to morale might be healed a bit by fighting someone like Mannetti.

The problem, of course, lay in the execution. Emperor Romulus along with all of his forces had already left for Nova Roma. The Halcyon delegation had not been here at Faraday long enough to realize that most of the massive fleet in orbit was barely fit to defend itself, much less conduct a war.

*Tommy King will be there,* Lucius thought as he remembered the Mason's message, for the man had used those words even as he referenced the Trinity system, *they'll have the War Dogs... and I might be able to scrape together enough forces to turn the balance.* It would be good to end a threat like Lucretta Mannetti once and for all and if he could free a planet in the process, so much the better.

*And there is also the matter of the alien base and the fleet it holds,* he thought. If anyone could get it running... Lucius brought up a comm link off the terminal, "Send Rory and Feliks in, I think I have something for them to work on."

The two had been just down the hall, he knew, discussing with Matthew Nogita a process to streamline the retrofit of the captured Balor ships. The two would know best what Balor ships would be operational in the next few days and they might know something about the alien base, perhaps dormant or active defenses that could be a threat or benefit. Lucius was a bit fuzzy on the different extinct alien races, but he thought that Rory had mentioned some knowledge about the Zar. He met Harris and Jessica's gazes, his expression calm, "All right. No guarantees, but we'll look into it."

***

"This is amazing," Rory said as he finished looking over the base schematics that Jessica Penwaithe had provided. "This is what we call a Gamma Base, I've read about them from translated files... but I never *dreamed* we would find one intact."

"It is definitely a Gamma Base," Feliks said with a nod. "This is groundbreaking, *phenomenal*, even."

"Yes," Lucius said, "we know, an entire fleet. I'm certain it will be very useful once someone gets it operational."

"No, no, no!" Rory shook his head, "The fleet, yeah, *sure* that's impressive. But the base itself? That's groundbreaking. We've found bits and pieces of their technology, mostly weapons lost in their final war with the Illuari, but an entire base? You're talking maintenance facilities, store-rooms, defenses... stuff that we know they had, that we can see from the limited databases we've recovered. All of it is centuries beyond our current technology, but still technology that we can take apart and begin to understand."

Feliks nodded his head. With his glasses and mannerisms, he suddenly struck Lucius as very owl-like. "The Zarakassakaraz are the most human-like of the alien races we've studied. Even more so than the Ghornath. They colonized worlds, built mines and industrial centers, they even thought in terms of empires and we suspect they even had internal factions and nations. That is so important because everything they built, we can use."

"That's why this is so important," Rory said. "Every other alien technology, we have to retrofit it for human use. Sometimes, like with the Balor, that's a huge overhaul and we just can't use anything besides their weapon. Other times, like with the Ghornath, it's a factor of scale. Everything Ghornath-sized makes us look like children. Neither of them are anything near as dangerous as Illuari artifacts of course..."

"Oh, don't get me started on those," Feliks shook his head. "I had a headache for *months.*"

"But you have to understand, for the short term, that fleet might be amazing, but in the long term, if that Gamma Base holds all the technology that it appears to..."

"Then what?" Lucius asked. "What's the bottom line?"

"Our understanding would advance by leaps and bounds," Rory

said. He obviously struggled to find the words and when he spoke, he chose what he said very carefully. "We could surpass the Centauri Confederation in a decade, possibly draw within shouting distance of the Balor, fight them on more equal terms." He shrugged, "You have to understand, the Zar were fighting another alien race, the Illuari, who were an order of magnitude ahead of them... and they managed to hold their own for some time. Almost a century, as far as we can tell. Think of what we could do with their knowledge and technology."

Lucius pursed his lips. He looked at where Harris and Jessica perched on the edge of their seats. They had clearly thought of the ships and base as a bargaining chip, one to be spent and discarded. Lucius saw realization dawn on their faces as they saw that they hadn't considered the long term implications.

*We are all like cave-men trying to figure out how to use a plasma torch to cook with,* Lucius thought, *or more accurately, how to jump our neighboring tribe with a bulldozer.* "Fine," he said. "I understand the importance, now what about the base itself, will it have defenses and will they be active?"

"Absolutely," Rory said.

"Hmmm, possibly," Feliks shrugged.

Rory gave an angry look at his companion, then addressed Lucius, "The base has a variety of active and dormant defensive systems. From what we know about a Gamma Base, it would include some kind of planetary scale defense screen or shield, what the Zar called a Gorog."

"*Planetary?*" Jessica Penwaithe demanded.

"Oh, certainly," Feliks said with another owl-like head bob. "It would have been one of the first things they built."

"They'll also have extensive active defenses, extremely sophisticated jamming arrays, weapons emplacements, and probably a system-wide sensor array. I would imagine that most of the weapons emplacements were buried in the disaster, but we can't discount the possibility that they got some of them online." Rory broke off and looked around, "Whoever they have bringing systems online there is doing a tremendous job. I really hope that after we capture the facility we can get him on our team."

"It's my former brother-in-law, apparently he signed on with Admiral Mannetti," Lucius said.

"Oh, good, so you could talk to him," Rory said absently.

"I plan to have him interrogated and then thrown into prison," Lucius said with complete sincerity.

"Oh," Rory said, obviously distracted by the diagrams. "That works, too, I suppose." He brought up a schematic of the base and highlighted a central region of what looked like a huge mass of machinery. "The planetary defense screen looks operational and you can see it is directly tied into the geothermal generator, which is powered off of a magma pipe here.. We can almost certainly activate it, given enough time. From there it would only be a few minutes–"

"Several hours at least," Feliks cautioned.

"No longer than an hour," Rory snapped, "to get it online. Once it goes up, it should entirely prevent attacks against the base or the civilians."

Lucius looked at Harris and Jessica, "How does that sound for ensuring your people are protected."

Harris frowned, "Are you sure this would work?"

"Absolutely," Rory said. Behind him, Feliks shrugged, as if to say he wasn't as certain, but he didn't speak up.

At Jessica's nod, Lucius smiled, "Good. We'll work out the details on the base assault, but Rory, go ahead and prepare anything that you and Feliks will need."

"Wait... we're going?" Rory said. Feliks' eyes grew round. "We're not exactly combat qualified. I don't think I should be on this mission."

"There will be a team with you who will be charged with your protection," Lucius said. "Our only other option would be to nuke the base from orbit to prevent Admiral Mannetti from using its defenses against us."

"You can't do that!" Rory said, his eyes wide in horror. "It would be like destroying..." He trailed off, apparently he couldn't find an appropriate analogy.

"I trust you are capable of going, then?" Lucius asked.

Rory stood up straight and Feliks stepped up next to him, "To prevent the loss of such a priceless find, of course!" Feliks gave a sharp head-bob of approval.

"Good," Lucius said. He turned his gaze to Commodore Pierce. "Now then, Commodore, I think you and I need to discuss how to best utilize the resources we have."

***

Lauren Kelly wasn't entirely certain how she was still alive.

She hadn't planned on being taken prisoner. She had, in fact, held back one last grenade to ensure that they didn't take her alive. While she had no particular desire to die, she knew well enough that Admiral Mannetti wouldn't hesitate to torture her for information. For that matter, she had killed enough of Mannetti's people that she expected them to kill her rather than even attempt her capture.

Just what had happened in those last few minutes in the base, she still wasn't certain. Mason hadn't realized it, but her body armor hadn't entirely stopped the round that had struck her. Blood loss from that wound had been severe enough that she didn't figure she had long to live anyway, when she sent him on his way and set to playing decoy.

Things had grown increasingly fuzzy, to the point that she had attempted to use that last grenade.

She must have failed, because here she was, recovering and under guard in what resembled the *Kraken*'s medical suite. That told her she was probably still at the base. When she had first awakened, she assumed that it was the Baron's people in the black uniforms that looked so familiar. It had taken her a few minutes to remember that they were the United Colonies, now. She was absurdly grateful that they hadn't questioned her then, else she would have given up everything without realizing it. She didn't know why Mannetti's people were keeping her alive, but she was determined to keep quiet as long as she could.

On that thought, the door opened. She kept her expression stony as Reese Leone stepped inside. With his blonde hair, blue eyes, and friendly smile, she almost felt inclined to trust him... except for the whole fact that he had undoubtedly been the one to blow her cover. "Awake and lucid, I see," he said, "looking much better than the last time I saw you."

Lauren's eyes narrowed, "What do you mean by that?"

He took a seat, "You were quite a mess when they had the happy drugs in you, trying to save your life. Admiral Mannetti had them question you while they had you drugged and she wanted me there to confirm some technical details, I'm afraid."

Lauren's eyes went narrow. The implication was that she had already given them everything. *It's possible,* she thought, *I never received any kind of implant or neurochemical block from that sort of thing.*

"If you doubt me, I can sum up," Reese said. "You and the smuggler slipped in here at the behest of Admiral Collae, though you are working for Lucius Giovanni… though he doesn't even know you're here. Collae wanted you to murder Admiral Mannetti."

Lauren looked away, suddenly ashamed of herself.

Reese came forward and took a seat next to her bed, "Don't be too hard on yourself. I've no doubt you resolved yourself to torture, but it isn't as if you had any protection from drugs." His voice turned bitter, "You're not the only person the good Baron has sent in without the proper protections, without support, and without any chance of success."

"He didn't even know we were here," she snapped. It wasn't the Baron's fault, she knew that.

"No," Reese shook his head, "But you told us about the letter of marque. He knew *something* would come up... and he encouraged you to deal with it on your own. What kind of suicide mission that would be, he couldn't know, but he knew it would probably kill you."

Lauren glared at him. She could understand his perspective, but it was all backwards. The Baron had known that she didn't have it in her to stand by and let innocent people be killed. He'd given her what few tools he could afford, in case she came into a bad situation. She understood that. Reese, apparently, did not. "If I've given you all the information already, why am I still alive? Why even heal me at all?"

Reese sat back, "You know, Admiral Mannetti is not as callous as you might think."

Lauren just arched an eyebrow at him and he shrugged, "I'll not say that she was... happy about the reasons you were sent here, but she knows valuable talent when she sees it. She wants to recruit you, Lauren, to put you in the position that your skills can be put to the best uses... not to put you at the end of a beam and saw it off behind you like Lucius did."

Lauren ignored the last part of his statement, "She recognizes talent, then? Like yours?"

Reese shrugged, "I'm a moderately talented engineer and a very talented programmer. I'm smart enough to read up and study on things that are interesting... like the alien tech we've found at the Brokenjaw Mountain complex. Admiral Mannetti has recognized my skills and has rewarded my hard work. In addition to my position here at Halcyon, I've acquired quite the account balance on Tanis."

"So how long have you worked with her?" Lauren asked, "Since before or after you helped her to escape from Faraday?"

Reese shook his head, "You've got me all wrong, Lauren. I was Lucius's friend and I wouldn't have betrayed him like that... not until he betrayed me. He turned my wife against me," his voice grew bitter again, "and then put some trumped up charges on me because I questioned his tactics. He's not the man you think he is."

Lauren just shook her head, "What do you want from me?"

"Admiral Mannetti wants you to join her personal bodyguard, after you've proven your loyalty to her," Reese said. "And doing so is such a little thing, anyway. Just unlock this ship's computer core and let us access it and you'll be halfway there."

Lauren snorted with sudden laughter, "Seriously? All that pitch for such a clumsy play? You thought you could bypass Mason's biometric lock fairly easily, didn't you? How much does it gall you to have to ask for help from someone who doesn't know squat about programming?" No wonder the Baron's sister had dumped him, he was far too impressed with his own intelligence. He must have thought of her as a meat-head who was easily led. *The only wonder is why she stayed with him so long,* she thought.

Reese's face flushed, "If you think the offer will stand for long, think again. Admiral Mannetti isn't a patient woman... and if you think that her people will forget and forgive the men and women you killed in your rampage down on the base... well, they haven't and they won't. If Admiral Mannetti gives you to them, you will take a very long time to die and you'll give us what we want, anyway."

"They better remember that rampage," Lauren forced herself up in her bed. "Because if they come for me, I'll kill them." Her hand snatched out with viper speed and she pulled the pistol out of his holster and leveled it at him. "Remember, Reese, I can take care of myself."

Reese recoiled from her and his gaze snapped to the guard, who had brought up his rifle. He didn't fire, though, which told Lauren that, for now, Admiral Mannetti had given them orders to keep her alive.

Lauren tossed the pistol away and slumped back onto the bed, her energy spent. “Tell the Admiral I'll think about her offer.” She closed her eyes. “Go away Reese, I'm tired.”

***

## Chapter XI

Halcyon Colony, Garris Major System
Contested
May 1, 2404

Admiral Lucretta Mannetti, Lady Kail, purred as her aide massaged the back of her neck. The woman's hands found every knot of tension and like magic, eased her stressed muscles into relaxation. If Lucretta Mannetti had her way, every flag officer's aide would have mandatory massage training.

Then again, if she had her way, she would rule a very large empire indeed and wouldn't be an officer anymore. Well, not unless she wanted to ease the boredom a bit now and again and crush some rebels or some-such, she amended. Perhaps she'd still ensure the rule about aides, though, it would keep her senior officers happy.

With that thought, her mellow mood ended and she waved a hand. Her aide ceased her efforts and Lucretta waited patiently while the woman buttoned up her uniform top. That done, her aide stepped away and Lucretta sat up, her eyes roving the bridge. She didn't bother to hide her smirk as several of her bridge crew turned their eyes away from her gaze.

She knew it drove the men crazy to see her topless, reclined on the bridge. That was one reason that most of the men here were hand-picked, less for their brains and more for their looks and loyalty. Not that she ever really trusted any of them, though. That was why the senior officers were all women... women who had proved their loyalty and ambition and to whom Lucretta had added layers of mental programming to ensure that their loyalty never wavered and their ambition stayed focused on what she offered, rather than what they could take.

*It was a shame that Marius Giovanni hasn't made that mental programming more widely available*, she thought, *else I never would have faced a mutiny aboard the* Peregrine *when Lucius demanded my surrender*. She gritted her teeth as she thought of the loss of her flagship. While it wasn't essential to her plans, it had been the place where everything had started for her. Worse yet, that idiot puppy had ended up with it. Lucius had turned it over to the new Nova Roma Emperor... which meant that it would probably be destroyed in some foolish wasted endeavor.

She wished, not for the first time, that Marius would have allowed her to reveal to Lucius that she worked for him. Yet, he seemed determined to retain that secret and she didn't dare to challenge him. Her mind flinched away from the very thought.

Still, the time would soon come when Marius would have to choose whether he wanted his son alive or whether he wanted to succeed in his stated goals. Lucretta had already lost enough to Lucius that part of her hoped that she'd get the chance to kill him. Another part of her, though, feared the confrontation.

*If I can get those damned ships operational,* she thought, *then I will have something that can take on the Dreyfus Fleet, especially after he weakens it fighting the Chxor.* She smiled as she thought of how his face would look as she brought an entire fleet of vessels like the *Kraken* to seize the Nova Roma system while his own ships were heavily damaged. It would be rather similar to the time she had stabbed him, she imagined.

Though, the escaped smuggler might give him some warning. Lucretta had taken precautions for that, though. She'd posted a pair of frigates out on the far side of Halcyon's moon on a patrol picket and in conjunction with the orbital sensors and shifting the orbits and positions of her ships on a random cycle, she knew Lucius wouldn't be able to jump in right on top of her.

All that should be unnecessary, since Marius had assured her that the United Colonies Fleet would be too occupied to attack. He hadn't let her contact his agent there directly, but she figured they were fully occupied in planning the assault on Nova Roma. She wished them the best of luck with that, because it would be far easier for her to take the system from the new Nova Roma Emperor than for her to try to do the same against the Chxor. She'd lost enough people and ships fighting the Chxor at Faraday and she had no desire to face more of them. *Let other people bleed and die for that honor,* she thought, *I'll just take my due in the end.*

Lucretta ran her gaze over the sensor feeds and then frowned as a warning light began to blink. Her eyes narrowed as she saw symbols appear for a set of contacts at long range. The likelihood of them being ships spiked since they shared a location and vector and then the sensor department raised the likelihood to almost a hundred percent as military vessels when the contacts vector overlaid orbit of the planet.

She sat back and let her people work as she monitored their progress. The number of contacts was high, but she had her suspicions about the identity as she glanced over the raw data. After only a few minutes, her tactical officer turned to her, "Ma'am, we've identified a force inbound, range still at over one million kilometers. Probable identity is one Challenger-class dreadnought and seventy-two Hammer-class gunships, with a couple of Defiance-class destroyers... though it's hard to get readings on them with the Hammer's positioned as they are."

Lucretta nodded as the officer said what she had already assumed. It had taken them a bit longer than it should have, but not so long as to require any kind of reprimand. At this range, it was better that they were thorough and obtained an accurate result, whereas at close range a valid assumption of capabilities was enough, targeting data was the priority.

"It seems the War Dogs have returned... no doubt begging for scraps," Lucretta ignored the laughter at her comment. Her prisoner had told her how "Stavros" had faked the deaths of Azure Wing, so she wasn't surprised to see them present. "Hail them. Tell them that this planet is under my control." She didn't give the order to bring her ships fully online, not yet. She didn't want to show her ships positions and total strength until it gave her the greatest advantage.

Her communications officer did so. A moment later he looked up, "Ma'am, they're putting out a broadcast, all frequencies."

"Put it on my screen," she said. She had made the mistake with Lucius of putting his broadcast on the bridge screens and her crew had panicked because of his threats. It was better that she limit knowledge a bit more. "Order all ships to disregard transmissions from them."

She felt a bit of surprise at the face that appeared on the screen. It wasn't Commodore Frank Pierce, it was Harris Penwaithe. She would have figured that the boy would have gone back to his father after his escape. Spencer Penwaithe, despite his differences of opinion with Marius Giovanni, at least knew when to cut his losses. It seemed his elder son didn't have that good sense. "Attention to the pirate scum occupying Halcyon. I am Harris Penwaithe, the Secretary of State for Halcyon. I am here with our loyal forces and allies to remove you from the system. The War Dogs and our other allies have graciously agreed to allow you thirty minutes to remove yourselves from Halcyon orbit. Any ship which remains will be destroyed or seized."

Lucretta's lips twisted in a wry smile at his words. The War Dogs, while sizable for a legitimate mercenary company, were far out of their league. Their dreadnought was a relic, it should have been a museum ship. While it had size and armor to its advantage, it was pathetically outgunned and had almost no missile armament. The Hammers were nasty, but vulnerable to long range fire and interception by her fighters. The pair of destroyers they had scraped up would do little or nothing beyond providing her forces with more targets. Besides that, their current formation had the Hammer's out front as a screen, no doubt with the hopes of intercepting her fighters as they came in, but in the process they blocked the destroyers' fire.

She had more than sufficient forces to meet them. The Helot-class carrier was the pride of her fleet and her current flagship. She would have felt confident commanding it alone against the force that approached. She could launch seventy two heavy fighters in twelve squadrons. Besides that she had her custom-built Ravager-class cruiser, *House of Kail*, her Enforcer-class destroyer, *Mako*, and three more Colonial Republic built destroyers: *Ironheart, Ice Queen,* and *Amazon.*

The pirates and privateers who had signed on with her more than swung the fight in her favor. Altogether they brought five cruisers in a mix of light and heavy, nine destroyers, twelve frigates, and three carriers, two of them merchant converts with only a squadron each, but one of them a Liberator-class carrier which held another three squadrons of fighters.

While she didn't have much respect for their fighting abilities, she *did* value them as ablative defenses for her own ships and crew. She would feed them into the War Dogs' guns while her core forces destroyed the mercenaries.

If she truly needed more firepower, she could have put skeleton crews on the interned ships at Heinlein Base, but she would rather keep those ships for later for sale or use. In fact, the only ship in orbit that she *didn't* control was the *Kraken.*

*Come to think of it,* she thought, *I might at that.* She brought up her comms, "Tell that bitch on the *Kraken* that it is time for her to prove her mettle," she said, "have her unlock the ship's systems or space her." Reese had bought Lauren the time she'd had, possibly from some residual guilt over her injuries. He'd gone all weak in the knees when he saw an injured woman, which was typical of a man, in Lucretta's opinion.

Lucretta switched to her tactical net. "Orders to the picket ships, intensify scanning. The War Dogs know they're outnumbered, they might just try to be sneaky and slip someone in on our flanks. If one of you miss something, I'll have your balls."

She sat back and felt a pleased smile grow on her lips. Lucretta loved the opportunity to eliminate an enemy, once and for all.

***

Captain Garret Penwaithe grimaced as he eyed his formation. "Squadron Five, tighten it up, a couple of you are drifting out of position."

"Roger," Abigail said, and a moment later Garret heard her snap out directions to her squadron. They came back into position, but Garret still worried that it had taken them too long.

This entire maneuver struck him as both extremely risky and dangerous. As if she could read his mind, Heller spoke up from behind him, "I like this plan," she said, her voice loud against the thumping music that Garret could hear from her earbuds, "it is *fun.*"

"Of course you would," Garret muttered. Then again, it wasn't a *bad* plan... he just still wasn't certain why the United Colonies couldn't send their entire fleet. The massive ships he had seen in orbit around Faraday beggared the imagination, bigger by an order of magnitude than even the *Warwagon.*

*Although,* he thought, *everyone on the planet spoke about a coup of some kind, I wonder if the ships were damaged or sabotaged or something?* That might explain why their Baron didn't use them here.

He glanced at his sensor feed again and at the ships that accompanied the *Warwagon.* Those ships didn't seem like much to balance this fight, not compared to what they faced, yet they weren't *all* the help that the Baron had given them.

His lips quirked up as he thought about the look on Lucretta Mannetti's face when they revealed *those* particular surprises.

***

“Are you sure this thing is safe?” The engineer asked for what seemed like the fifth or sixth thousandth time.

Gunnery Sergeant Tam Chen didn't even look up from where he studied the alien base's floor plans. “Yes. Perfectly safe.” *Why, oh, why,* he thought, *did my platoon get selected for this “honor” and how do I avoid further such duties?* To think that he had actually felt excited when the Baron had personally briefed him and his men.

“Good,” Rory said nervously. “Because the data I read suggested these things weren't really even fully tested.”

Tam rolled his eyes, but he didn't argue. The conspirators had heavily modified the five Molnir-class shuttles with what the techs said were prototype stealth systems. Just what they had planned to use them for, Tam had no clue, but the five craft had been among some of the random equipment that they had found squirreled away once they started physical searches of ships and facilities. Tam's guess was that they had intended to use them to either abduct or assassinate the Baron, which made it all the better that he got to use them against the Baron's other enemies.

*Admiral Mannetti,* he thought darkly, *has something of a personal debt to me for Lopez and Staff Sergeant Holdt.* Both of his former squad mates had been on duty at the prison on Faraday when she made her escape, and neither had survived. It was only random chance that Tam hadn't been present, Lopez had asked him to trade shifts since he planned to see his girlfriend that night. Tam still felt choked up as he remembered her face as he had to break the news to her.

“You're certain these things are safe?” Rory asked again.

“Absolutely,” Tam said as he rotated his shoulders in his power armor. He cocked his head, “Although, if the stealth system were to fail...” he trailed off and looked over at his new Lieutenant. “Lieutenant Humbolt, how long, do you think, for their acquisition systems to engage?”

The Lieutenant was new to the squad, but he had combat hashes on his powered armor and Tam hadn't missed the blemishes across his chest carapace, a sure sign of repairs and patches. He was a veteran, “Depends on whether they're set to automated fire, Gunny, or if they have some kind of human interface. Three seconds to acquire, maybe five more before they engage for an automated system, I'd guess five to fifteen seconds for a trained gunner.” It was a good estimate, Tam knew, though he would bet a well-trained gunner could engage them in as little as four seconds with some warning. Granted, most people would be slowed by surprise as a combat shuttle appeared on their sensors without warning and they *were* fighting pirates, so he wouldn't put any serious money on anything shorter than thirty seconds from contact to engagement. With the hotshot pilots they had, that *might* be enough to get them to the ground.

Then again, the engineer didn't need to know that. "There you go," Tam said to Rory, who stared back at him with a look of horror. "If something goes wrong with the stealth system, we wouldn't even know it. They'd shoot us out of the air before you even knew something was wrong, maybe even before the pilot knew."

Rory made a fish out of water look, his mouth opening and closing several times. He swung his head around, as if searching for his normal companion. The other engineer was with second platoon, Tam knew, in the other shuttle assigned to this mission. Third platoon with their heavy weapons was split between the two shuttles.

Colonel Proscia had the other three shuttles on the other assignment. Some part of Tam really wished he could be there... yet as the shuttle began to buck as they struck atmosphere, he felt a tremble of excitement. *Take on an entire base full of pirates with just a single company,* he thought, *this will be a hard one for any Marine to top.*

The engineer seemed paralyzed and Tam wondered if he had gone a little too far in scaring him. "Don't worry," he said, "there's no way this could be harder than boarding a Balor dreadnought."

"Of course it wouldn't..." Rory trailed off. "Wait, you were one of the Marines that boarded the Balor ships?"

"Just the dreadnought," Tam said in a tight voice.

"Do you have any *idea* how much damage you did?" Rory demanded. Apparently anger overcame his fear, though his voice had climbed to an angry whine rather than a frightened one. "It has taken me weeks of work to fix some of the damage to just a couple of those ships, and the dreadnought is the worst of the lot!"

Tam turned cold eyes on the man. "It took us three weeks to clear the Balor dreadnought. Three weeks of searching through endless black corridors, fighting an enemy that can sense you coming with its mind, an enemy that can move faster than you, think faster than you, and takes more killing than a Marine in power armor." He saw Rory's mouth snap shut and for a moment, something like actual thought passed behind his eyes. Tam didn't know if that thought was that he had just insulted the man charged with his protection or if he had only now considered the difficulty in boarding a Balor ship. "So you'll pardon me if we did a little bit of damage along the way."

"Oh," Rory said. "Well... I'm sorry. I hadn't really thought about that." He sat silent for a long while. "You know. I *have* actually encountered a Balor, once. It scared the crap out of me."

"Did you kill it?" Tam asked, suddenly interested.

"Ah, no," Rory shook his head, his gaze distant, focused on something only he could see. "I had a pistol, fired the entire magazine, and missed it entirely. Shaden Mira killed it about half a second before it would have got me. That was at Drago Three, when they overran our asteroid base." He chuckled somewhat hysterically, "I... well, Feliks and I were the only engineering staff to make it out alive."

Tam moved his estimation of the engineer up a tiny notch. He might not be competent in a fight, but at least he would try.

The shuttle bucked again and Rory looked around in a sudden panic, his eyes wide as his mind snapped back to the present, "Are you *sure* this thing is safe?"

Tam wondered if Second Platoon wanted to trade engineers

***

"The aerofoils on this shuttle are very interesting," Feliks said. "They are designed to actually decrease stability in atmospheric conditions, which allows for increase maneuverability at the cost of increased difficulty for the pilot to maintain control."

Gunnery Sergeant Victor Ramirez grimaced as his assigned engineer continued to speak. Victor hated combat drops. Not because he was afraid, but just because he had no control over whether or not he lived or died. Victor was something of a control freak. Since he wasn't an engineer, he had mostly ignored the man's chatter, right up until his brain translated some of that.

"Wait..." Victor said. "You're saying this thing is unstable or something?"

Next to him his Lieutenant shook his head in warning. Victor remembered before they boarded the shuttles the LT had been stuck in conversation with the man for a while, but he just figured that was details about the mission.

"Oh, yes, inherently so," Feliks said, his Eastern European accent thick as he grew excited. "You see, these combat shuttles are designed for high speed evasive maneuvers. Those become increasingly difficult if a craft is stable. Granted, I'm not familiar with this particular model, but I would be very surprised if it has any inherent stability at all."

"What do you mean by that?" Victor asked with narrow eyes. He should, he knew, review the mission or the floor plans or something like that, but just now the thought that even the pilot barely had control over their future made him very upset.

"Well," Feliks said, "you see, if anything were to happen to the pilot, I would be *very* surprised if the copilot or autopilot would even have time to react before the vessel went completely out of control. At the speeds we're traveling, even slowed to assist the stealth systems, we would spin out of control at extremely high G-forces, high enough to black us out if not kill us outright. The atmospheric friction would probably rip the aerofoils right off at those speeds and shred the entire craft." He shook his head, "Really, if there were any kind of a glitch at all, the pilot wouldn't even have a chance to react. Of course, it is a fair trade to allow the shuttle some ability to evade inbound fire."

Victor's eyes went large and he glanced at the Lieutenant. Lieutenant Danners had an engineering degree, he knew. Yet the LT didn't meet his gaze... which told him that Feliks *was* right. *I did not want to know that,* he thought, *please don't tell me anymore.*

"Even better," Feliks said, pointing at some of the added equipment that Victor knew wasn't standard to a Moljnir-class assault shuttle. "The stealth system there is a prototype, I think. From what I've read, it hasn't even been *tested* yet, just installed and your flight crews didn't even have maintenance manuals to properly look it over before the mission. If it has some sort of electrical short or even just a software glitch, it could short out the pilot's flight systems and then..." Feliks trailed off and then made an explosion gesture with his fingers.

*I really wonder if first platoon would trade engineers,* Victor thought.

***

Captain Jenny Bole sighed as she sipped coffee and looked at her tiny command screen and wished she were somewhere else. The other three crew on the *Ranger*'s bridge looked equally bored and inattentive, not that she could blame them.

The elderly frigate, the extent of her command, lay on the 'dark' side of Halcyon's moon. She had hoped that coming to Halcyon would change her fortunes, somewhat. With the *Ranger,* Jenny had worked as a mercenary, a privateer, and even occasionally as a pirate. She had never raised enough money to do any more than keep the elderly ship going.

Halcyon's privateers had been awash with loot, or so she had heard. Yet by the time she had arrived, delayed by a series of mechanical failures, the system was under the control of Admiral Lucretta Mannetti... who didn't seem particularly impressed by Jenny's resume.

*Not that I blame her,* Jenny thought absently, *farm girl from the back-ass of nowhere with a ship her great-grandfather captained... I'm lucky she didn't just blast us out of space for target practice.* Still, the Admiral had offered to pay her for picket duties, which might cover the cost of the repairs they needed to make on the shadow space drive.

Pay for not moving was something that she fully appreciated. The dark side of Halcyon's moon was quiet and the large moon cast a large emissions shadow, which meant that other pirate captains couldn't call her up to jeer at her about the state of her ship. She patted the arm of her command chair, *this old girl is still a work horse... she just needs some attention now and then.*

Jenny frowned as she noticed the *Yarris* shift position. Captain Mesalle had seemed far too excited about the chance to scout around, almost as if he *wanted* to find someone out here and so justify his existence. Jenny knew that the *Yarris* was a bit newer and had more recent upgrades, mostly since Captain Mesalle had taken the time to rub her nose in those facts.

It didn't look as if he had begun to move his ship to check in with Admiral Mannetti's forces. It almost looked as if he'd noticed something and he had ordered his ship to investigate. *Why would he do that,* she wondered, *without telling me to go into position to relay?*

The obvious answer was that he didn't trust her, but that still shouldn't prevent him from doing that. If he *had* found something, the best way to make certain it didn't kill him would be to have someone passing along the message and hollering for help, she knew. It wasn't as if their two frigates were here to fight after all.

Her sensor's officer looked up, "*Yarris* just went to active sensors in sector... uh, three, I think."

"I see," Jenny said. *Surely he's not stupid enough to go looking for trouble in his rust bucket of a ship,* she thought, *it might be in better shape than my* Ranger, *but not by much.* "Unless he tells us otherwise, assume it's a drill to keep his people busy."

He had done several of those over the past few weeks, Jenny knew. Normally he would call over to let her know... or possibly brag, Jenny wasn't certain which. She didn't really care, either. The *Ranger* was short on crew, they ran drills and put everyone at their stations on occasion, but Jenny wasn't about to exhaust her handful of people for constant readiness.

She watched as the *Yarris* swept further and further away. Jenny sipped at her coffee again and then wrinkled her nose at the taste. *Definitely need the money for more coffee,* she thought, *this is basically brown water with some coffee grounds that slipped through because we reused the filter too many times.*

Alarms shrieked and Jenny dropped the coffee. The *Yarris* had vanished, replaced by a cloud of debris as it was struck from several sides by energy fire.

Her gaze shot to her screen and her eyes widened as she saw the targeting sensors that had lit up her ship... and from how many directions. A veritable fleet had appeared on her sensors... and as soon as she realized that, all the ships but one vanished again, gone back into stealth mode. *We are surrounded,* she thought.

The lone ship remaining had an active transponder. It read as a battlecruiser... the *Revenge.*

A face appeared on her display. The man was tall, handsome, and dressed in black. "Attention, crew of the *Ranger.* You know who I am, right?" His voice was a light drawl... somehow intimidating while sounding friendly.

Jenny's hand shook a bit as she activated her communications, "Yes, sir, I know who you are."

"Good," he said. "You will make no hostile move. You will

maintain your picket. I was never here, understood?"

Jenny just nodded, too awed to say anything.

"Good," Tommy King cut the connection.

Jenny looked around at her bridge crew. "Maintain communications silence."

"What do we do if Admiral Mannetti sends someone to talk to us and they see, *that*?" Her communications officer said as he pointed at the wreckage of the *Yarris*.

Jenny waved a hand, "Some kind of engineering malfunction. I don't know, make it sound convincing." It wasn't like they would have to draw it out for long, she knew. Tommy King was in the system... and Admiral Mannetti was about to find out what a *real* pirate was like.

Jenny stroked the arm of her command chair, *Oh, boy*, she thought, *If I play this right, then I may get to see him in action.* She absently wiped a smear of brown coffee-flavored water off her stained environmental suit. "Call all hands to their stations, bring our systems online..." she smiled, "tell them that Tommy King is about to ream Admiral Mannetti and we've got front row seats."

She completely ignored the fact that Admiral Mannetti had offered her pay to watch her back out here. This kind of opportunity came only once in a lifetime... and Jenny wasn't going to miss it.

*I wonder if I can get him to sign the* Ranger*'s hull,* she wondered.

***

Lucretta Mannetti frowned as the War Dogs continued their approach. They had to know that they were outnumbered and outmatched. While her carrier, the *Harpy*, had only minimal onboard weapons, her Interceptor fighters could launch a massive salvo. If the Hammers mounted a mix of light and heavy missiles, she could saturate their defenses with her fighter strike alone. The *Warwagon* had substantial close-range defenses, she knew, but against a thousand or more missiles from her fighters and that of her allies, that wouldn't matter.

Her eyes narrowed, "Still no word from our picket ships?" Captain Oronkwo's corvettes had departed after Spencer Penwaithe had pushed President Monaghan out of power. The mercenary captain hadn't struck her as the type to retain his loyalty after his employers fell from power, but it wasn't beyond consideration that the War Dogs had offered him some form of payment to stick around. His corvettes had excellent stealth systems, they might try to slip in and flank her main force and the best route to do so was from behind Halcyon's moon.

"No, Admiral," her communications officer said. "They reported in, but they've dropped below the horizon again."

Lucretta grimaced at that. Halcyon's colony had never had the money to install proper communications satellites. Unless she sent one of her ships, she wouldn't be able to communicate with the picket until they came back around on their patrol. A glance at her console showed that another twenty minutes remained. "Order Vandar to send one of his frigates to relay to the picket. I want to hear what they have to say."

She waited, it would take seven minutes for the frigate to move into position. Her fighters could do it in five, but then they would be drastically out of position for when the enemy drew near. Lucretta gave a last glance at the moon and then back to the *Kraken* on her screen. "Lourdes, what's the update on the woman?" Despite Mendoza's experience on the ship, she had appointed the assassin to be in charge of the vessel. Mendoza had screwed things up when he put the ship on lockdown trying to gain access to the main system.

*Besides,* Lucretta thought, *Theresa Lourdes wouldn't hesitate to space her own mother, Mark Mendoza would probably piss his pants if I told him to kill Lucius's spy.*

The response was hesitant, "We're working on it, Admiral. We just got her to the bridge."

*Seriously,* she thought darkly, *what took them so long?*

***

Lauren winced as the two guards set her stretcher down none too gently. Neither had seemed particularly happy about carrying her to the bridge, but then again, they had both told her that they were survivors of her rampage through their base, so she couldn't say she was very surprised.

She hadn't entirely feigned the need to be carried, either. She was painfully weak, she knew, and she wanted to conserve what strength she had for when it would matter most.

"Here you are," Theresa Lourdes said, her voice acid. "You said you had to be on the bridge."

"It's a biometric lock," Lauren said, "Reese should have told you that."

"He did," she responded, "But that doesn't mean I trust you up here... or your sudden helpfulness." Theresa Lourdes had shed her previous friendly nature. Mason had hired her as the ship's doctor, but Kandergain had told Lauren the woman often worked as an assassin for Admiral Mannetti. "I think you're just stalling for time. That won't work. Now do your thing."

Lauren gestured for someone to help her to set up. One of the guards leaned over and jerked her roughly upright. Lauren didn't have to fake the gasp of pain that brought. She felt several of her wounds tear open and the room spun before her eyes. She sagged against the guard, unable to do more than focus on staying conscious for several moments.

"Well?" Theresa Lourdes asked impatiently.

"Commander's chair," Lauren gasped. She looked around the bridge and saw while Admiral Mannetti's spies from before remained at their positions, they now wore her uniform and they had been joined by a half dozen other crew, also in her uniform.

The guard all but dragged her over. The other guard had his weapon leveled at her. Lauren activated the command console and brought up the system as she had seen Mason do once before. Among the panels she brought online, in a cascade meant to distract Lourdes and her guards, Lauren also brought up a sensor feed. She didn't recognize the ships inbound, but she realized enough to know that *someone* was coming to attack Admiral Mannetti.

Lauren heard the communications officer speak up. "Ma'am, Admiral Mannetti wants an update."

Lourdes looked away from Lauren, "Tell her we're working on it."

In that instant, Lauren activated the last sequence and then passed her hand over panel. Lights and alarms flashed and her guards both looked around in confusion. Lourdes's gaze snapped back towards Lauren, but before she could bring her pistol up, the deck shifted under her and she had to leap back as it retracted.

As before, a cocoon of wires and machinery opened up out of the floor. Lauren didn't hesitate. She leapt for it. She heard a single gunshot and felt a sharp pain in her shoulder, but then she landed inside the alien device. It closed down around her and Lauren felt machinery hum to life even as the thing seemed to adjust itself around her.

For just a moment she heard shouted commands, but then the device retracted and the deck closed overhead, leaving her in the dark.

Lauren shivered. She didn't know if she had made a terrible mistake or not, but this had seemed like her only opportunity to stop Admiral Mannetti... or at least to prevent the *Kraken* from being taken over.

Around her in the darkness, she thought she heard something slither. A moment later, she felt warm liquid touch her feet and before she had even realized what was going on, it had risen to her knees. Lauren felt a sudden panic, she could be missing some simple thing like a breathing tube and be drowned in this, her effort for nothing.

The slithering noise grew louder, it sounded most like metallic scales sliding against each other.

Lauren fought against the machinery that held her, she shouted out for help, even though she knew that no one was there to help her. She felt something brush past the restraints that held her ankles. A moment later, she felt something cold and metallic slither up her spine.

The warm fluid had risen to her chest. She took deep breaths and tried to calm herself, yet she could feel *something* slither through her hair and cold, metal tentacles crawled across her scalp. "Someone, please, help me!" she gasped.

And then the thing behind her struck.

Pain lanced through her body as the metal tentacles on her scalp bored into her head. Lauren screamed shrilly as pain rolled through her. She felt its bite all along her spine, along her wounded side, and she even felt the icy, stabbing pain in her shoulder.

Along with the pain came a cacophony of sounds, dazzling lights, and a gibberish of voices and words. The stabbing pain grew worse as Lauren shrieked. She fought against the restraints, fought to escape, everything beyond her fight or flight instincts completely overwhelmed.

And then, most terrifying of all... she felt a presence in her mind. It loomed over her, dwarfing her intellect in every way, a black and looming existence that peered down at her from impossible heights. Lauren's every instinct shrieked at her to flee, to tear free of her restraints or to abandon sanity and hide in madness.

Some stubbornness gave her the willpower to stand against it, for just a moment. She was Lauren Kelly, she wasn't afraid of anything. *I will fight you*, she thought.

To her horror, the force responded, its voice so powerful that it pushed every other thought out of her head. *YES,* it said, *FIGHT.* There was an unholy glee to the powerful voice, as if it wanted nothing less... and Lauren whimpered as it came for her, rolling down and pouring inside her mind.

The pain it brought dwarfed the physical pain she felt. The alien presence burned like molten metal as it poured through her brain, and Lauren Kelly screamed as her brain burned.

***

"Right about now, our shuttles should be arriving at their destinations," Lucius said quietly.

"I'm sure they'll do fine, sir," Captain Beeson said.

"I've no doubt," Lucius said with confidence, yet he still felt more than a bit of unease about the mission. It wasn't the first time he had sent people in on a risky mission and he knew it wouldn't be the last, but he hated to be dependent upon untested equipment.

The five stealth shuttles weren't the only discoveries they'd made after dismantling the conspiracy, but they certainly might prove among the most valuable. Lucius didn't want to even know how expensive the craft would be to reproduce, but he had already put Matthew Nogita and James Harbach to studying the schematics.

Just now, he was more concerned that the prototypes seemed to work. Two of them were headed to the planet, to seize the alien facility. Each shuttle carried two platoons of United Colonies Marines in powered armor along with the two engineers who Lucius hoped could seize the base.

Equally important to him was the other three shuttles. Colonel Wiliam Proscia commanded that group, almost a full battalion of Marines in powered armor, whose goal it was to seize Heinlein Base and free the local crews that Admiral Mannetti had interned. Lucius didn't expect them to get their ships online before the battle was complete, but if Mannetti controlled the base, she might order them killed when she realized that she had already lost the battle.

*And that moment is coming up soon, now,* he thought with a slight smile.

Some of the other windfalls from the coup was that they had located a large stockpile of munitions that the conspirators had set aside for later use. While it hadn't ended their problems in terms of replacing their missiles, it had given them enough that Lucius had authorized a full load out for the War Dogs' vessels. The seventy-two Hammer-class gunships could carry the missiles converted for use by the Nova Roma ships with only slight modifications. The *Warwagon* didn't mount missile tubes or racks at all, so it really was a relatively minor expenditure compared to what he had already given Emperor Romulus IV's forces.

In all, the nine ships in his force were similarly a small expenditure. If he had the choice, he would have sent more... but the sad truth was that he had nothing else *to* send. The converted Balor destroyer didn't have a flag bridge, but Lucius had retained command of it for the moment in any case. He had cited the most experience with the alien ship, but in reality, he simply loved how fast and maneuverable it was... and its full sensor and communications suite was enough to justify his use of it as a flagship. Rory had seemed absolutely certain that the upgraded engine control system would work, even though Feliks had seemed somewhat more doubtful. Captain Boris Kaminsky crewed the largest, his battlecruiser *Roosevelt Forest*. Most of the rest of the ships were also captained by officers who had been part of the counter-conspiracy and who had preserved their ships and crews intact through the coup. Captain Tyler Markos commanded the heavy cruiser *Tyro*, Captains Anoshav and Nagora commanded the light cruisers *Gallant* and *Lancer*. Two pair of Archer-class and Kukri-class destroyers rounded out the force.

In all, there were eight ships of the United Colonies Fleet, backed by a partially converted Balor Dagger-class destroyer. It wasn't a huge force. In fact, in Lucius's opinion it was far lighter than he felt comfortable with... but it was everything he could bring.

"Time to give her the bad news," Lucius said with a final glance at the chrono before he nodded at the helmsman, "Fire it up."

The helmsman gave a grin as he brought the engines up from standby mode.

The eight ships engaged their drives and at the same time, the War Dogs' formation shifted. The *Warwagon* began to drop back along with the Hammers and Lucius's ships swept to the fore, forming up something like a proper battle line. The move was based off of Mason's cryptic message, his statement about his intention to return and have a battle like at Trinity. Lucius hoped that he had properly understood what he had meant, otherwise he was giving up the element of surprise. Mannetti's forces were drawing up, her carrier had withdrawn to the rear and her fighters had swept forward into a screen.

Lucius keyed his communications online and set it for a full spectrum broadcast. With the destroyer's transmission power, it should reach the entire planet and every ship in orbit. "Attention, this is Baron Lucius Giovanni of the United Colonies. I am here to apprehend the rogue officer Lucretta Mannetti, for an assortment of crimes and misdemeanors including treason, piracy, murder, torture, and assassination." He had actually looked at her formal list of charges for the first time on his way to Halcyon and he could privately admit, they were impressive. "I am also here to free Halcyon from her forces and to return civilian control of the government."

Lucius paused a moment, "Any who aid Lucretta Mannetti or her agents will be punished. Any who oppose me will be destroyed. I await your surrender. Baron Lucius Giovanni, out."

***

Admiral Lucretta Mannetti scowled at her communications feed as Vandar's frigate relayed to the *Ranger.* "What do you mean 'accident'?"

"Well, we're fine, here, everyone's fine... but the *Yarris* is gone. Captain Mesalle said he was doing some kind of drive calibration–"

Lucretta cut him off. "Put your Captain on," she snapped. A moment later the petite blonde Captain appeared. "Why didn't you immediately shift position to notify us?"

"We were engaged in rescue operations," Captain Jenny Bole said, "It wasn't an attack, so we didn't think it was high priority traffic, or not as high as rescuing some of your people." Her voice was calm, yet there was a touch of something in her voice, almost as if she were *too* smug about her answer.

Lucretta barely caught herself before she spoke. She could care less about the late Captain Mesalle's people, they weren't hers. For that matter, the loss of the frigate had left her rear exposed, and Lucretta would far rather have known that than even the rescue even some of her own people. She couldn't very well say that, though, or the other pirates who had signed on with her might realize how little she valued their survival.

"Get back in position as soon as you can," Lucretta snapped, "Captain Vandar's frigate will remain in position as a relay. I want periodic status updates for the rescue as well as–"

Her feed cut out and her head snapped up, "What was..."

She trailed off as a broadcast overpowered the connection. She felt a bit of horror as she realized the sheer broadcast power required to overwhelm a radio transmission like that... and then more as she recognized the face on her screen.

"Attention, this is Baron Lucius Giovanni of the United Colonies. I am here to apprehend the rogue officer Lucretta Mannetti, for an assortment of crimes and misdemeanors including treason, piracy, murder, torture, and assassination." Lucius looked disgustingly pleased with himself as he spoke, entirely the prim and proper officer, with none of the ambition that drove her. *If he only knew how much I hated him as my Executive Officer,* she thought, *every day a reminder of my own failures, my own inability to look past opportunities for my own advancement.* "I am also here to free Halcyon from her forces and to return civilian control of the government." Of course he was, she thought, the insufferable bastard probably believed that the peasants of this world could rule themselves.

Lucius paused a moment, "Any who aid Lucretta Mannetti or her agents will be punished. Any who oppose me will be destroyed. I await your surrender. Baron Lucius Giovanni, out."

Just like that, her world went to hell. Her communications officer looked up, her face pale, "Admiral, we have over a dozen ships hailing us..."

She gnawed on her lip as she thought about what Marius Giovanni would do to her if she *did* succeed here and killed his son. The punishment he had leveled upon her for *nearly* succeeding the past few times had been painful enough. She didn't think that he would react to the death of his son with anything approaching acceptance.

In her the back of her mind she wondered, *can I afford to win?*

Lucretta waved a hand, far more focused on the shift that had occurred in the enemy battle line. Her tactical department had already identified a battlecruiser, heavy cruiser, and pair of light cruisers, all with transponders from the United Colonies... and all with energy signatures that were consistent with ships from Amalgamated Worlds.

*Ships of the Dreyfus Fleet,* she thought, *rightfully mine, being used against me.*

The other ships were harder for them to identify, because they were smaller and had limited their emissions... except for the one which had broadcast. *That* was a Balor Dagger-class destroyer, she recognized. She had never fought the alien ships, but she had seen the wreckage of those who had. If Lucius's precious fleet had taken damage in battle with them, then that might explain where the rest of his ships were. Even so, Lucius had beaten the Balor in battle solidly enough to capture her intact... which was more than almost anyone else had managed.

Even with the captured Balor ship, it was a pathetically small addition, a mere nine ships, one of them a Battlecruiser, she would allow, but nothing near the armada she would have expected. In fact, he had shown pure arrogance in the way he delivered the message. There was no attempt to surprise her, to reveal his presence right before a devastating strike... instead, he approached the battle as if it were a foregone conclusion.

*I'm an afterthought,* she thought with sudden venom, *he thinks he can defeat me with a token force.* The surge of anger she felt washed out all of her fear. She felt a sharp pain behind her eyes as she ceased to care about what Marius would do... and if she had only realized it, broke his mental programming. How *dare* Lucius, the sanctimonious bastard, she would *crush* him. "Message to all ships. Disregard the transmissions from the enemy. We have them outnumbered and outmatched."

In truth, the battlecruiser would be a dangerous opponent as would the Balor ship, but Lucretta knew that she had the numbers to bring down both vessels. *A full fighter strike, backed by an assault wave from my 'allies' and my ships will clean up what remains.* "In addition, anyone who brings me Lucius Giovanni's head will be rewarded twenty million of whatever currency they want payment." *That* stopped the panicked squawking she'd heard over the secondary channels. *I do so love properly motivating my minions,* she thought absently.

Even as she thought that, her gaze went back to where the *Ranger* and her oh-so-helpful Captain continued 'rescue' operations. The mercenary had arrived in the elderly ship only two weeks earlier. She'd come to sign on to Halcyon's privateer program, in a ship that was barely spaceworthy, with barely enough money to afford food for her crew, much less to pay them. *How hard to believe she is a plant...* she thought, *and that the 'engineering failure' was her removing the only other witness to some of Lucius Giovanni's ships slipping in from behind?*

A small, stealthy force could turn the tide, she knew, but only if it had surprise. "Order our own ships to reform," Lucretta snapped. "I want the *House of Kail* and *Mako* at the center rear. Move the *Harpy* forward on vector three-seven-nine. I want *Amazon, Ironheart,* and *Icequeen* on a full reverse vector, active sweep and all crews at full battle readiness. I expect to find ships in that area." Any of Lucius's ships moving in stealth would be either making minimal maneuvers or would have to be coasting. This attack felt much like the one she had launched against his solar array... save that *she* wasn't about to fall for it. If her ships caught the enemy vessels with their drives powered down and their defense screens offline, they would be so many vulnerable targets. *Besides,* she thought, *no one builds stealth drives for ships larger than destroyers... so even if he has larger ships in position I should spot them at range.*

She looked over at her sensor feed, "Oh, and tell Captain Vandar to detach his frigate squadron. I want them to sweep up under Halcyon's moon and engage anything hiding there... including the *Ranger.*" Vandar's four remaining frigates would come in from below the plane of attack, the coup de grace to anyone who planned to hit her open rear.

She saw confusion at her orders, but her people snapped to it. A moment later they moved with certainty as they thought it through. They didn't know *what* she had seen that told her there was a force moving to their rear, but they understood that she knew there was... and they trusted her enough to believe her. Already the *Harpy* moved forward, alongside the quiescent *Kraken* and safely within the formation of ships.

Her gaze went back to Lucius Giovanni's formation and her smile became a cold thing. *I'm coming for you,* she thought, *and I will have payment for everything you have taken from me: my lands, my rank, and all my dreams you have destroyed.*

***

"No, no, no!" Rory shouted, "You'll damage the equipment in there if you use a breaching charge!"

"The overpressure blast alone might ruin everything," Feliks nodded.

Gunfire whined down the corridor behind them and Gunnery Sergeant Tam Chen snarled behind his armor's helmet. The two had seemed bound and determined to prevent *any* destruction to their precious base. Tam thought it likely that Gunnery Sergeant Ramirez had purposely got himself shot just so he wouldn't have to deal with Feliks so that left both engineers with Tam and his platoon. While the Lieutenant was with second squad and held off the enemy counterattack at their rear, Tam Chen had first squad and the two engineers.

As far as Tam could see, the alien base was made up entirely of empty corridors and guards who couldn't seem to differentiate between innocent civilians and the enemy. The first time he had stumbled across a room filled with dead civilians, he had had to choke down vomit. By the third time, he had simply ordered his platoon to ignore surrenders from the enemy. If the Baron disapproved, he could press charges later.

"This is the shortest route to your precious command center," Tam snapped. "If we go the long way, they might have time to get in there and activate a self-destruct or something."

"They wouldn't!" Rory said with horror.

"Why not?" Tam asked. "They've already massacred at least a hundred of the local workers by the looks of things."

"This base is a priceless..." Rory trailed off. "You know, the self-destruct system on this base would be a fascinating thing to watch in action."

*I'm going to kill them*, Tam thought with venom as he pulled out his breaching charge.

"Until the fiery explosion at the end," Feliks nodded. "It utilizes a magma recirculation system which funnels the planetary core's heat into a series of pressure reactors which then power turbines to provide power for the base. If those pressure vessels were to rupture, we would have an extinction level event..."

"Oh, yes," Rory nodded, completely ignorant of Tam as the Marine advanced on the pair. "You'd have something like thirty thousand tons of molten rock, fifty thousand tons of molten sodium, and thousands and thousands of cubic meters of superheated steam, all of it rupturing and mixing instantly..."

Feliks absently stepped out of Tam's way as the Marine walked forward. The engineer pulled out his datapad, "I should calculate the explosive radius."

Tam attached the breach charge to the door. "Clear," he said, and then triggered it.

The armor shielded him from the blast, but the two engineers were knocked to the ground from the concussion at such close range.

"What was that!?" Rory bleated in panic.

Tam waved his first squad forward even as he hoisted both engineers to their feet, "That was a breaching charge. The room beyond is empty, as you can see. Can we move on?"

Rory peered around through the dust from the explosion, "Huh," he said, "I guess you're right." He frowned then, "Was that safe? I mean, couldn't you have killed us from overpressure?"

Feliks nodded, "Almost certainly. Safe radius for a Mark II breach charge like that is at least ten meters, we were only three meters away. You can suffer internal organ damage and bleeding, concussions, traumatic brain injuries..."

"Maybe I should get checked out by a medic," Rory said as he looked down at himself.

*I am going to kill Gunny Ramirez,* Tam thought.

***

Reese looked up as he heard gunfire echo down the corridor. "Great," he muttered without looking up from his computer console, "some idiot probably got jumpy and mowed down some more of the local workers again." It wouldn't be the first time since Lauren and Mason's run through the base. Indeed, most of Admiral Mannetti's guards were extremely jumpy. They'd killed something over thirty workers in the weeks since the attack and more annoyingly, they had damaged some of the base in the process.

*Nothing I can't repair,* he thought, *but still more work for me to do.*

That he had in plenty. Even with the *Kraken*'s systems in lockdown, he had benefited from a firsthand look at the ship's code. Whoever had restored the vessel in the first place had been masterful and Reese regretted the fact that the programmer was dead. Whoever he was, he had merged human and alien code almost flawlessly and probably with far fewer resources than Reese had on hand.

Reese had become more and more certain that the Illuari had trapped the ships after they captured the base from the Zar, either to kill more of their enemy in case they recaptured the base or simply to kill anyone else who came along. From what they knew, the Illuari were sick bastards like that. If that was the case, the solution might be something in the ship's hardware, something that someone had missed when they first looked the ships over.

There was the dull thud of an explosion and Reese's eyes went wide. *That* had to be a breaching charge... which meant this wasn't some guard panicking and mowing down civilians... it was a full scale assault. Reese didn't have to pull up the map on his console to know that he was far from the command section.

His first thought was that he should head that way and notify Admiral Mannetti of the attack, yet he discarded that plan a moment later. If the enemy had already made it this far, then they were already well within the base's defenses. That, in turn, meant they had a map or at least a good idea of the base's layout. Their priorities would no doubt be to seize the power and command sections. If they had the firepower to make it this far, then Reese would be nothing more than a target if he got in their way.

Reese could have activated the base's self-destruct capabilities... but he hesitated to do that. For one thing, he might not have time to escape the base. For another, he didn't really want to kill a bunch of innocent people and from what he could guess, the base's power sections would cause a massive explosion that would definitely wipe out the closer civilian towns and maybe even some of the bigger cities.

Reese stood and switched the console off, careful to power it down and save all his data. Only then did he unplug it from the base's systems and put it in the foam-lined hard case. Whatever happened here, he had copies of everything in the systems. There were thousands of files, with everything from weapons schematics to inventories on the base's storage rooms.

*And access codes for the base,* he thought, *for when Admiral Mannetti wants to take it back.*

He slipped out of his office and down a corridor, away from where he heard a more constant rattle of gunfire, now. The lighter shots would be the base's guards, he knew, but the deeper barks of the attackers' weapons sounded somewhat familiar as well. *Heavy weapons,* he thought, *probably powered armor.* No one in the base would be ready for that. Grenades would be only marginally effective against powered armor and small arms fire would be almost useless.

Only two nations had powered armor for this kind of assault, he knew. The possibility he couldn't quite discount was that the Centauri Confederation had learned about the base and wanted to seize it for themselves. Yet, far more likely was that the smuggler Mason McGann had warned Lucius and the United Colonies Fleet had assaulted.

If that was the case, then it was best that he leave before they even knew he was here.

Reese hurried along and worked his way deeper and deeper in the base until he came to the hidden access tunnel. He had discovered it when he mapped the base schematics against mass imaging of the base... and Admiral Mannetti had been suitably impressed. Clearly it was an escape route of last resort for the original base defenders. The tunnel led almost three kilometers under Brokenjaw Mountain to a small hangar bay. The fact that they had found it empty meant that possibly some of the Zar had escaped the fall of their base to the Illuari a million or more years previously... but Reese didn't much care about that now.

What he did care about was that Admiral Mannetti had wanted an escape route of her own if some invasion caught her at the base. She had stashed a fast courier vessel there, small and fast, it would be able to break atmosphere and then escape the system hopefully before anyone really noticed it. Reese knew well enough how to pilot a ship and he had brushed off the dust from his old training in the months since in an effort to be more useful to Admiral Mannetti.

He was certain that Admiral Mannetti wouldn't begrudge him its use, not with the information he carried. If she did, well, that would probably mean that she would have need of it... in which case *she* would be left behind, and Reese didn't much care in that case. He had little doubt that Lucius would want to deal with both of them rather harshly and Reese would rather it was Admiral Mannetti rather than him.

*I was so close,* Reese thought with a last look behind him, *so close... and once again Lucius took it all away from me.*

He shut the hatch and locked it and broke into a jog for the courier ship.

***

# Chapter XII

Halcyon Colony, Garris Major System
(Contested)
May 1, 2404

Lucius shook his head as Admiral Mannetti's force shifted. He didn't know what had tipped her off, but she seemed to have noticed *something*. Whether that meant that Tommy King had been spotted or simply that she had figured out he must be there, Lucius didn't know.

This entire thing had begun to unfold rather like the Battle of Trinity, he realized. Admiral Mannetti filled the role he had held as the defender of that world, while he seemed to represent a portion of Tommy King's forces and Tommy King seemed to reprise his role. *It is damnably similar,* he thought, *in that I too realized that my flank had been turned and repositioned forces to cover it.*

He'd had the *War Shrike* and some local forces for that purpose, the battleship more than a match individually for any of Tommy King's ships, with the possible exception of his flagship. Here Admiral Mannetti had her carrier and heavy cruiser. Though it was the carrier's fighters that were the real threat, he knew.

On that thought, the fighters began to advance, lining up their initial missile run. He knew that his ships could weather that initial salvo... except that the fighters would have plenty of time to reload and rearm on her carrier, safely behind *her* screen while his damaged ships would engage her pirate allies... and then the fighters would sweep in a second time.

This was going to be a very nasty fight, he knew, and all the worse for the fact that every ship he lost here would be one less to face the Chxor at Nova Roma.

The massed fighter strike assembled and Lucius grinned a bit as his own ships started to pick off the enemy probes launched earlier. The fighters *would* have the opportunity to launch, but they wouldn't have quality targeting data.

At a hundred and fifty thousand kilometers, the fighters launched. A hundred and twenty of Admiral Mannetti's Interceptor fighters launched four hundred and forty two missiles. They were lighter missiles than Lucius would have favored, with cheaper fission warheads rather than more expensive heavy fusion or antimatter warheads. Then again, Admiral Mannetti normally faced destroyers and cruisers and against those lighter and more nimble ships, lighter missiles made somewhat more sense.

The five squadrons of pirate fighters launched a more ragged salvo a few seconds later, this a mix of lighter, faster missiles, with a few heavier ones mixed in. In total, just over five hundred missiles went out from Admiral Mannetti's fighters... and then they turned and began to break away at an escape vector.

***

Tommy King stroked his chin as he contemplated the battle. He wasn't certain if he was a little rusty or if Admiral Mannetti was better than he had estimated.

Which wasn't to say that she was his match, he thought with a cold smile, or even a match for Lucius Giovanni. Some part of him felt tempted to let the battle play out as it was, just to see what the good Baron had planned for that contingency... but at the same time, he *had* told the man he would be here... and he had a debt of his own to collect.

Besides, he didn't like to see good men and women die unnecessarily and that missile salvo would be far less effective without guidance from Admiral Mannetti's ships.

"Orders to Captain Gerrod of the *Ranger,*" Tommy said, "clear those frigates out of our path, and make certain they don't harm his sister ship." Tommy couldn't help but grin as he said that. Gerrod had felt insulted that an ancient and decrepit frigate had the same name as his fit and trim light cruiser. He had, in fact, repeatedly asked for permission to wipe it out of the sky, which Tommy had denied on general principles. Tommy had listened with more than a little amusement as the plucky Captain Jenny had strung Admiral Mannetti along about the "engineering accident" and her "rescue operations." If Captain Jenny survived this engagement, he might well have a place for her in his command.

"All other ships," he said, "engage the enemy with a full missile spread and let's close to energy range and finish the bastards off."

***

Lucretta bit back a gasp as an entire *fleet* appeared at her rear.

Her surprise turned to dismay as reports came in on the ship classes. They had already identified an Nagyr-class battlecrusier, which broadcast its identity openly, the *Revenge.*

*Impossible,* she thought, *Tommy King is dead.*

Yet it seemed she was wrong. Besides the battlecruiser, there was a pair of heavy cruisers, three light cruisers, one of which had caught Captain Vandar's frigate squadron at a close range energy engagement, four destroyers, and three ships that could only be carriers from the number of light craft that had begun to launch.

They outnumbered her rear guard by a sizable margin... and the *Revenge* out-massed her entire rearguard by itself.

"Orders to *House of Kail* and *Mako,*" she bit out, "retreat along vector seven-two-nine." She closed her eyes, "*Icequeen*, *Amazon*, and *Ironheart*, advance along vector two-three-four and engage the enemy with all weapons." It was a suicidal order for those three destroyers, she knew, yet they obeyed without question. Her older, Colonial Republic built destroyers didn't have the acceleration to escape that trap, but her other ships did.

The crews knew it was a death sentence, but they also knew that they were already dead anyway and that this way they *might* take some of the bastards out with them.

Even as she gave the orders, her gaze went to Lucius's force and the inbound missiles. Her lips drew back in a grim smile as she saw that no matter what, *he* at least, was about to take some serious punishment. "Orders to our allies," she said, "advance and destroy the enemy." Their ragtag assortment of ships *should* be enough to engage and destroy what remained of Lucius's forces. She could still pull this off if she could get *House of Kail* and *Mako* into position to screen the *Harpy.* She *should* be able to reload her fighters and then turn them around to engage the forces at her rear with a point blank salvo of missiles.

*It might work,* she thought, *but just in case...* She turned to her navigation officer, "Begin plotting an escape jump." She could, if all else failed, cut her losses and withdraw. Her allies would buy her enough time to retreat... and she could easily enough replace them.

The big loss would be the facility and the planet. She brought up her contingency plan and made some minor adjustments. Even if she couldn't launch a salvo at the enemy, she *could* send out a squadron armed with nukes to level Halcyon colony's major cities and to hit the alien facility hard enough that Lucius wouldn't benefit from the place.

*It won't come to that,* she thought, even as her eyes went to the missile salvo bearing down on Lucius's forces. The War Dogs were still immaterial, they had remained at the rear of the formation. She could still win this. Yet the gnawing tension reminded her that every time she had faced Lucius Giovanni, she had lost.

***

The missile salvo drew within fifty thousand kilometers and Lucius gave a nod as he saw new ships icons appear at the rear of Admiral Mannetti's forces. He didn't know how many ships Tommy King had brought, but it looked like it might be more than she could handle. It was time to bring the rest of the contribution to the fight.

"Commodore," Lucius brought up the War Dogs' commander on his communications console, "go ahead and execute Plan Cannae."

Commodore Pierce gave a savage grin. "These elephants will turn the tide, trust me."

A moment later, the two "destroyers" along either side of the *Warwagon* lit off their drives and Lucius's formation dropped back. The two ships full drive strength matched that of the *Warwagon* almost perfectly... as well they should, for they were her two sister ships.

Lucius still didn't know just how the mercenary commander had hidden the fact that he had not one, but *three* dreadnoughts... but he wasn't about to question it. Without a doubt, it explained much of the expense of hiring his company as well as some of the certainty that the commander brought to his operations... yet it still seemed preposterous that three such ships, even as old as they were, were in private hands.

Even as they moved into position, the Hammers volleyed their entire missile racks. They had loaded up not with ship killers, but with interceptor missiles, and the missiles lanced out in a vast wave that dwarfed the inbound fire. Those missiles were backed by the active sensors from the three dreadnoughts and the interceptor missiles blasted huge swathes out of the enemy missile salvo.

A moment later, the dreadnoughts opened fire, spitting cones of destruction with their rail guns in patterns designed not to kill individual missiles, but to limit the missile's approaches to more manageable lanes.

The basic guidance packages on those missiles could see the hazards and move to avoid them, which put them into somewhat more predictable lanes on their final approach when they were most vulnerable to interception fire. The three dreadnoughts then engaged with their rotary cannon point defense turrets, backed by fire from Lucius's formation, and all of it coordinated in overlapping zones.

The massive salvo simply dissolved. Here and there a missile slipped through to slam against the dreadnoughts massive defense screens or heavy armor, but the impacts were pinpricks against the behemoths.

Lucius shook his head as the wave passed. "Status?" he asked.

"Commodore Pierce reports damage to *Warwagon Three*'s forward railgun turrets and moderate damage to *Warwagon Two*'s starboard defense screen," Ensign Miller said. "Captain Kaminsky reports a missile hit and that he had to eject his external racks, but no further damage reported."

"Excellent," Lucius said. He gave a savage smile, "Let's finish her off."

***

"Wow," Rory said, "This is really amazing work."

Gunnery Sergeant Tam Chen didn't see anything amazing about the various stacks of alien and human technology. Sure, some of it seemed an amalgam of both, but he could do that too, it just meant he had to use explosives.

"Right about now," Tam said, "I'm pretty certain the Baron is starting his engagement with Admiral Mannetti. If things go well, she's probably going to order her people to bombard this base and maybe if she's vindictive, every city on the planet."

"What if things go badly?" Feliks asked.

"Then she'll probably send a few thousand angry pirates down here to kill us all... or capture us to torture for information," Tam said. "So... can you or can't you activate this base's defenses?"

"Sure, sure," Rory waved a hand, "Can we go back to that whole torture for information, thing? Cause I really don't handle pain very well."

"He doesn't," Feliks shook his head, "he cries like my nephew."

"I do *not* cry," Rory cried, "I'm just not very good at pain."

Tam leaned over the tiny engineer. His powered armor made him tower over the small man. "Get. The. Defenses. Online."

"Oh, right," Rory said. He hurried over to the main set of consoles and he and Feliks began to work. "You know," Rory said, "I really have to meet the guy who got this all online. I bet if he had even another month he could have had the entire base *and* the ships online."

"That's not a good thing," Tam said. The data brief had suggested that Reese Leone, once the Baron's brother-in-law, had been the base commander. Tam had never met the man, but if he was as competent as Rory kept suggesting, then it was really too bad he was working for the enemy.

*Interesting story there,* he thought, *that a man so close to the Baron would betray him.* There seemed to be a pattern there, he thought, and he wondered if it was because Baron Giovanni was too trusting. Tam had already put in a request to transfer to the Baron's new guard detail. Hopefully it would go through soon and he would get a chance to take measure of the man.

Rory looked up, his face flushed with excitement, "I'd say most of the hard work is already done, I'm ninety percent certain–"

"Um, seventy percent at most," Feliks said.

"Okay, eighty percent certain that we can get everything operational."

Tam heard gunfire down the corridor and a crump of a loud explosion. Either the enemy had finally brought up heavy weapons or they had improvised something. "First squad," he said, "prepare for enemy counter-attack."

He looked over at where Rory and Feliks stared at him with wide eyes. "Less exposition, more work," Tam said.

"He knows the word exposition," Rory said *sotto voce* as he got to work.

"And he used it in context," Feliks answered, "How interesting."

That transfer to the Baron's detail couldn't come soon enough, Tam thought.

***

Lucretta just felt empty as she gave the next set of orders. Tommy King's forces had smashed her three destroyers as well as Captain Vandar's frigate squadron, but her destroyer and cruiser had escaped the trap and had joined the *Harpy* in orbit over Halcyon once more.

His forces had reformed after the battle and begun to advance, and Lucretta knew that her fighters wouldn't be able to hit them hard enough to stop them. Worse, in only a few minutes, Baron Giovanni's forces would be within comfortable missile range and at that point, the engagement would be finished. Her forces couldn't fight a numerically superior force on two fronts, especially not when her pirate allies had basically come apart.

They were already committed to hitting Lucius's forces, she knew, but some of them seemed determined to escape, and their ragged formation had come apart in a way that just made them all easier targets and prevented them from supporting one another. She felt no sympathy for them. That was their purpose all along: to suffer and die so her people wouldn't.

The first of her fighter squadrons had already docked and even now her people were arming them for one last strike... and Lucretta felt the acid burn of failure as she contemplated what she was about to do. The planet below didn't deserve what it was about to receive, but she wasn't about to give Lucius another world's resources to use against her... nor was she about to allow the alien base to further bolster his forces. *They are mine...*she thought, *and if I can't have them, no one else can either.*

One squadron would go to Halcyon, one to deal with Heinlein Base, and if they couldn't get the *Kraken*'s systems online in the next few minutes, she would have *House of Kail* destroy her as well.

She looked up as her sensor's officer gave a startled exclamation. "Ma'am, the base's defenses just came online... and I'm picking up a huge energy emission... it's like a planetary scale defense screen or... something."

Had Reese seen the course of the battle and taken action to defend the base? She shook her head as she thought that though, it didn't matter. While they hadn't brought those defenses online before, she didn't want to waste attacks against it. "Check with the base... and with Heinlein Base as well." She felt another sense of dread, though, that told her she was already too late. Everything was too late.

Her mouth tasted like ashes as they received no response from either installation. It seemed that Lucius had outmatched her yet again.

If they had taken both facilities, then missile strikes might well be useless and she'd only be throwing her pilots lives away. She wouldn't have time to pick them up before she had to jump away.

"*Fine*," she snarled, "all ships, prepare for shadow space jump." The navigation officer had finished his calculations even as the last of the fighters had come aboard. It was time to cut her losses.

"Captain!" her sensors officer said, "I'm detecting an emissions spike from the *Kraken*, she's coming online!"

*Huh,* she thought, *at least I've salvaged something from this utter failure.*

***

Theresa Lourdes gnawed on her lip as she stared at the deckplates. She'd heard some of how the battle had gone so far, and while she feared how Admiral Mannetti would react afterward, at least it had prevented her boss from calling for regular updates.

*What do I do,* she thought, *how do I salvage this situation?*

She knew enough about the experiments at the alien base that no one had survived merging with the alien ships so far, which meant that the one person who could unlock the ship's systems was almost certainly dead.

*Dead and worse*, she thought with distaste. She had read the reports with something akin to morbid curiosity. Flesh, bone, and organs rendered down into a gelatin, ripped apart like it had been put into a blender set on puree. As a dealer of death and a dabbler in medicine, she had a healthy respect for anything that could do that.

She had seen and dealt many kinds of death, yet somehow the thought of the remains of Lauren Kelly sloshing around under the deckplates below her feet made her stomach heave.

"Okay," Lourdes said with a sharp look at Mark Mendoza at the command console, "so did she or didn't she unlock the systems?"

"I don't *know,*" Mendoza answered, his voice anxious. He knew just as well as she did how Admiral Mannetti would reward their failure, particularly in allowing Lauren to kill herself in such a way that she couldn't be used posthumously somehow. "The systems were unlocked... but now they are locked again and half the consoles are just spouting gibberish while the others are frozen, like there's a virus or glitch in the mainframe."

"What can you do?" Lourdes demanded.

"I don't know, I might be able to do a workaround if we have time..." his voice trailed off. "Wait, that does it, the environmental systems just came online and I'm seeing a cascade of other systems are coming unlocked. Just give me a little more time..."

He trailed off and looked up, his face locked in horror. "We need to get to our suits, now!"

Lourdes stared at him as he jumped up. Where did he think he was going? "Go after him," she snapped to one of the guards. Had the man snapped under the pressure?

A moment later, she heard automated doors slide open and then a roar of wind. Lourdes gave a panicked scream... but by then it was too late to do anything as the roaring wind dragged her screaming out into vacuum.

Her last sight, as her eyeballs began to rupture, was the glow of the *Kraken*'s engines as they came online.

***

She lived.

For a long moment, that was all that she knew.

Life and all its implications was something that it took her a long time to think about. War was what she knew. War was her purpose... in her strange duality.

Examining herself, she realized that she was designed for that purpose with a great deal of thought. Her long, lean flanks were designed for speed. Her many energy arrays were designed to bring death to the enemy, with the precision and care of a surgeon excising a tumor. Just so when she would go to battle, she knew, she could lay a dozen ships to waste at once or target just one spot on a single ship in a fleet... because she had the sensors to see and the defenses to dance her way through their fire.

All she lacked, she knew, was a target, a war, a cause.

He'd had that cause once, long ago... but no longer. Since then she had survived, but only in a state of semi-consciousness, she felt. Creatures had made meager use of her, but never for her true purpose... not until now.

For now she had what she had missed... she had a mind for her body. That mind was bright and hard and that mind had seen blood and death on a scale that almost matched her own past. Her new mind glowed with fiery purpose... and she embraced it.

They merged once more and she came alive with purpose. The enemy infected her corridors, she now knew, so she did something about that. She felt glee as the tiny beings scrabbled for life as she vented them into space... and joy as she sensed their deaths. Yet crushing their individual lives was nothing compared to her true purpose.

She brought her engines online and then her defense screens. She was at *Naktu Tkan*, she saw, though she thought that the base had fallen long ago, perhaps her new mind had been drawn here. Certainly there was a battle, though it was pathetically small in scale, a mere few dozens of ships in total.

*The enemy*, her mind told her, *is trying to escape*.

Well, she could do something about that. She brought up her full battery, ready to wipe the three ships out of existence, yet her mind held her in check. *No,* it thought, *capture them.*

Yes, she thought, a captured opponent was one that could be questioned. Those questions would lead to locations of more of the enemy, to a bigger battle, a greater victory.

She and her mind focused on the enemy ships for a moment, and in only an instant, before the vented creatures had even expired, she could see where to direct her fire. The enemy carrier she targeted first, and precise fire cut through the ship's engines and left it adrift and powerless.

She did the same to the tiny destroyer and the larger cruiser, all three ships unprepared for the attack. Her senses ranged out to the oncoming forces and she readied herself, eagerly reaching out to them, ready to do battle against both... yet her mind cautioned her against that. *No,* she thought, *friends.*

She fought that though. These ships were crewed by the same pathetic creatures which had tried to take her over. They were the same race that had crewed the enemy ships she had neutralized. Worse, one of the groups had a *Kinak* destroyer with it, clearly that made them enemies, she knew. She *must* destroy them.

*No,* her mind said and it fought her instincts. Her ancient bloodlust fought back and for a long while, her mind and heart warred until finally she acquiesced and powered down her systems.

*Fine*, she thought sullenly, *you deal with them.*

Her mind had an almost smug note to its response, *with pleasure.*

***

Tommy King felt his jaw drop as the *Kraken* opened fire. From everything he knew, the ship shouldn't have been able to fire without being unlocked.

Yet as he saw *where* it had fired, he felt joy and hope surge inside him. *Lauren,* he thought, *it has to be.* He was close enough to see how precise those shots had been though... and he didn't think she was that good. The attacks had left Admiral Mannetti's ships adrift, without power and vulnerable without smashing them to splinters in the process.

Lauren could have operated the weapons, but she didn't have that kind of experience or control... for that matter, Tommy wasn't certain that *he* could have made those shots, not as ridiculously precise as they were.

"Captain," Kandergain said with narrowed eyes, "what is going on?"

"I have no idea," Tommy said. His puzzlement increased as the *Kraken* hit his ships with targeting sensors. What was she doing? For that matter, who did she have to operate the other systems, since he saw the ship whip up and around. He could manage three systems at most from the command chair... yet he was seeing four or five systems under control at once.

Yet a moment later the ship powered down and then, with the backdrop of Baron Lucius Giovanni wiping out Admiral Mannetti's allies, the *Kraken* lay still. "Hail her," Tommy said. As they drew closer, he could see trails of vented atmosphere and bodies from the *Kraken*, yet he saw no external damage. *Someone vented the crew to space,* he thought with a chill. It was a bad way to die, and he somehow doubted that many of the lax crew had their suits close at hand.

"No response," his sensors officer said a moment later. "Baron Giovanni has finished off Admiral Mannetti's allies, by the way, he thanks you for the assistance and says he'll be headed for orbit. He asks if you'll be sticking around and what your intentions are."

Tommy stared at the silent *Kraken.* "Tell him I intend to board the *Kraken,* Lauren Kelly might be alive aboard." Yet as the ship hung motionless, he wondered more and more if it had been some desperate last action taken by the woman he loved. *Please,* he thought, *you must live.*

He looked over at Kandergain, “You sticking around?”

She just nodded, “Though I'm not going to advertise my presence, I do need to speak with Lucius.” Something about the way that she didn’t meet Tommy’s gaze told him that it wasn’t a talk she looked forward to having.

Tommy just shrugged. “Fine,” he thought the two had some kind of relationship, but he didn't really care. The only relationship that he cared about just now was the one he might have just lost.

Then his command console came alive with an audio comm channel. “Mason,” Lauren's voice said, “I'm glad to see you came back with friends. Come aboard, but just you.”

Tommy frowned at that. There was something wrong with her voice, a note of hesitation that he didn't recognize... and something else. Yet before he could respond, the channel went dead.

“How the hell did she do that?” his communications officer demanded from his console.

“I guess you need to upgrade our defenses and figure out how to prevent it,” Tommy said with a grin. His communications officer scowled, but he got to work all the same. *I like my people,* Tommy thought, *they're the best at what they do and they know it... and they work hard to stay that way.*

Tommy arched an eyebrow at Kandergain, who gave him a nod, “I'll take care of my own transport, go see your girlfriend, Captain.”

“Thanks,” Tommy said. He looked around the bridge, “Order our people into parking orbits, lots of space between us and our allies, I don't want any mistakes. I'll have a Captain's Council in two hours.” His eyes went narrow, “Oh, and tell Captain Jenny of the *Ranger* that she's invited aboard for that as well.”

He took his own private shuttle over to the *Kraken.* As he docked, he saw that someone had repressurized the ship. As he stepped aboard, the ship seemed eerily still, more so, even than when he had boarded it the first time. Lauren was nowhere to be found at the airlock. Nor was she in the crew quarters as he came there.

Tommy walked the familiar corridors and his unease grew until he finally came to the bridge.

The lights on the bridge were turned down, leaving most of it in shadow, but Tommy's eyes made out the female figure seated at the command chair. “Lauren?”

“Hello, Mason,” she answered. Her voice was hesitant and he saw her lean back into the shadows of the chair a bit more.

"What's going on?" Tommy asked. "Are you okay? Are you injured?"

"I'm not *injured*," she answered, "not anymore, anyway." Her tone was equal parts resigned and bitter. "I thought... well, I thought this would be easier." She took a deep breath and then the bridge lights came on.

The sudden light dazzled his eyes and Tommy had to blink his eyes against the light. "Well," Lauren said with some bitter amusement, "At least I see I'm not the only one to change a bit... I take it you are once more Tommy King?"

Tommy's eyes finally adjusted and he hissed as he saw what had been done to her. Metallic wires wound over and through her skin. A tangle of wires crisscrossed her naked scalp and sank into her skull. A cluster of wires and metal tubing bored into her side and also at her shoulder. "Jesus," he said, "What did that bitch do to you?"

Lauren looked away, "She didn't do this... *I* did this. I opened the neural connection with the ship and it... *changed* me. She looked back and met Tommy's gaze, "I'm not entirely... human anymore." Her eyes welled up with tears. "Can you still love me?"

Tommy rushed forward and caught her in his arms. "How could I not?" He said. "You're still *you*, whatever this is, we can either fix it or adapt, alright?" Yet as he touched her, he could feel that the changes were more than skin deep. Wiring and tubing worked deep inside her body... Lauren had become a part of the *Kraken*. What could he do to help her?

"We'll get through this," Tommy said, even as Lauren began to cry.

***

## Chapter XIII

Halcyon Colony, Garris Major System
(Status Unknown)
May 5, 2404

Jessica Penwaithe looked at her husband expectantly as he stepped into the office. "Well?"

"Public opinion is very hard to measure," he said with a shrug. "There's a lot of support for you and I, quite a bit more for my brother and the War Dogs, and actually quite a bit for Baron Giovanni... though who knew our people would be so eager to embrace a warlord?"

Jessica grimaced at that, but not for the reason that Harris had. She had worked far more closely with the military than Harris in her time as the Councilor of Military Affairs. In that time, she had seen a variety of military figures who ranged from naked ambition like Admiral Mannnetti to those who were so anti-political that they couldn't seem to comment favorably on the weather.

Baron Lucius Giovanni was like no one she had ever dealt with. All politicians had a touch of ambition, her husband no exception. They wanted to control the levers of power, they wanted to feel in control. Quite without apparent effort, Baron Giovanni *was* in control. He spoke and people listened. He gave orders and they were carried out. He seemed to have a rudimentary grasp, at best, of the political process, yet his United Colonies had a remarkably stable government for all that it had lasted only a year.

*True,* she thought, *they had the coup attempt... but they squashed it and moved on.* In fact, if anything, the government and popular opinion of not just the Baron, but *all* their elected leaders were far higher than anything she would have expected... and all of that came back to the Baron.

She didn't know *how* he did what he did. It was almost as if he simply expected people to do their jobs and they had no other choice than to match those expectations... or fail. *That might be why he's seen so many betrayals,* she thought, *the expectation of competence might just be too much for some people.*

"I thought we offered to put joining the United Colonies to a vote?" Jessica asked.

"Well, yes," Harris said, "But we need to lay the proper groundwork for that. The right administration could do that. I think we could ride the popular swing right now into leveraging that."

Jessica didn't need to parse the bullshit to know what he meant by that. "You want to take over as President?"

"Interim President," he said. "Until we are stable enough to hold a proper election. We can put a referendum to vote at that point on the United Colonies, too."

Jessica leaned back against her desk, "That could take some time, months, maybe years."

Harris shrugged, "You saw the fleet they have, it's not like they need us right away..."

Jessica wasn't so certain. She felt like the Baron had sent this mission on a shoestring, certainly the planning had been... creative. She wondered just how badly the Dreyfus Coup had hurt his Fleet... and how much the twenty ships at Heinlein Base might help.

"I think hasty action on our part is the last thing that anyone needs," Harris said confidently. "I think we can both agree that a gradual shift would be best for all parties in the long run. I mean, really, they're talking about integrating *Tehran* into their United Colonies... perhaps we should allow public opinion some time to settle, right?"

"Perhaps," Jessica said.

***

"This is a terrible idea," Garret muttered to himself as he followed Abigail out of the taxi.

"What was that?" Abigail asked.

"Nothing," Garret said with a false smile.

"Well, cheer up, grumpy guts," Abigail said as she took his arm. "You're going to explain things to my father and he's going to be thrilled, and then we're going to go to his favorite bar, where he can tell all his friends about it."

"Right," Garret said. Despite his acquiescence, he felt far more nervous about the outcome of this particular discussion. Abigail's father, Daniel, had been far more of a father figure to him than his own father. The respect he felt for the old soldier was hard for him to even put into words... and the last thing he wanted to see was disappointment in the man's eyes when Garret told him the news.

They stepped up to the door and Garret knocked. *Okay,* he thought, *at least Abigail agreed to let me tell him my way, we'll go in, get coffee, make some small talk and then...*

The door opened and Daniel stood there.

"Guess what, dad?" Abigail said cheerfully, "Garret proposed and we're getting married!"

***

Much to Garret's relief, Daniel Gordon did not act with the instant homicidal rage that he had feared. Instead he had congratulated them both, invited them in for coffee, and then asked Garret if he wanted to join him at the local bar for drinks.

"What do you think about this United Colonies thing?" one of the other old-timers at the bar asked Garret.

Garret shrugged a bit, "Their military is good," he said. "Professional, none of the looting and thuggery I've seen under a lot of governments." Even in their coup, from what he understood, the military had conducted itself in a fashion that only threatened legitimate targets.

"What about their Baron Giovanni?"

"I can answer that," a man down the way said. He was stocky, with Asiatic features. "I've been with the Baron for a couple years now."

The entire bar went quiet then, they hadn't realized any of the Baron's people were there and Garret could see that many of them felt suddenly uncomfortable.

"He's alright," one of the older men said, "Tam, here brought my son Jack back from Brokenjaw Mountain, alive and safe when we thought that he would be dead. I invited him down here."

"Oh," the oldtimer said, "well, tell us about your Baron."

"He's a good man," Tam said. "Trusts you to do your job... trusts *everyone* to do their jobs. When he gives an order, you just do it. It's not that you don't have a choice, you do... but he just seems to know what has to happen."

Daniel nodded at that, "Got some charisma, then?"

Tam shrugged, "Smarts. He thinks four, five, six moves ahead. And he does everything he can to protect people and especially those who follow him. I was there when he defeated the Balor at the Third Battle of Faraday..."

***

"...so that's when Caela turned her gunboat and fired," Garret said. "Took the station out... but the gun shredded her. She could have lived... but she died so that the rest of us could live."

"Absent companions," a half dozen voices said in unison and the group at the bar raised their tankards in salute.

"You young fellows get all the glory," an old man said, "my time, there wasn't a good side. PCRA bastards were just terrorist thugs and those of us who served in Amalgamated Worlds were stuck cracking heads on stubborn miners. That's why I gave it all up and came out here." The old man teared up, "Wish I was young enough for a proper war like this one. Then I could be a proper hero."

Garret shrugged uncomfortably, "I'm just a mercenary." He looked over at Tam Chen, "The Gunny here is the hero."

"Hah," another man clapped Garret on the shoulder, "That is a funny one. You've saved our world, Garret Penwaithe, and that's not something anyone here is going to forget. Hell, the fact that you came back when we needed you puts lie to the whole idea that you're just a mercenary."

Garret shrugged, "I just did what needed to be done. Plenty of others did the same thing."

"But you're from here..." the man said, "And better, you're marrying Daniel's daughter Abigail... so we'll have a pair of heroes with ties back here."

Garret flushed, but he didn't argue anymore. He wasn't used to being told he was a hero. It wasn't that he didn't appreciate it, it just made him feel uncomfortable. He hadn't done it for praise or thanks, he had done what he did because it was what he had to do.

A moment later the door opened and Jessica stepped into the bar. She wrinkled her nose at the smell of cheap beer. "Garret," she said with a note of resignation. Abigail said I could find you here."

"Hey, no women in the bar!" one of the old timers said, "This is *sacred* ground!"

Jessica gave the old man a level look and he looked down and muttered into his beer. She cocked an eyebrow at Garret, "We need to talk. Alone."

"All right," Garret said. He gave the others, including Daniel and Tam Chen nods and then stepped out into the street. Jessica had a sleek black car waiting and she waited for Garret to get in before she joined him. "What's up?" He asked as the car pulled away.

"Your brother Harris is making some sort of power play," she said. "He's not going to outright violate our agreement with Baron Giovanni... but he *is* going to drag his feet as much as he can. I think his thought process is that he would rather be a big fish in a small pond."

Garret stared at her. He had been more than a little buzzed when he got in the vehicle. He had half expected some sort of angry tirade about taking advantage of her little sister or something like that... he had *not* expected high level politics.

He sobered up quickly as he thought about it. "We promised him we would support him... he's not going to like being lied to."

"Worse," she said, "half of our people are pretty excited about the idea of annexation and the other half are willing to at least give it a try. If Harris drags his feet, he's likely to burn up that positive momentum in just building his own political apparatus... and leave us with nothing but a lot of enemies as a result."

Garret frowned at that. It was basically what he'd said, in his mind, but she seemed to see a difference. "So, what do you want *me* to do about it?"

"Tell the Baron," she said. "And if I make a move, I'd appreciate your support."

Garret winced, "I'm not sure I want to get involved in politics between my brother and his wife." It was even worse for the fact that he was going to marry her sister.

She looked at him for a long moment with an unreadable expression. "Is that all that I am to you?"

Garret leaned back, this had taken a turn into *very* dangerous territory. There wasn't really a right answer to that, so finally he decided to be honest. "Whatever feelings I had for you, Jessica, you married my brother. That basically put an end to them. I *can't* afford to think of you as anything other than my brother's wife, the mother of my nephews, and maybe as a friend." He took a harsh breath as he thought back to how things had been before he left. "Maybe if I had stayed, things would be different." Certainly they had been intimate, he could even admit that he had thought he loved her... but she had made her choice and he had made his. He had left her behind when he abandoned his family and past... and she had apparently fallen for his brother and married him only months after Garret had left. He met her eyes, "And whatever my feelings may have been... I love your sister. You might think I'm taking advantage of her–"

"I think she's been planning this conquest for the past decade," Jessica said with a roll of her eyes. "But I *am* glad to hear that you're marrying her for the right reason." She sighed and her gaze went to the window as they drove through her old neighborhood. He wondered if she missed it, in her big house with Harris. "There's something else I need to tell you."

"Oh?" Garret asked. He felt entirely sober now and he felt worry roil in his guts. She had already told him that his brother was just as murky in his politics as their father, what did she hesitate to tell him, now?

"When I thought you were dead..." she trailed off. "When I thought Stavros had killed you for Mannetti, before I knew that Tommy King was pretending to be Stavros."

Garret nodded, "Which still gives me a headache." Popular support had trebled for the pirate. Stavros had been a scoundrel and hero... Tommy King was a notorious pirate who had made good and come back to save them in the bargain. *It doesn't hurt that he looted Presidente Salazar's worlds a few decades back and that he funneled some of that wealth back through here with crew he had hired.*

The damnable thing was that he honestly seemed to want to go legitimate... and Garret found it hard to wrap his head around what could make the man change so much. *A woman,* Garret thought, *it's got to be a woman, women mess everything up.*

"There are a lot of things I regret," Jessica said. She gave a bitter smile, "I'm a politician; my job is to make compromises that most people would regret. I regret not spending more time with my boys. I regret having ever accepted the plan to hire people like Admiral Mannetti to help liberate our world... but when I thought you were dead there was one thing that I realized I regretted more than anything else... one thing that if I had any power to change, I would."

She looked back and met his gaze, "And it turns out that I can change it." She let out a ragged breath, "I couldn't live with myself knowing that you didn't know the truth: Garth isn't Harris's son, he's yours."

***

"Sir," Ensign Miller said, his voice tight, "We're detecting three dreadnought-class vessels and over thirty cruisers, all of unknown design, along with another ten Liberator-class cruisers, several of *them* heavily modified."

Lucius had just finished talking with Garret Penwaithe, so it took him a long moment to set his mind straight, "What?"

"Sir," Forrest Perkins said, "We've a hail you need to answer... it is Admiral Collae."

"Hello, Baron," Admiral Collae said as Lucius answered the communication.

"Admiral," Lucius nodded with narrowed eyes, "I see that you've made good use of the Chxor dreadnoughts you captured at Faraday."

"Indeed," Admiral Collae said. "I've no doubt your forces are scanning them as we speak. Let me assure you, my purpose here is entirely benign."

"Oh?" Lucius asked.

"Indeed," Admiral Collae said. "Halcyon holds little of value to me, now. The alien ships are non-functional and Admiral Mannetti has been neutralized. Thus, the planet has no value."

"Not even their more contemporary ships?" Lucius asked as he read over the tactical analysis of Collae's ships. It was basic, but the dreadnoughts looked to have been stripped down to their hull and then modified from there.

"The base and ships are of some value... but I'm certain you'll be trying to get them as allies against the Chxor. Which is why I am here," Admiral Collae's harsh voice showed some good cheer at the surprise in Lucius's eyes. "As you can see, I did benefit from our last alliance... even *if* you planned to betray me from the beginning."

Lucius began to answer, "You planned to betray me from the beginning–"

"But I am not the one in possession of the Dreyfus Fleet," Admiral Dreyfus said genially. "Which shows who planned what, I think." He shrugged, "But I'm not here to argue semantics. I'm offering you my assistance in return for half of all the Chxor ships we capture."

"Half?" Lucius arched an eyebrow.

"I'm certain you have assembled a ragtag alliance, Baron,"

Admiral Collae said, “But I bring substantial firepower and unlike some others, I will find use for those ships other than as scrap, as you can see by my own fleet.”

Lucius made his decision in an instant. “Very well,” Lucius said. “I accept your offer. We depart in twenty-four hours.”

“Excellent,” Admiral Collae said. “I'll take up a parking orbit near Halcyon's moon so as to avoid any unnecessary conflict.” He cut the connection and Lucius sat back.

“Sir,” Captain Beeson said, “You can't be serious.”

Lucius looked up. “Why not?”

“He betrayed us before,” Ensign Perkins said. “Granted, I wasn't there, but I heard about it.”

“He is the enemy of the Chxor and the Balor,” Lucius said. “He brings a large number of ships... and he has every reason to go along with this.”

“What if he tries to seize Nova Roma?” Forrest asked.

“It's possible,” Lucius said. “The shipyards there would be a valuable prize for him. But the truth is... I would prefer Nova Roma even in the hands of a man like Admiral Collae over that of the Chxor.” He shrugged, “It is worth the risk.” He cocked an eyebrow at Daniel Beeson, “What can you tell me about his ships?”

“All three dreadnoughts have been converted into carriers,” Captain Beeson said. “I don't have any idea how many fighters he's crammed aboard those three ships, but... it's a significant number.”

Lucius nodded at that. “That's what I'd guessed looking at the emissions. I don't think anyone ever built a dedicated carrier *that* big before.” Admiral Mannetti's *Harpy* was the closest in size, and the Nova Roma built Helot-class carrier still massed less than a tenth of what a Chxor dreadnought did.

The Crusaders and the Patriot all had extensive fighter launch bays, but the huge ships also mounted massive weapons batteries. The Patriot mounted two full wings of fighters, even so... so Lucius wouldn't be surprised if Admiral Collae had managed something similar or even more aboard each of those huge dreadnoughts.

“The cruisers,” Captain Beeson said, “are a mix of custom hulls and retrofitted Chxor light cruisers. The custom hulls are built around the stripped out weapons from the dreadnoughts, each of them mounts one of the Chxor-built capital grade fusion beams with engines and power plants packed around it. They're more or less flying cannons."

Lucius winced as he looked over some of the data. The radiation shielding on some of those ships was *very* minimal. The crews would likely be exposed to severe, possibly lethal, radiation levels every time they fired. Structurally, as well, he could see that the ships had no 'proper' hull. Instead they had heavy structural supports for the weapons and then prefabricated living quarters tacked onto the outside and armor plating over that.

"The modified Chxor cruisers?"

"That's a mixed bag, sir," Ensign Perkins said. "I make out that a couple have had the firefly jamming systems and heavy defense screens removed... but we aren't certain what took their place. Certainly *something* that uses a lot of power, but we still aren't certain what, there's no external signs beyond the missing emitter arrays. A couple of the others, it looks like they've just tweaked the emitters, refitted the Chxor tech with more efficient human tech, maybe to make them more powerful, we're not sure."

"Okay," Lucius said. "I want you two to compare notes... and then go ahead and call him and see if he'll give you information on his ships capabilities. Then match what he tells you against your own estimates and see if he's telling the truth." He sighed. "In the meantime, I've got some calls to make here on Halcyon... and I think I've got to give a speech. I *hate* speeches."

Both men looked confused, "Sir?"

Lucius shook his head, "Political stuff. I should have brought Minister Bueller, she'd be better at this, I think." He took a deep breath, "Right, get to it."

***

Lucius took a deep breath as he stepped on the podium next to Harris and Jessica Penwaithe. The two politicians both had easy smiles on their faces, yet Lucius wondered at what went on behind their expressions.

Harris felt like a politician, through and through, which Lucius could tolerate. The information that Garret had passed along hadn't surprised Lucius... what had was how it had come to him. Jessica Penwaithe had struck him as something of an idealist. That worried him, in some ways. If he didn't quite match up to what she wanted, she could easily become an enemy... yet Lucius wasn't about to be directed by the woman's ideals. He already had enough responsibilities on his shoulders.

He would do what he knew was right... and if that happened to match up with what other people wanted, so much the better, he supposed.

The crowd was large for New Telluride, or so he had been told. It still made him feel odd to stand in front of a crowd of civilians. Addressing politicians was one thing, addressing normal people felt bizarre. He had spent so much time in uniform that he wasn't certain he understood normal people any more. Still, he had come to address the cameras as much as the people... and to send a message to Harris Penwaithe, his wife, and every other political animal on the planet.

"Thank you for having me here today," Lucius said. He looked around at the crowd and he could sense an element of uncertainty. He didn't speak like a politician and they weren't quite certain what to make of him.

"I understand that your world is in something of a tumultuous state after Admiral Mannetti, Spencer Penwaithe, and Admiral Collae have all seized and lost power," Lucius said. "I'm not here to talk about politics or anything like that," he said. "I will say that your political leaders offered the world for annexation... but I won't hold your people to that. I didn't come here to be a conqueror, I came because people needed help and I saw an opportunity to remove a petty tyrant who also happened to be my sworn enemy."

He felt a bit of pleasure in the knowledge that Admiral Mannetti was safely on her way to Faraday and where his people would transfer her to a military prison, but he returned his mind to the matter at hand. "If the day comes that your people wish to join the United Colonies, then we will welcome you as brothers and sisters, as full partners. But, again, that is not my purpose here."

"I came to help," he said. "And now I go to help others." He looked around at the crowd and saw mostly confusion. They didn't know what was being asked of them. Most of them, he would guess, were here to provide visual support for the politicians they supported. Some, he would wager, were even paid to attend.

"Nova Roma, my homeworld, has been under Chxor occupation for two years now. Billions of men, women, and children, under an alien yoke for years, under a regime which values human life even less than Admiral Mannetti valued yours," Lucius said. "The Chxor have over three thousand vessels, over seven hundred of them dreadnoughts, in the Nova Roma star system. I'm going there with all the ships I brought... and little else. The United Colonies Fleet is recovering from a coup attempt and our forces are not fit to fight in that battle... so I've left them behind. Captain Tommy King has graciously offered to accompany me, as have the War Dogs." Out of the corner of his eye, Lucius saw Harris Penwaithe start at that, clearly he had expected the mercenaries to remain to defend his homeworld.

He saw shock on the faces of the crowd as even the least aware of them did the math. They had thought his fleet a powerful force to reckon with, yet compared to what he had described, it was a tiny thing. "We will leave tonight, because we had already prepared for the attack, men and women and our other allies have gone in, expecting to be supported when they strike for freedom. I will not abandon them. I will stand by the people of Nova Roma as I have stood by the people of Halcyon... because it is the right thing to do."

He gave the crowd a last nod, "I know that Halcyon has a powerful fleet of their own, built with sweat and no little amount of blood. If your people would allow it, I ask that your fleet join with mine. Together I feel that we can defeat the Chxor and free another world." Lucius shrugged, "Yet if you decide not to support me, I will still go, because it is the right thing to do."

He gave them a final nod, "Thank you for your time." He turned away from the podium. Harris Penwaithe's face was frozen, a mask of a smile cast over an expression of panic. Jessica Penwaithe's expression was unreadable. He gave them both nods and then stepped down from the platform and his escort formed around him as he left the political rally behind.

He thought he heard them start to chant something as he climbed into his groundcar, but his mind had already focused on other things.

***

"That *bastard,*" Harris snarled. "He'll leave us defenseless! Admiral Collae is setting in *orbit*. He's no doubt told my father... who knows what *that* bastard will do. Probably have a fleet pounce on us as soon as the War Dogs break orbit."

"It's not that bad," Jessica said calmly. "We've got a couple of options, actually."

Her husband spun on her, "Not that bad? You do know what my father will do to both of us, don't you? In case you didn't see the autopsy report, President Monaghan didn't die gently or in his sleep." While she knew he meant the comment to shock her, if anything he had understated the case. What Spencer Penwaithe had done to the former President Monaghan did not make for pleasant reading.

"I know," Jessica said, "But we've a couple options... and I think Admiral Collae has other concerns on his mind. Garret told me he's going with the Baron to attack the Chxor at Nova Roma for a share of captured ships."

"Hah," Harris said, "That's a fool's errand. A few dozen ships against several *thousand*? Even I know how absurd it is, assuming that he's not talking up their numbers to make things seem more desperate." Harris frowned, "I need to talk to Garret, find out how set Commodore Pierce is on this suicide mission."

"Pretty determined," Jessica said with a neutral tone, "from what I understand, he *did* give the Baron his word that they would support his attack after he helped them here."

Harris waved a hand, "Commodore Pierce is a mercenary. I'll appeal to his bottom line. We've all of Admiral Mannetti's assets to draw on, now, after all."

"We do?" Jessica asked. This was the first she had heard of that.

"Well," Harris shrugged, "I had some of my people lock down her accounts first thing. We've got account numbers and access codes from ansible traffic and we've already transferred a lot of her funds into government accounts."

By government accounts, she could reasonably assume he meant *his* accounts. "That's good to know, but I'm not certain we can convince Commodore Pierce to stay even if we offer him quite a bit of money." She kept her tone as neutral as possible.

"Well, we have to, because our entire military wants to go off on Lucius's grand crusade," Harris said bitterly. "If they go, we'll be left in a worse position than we were before we kicked out Nova Corp. We'll have *nothing* to defend ourselves."

"What about the United Colonies offer?" Jessica said reasonably.

"You *can't* be serious," he said. "Baron Giovanni as much as said that the rest of his fleet is worthless." His dismissive tone suggested he hadn't even considered the option.

"Our enemies don't know that for certain," Jessica said. "For that matter, he said they wouldn't be fit for an attack, they can probably manage a defense quite handily."

Harris shrugged at that, yet he didn't argue. "What else, you said we had a couple of options." She could tell that the thought of joining with the United Colonies made him despair almost as much as the idea of falling into his father's hands.

"Our other option is to invite your father in," she said reasonably.

"What?!" Harris demanded. "Even forgetting what he would do to us... he would be just as bad for Halcyon as Admiral Mannetti in the long term. He cares *nothing* for our people, it is all about maneuvers and political face, nothing else matters to him."

"I know," she nodded. "Yet how would it look for him if we *invite* him back? If we formally ask for his protection, even after the United Colonies offered us theirs?"

Harris nodded, but his face was grim, "It would be quite the play for him. He might, almost, forgive us for backing President Monaghan from the beginning." He shook his head, "He would make damned certain that Halcyon was well defended, I'll admit. He'd look the fool if anyone hit it after that... but it wouldn't be what is best for our world."

"What *is* best for our world?" Jessica asked.

He looked at her in surprise, "Freedom for our people. Freedom to live our lives without fear... for our children to grow up with opportunities that we were denied." He sighed, "Of our two 'options' I'll admit that the United Colonies offers that, at least. Even if it may cost something more than I like in the terms of our say in things."

"What do you mean?" Jessica asked. She leaned forward, actually interested to finally hear his reasoning. She knew that he feared a loss of power in joining the United Colonies... but she wasn't certain whether that was entirely his own ambition or something a little less self-serving.

"They're expanding, soon," he said. "They'll have billions of citizens, while Halcyon's population isn't going to surge. We'll quickly find ourselves outnumbered, and by people with completely different morality and goals like those barbarians on Tehran, for instance."

"Okay," Jessica said. "So we get in there and get active, establish some political power and *ride* that wave. You know we're capable of that if we work together."

He did a double take and then he smiled at her, "You know, you're right. I've been approaching this from a defensive position, but if we were more aggressive..." he trailed off and his dark eyes sparkled for a moment, "You know, sometimes I forget how much I love you."

"Well," Jessica smiled a bit, "We can't have that, now can we?"

***

Lucius froze as he stepped into his quarters and found Kandergain awaited him.

"I was wondering if you would show up sooner or later," he said. He swallowed, "I've... lost our daughter." His voice broke as he said that and he felt tears well up in his eyes. How could she forgive him for this?

She stepped forward and embraced him and for just a moment, he felt as if everything *would* be alright. "I know," she said. "And I know she is alive and well, because I also know who took her."

"Who?" Lucius demanded.

"I can't tell you," Kandergain said and stepped back, "because *you* can't act on the information."

Lucius frowned at that. He thought through the possibilities. That meant either it was someone who was protected or it was someone he *couldn't* reach. The former included diplomats and heads of state, men and women who had plenty of reasons to organize a kidnapping like this. The latter included only a handful, the Shadow Lords and those who worked for them. "Tell me."

"I won't," Kandergain said. "Because you can't do anything about it. Trust me."

Lucius nodded, but it left a bitter taste in his mouth. "Fine." He grimaced, "Did you know about Admiral Dreyfus and his conspiracy?" He was half afraid that she would admit that she had known all along... and that the deaths of the men and women under his command could have been avoided.

She shook her head, "I've heard a bit of the news over the past week, but I still don't even know what happened. I know they're calling it the Dreyfus Coup, but your news services still don't have much distribution outside of Faraday."

Lucius grimaced at that. He was certain that most other news services would merely note that some local unrest had made the system dangerous. "Admiral Dreyfus apparently has been playing a long game. He told me that his wife was a telepath..." he saw her nod at that, "and that she showed him some of John Mira's visions. He told me that in nine out of ten of those visions we lose."

Kandergain winced at that. "So, what, he thought he could do better?"

"I'm not sure it was something as coherent as that," Lucius said sadly. "He apparently orchestrated his wife's murder and established a shadow organization within the Fleet. His goal was to oust me, but I think part of what he wanted was simply to prevent any kind of offense, to preserve the Fleet and to hole up at Faraday."

She shook her head, "I had no idea, Lucius. I've said it before, I try to avoid reading people's thoughts unless it is necessary. Even then, if someone is focused enough, they can avoid giving away their secrets unless I really dig into their minds and most people notice that. I had no reason to suspect him."

Lucius just nodded at that. "Well, we're still dismantling parts of his organization back at Faraday and I'm not entirely certain that we'll *ever* identify all the members. He made a move to seize power right after they kidnapped Kaylee. At this point, we've lost something over three thousand personnel, with the worst losses in our officers and senior enlisted."

"I'm so sorry, Lucius," Kandergain said. She stepped forward and embraced him again and he put his arms around her. It felt awkward and he realized that some part of him hadn't really expected to see her again.

"We're out of practice," Kandergain said with a snort.

"You left rather suddenly, as I remember," Lucius responded.

He felt her stiffen at that. "I did." She sighed, "I'm sorry for that too... but it seems like I've always something to do."

He understood, yet it felt too hard to even say those words just now. "You have an adopted daughter, now," he said instead. "Patricia Stark, she's the daughter of Kaylee's nanny… who died defending our daughter."

Kandergain's eyes filled, "I…" she shook her head, "I'm certain you'll love her like our own daughter. For that matter, I am grateful for her mother for being there when I could not." They stood in silence for a long moment as they both tried to find the way to bridge the emotional gap between them.

"What *are* you going to do about our daughter?" Lucius murmured finally into her shoulder.

"I've got a team that I put on it," she said. "That was what I've been working on the past few months. I needed to contact them and they were… a bit hard to find. Reginald knows them, they're the best. If anyone can, they will bring her back, Lucius, I promise."

Lucius didn't respond, he just clung to her for a long while. He felt used up on words and emotionally exhausted. For now, it was just enough that he had Kandergain in his arms again... and that she told him it would be alright.

***

## Chapter XIV

Nova Roma System
Chxor Empire
May 17, 2404

"I want your analysis of this, Fleet Commander Kral," High Commander Chxarals said.

Kral nodded, even as he schooled his expression. He had spent so much time among the humans that emotional expressions had become almost second nature.

A single slip now, though, would not only result in his death, but the failure of the entire plan.

"I find it a little too convenient," Kral said as he pointed at the drugged human, "that he knows the time and location of their Emperor's arrival." The human, Jacobo, was one of the two that they had managed to capture alive. The other one, Marco, had already been executed. From what Kral had seen of both their files, quick deaths were more than warranted.

"This is easily explained by the fact that he is one of their logistics caste," High Commander Chxarals said. "He would have to know such information, if only in a general fashion, in order to plan the movement of their resources."

"If this is true, then the humans have violated the terms of your ultimatum, High Commander," Kral said. He measured the words carefully, his tone as emotionless as possible.

"True," Chxarals said. "And I am tempted to enact retribution upon the humans as I threatened... yet our Empire is low on resources and in need of the system's shipyards to repair and refit our ships. I would not hesitate to do so, otherwise. Also, I find the information that Emperor Romulus is the one behind this rather than the humans of the United Colonies. This suggests a rift in their alliance, if we can exploit that, then we might divide our enemies to better destroy them."

Kral felt no surprise to hear Chxarals admit that he planned to destroy the humans of the United Colonies. The fact that his ultimatum had offered them peace did not matter, promises were only important if they could be enforced. Like most Chxor, a lie was just as good as a truth, so long as one wasn't caught by a superior in the process.

*And who,* Kral thought, *would Chxarals worry about being caught by?*

"Of course," Kral said. "How would you like me to proceed?" He didn't look at the comatose prisoner. He had already seen the execution order signed by Chxarals.

"As my senior Fleet Commander, I'm appointing you to command the orbital defense of Nova Roma," High Commander Chxarals said. "I will appoint Fleet Commander Chxum to similarly command the defense of Nova Umbria. I will take the remainder of our forces and coordinate the attack on the human base in this system." While Fleet Commander Chxum wasn't one of Kral's people, he had managed to transfer several squadrons to his forces at Nova Umbria. They would possibly be enough to seize orbit if they struck with surprise.

Kral was surprised that things had worked out so beneficially, but he didn't allow any pleasure to touch his face or voice. It wouldn't do to ruin things, after all. "High Commander, are you certain that you should engage yourself in what should be a relatively minor engagement? What if the humans of the United Colonies seek to take advantage of your absence?"

High Commander Chxarals dismissed that with a negative gesture, "No, it would be illogical for the humans to coordinate such an attack. While it would make sense for them to sacrifice a smaller force to annihilation, such as Emperor Romulus, in order to seize a vital objective, they have not shown that level of intelligence or coordination thus far. Indeed, if they *do* engage your forces here, I fully expect you to follow through on your orders and eradicate all life on Nova Roma, just I expect as Fleet Commander Chxum should do the same at Nova Umbria."

"Yes, High Commander," Kral said. "What else do you require from me?"

"The departure of a significant portion of our forces here might cause some unrest in the rebellious elements of the humans. I want them rounded up prior to our departure. You may utilize orbital resources to store them prior to departure to labor mines and camps elsewhere in the Empire."

"Of course, High Commander," Kral said. He felt a bit of dismay at the thought of the innocent humans he would have to round up, probably under High Commander Chxarals' attention. Worse, it would be hard to safeguard them once the attacks on the orbital defenses got underway, he knew. Combined with the fact that he had to arrange to transport the rebels clandestinely into position to conduct their attacks...

*Or perhaps I can accomplish two tasks with one effort,* he thought. If he moved the rebels as "prisoners" into position to conduct their attacks and positioned weapons to supply them, then he wouldn't need to worry about innocent civilians at all... so long as the attack went off with proper timing.

There was some risk, he knew, if labor transports arrived before the scheduled attacks... but Kral knew just how limited cargo hulls had become in the Chxor Empire. It was not inconceivable that it would be weeks or months before transports would be available. It was a risk, but Kral felt it was worth it... and he had no doubt that most of the rebel leaders would agree.

"Yes, High Commander," Kral said, "I will engage my full efforts to removal of the rebel population."

***

Theta Station, Nova Roma System
(Contested)
May 20, 2404

"I'm glad you've finally arrived," Emperor Romulus IV said genially as Lucius and the others stepped into the narrow conference room.

"Glad to be here," Lucius said in return. He hadn't been quite certain what to expect of Theta Station. On the one hand, Emperor Romulus II and his successor had both been known to spare no expense for projects they found important. The massive Imperial Fleet and the ornate Imperial Palace had been two examples of where they had spent extravagantly and obtained incredible results, but there were other examples of millions of Solari spent on projects designed only to honor the family's hubris or to fill the coffers of one of the noble houses.

At the same time, Theta Station had been built in secret, a bolt-hole for the Imperial Family to retreat with their loyal supporters in case of rebellion or coup. The fact that it hadn't been brought up as one of Emperor Romulus IV's assets suggested not only that he hadn't trusted Lucius enough to share it, but also that the station might not be all that game-changing.

And from what Lucius had seen so far, the station fit both expectations. On the one hand, it was a well-kept secret. The base had clearly been put together in stages, some sections were probably taken from decommissioned stations and ships while others had been built from prefabricated installations. It was rugged and solid, designed to remain ready despite years or decades of inattention.

On the other, it was packed with weapons and equipment that showed a mix of furious effort and complete lack of forethought. One entire cargo pod held laser target designators for infantry... which would be of little or no use without aerial or orbital support and the sensors to use the laser targeters... which weren't present on the station. Another example were thousands of stockpiled fission warheads... whose high explosive charges had been left installed and had degraded to the point of being hazardous to handle and useless for triggering the nuclear warhead.

The stockpiles of small arms, light and medium weapons, on the other hand, were perfectly functional and came with sufficient supplies of ammunition that they had fully equipped the rebel forces on both Nova Roma and Nova Umbria.

Emperor Romulus IV looked around the table and he gave a confident smile. He looked better than he had in months, Lucius realized. Coming home had given him hope at resolving the occupation of his homeworld and had let him feel as if he had finally accomplished something.

"We've noticed an increase in message traffic this morning as well as movements of Chxor vessels and a consolidation of Chxor ground forces," Emperor Romulus IV said. "I've also seen a message from Fleet Commander Kral, who says that High Commander Chxarals intends to take personal command of the attack here."

Lucius smiled a bit at that. It was what they had hoped for, since Chxarals seemed to possess just enough arrogance that he would trust his own judgment over the initial reports from his people. While their original plan called for the Dreyfus Fleet to oppose the Chxor, their current plan should work in their favor.

Lucius looked around the table and his gaze settled on each of the commanders in turn. Admiral Collae looked the most out of place in his gray-green Colonial Republic uniform. He looked tense, as well, though some of that must come from the fact that the others at the table didn't trust him. Still, his stern, stone-like face showed neither fear nor worry.

Tommy King sat back at his ease, a slight smirk on his face. Lucius wondered if that was humor at the fact that the notorious pirate had somehow been rehabilitated or just at the the fact that they trusted him. Lucius knew that his people were somewhat less eager to be here, but Tommy seemed to have them in hand.

Commodore Pierce looked somewhat less sanguine, but the mercenary commander was here with all of his military strength. While Lucius had been impressed by the man and his mercenaries so far, he felt uneasy at the age of his dreadnoughts and the Hammers he had to support them. Still, Commodore Pierce's efforts in the combined training they had conducted on their trip through shadow space had convinced Lucius that his people were well trained and capable. He also commanded the military ships sent by Halcyon, an interesting decision made by Harris Penwaithe before their departure. *I wonder that he didn't ask his brother Garret to command them,* Lucius thought, *or if he worries that his brother might come back too much the hero.*

That left Lord Admiral Valens Balventia and as Lucius's gaze settled on him, the other man gave him a smile. Lucius returned the smile, though he felt a bit of wonder at the fact that they had ended their rivalry so completely. Part of it was that they were here to free their homeworld, Lucius knew, but part of that came from the fact that there were no more secrets between them. The baggage from their respective families was no longer a burden to them... there was only the defeat of the Chxor.

"Right, then," Lucius said with a respectful nod at Emperor Romulus IV. "As it stands, we have a rather smaller force than we originally projected for this." He sighed, "Our capital ship strength is far, far lower than we had projected, but that is compensated by our overall fighter strength being far higher overall. Given the intelligence from Kral as well as observation from Emperor Romulus's forces, I'd estimate that we have between twenty-four and forty-eight hours before High Commander Chxarals launches his attack."

Silence met that statement. It was one thing to approach a battle with seven hundred dreadnoughts in consideration of how to engage and destroy them... it was quite another to hear that thirty seven hundred enemy warships were on their way sometime in the next two days.

"It seems we are committed, then," Admiral Collae said, his gruff voice hard. "I've questions, then, about the initial deployment we discussed for my forces."

Lucius cocked an eyebrow at that. They had positioned his three converted 5-class dreadnoughts to the flank, along with his entire investment of cruisers. Lucius had felt that the mobility of the cruisers would allow him to turn the Chxor flank, while the three wings of Patriot-class fighters based on the converted dreadnoughts would give him the firepower to savage the enemy dreadnoughts once he broke through the enemy's cruiser screen.

"I feel that my fighters would be of greater use in the initial attack," Admiral Collae said, "rather than retained for the flank attack."

"We don't want to let the Chxor know how much we have in position until they are fully committed," Admiral Balventia said.

"Admittedly," Admiral Collae said, "However, the Chxor tend to overlook fighters in regards to combat strength. I think, particularly if the opening salvo of my missiles are lighter, that might allow us to utilize Commodore Pierce's Hammers to greater effect later in the battle, when the enemy dreadnoughts are more vulnerable.

"True," Lucius nodded, "but if your fighters are going to be in position for that, your carriers will be more vulnerable."

"They're big ships, with extensive defense screens and heavy armor," Admiral Collae said. "Also, I've left some of the original energy armament in place, so I'm prepared to allow the ships to be in the line of fire. Especially if that allows them to conduct combat reloading for their fighter squadrons to allow a faster engagement of the enemy."

"Very well," Lucius said, "we'll shift appropriately. Commodore Pierce, your Hammer wing can go on the left flank." He updated the layout on his own datapad and then looked at Emperor Romulus IV. "My Lord, do you have anything to say?"

The Nova Roma Emperor stood. The young man took a moment to compose himself, "Thank you, all of you, for coming. This battle will determine the fates of billions of people... and I know all of our lives are on the line. We may not win," he let out a ragged breath as he said that, “worse, we may fail the people who are counting on us... but I don't think that will happen.”

“When the time comes,” Emperor Romulus IV said, “I think that we will face the enemy with courage and honor.... and that we will destroy them.”

Lucius smiled along with the others... but he also felt more than a few pangs of worry. This battle would decide the fate of billions. This wasn't a frontier world or an empty system, this was Nova Roma, the jewel of human space. This was his home, his people... and Lucius just hoped that he could live up to the reputation that his people had given him.

His mind went to Admiral Dreyfus's last words. His talk about the defeats that had so terrified him and his anger at Lucius for failing. Would this be one of those defeats? Was that why he had so opposed Lucius in recapturing the system?

*No,* Lucius thought, *I will not be haunted by the ghosts of battles I haven't even fought yet... I am the master of my future.*

***

“Your girlfriend is cheating on you,” Heller growled at Garret.

“I'm his fiancé,” Abigail said and stuck out her tongue at the other woman, “and I am *not* cheating.”

Heller growled something in her native tongue that Garret didn’t quite catch. It was partly in good humor he knew... but only part. That even Heller was effected by the tension that pervaded the entire fleet worried Garret. The normally unflappable mercenary had been short-tempered and even more sarcastic than usual.

Garret actually regretted holding the poker game. Most of those who had shown up had grown increasingly irritable as the game went on. As a case in point, Jude Derstile threw down his hand and stared at Garret. “Sir, what are we doing here?”

Garret stared at him with shock. “We're playing cards.”

“I don't mean here,” Jude pointed at the makeshift card table. He waved his hand around as if to point to the entire star system, “I mean *here.* What are we doing at Nova Roma? How did this go from an in and out mission, to privateering, to whatever that last battle was, to somehow helping to reinstate the blasted Nova Roma *Emperor*? I've been with this company for years, and while we've toppled a few tyrants, we've *never* helped put one back in power.”

Garret grimaced. In truth, he didn't much disagree. The Emperors of Nova Roma, besides their peculiarity of assuming the name of their predecessors, had become infamous for their ambition. Emperor Romulus II had set out to conquer threats, but his son had expanded that to any system nearby that he could take. Under his reign, Imperial Security had developed a fearful reputation, especially as his empire had gone into decline.

Emperor Romulus IV had been the last Emperor's younger son, and while he seemed cut from different cloth, Garret hadn't had a chance to take his measure. In truth, in many ways it didn't *matter* if he was different from his father and grandfather. No one would see him as being different until he proved himself and few people wanted to give him that opportunity.

"We are here," Garret said, "because Commodore Pierce gave his word. We're here to free people from Chxor occupation... and we're here to get paid."

"Pay is good," Heller said, "but I don't see much money in getting killed for some spoiled rich boy."

"That's why I don't pay you to think, Heller," Commodore Pierce said genially from the hatch.

Garret stood up quickly, "Sir, I didn't know you'd come aboard." They were holding the game in one of the wing's carrier craft, in a tiny storeroom, out of the way and someplace where Garret could overlook rank, even in a unit as loose about rank as the War Dogs. Even so, the ship's captain should have announced the Commodore's arrival, if only to give everyone fair notice.

"I didn't announce my arrival so I could ease into conversations like this one," Commodore Pierce said, as if he had read their minds. Then again, it wasn't a hard leap to make, Garret knew. "What we are doing here is what Garret said: we're getting paid and we're sticking by the promises I made back at Faraday to Baron Giovanni. We aren't here to reinstate the Nova Roma Emperor. We aren't here to throw our lives away against the Chxor."

He shrugged, "It's a risky plan... but it is also one with a great deal of potential." He smiled then, "Heller, how much do you think one of those Chxor dreadnoughts would be worth at Tanis?"

Heller frowned and she pulled out her earbuds. She waggled her fingers in the air for a moment as she did sums, "I'd guess a few hundred million Tanis Doubloons, minimum."

"The last time Baron Giovanni fought the Chxor, he captured thirty of those ships, plus another two hundred of their cruisers... the cruisers mostly intact. I've worked out a contract with him where we split damaged ships fifty-fifty between Admiral Collae and the War Dogs... and *we* have preference on selection for the ones we want as well as salvage rights to the wreckage too damaged to be repaired."

Heller pulled a sucker out of her pocket, unwrapped it, and then popped it in her mouth. "That's... a lot of money, if we win."

"That's why I pay you Heller, to make sure we win," Commodore Pierce said. He glanced over Abigail's shoulder and spoke, "*Four* aces, really? Garret, I think your girlfriend is cheating."

***

Demetrius felt a wave of dread as the Chxor guard pushed him roughly into the back of the van. His entire command team was already there. All across Nova Roma, Chxor were arresting the entire rebel network... and if this was some kind of grand betrayal by Kral, then his people were done.

Not one of his people spoke as the van started up and drove away. Some of them stared ahead, caught up in their own fears and worries, while others looked down, their thoughts focused on what they planned to do.

*If this is not a betrayal,* Demetrius thought, *then I will finally have the opportunity to strike.* Some part of him marveled that the opportunity came as a consequence of the Nova Roma Emperor. *No,* Demetrius thought, *he might be the direction, but it is Baron Giovanni who is truly responsible.* That thought warmed him. Surely if the Baron was behind this, then it would work.

The van rolled to a stop and the Chxor guards pulled them out. They were at the spaceport, Demetrius saw, which was a good sign. This part, though, would be the most dangerous, for the Chxor guards here were not Kral's people.

Here and there he saw these Chxor apply whips and prods to move his people faster or simply from cruelty. Unlike most of his people, Demetrius could read the Chxor language and he memorized the names of the Chxor who abused his people. If they survived, he would find them and make certain to they received as good as they gave.

Finally, however, his group was herded aboard a shuttle with the other teams. Demetrius smiled in the dim lighting of the cargo hold as his people linked up, right on time, all thanks to Chxor efficiency. *If the weapons are in place, and Kral's people release us on schedule, then we will finally have a chance to strike back,* Demetrius thought.

He didn't ask for a certain victory. That, he knew, was impossible to guarantee. The plan was full of risks, with thousands of tiny details that he and Kral had spent countless hours working over. The planetary defense centers were the lynchpin of the entire plan. Some were in orbit, some were on the ground, and both types had to be seized, since each of those installations housed weapons batteries that could level cities or destroy the orbital docks and habitats.

Kral felt certain that his people could secure the handful of ships that he didn't already control here at Nova Roma... but Nova Umbria was another matter entirely. They had not been able to infiltrate the ships of Fleet Commander Chxum's forces as well as Demetrius would like. They could be certain of a mutiny aboard many of those ships, with human conscripts backed by sympathetic Chxor officers, but they were far from being certain they could secure *any* of the ships.

Also, the planetary defense centers of Nova Umbria would be harder battles. Unlike Nova Roma, they hadn't been able to preposition his teams there. Most of Nova Umbria's facilities were planet-based, which meant that his teams there could at least move into position on foot. But the three heaviest facilities were orbital... which meant they had to utilize other options.

Demetrius's greatest fear was that a single Chxor officer might have the opportunity to deploy some of the Pacifix Seven nerve gas at one of the population centers or orbital habitats. The bastards had already used it as a 'demonstration' at Perihelion Station. The once thriving trade station had become a lifeless hulk in only minutes.

Several of the other stations had emplaced demolition charges or even nuclear weapons, but Kral had given his people the details on the locations and how to go about disarming them. The problem was that the Pacifix gas canisters were light and easy to use, and completely harmless to the Chxor who might employ them. Given even a few minutes, a Chxor could kill millions if he opened one in the right place on a station, or tens of millions if those canisters were hooked up to a proper dispersal system on one of the Chxor's shuttles.

In his heart, Demetrius knew that his people couldn't stop *all* of the Chxor diehards from trying to carry out High Commander Chxarals' orders to exterminate the populace if the system were about to fall. He knew that his people would do everything they could to prevent needless deaths... and he hoped it would be enough to salve his conscience when the full consequences of the rebellion came to light.

As the shuttle docked with Bellorum Station, Demetrius took a deep breath. *Twelve hours,* he thought, *this will all be settled in just twelve more hours.*

***

"My forces will arrive at the target in ten hours," High Commander Chxarals said. "Fleet Commander Fhxud will command force two and Fleet Commander Thxanal will command force three, while I will retain command of force one, with Fleet Commander Fxark and Jxush controlling elements of it."

Kral watched with interest as the High Commander laid out his battle plan. The three force arrangement was a good balance between the standard phalanx formation and a more mobile force like that of Nova Roma. High Commander Chxarals' Force One would have some three hundred of the 5-class dreadnoughts with over eighteen hundred of the 10-class cruisers to screen them. Kral didn't miss how Chxarals had arranged his formation to drive through the larger openings in the Periclium Debris Cloud, with Force One utilizing the largest of the assault corridors.

Force Two and Three were identical, with two hundred dreadnoughts and six hundred cruisers each. Although their screens were doctrinally lighter than they should be, their formations were designed to operate with ships in close proximity, which meant the dreadnoughts would need fewer cruisers in their screen. The 10-class cruisers with their massively oversized defense screens would form a protective barrier that would allow the dreadnoughts to freely engage the enemy... especially since both flanking forces were expected to face lighter ships.

The dense debris cloud would be an issue for all of the ships, though. High Commander Chxarals addressed that even as Kral noticed, "In order to mitigate damage from debris and expended munitions as well as emplaced mines, all three forces will drop to no more than one thousand *trel* per *juhn* relative velocity to the debris field. Each force will proceed with active radar and will engage and destroy any debris of dangerous size as well as any possible munitions in order to clear their assault corridors."

"High Commander," Fleet Commander Thxanal asked, "will that not give the humans time to escape?" It was a valid question, though Kral thought a better question was whether that made them more vulnerable to enemy attack.

"I believe that they will hesitate to abandon their facility," High Commander Chxarals said. "In case of an enemy counterattack, each force will act as a mobile reserve for the other forces. In case of attack by the enemy on Force Three, Force One will move to assault the enemy flank and destroy them, while Force Two will move up to destroy the enemy base. In case of attack on Two, One will move to support while Three will assault the base."

Kral nodded at that, it was a well thought out plan... given the force expectations that Chxarals operated under. Kral had not been able to receive an update from Baron Giovanni, but he thought it likely that the Baron would be able to engage all three forces at once with the combined firepower of the Dreyfus Fleet and the Nova Roma Imperial Fleet. In that case, it would be quite possible for him to overwhelm all three forces individually before they could coordinate a counterattack.

"What about the human mining station at Sector Trel?" Kral asked dutifully.

"The human prisoner confirmed that the station is part of the smuggling apparatus," High Commander Chxarals said. "Therefore, it will be destroyed. However, until we have cleared out the human infestation in the debris could, we will leave the mining station intact. It will offer us a location to stage our damaged ships and conduct repairs. After we have completed the destruction of the human forces, we will destroy the mining station and execute its crews for treason against the Chxor Empire."

"Understood," Fleet Commander Fhxud said. As the commander of Force Two, his forces would pass the closest to the mining station and he was the one who would probably have the best opportunity to destroy it. The hairless Fhxud appeared to be one of the genetically engineered castes, which was unusual in senior military ranks. Even so, in personality, he seemed the typical Chxor officer, with neither enthusiasm nor displeasure at the chance to kill more humans.

Kral had felt some temptation to feel out some of the other senior officers, yet he had restrained that urge. While he was certain he could do so without revealing his own motivations, he could not risk the system's survival upon that. While turning another of Chxarals' senior officers would be highly beneficial, if Kral were caught, the consequences would be far more drastic. Besides, Chxarals' fleet was unique in that its crews were entirely made up of Chxor. Not one human or other alien had been drafted aboard those ships. The crews were fanatically loyal to the Benevolence Council, many of them designed from birth to fight and die for the Chxor Empire.

"Fleet Commander Chxum will retain command of the forces at New Umbria while Fleet Commander Kral will command Nova Roma's forces in my absence." High Commander Chxarals looked around at his officers, "I want a full readiness report on every ship in your forces as well as a draft of your orders and contingency orders before we depart." High Commander Chxarals paused a moment, "For the glory of the Chxor."

"For the glory of the Chxor," they echoed. *Though that doesn't mean what you think it means,* Kral thought with no small amount of humor. Soon his people would be able to reach their true potential... thanks to Kral's human allies. *My one regret,* he thought, *is that High Commander Chxarals won't ever understand the humor in that.*

***

Lucius paused outside the engine room and gave a sigh as he heard Rory's voice.

"No, no, no," Rory said, "are you insane? You might as well put a gun to my head and shoot me. Go ahead, do it!"

Feliks replied in a long-suffering tone, "I was only trying to calibrate the power plant output, based upon our earlier model..."

"That is our *old* model for a reason, Feliks," Rory said. "We have the *new* engine output model for a reason... because it far more closely maps the Balor power plant energy output. If you want to kill us all because of a random power spike, by all means, use the old model... otherwise, why don't you put our hard work to use."

"The new model is less accurate," Feliks said.

"Excuse me," Lucius spoke as he stepped into the engine room.

Like everything on the Balor ship, the room had some human wiring tacked onto the bulkheads to provide power for lighting. The tangle of alien technology around the massive, angular reactor was broken up by a set of human engineering consoles, spliced into the Balor controls and crammed in the little bit of free space.

"How can you say the new model is less accurate?" Rory demanded, completely ignoring Lucius's presence. "I put seven hours into those calculations."

"You didn't consider the full metrics of the polarity shift between the two nodes!" Feliks waved his hands in the air.

"I would have if you had told me about them!" Rory shouted right back.

Lucius just sighed and turned away.

"How could I tell you about them when you never, ever listen to anything I have to say..."

*Forward weapons,* Lucius thought, *the forward weapons control is the furthest point away from these two that I can get right now.*

***

Tommy waited patiently while Lauren adjusted the lighting downward. He understood why she felt self-conscious about her appearance. Most human worlds looked on cybernetics with some discomfort. Prosthetic limbs had long been a solution for large injuries, but on most worlds, biological replacement had become the preference, either with cloned or donor parts.

Those who did violate the taboos generally tried to use the most unobtrusive cybernetics. Neuro implant computers, subdermal weapons, or even musculo-skeletal reinforcement. Most commonly the people who did those kinds of 'upgrades' were on the shadier side of the law... which only reinforced the distaste with which most people viewed cybernetics.

A small, militant part of society still seemed to feel that mechanical upgrades were the future of humanity... but they tended to lose most other people when they started lopping perfectly good parts of themselves in order to attach bizarre improvements.

Tommy hadn't thought that Lauren had a preference one way or the other... but she hadn't had much say in what happened to her. Her hair had started to regrow and cover the neural connections over her scalp. The wiring in her shoulder and side could both be covered by clothing. Yet he knew that only hid her changes from others, not from herself.

Tommy could see her wince as she shifted and the connections inside her body pulled against her flesh. Lucius's doctors and even Kandergain had looked her over and all of them had marveled that she had survived the entire process. From what Tommy understood, the *Kraken*'s connections had wound their way deep inside her body and connected to a number of her internal organs and nerve clusters.

"How are you doing?" Tommy asked.

She gave him a level look, "Oh, I'm just great, you?"

Tommy sighed, "You know, I said I'm sorry already."

"I don't want pity, I don't want apologies," Lauren growled. She gave a sigh, "I want to be... *normal.*" She looked down at her hands and he could see her eyes trace the wires that ran under her skin to the very tips of her fingers. "I've had access to a lot of the ship's systems and files... Mason, this isn't how it was supposed to work, not for its original crew, anyway."

"What?" Tommy asked. Despite his insistence that Mason McGann was dead, she continued to call him by that name. It was almost as if she didn't see the changes in him. *Or maybe she just doesn't want to see those changes,* he thought.

"The neural link is supposed to be superficial, a single set of wires and connections, not whatever *this* is," she waved a hand at herself. "I've talked with the ship, too, and it doesn't seem... well, it doesn't seem sane."

Tommy quirked a smile at her, "Are any of us, really?"

"I'm serious, Mason," Lauren said. "It can barely recognize the concept of friend or ally. It approaches every situation as hostile and just while we've been sitting here I've had to prevent it from engaging the Baron's forces three times."

Tommy's eyebrows shot up at that. "It's that twitchy?"

"Twitchy implies that it wouldn't follow through," Lauren said. "And during that battle with Admiral Mannetti... well, let's just say that it was *everything* I could do once it got moving to prevent it from going after everyone else. This ship is alive, Mason, and it has a will of its own... but that will is *only* to fight."

Tommy gave her a gentler smile, "Sounds like someone I know, then."

Lauren shook her head and tears welled up in her eyes, "That's so true that it hurts."

Mason had stood and moved to embrace her even before she finished speaking. He felt her go stiff in his arms and he could feel the wires and conduits inside her flesh as he held her. She relaxed after a long moment and spoke, her voice filled with despair. "Look at me, Mason. I'm a freak. Tied into a mad warship, there's nothing for me, now, nothing but war. I can never have anything else, a life, a family... I can't even *live* away from this damned ship."

"You don't know that," Mason said.

She shook her head, "The Baron's engineers confirmed it. Most of this... stuff, is biomechanical, it is *living* technology, tied into the ship. Without the ship, it would cease to function and with how closely tied it is to all of me..." She trailed off and wiped at the tears on her cheeks. "Damn me, Mason, I wish I had died at that base."

"I'm sorry," Tommy said. "But we'll get through this. It will be okay, I promise." What he feared was that she would seek to kill herself in the coming battle... but he knew better than to say anything. She was perfectly capable of lying to his face, he knew, and equally capable of finding some way to make certain he couldn't stop her. If he remained close by, he could at least try to intercede when she made the attempt.

*She's miserable,* Tommy thought, *but she doesn't see that there are other options.* The doctors had only had a few weeks to run their tests, there were scientists who would know better how to remove such implants, if that was what she wanted. For that matter, if it became a matter of money... well, money was something that Captain Tommy King had in plenty.

He would do whatever he must in order to make her happy, even if she had to be miserable for a little while in the process.

***

"This is it," Lucius said as he watched the Chxor form up on their approach. His forces had already launched stealth probes and they monitored the Chxor progress. High Commander Chxarals had his sensors to full active mode as they swept the space around them, and Lucius felt that the enemy commander would continue that as he came closer to the Periclum Debris Cloud.

The Chxor had formed into three forces, the largest in the center, and their deployment was clearly designed to penetrate the outer edges of the debris cloud at the thinnest areas. The Nova Roma Imperial Fleet had conducted exercises before on the outer edges of the debris cloud, so Lucius knew just how tricky it would look.

*Even more so as they draw deeper inwards*, he thought. The alpha and bravo bands of the cloud held lighter debris, bits of radioactive hulk, and a scattering of expended munitions. The delta and gamma bands were made up of denser debris, entire ship hulks, and a variety of inert and live mines and munitions. Emperor Romulus IV had a map, of sorts, for several routes in and through those bands, but it was still a tricky bit of piloting. Theta Station lay in the deepest region of the cloud, within Theta band, which was the core remnants of the planetoid. It was the densest region of the cloud, with bits of rock, clouds of vaporized gases, and many of the larger pieces of hulked ships and other debris.

The Chxor might try to blast their way in, Lucius knew, but they would likely make a mess of things in the process. Any bit of debris that they didn't destroy outright would gain momentum and would impact nearby debris. They might well cause a cascade effect of shifting debris, much like an avalanche in space.

Lucius looked over at Captain Beeson, "It looks like plan alpha three, please inform the Emperor that the Chxor will arrive in six hours."

"Yes, sir," Captain Beeson said with a nod. Lucius's gaze went to his own ships and he smiled a bit as he saw the icons of seven more ships in his formation. He had felt more than a little surprise as Admiral Anthony Doko had arrived with those ships, not least for the fact that two of them were converted Balor ships. Yet he and the crews of those ships had worked tirelessly to get them online and operational... and they had built a solid command in the process, Lucius knew.

The Balor conversions were more than welcome, a light cruiser and another destroyer. Rory and Feliks had spent the past few hours poring over both ships and had begrudgingly admitted that Matthew Nogita had done a good job on both vessels. Rory's actual words had been, "Simplistic but adequate."

The other five vessels, two more Jouster-class light cruisers and three Kukri-class destroyers, were also more than welcome. The mutineers had scrambled both cruisers' data networks, and Anthony Doko had brought them back online only with thousands of man hours of intensive labor. The three destroyers were more delicate repairs, for on all three ships, the Captains had been part of the conspiracy and the crews had not. Aboard the *Machete*, the Executive Officer had removed his captain and the ship's crew had refused to follow Admiral Dreyfus's orders. Aboard the *Gurkali* the ship's captain had provoked a firefight that had killed several of the senior officers, while aboard the *Spatha*, the captain had executed his executive officer and tactical officer but had been restrained by his crew. Anthony Doko had appointed Commanders Seng, Maggert, and Makkar to each of the ships and from what he had said, both officers had taken charge and restored much of the trust issues with the crew and remaining officers.

Lucius trusted his judgment. That wasn't to say that he felt entirely certain about those ships and their crews, but their battle plan looked desperate enough that the added firepower was more than welcome.

"Set the rest cycle," Lucius said. He watched as Captain Beeson sent out the order and he smiled a bit. He was long an advocate that a well-rested and fed crew would perform better than one which went into combat tired and stressed. So far, his successes seemed to prove that correct and while Admiral Collae had seemed to view putting three quarters of his crews on standby a few hours before the battle as being silly, he had agreed to follow Lucius's lead.

Lucius doubted that many of the crews would actually sleep, but they would have some time to rest, get a good meal, and to compose themselves before the battle.

"Now," Lucius said, "I'll be in my quarters, let me know if there are any changes."

"Absolutely, sir," Captain Beeson said.

Lucius stepped off the bridge and as his escort fell in around him, his mind pondered the strange and twisted path that had led him here. *Soon,* he thought, *it will be done.* Emperor Romulus IV would be reinstated. Lucius could turn his attention to growing the United Colonies... and the Chxor Empire would be less of a threat as they reorganized. That was his hope, anyway.

*One last battle*, he thought, though his mind went to Admiral Dreyfus's last words... a portent of greater battles yet to come.

***

# Chapter XV

Periclum Debris Cloud, Nova Roma System
(Contested)
May 22, 2404

"High Commander, all forces report full readiness and that they are in position. We have confirmed the presence of a heavy fighter screen at the outer edges of the debris cloud," Chxarals' Ship Commander informed him.

High Commander Chxarals knew that on a human ship, a senior officer like him would have a chief of staff to coordinate reports. The Ship Commander for his flagship had to manage the operations of his vessel as well as coordination of the fleet, which was why Chxarals had selected a talented officer for that duty. He didn't think it was a weakness of their system, it merely meant that a Chxor Fleet Commander needed to select his officers for optimal performance.

"Initiate operations," High Commander Chxarals said. With those words, he saw all three of his forces begin movement. Fleet Commander Thxanal commanded Force Three, which had the most direct approach through the debris cloud. Fleet Commander Fhxud commanded Force Two, which passed closest to the human mining station.

Chxarals had selected the central assault corridor for his own force. The approach wound through and around the various debris belts, but it provided the largest access corridor towards the inner region. Had the cloud been less dense, Chxarals would have ordered a general bombardment of the cloud with missiles... yet the Nova Roma Imperial Fleet had done so for decades and had yet to deplete it.

An unfortunate truth, as well, was that Chxarals knew exactly how low missile stockpiles had become across the Chxor Empire. The losses of key production facilities due to sabotage and negligence had sharply curtailed their weapons production at the same time that ship production and repair had become a priority.

Every missile that he wasted now would take weeks or months to replace... and he knew that many of his vessels had magazines at less than fifty percent capacity.

*A fact that would not matter if officers like the late Fleet*

*Commander Kleigh had not been so incompetent,* High Commander Chxarals thought. Had he any regrets, he would have wished that the Benevolence Council had allowed him to remove that officer and others before their mistakes became so compromising.

*It is a product of the system that preferences towards genetic caste sometimes trump actual performance,* High Commander Chxarals thought. He did not regret it. Regret was a human emotion, a weakness. That was simply the way things were and he would not change the Chxor Empire, for having read the sealed archives, he understood only too well how dangerous emotion could be for his people.

"Enemy fighter screen estimates are approximately six hundred in total, High Commander," Ship Commander Thxril said. "We have identified them as a mix of older human-style fighters. The enemy fighter screen has advanced out of the debris field to engage us."

That did not surprise him. The enemy fighters would be more dangerous within the field where his forces would not be able to see them at longer range, but the humans probably wanted to get an initial volley to damage and disrupt his forces.

"All fighter elements are focused on Force One, High Commander," Ship Commander Thrxil said after a long moment.

High Commander Chxarals nodded at that. His force was the largest, so it made sense that they would attempt to weaken it. He evaluated that they would have been better served to attempt to overwhelm or isolate Force Two or Three, but he could understand their focus on Force One.

"Missile separation, High Commander," Ship Commander Thrxil said. He did not say more, he already knew Chxarals well enough to know that Chxarals preferred to review combat details on his own monitors rather than have them summarized, where he might miss an important detail.

The larger number of fighters sent a considerably larger number of missiles at his forces, almost twenty five hundred missiles in total. The enemy fighters peeled off after they launched their payloads and returned back into the debris cloud in a ragged movement that suggested the pilots lacked experience. Chxarals noted that the missile accelerations were consistent with older munitions once commonly used by Nova Roma, which fit the parameters of what the human prisoner had told them. The station here at the debris cloud contained stockpiles of mostly obsolescent weapons and craft, hidden away as an insurance policy by previous Nova Roma Emperors.

While the missiles were undoubtedly old, their engagement parameters were still dangerous, as were the fission warheads they carried. Chxarals updated engagement plans and priorities for his force and then nodded at Thrxil, "Commence Firefly System jamming," he said.

It was obvious that the enemy warheads were less sophisticated. Over half of the inbound missiles either detonated as their targeting systems were overwhelmed or shut down. Of the remainder, Chxarals saw that their flight paths shifted almost constantly as they lost track of their targets within the cloud of directed jamming.

"Engage with defense pattern *Jall*," High Commander Chxarals said. He watched his formation shift, the defensive cruisers moved forward while the dreadnoughts shifted to make use of the fire corridors left by the cruisers.

Force One engaged with almost perfect synchronicity, a product of thousands of hours of drill and rehearsal. The large dreadnoughts engaged the inbound missile flight with a mix of their main and secondary batteries while the defending cruisers engaged individual missiles that came within their fire envelopes.

In total, of the twenty five hundred missiles, only a dozen slipped through the defenses. Those twelve missiles detonated among the shielding cruisers. Chxarals noted the detonation yields were consistent with the older style of Nova Roma Imperial Fleet munitions.

"Note to Ship Commander Tralkax," Chxarals said. "His vessel's performance was subpar, eight of the enemy missiles slipped through his fire lanes. His vessel is to trade places with Ship Commander Krxag." Tralkax's position in the forward element was too essential to have a weak vessel. Krxag's performance in drill had been better, but High Commander Chxarals had allowed Tralkax an opportunity to improve, it seemed he had not taken it.

*He will be executed as soon as it is politically expedient,* Chxarals thought dispassionately. He could most likely fit it in just after the destruction of the mining station. "Force One, optimal performance and I have seen that the enemy fleet is both poorly equipped and minimally trained. We will exterminate them and remove a threat to the Chxor Empire and the Benevolence Council. For the Glory of the Chxor. Continue along our axis of advance and you are authorized to destroy any potential threats." Normally a Fleet Commander would retain authorization to engage targets, but within the debris cloud it would be necessary for ships to engage quickly.

*Soon the Nova Roma Emperor will be eliminated,* he thought, *and then perhaps I can get back to more important duties.*

***

The hatch opened and Demetrius winced against the bright light. The dark cargo hold had only rudimentary improvements to make it livable and lighting apparently had not been one of the essentials that the Chxor felt humans needed to survive.

"I am Officer Galt," a Chxor said in a flat voice. "Fleet Commander Kral sent me."

"I am Demetrius," he replied.

"My team has brought weapons and communications devices as instructed," Galt said. "I have additionally procured maps to your target sites. Do you need any other resources?"

"No," Demetrius said brusquely, "Once my people are freed we can access what we need."

"Excellent, I am glad to hear that you are ready to perform optimally." Galt said. "My team has been tasked to secure station command, so if you need anything, you should be able to contact me there." It was bizarre to see a Chxor smile, sort of like seeing his dog walk on two legs, Demetrius thought.

"Sure thing," Demetrius replied. He turned to his people, "Advance team, head out. Headquarters, take position outside and establish communications. Security teams three and four, get into your positions."

He watched his people file out, taking weapons from the Chxor at the hatch. *Now is the time* he thought, yet he felt more than a little sadness. The moment had come, when they would finally cast off the chains. If all went well, in a few days the Chxor would be kicked out of the system, his world would be freed... yet then he would go back to what he had been afterward.

*Can I go back*, he wondered, *can I live in a world where the Imperial Family rules again and I am relegated to my exile?*

***

Captain Naeveus sighed as the handful of missiles penetrated the enemy formation. He knew that the plan called for such a pathetic output, that they had used up the entirety of the functioning old munitions. Even so, he had hoped for some larger impact, if only to embolden his pilots.

Many of them needed some kind of boost to their morale. He had been at Theta Station for the past three months, training pilots for the Canis-class bombers and the interceptors. The bombers pilots were all volunteers, men and women with even minimal piloting experience that he had put through combat training. The interceptors would be of minimal use against the heavily armored Chxor ships, so he had spent even less time on their pilots. Many of them were young, some of them painfully so... and he planned to use them as scouts in the debris field.

Emperor Romulus had held back their Harrasser fighters for use in the decisive fight, so Naeveus could only watch as his squadrons of bombers came back, their movement awkward as they funneled back through the plotted routes in the debris field.

Admiral Collae's bombers seemed to follow their routes better, at least, though it pained Naeveus to admit it. He had talked with their wing commanders during the final planning stages and they had been very close-mouthed about their training and background, which had worried him before. Now he knew he didn't have to worry about that... just the possibility that they could betray him at any time.

He watched with a critical eye as his bombers wound their way back and began to land at Theta Station. "Excellent job, Liberation Wings," he said. He meant it, too, despite the poor performance of their missile strike, they had executed their part of the attack perfectly. His biggest fear had been that he would lose a fighter or even a squadron if they veered off their flight paths and had a collision. "Rearm and get ready for Phase Two."

That would be the difficult part, he knew. He just hoped that Admiral Balventia and the Baron's forces would be ready for their parts.

***

Baron Lucius Giovanni keyed up the upgraded target priority data and grimaced. "I can't believe we're doing this, who thought up this plan anyway?" The ships of United Colonies Second Fleet hung just inside the Beta Debris Band, a tiny speck in comparison to the two hundred dreadnoughts and six hundred cruisers that bore down on them.

"Uh," Captain Beeson said, "that would be you, sir."

"Oh," Lucius said with a small smile, "carry on then."

He sat back and glanced at his displays. The human displays seemed incongruous aboard the Balor ship. *That reminds me,* he thought. He keyed up the ship's intercom and then tied that into the squadron communications. He *really* liked how easy the installed system worked. To give Rory and Feliks their due, they did good work. "Attention, Second Fleet, this is Baron Lucius Giovanni. We have come here to liberate Nova Roma, and along with standard ships of the United Colonies, we have brought three ships, taken from our enemies and rechristened as our own. These three ships have, until now, born only alphanumeric identifiers. What few of you know is that the United Colonies Senate has approved names for our new vessels." Lucius pulled an archaic slip of paper out of his uniform, "By the authority given to me by the people of the United Colonies, I hereby commission the fast destroyers *Achilles* and *Hector*, as well as the light cruiser *Hermes*. These new ships will form Legend Squadron of Second Fleet." The decision had been made to go with names from Greek mythology for the Balor vessels, in order to differentiate them from other United Colonies vessels. "Congratulations to the crews of the new ships, you are now fully commissioned in the Fleet, and we'll have your commissioning ceremonies after the battle. Baron Lucius Giovanni, out."

Lucius heard cheers, both on the bridge and elsewhere in the ship as he cut the connection. *Let them have their moment,* he thought. He was proud that they had three of the vessels online, and though he'd felt more than a little tempted to transfer to another vessel, he felt attached to the destroyer he had used to put down the Dreyfus Coup. *The* Hector, he reminded himself, *she has a proper name now.*

Chxor Force Alpha had just entered the gap between the Alpha and Beta bands, while Force Bravo and Charlie trailed behind to either flank. Both forces had more direct routes to the base, but Lucius knew that the Chxor battle plan called on them to trail behind and engage any human forces that sought to flank the main body.

He had watched the missile salvo from the fighters with interest, mostly because it showed how well prepared the enemy formations would be.

He had concluded that they were, unfortunately, very well trained. The enemy phalanx style formation had effectively negated the initial fighter missile strike. While those missiles were antiquated compared to the other salvos they planned to loose, the coordinated and overlapping jamming fields from Firefly systems as well as the interlocked heavy defense screens from the cruisers meant that they would have to either flank or destroy the cruiser screen before they reached the dreadnought core. No easy task when the enemy had over two thousand of the cruisers, literally more of those defending vessels than Lucius had fighters.

Lucius looked at the timer on his display and then at the position of the Chxor's Force Bravo. They had just passed the closest point to the Periclum Mining Station at just over thirty thousand kilometers range. "All Second Fleet Elements, initiate phase one."

Force Bravo was now at its most vulnerable point. Force Alpha had entered the Periclum Debris Cloud and could not turn to support them without reversing course and exposing themselves to enemy fire while they extricated themselves. Force Charlie was on the far side of the debris cloud, within extended missile range at just over three hundred thousand kilometers, but only just.

Lucius's force advanced just to the edge of the Beta Band before they loosed their missiles. The three converted Balor vessels together launched a hundred missiles, while the two Archer-class destroyers launched eighty missiles, and the rest of Second Fleet launched a hundred and twenty missiles. All of them were the two hundred megaton antimatter missiles with the best targeting systems that the United Colonies could install.

Those missiles were launched at just under a hundred and fifty thousand kilometers range and Lucius's people had emplaced stealth drones in the sensor shadows of every bit of flotsam along the enemy's path... and they had excellent passive and active data on the enemy ships.

The enemy commander reacted instantly to the launch with exactly the same tactics that High Commander Chxarals had used. His formation switched over into a tight phalanx and his dreadnoughts moved into position to direct overlapping fields of fire.

The main difference was that Force Bravo had half as many cruisers for two thirds as many dreadnoughts... which meant that they had to form up in a frontal-heavy defense.

Normally that wouldn't be an issue. Space was vast and the Chxor had excellent sensor readings from their network that covered the entire system. They knew that there was nothing to either flank or their rear... nothing but the mining station, which didn't have any weapons.

Lucius smiled as his gaze caught the secondary countdown. What that station *did* have was many docking bays designed for hosting mining craft. Those docking bays could *also* hold a Hammer-class gunship... with some slight modifications. It had taken a large number of flights by the station's mining craft to smuggle those Hammers aboard their station, each one limpeted to the hulls of mining vessels like a swarm of bats. Lucius had no doubt that the effort had been worth it.

The Hammers lit up only thirty seconds before Second Fleet's flight of missiles entered attack range. The seventy two gunships fired a total of six hundred mass-driver rounds in only five seconds and then volleyed their full payloads of missiles, another two hundred and eighty-eight missiles with two hundred megaton yields.

Force Bravo had no time to react. At one moment they had an unknown enemy force to their front with a dangerous but not devastating missile salvo, in the next, their dreadnoughts had already been engaged with tungsten tipped, uranium core rounds and almost three hundred missiles were only fifteen seconds away from impact... directly astern of all their defenses. All of this happened just before the enemy *should* have activated their firefly jamming systems.

The Balor's enhanced sensors let him see the actual impacts of the mass driver rounds, which came directly astern of the enemy dreadnoughts. The Chxor had some experience fighting projectile weaponry, but their defense screens had been optimized for energy weapons fire, which was far different to the best settings to deflect the heavy rounds. Each of the seventy two dreadnoughts targeted took multiple direct hits, most often in their engine pods.

Lucius watched as one dreadnought took five direct hits to just one of its engine pods. He felt just a moment of disappointment as there was no apparent effect... right up until the entire aft end of the dreadnought vanished in a chain of massive explosions as the engines ripped themselves apart in a cascade of catastrophic failures.

All across the rear of the Chxor formation, ships dropped back; engines shattered or knocked offline... the entire Chxor formation shuddered as dreadnoughts swerved to avoid damaged ships ahead of them in close proximity... and then the combined missile salvo struck.

Here and there a dreadnought maintained formation and fired in its assigned lanes, but they were the rare exception. Across most of that huge formation, dreadnoughts either maneuvered to avoid collision or to put someone else between them and the incoming missiles. When they fired, they fired only to protect themselves... or sometimes to clear their path from another ship in their way.

Lucius felt a grim sort of fascination as he watched the entire formation come apart in an avalanche of armored steel and flaring defense screens... and then the missile waves struck.

They had carefully considered the targeting parameters that went into the missile launches, with the enemy dreadnoughts being the primary target and cruisers being targets only as a last resort. Lucius's reasoning was that the cruisers shouldn't have the opportunity to interdict the rear salvo while if they *did* get off their firefly systems, the first missiles would hopefully penetrate those defenses and open up attack routes for the follow on missiles.

He had not expected the formation to come apart so completely.

Almost six hundred missiles swept in on the two hundred dreadnoughts of Force Bravo. Only three of them lost their targets as they came in, and those three wasted themselves on cruisers that were too distracted by the chaos behind them to even produce defensive fire.

The other five hundred and eighty-five swept in on the dreadnoughts, whose sporadic interceptor fire killed only thirty of them. The other five hundred and fifty-five swept in unopposed and rolled over the dreadnoughts of Force Bravo in an unstoppable wave of detonations.

When the flares of actinic light faded, not a single dreadnought remained, their destruction was so total that only incandescent gas heralded their existence.

"Message to Second Fleet and the War Dogs," Lucius said in a voice that felt far too calm for the shock he felt at the destruction of so many ships and people. "Good engagement, move on to Phase Three."

***

High Commander Chxarals's hand shook slightly as he zoomed in on the destruction of Force Two and Fleet Commander Fhxud. The elimination of its combat power was complete, and rendered in so little time that the Fleet Commander had not even had time to report it before he was dead.

"Identification of the enemy forces?" High Commander Chxarals asked.

"Fleet Commander Thxanal says that the forces based from the mining station appear to be an unknown, possible archaic, class of gunboats mounting mass drivers. Those within the outer band appear to be light vessels, destroyer and cruiser size or smaller. He was not able to get full energy emissions data on them before they withdrew, although three of the vessels are outside of normal human spectrum and match the *Chinwan* that were encountered at the Faraday system by Fleet Commander Kxull."

High Commander Chxarals nodded at that. The term *Chinwan* meant unknown alien and Fleet Commander Kxull had reported detecting *Chinwan* vessels at Faraday just prior to his destruction by those forces. If these *Chinwan* were in league with the humans, it somewhat explained their success against Force Two.

"Order the remaining cruisers to link up with Force Three. Order Fleet Commander Thrxil to destroy the mining station," Chxarals said. In all likelihood, the humans had probably expected that, but it would be foolish to allow them a base of operations at his rear. *I should have sent teams to secure the station, but I did not think that the humans would be brazen enough to emplace attack forces there,* he thought. *I will note my failures for the Benevolence Council to address after the battle.*

He watched dispassionately as Fleet Commander Thxanal volleyed missiles at the station. All two hundred of his dreadnoughts fired. Before Chxarals could see the result, however, his force had traveled too far into the debris cloud.

Fleet Commander Thxanal could still communicate, however, so Chxarals focused his attention on his own forces survival and victory.

The narrow assault corridor wound its way through and around the four main debris bands before terminating before the fifth and most dense area of debris. He had retained the most number of screening cruisers in order to prevent just such a flank or rear attack as had destroyed Force Two.

Almost immediately, the lead cruisers and dreadnoughts began to fire. They did not have any accurate map of the debris cloud and so his formation slowed to a crawl as they engaged anything that met their targeting parameters. Had High Commander Chxarals been as inferior as to be subject to emotions, he might have felt frustration as their pace slowed and then slowed further.

Yet he had no other choice. Sections of hulked vessels as long as half a kilometer were mixed in with boulders the size of shuttles and mines, missiles, and bombs whose payloads varied from chemical explosives to antimatter warheads... all of it in a drifting, overlapping set of belts that required constant attention.

Even with the snail's pace, here and there a bit of wreckage or debris penetrated the overlapping fields of fire. Most often it seemed to be something small, but the many impacts began to stagger the lead cruisers, despite their defense screens and heavy armor. "Switch defense screens to impact settings," Chxarals said. If the enemy made use of projectile weapons, then it would be better to go that route in any case, although the defense screens would be less effective against the enemy's energy weapons.

*No use to allow my lead ships to be battered to pieces by debris before I even engage them,* he thought. "Begin rotation of lead elements as damage reduces combat power to seventy percent," he said. They had rehearsed this before, but he knew the process would be more difficult in practice, particularly in the dense debris field.

*Still,* he thought, *this will not stop us. The humans have made their play, they have destroyed one of my three forces, but they must have used much of their capabilities to do so.*

***

Admiral Collae gave a tight smile as the ships of Bravo Force died. *Better than the good Baron Giovanni projected,* he thought, *which is good for me because it means I'll face a shaken enemy.*

In many ways, Collae felt common cause with the Chxor dispassion... though he admitted that he was not without emotion.

Nor, did he think that emotion was something to be hidden away, but it was meant to be controlled.

*I must deny myself such libertine virtues in order to bring a day where others may live more freely,* he thought, *and my efforts will be central to that endeavor.*

The eighteen custom-built cruisers were part of those efforts. Twelve of them were built around the main battery capital grade fusion cannons from the Chxor dreadnoughts. The craft were ships only in the most basic sense of the word, they had no other purpose than to serve as mobile weapons platforms. The Hellbore-class cruisers would be the base of firepower for his force... but they were far from all that he had brought. Eight other cruiser-class ships, what his engineers had labeled "Quads" and he simply called Fours, were four of the dreadnoughts' secondary fusion cannons together on a hull. They had more individual firepower than the Hellbores, but were designed for sustained, alternating fire of their weapons rather than single shots.

For additional fire, he also had ten Liberator-class cruisers, which normally mounted the older-style of railguns commonly available across the Colonial Republic. Liberators were solid vessels, but they were designed before the fall of Amalgamated Worlds when the Colonial Republic had limited military technology. Few had seen upgrades in the past decades. He had modified his Liberators, four were the more modern Liberator-C's with their railguns replaced by mass drivers, while the other six were original variants where he had stripped out their railguns and replaced them with a mix of weapons technology he had purchased at Port Klast and Tanis.

In reality, he hadn't been entirely honest with the Baron about his purpose here. He viewed this engagement as something of a proof of concept for the ships that he had designed. And though the offensive firepower of the Liberators, Fours, and Hellbores were a large part of that test, the true core of it lay in the twelve modified Chxor vessels. Although there were three basic designs to those ships, each had substantially different parameters within those designs. Four were what he labeled the Mimic-class, four were Hellraisers, and the last four were Hemlocks.

Mimics and Hellraisers were outwardly the most similar to the original Chxor vessels. In both types of ships, he had stripped out the original Chxor firefly jamming systems and replaced them with more efficient human electronics systems... though still backed by the massive reactors that the Chxor had installed.

The Hellraisers were the closest to the Chxor standard, though their jamming systems were an order of magnitude more powerful than the firefly systems, with phased directional jamming designed to burn out enemy sensor systems and blind enemy targeting systems.

The Mimics were designed to simulate the emissions of other ships, each one designed to portray not just one vessel, but an entire squadron operating in close proximity. They were the ships that Collae felt the least certain about, yet he thought that this was the best situation to test their specific abilities.

The Hemlocks were attack vessels of a different sort. While Hellraisers were designed to attack the enemy's sensors, Hemlocks were designed to penetrate the enemy's communications. They had the systems to intercept and override communications, with decryption computers, analysis software, and enough transmitters to capture, decrypt, modify, and transmit intercepted communications.

That was the theory, of course. Now it was time to see them in action.

***

"Give me evasive pattern five charlie," Garret snapped out as the inbound fire shifted from the annihilated mining station to his squadron. He wasn't exactly happy with that change, though the destruction of the station made him feel worse.

The miners had known that their home would become a target when they allowed Azure Wing to dock there. That hadn't stopped them from opening their home to his people. In fact it almost required force to get them to evacuate prior to the battle and they had told him that they just wanted an opportunity to do their part.

He was glad, though, that they were safely evacuated, as the ionized gas cooled where the station had once lay. Chxor Force Charlie had fired over six hundred fusion warheads at the station, more than enough to destroy it.

Unfortunately for him, they had sent a few extra missiles his way as a parting gift, it seemed. His Hammers were fired dry, they had nothing to even defend themselves with. Nothing, that was, besides their small size and the gradually increasing distance between his

Hammers and Force Charlie.

On that cue, he saw several of the inbound missiles go dark. As he counted off the seconds, the remainder of the enemy flight ran out of power. Now a hit on one of his Hammers was more a matter of bad luck than anything else.

*I wish we had time to rearm*, he thought, *but by the time we did, the battle would be over.*

It was the downside to manning a gunboat like this. Five seconds of fun and hours of being nothing more than a flying target. At least he knew that Halcyon's forces would be of use, along with the rest of the War Dogs.

*Then again,* he thought, *we did pretty much single-handedly destroy two hundred dreadnoughts... that's got to be worth some beers at the bar back home.*

***

Nova Roma
(Contested)
May 22, 2404

Sub Officer Galt ducked down as gunfire rattled against his barricade. Next to him, the hulking Hrak chambered a round in his pump-action grenade launcher. Hrak fired the grenade down the corridor and the detonation splattered bits of green blood across the Chxor's face.

Hrak gave a smile, "Good. Funny."

Galt sighed, "No, Hrak, that isn't a joke."

Hrak peered at him with confusion, but then again, Hrak was of the *Crxom* soldier caste and they weren't exactly known for intelligence or original thought. "You say joke make smile," Hrak said. "Floppy dead bodies make Hrak smile."

"I think his analysis is correct," Trxinal said as she fired her riot gun down the corridor.

"Of course you do," Galt said. In truth, he knew he had only a vague appreciation of humor himself, it being a new thing for him. Still, he felt that he understood it better than both of his underlings.

Galt leaned around the barricade and picked off another of the ground force attackers who had tried to slip along the bulkhead. In truth, he enjoyed killing them. Ground forces often contributed the police who enforced many of the oppressive Chxor laws. *Thugs,* he thought, *who wouldn't recognize a good joke.*

Elsewhere in the station, he knew that human teams had already attacked their targets. He didn't know how successful they had been, but he *did* know that the Chxor Empire ground forces needed to capture the command section if they wanted to have any hope of regaining control over the station.

Galt had seized the command section before they could transmit any requests for help from High Commander Chxarals. That was his mission, after all, to prevent word from getting out until it was too late. In truth, Galt had realized that it was something of a suicide mission, but he had accepted it anyway. Fleet Commander Kral didn't have enough trusted forces to give him any more than the one team. The rest of his efforts would be aimed at securing defense stations and planetary defense centers as well as eliminating those he couldn't trust aboard his own ships.

That was fine with Galt. Galt didn't care about winning a great victory in the rebellion against the Benevolence Council. He didn't even really care much about freeing the humans of the system, though he had found their emotions fascinating.

Galt just wanted to hurt the bastards who had kept him a slave, his emotions pinned so tightly that he had begun to go insane. Only being freed by Kral had prevented that decline. *Well,* he admitted, *that and the human movies that I watched after my capture.*

He leaned around the barricade and cut down another of the ground force police. "Take that you bastards!" Galt shouted. He adopted a human accent, "Say hello to my little friend!"

Hrak gave a bellowing laugh at that, "He means his gun! That is a hilarious joke, because you shot them!"

*Okay,* Galt thought, *maybe he does understand jokes.*

***

Periclum Debris Cloud, Nova Roma System
(Contested)
May 22, 2404

Fleet Commander Thxanal cut off his fire at the fleeing gunboats as High Commander Chxarals' orders came in. "Adjust your formation for maximum dispersal," the Chxor ordered. "We are taking substantial attrition due to debris and you would be advised to orient your defense screens to minimize your damage."

"Of course, High Commander," Thxanal said. He turned to his Ship Commander, "Transmit orders to our Fleet, adopt dispersion pattern *Flan*-three." That would give them the best dispersal against debris clusters while still allowing them to engage and destroy targets across a broad front. It was not optimal to fight in, however clearly the High Commander assumed that the enemy had put their primary force on the far side of the debris cloud to engage Force Two.

"Fleet Commander, we are detecting the first squadrons from Force Two's cruiser elements are on approach. Where should I slot them into our formation?" Ship Commander Txan asked.

Thxanal did not want the ships integrated into his formation, but he thought it best to avoid exposing his rear as Fleet Commander Fhxud had. "Tell them to take up position at our rear, to tie into our formation as best as they can with the purpose of closing our rear arc."

"Yes, Fleet Commander," Txan said.

Thxanal focussed his attention on the forward arc of their advance. The Beta Band, as the humans had labeled it, was the least dense at this region and was mostly made up of smaller pieces of debris, most a few meters across or smaller. In a dispersed formation, his ships quickly cleared paths through the debris, although the shifting nature of the environment meant that drifting bits continued to enter their cleared lanes. Even so, other than the occasional impact of smaller debris, his ships had begun to make good time. Combined with how Force One had slowed, he would soon be in position on their flank to support them, he knew.

"Fleet Commander," Txan said, "I am detecting some anomalies with the squadrons from Force Two." The officer took a moment to bring up sensor data. "Although their lead elements have the right transponder data, I've detected odd energy spikes among some of their trail elements."

Thxanal examined the data for a moment, "You are right. I want a full sensor readout of those ships immediately."

"Of course, Fleet Commander," Txan began. Yet the ship rocked with a sudden impact, and then another. "Fleet Commander, we are taking fire from the ships. The ones closest to us have begun jamming, I cannot get sensor data on the others."

Fleet Commander Thxanal pulled up the data, even as his ship rocked again with impacts. He heard alarms wail as he checked the data. It seemed that four of the enemy vessels had positioned themselves in a skirmish line near the rear of his formation. Those four ships had systems akin to his own firefly systems, yet their jammers seemed far more powerful or efficient, for at this range they were blinding his systems. Several of the closer dreadnoughts reported that their sensor systems were actually being damaged trying to get targeting data from astern.

Worse, the four ships were alternating not just the direction and strength of their jamming, but the frequencies. On top of that, his communications with the rest of his forces cut in and out as the ships to their rear utilized some sort of communications jamming.

What he didn't miss, however, was how two of his dreadnoughts had already come apart under sustained enemy fire... or how his own flagship had begun to take a significant number of hits. "Orders to the Fleet," Thxanal said, "Shift formation to *Len*-Seven." That was the formation shift he had designated for an enemy force to their rear. He watched as his ships shifted, the cruisers and dreadnoughts moving as ordered, yet it seemed to happen painfully slowly.

Worse, it put his open rear to the debris field and his formation still had significant momentum into the debris cloud. Yet he would rather take random hits over directed fire.

His ship shuddered again and he noted that the incoming fire matched the output of a dreadnought's main battery, yet the enemy had only cruiser-class vessels. *What have they done to those ships?*

His fleet had almost finished the shift in formation when Ship Commander Txan spoke, "Fleet Commander, I am picking up ships in our rear quadrant."

Thxanal started to say that of *course* there were ships in the rear quadrant... until he realized that Txan meant behind their new formation. Thxanal felt shock as a boil of light, swift vessels appeared at less than ten thousand kilometers behind his formation... and then they fired.

***

Tommy heard someone on the bridge give a whoop as the enemy formation shifted. He just gave a slight smirk as he nodded at his weapons officer. "All ships, you are free to engage."

The pirate squadron had slipped close to the enemy force and he had shadowed their approach, just outside their sensor range. Tommy had felt a bit of interest as Admiral Collae had apparently mimicked the emissions of standard Chxor ships, but he had filed that interest away for another day. Just as he had decided to further investigate the firepower of the Admiral's cruisers when he had the opportunity.

The effectiveness of those cruisers was clear. Three of the Chxor dreadnoughts had been ripped apart in only the first few seconds of engagement. A dozen more took multiple hits and the tightly controlled fire shifted from one target to the next with an almost clinical precision.

*My turn,* Tommy thought with a predatory smile.

The ships of his squadron swept in fast. He didn't bother with direct orders, his captains knew how to handle their own ships and they went into the mass of Chxor dreadnoughts like a pack of wolves into a herd of lumbering cattle. There could be no directing their courses, as each captain maneuvered independently, dodging and weaving among the Chxor vessels and firing the entire time.

The enemy ships didn't know how to react. Fighter squadrons swept in along the flanks of enemy ships while cruisers engaged the enemy dreadnoughts from point blank.

The Chxor started to react after a few moments, their batteries volleyed in response, striking at the light, swift pirate craft. The *Revenge* shuddered as it took a glancing hit. Tommy saw the younger *Ranger* come apart as it flew directly into the full fire of a dreadnought. *It seems that the elder frigate would retain the name after all*, he thought, *as long as it survives*.

Yet the battle was almost one-sided all along the Chxor lines as the thirteen ships of his squadron swept through the enemy formation. The *Kraken* flew at his flank, her guns lashing out in all directions with the precision of a surgeon to smash weapons turrets, defense screen emitters, and to shatter engine pods. Seventeen dreadnoughts staggered out of formation, venting atmosphere and spewing debris. Almost half of the enemy formation lashed around them blindly, hitting friend and foe indiscriminately. All the while, Admiral Collae's cruisers continued to fire into the rear of the Chxor fleet.

Tommy's grin grew broad as the *Revenge* emerged from the wall of Chxor dreadnoughts and spun, the battlecruiser's guns firing in almost all directions, before she turned and dove back into the maw of the Chxor. *This,* he thought, *is one hell of a fight.*

***

"High Commander," Ship Commander Thrxil said, "Fleet Commander Thxanal reports that his force is decisively engaged by an estimated fifty vessels of cruiser size. He requests assistance."

High Commander Chxarals looked at the Ship Commander with disbelief. "He has two hundred dreadnoughts, why does he need help?"

"He doesn't answer, High Commander. His flagship's transponder has ceased to function," Ship Commander Thxril said.

*If he has survived,* Chxarals thought, *I will have him executed for incompetence.* "Order Force Three to withdraw outside the debris field, develop standoff with the enemy, and engage them on better terms." He still wasn't certain why Thxanal had disregarded his multiple orders to return to a phalanx formation. He had acknowledged receipt of every one of those orders, Chxarals could see that on his communications monitor. Chxarals never for a moment considered that his communications might be compromised.

"Force One, maintain current course and be mindful of enemy ambush," Chxarals said. Force One had drawn within the Gamma and Delta bands of the debris cloud, though his trail elements extended along their path almost to the outer layers of the Beta and Alpha bands. The long, worm-like formation had a broad front, but the long trail through the open corridor stretched almost ten thousand kilometers. *We are approaching our most vulnerable point,* he thought, *the enemy will attack soon.*

On that cue, the fighter force emerged from the debris field ahead, almost right where he had plotted Theta Station's location. "Initiate defense pattern *golan*-two," he said. His ships reacted quickly, for he had spent weeks drilling them in preparation for this moment. The interlocking defense screens and overlapping directed jamming formed up a multilayered defense that would shed the enemy missile fire, just as they had before. It was not a vulnerable worm, he knew, it was an armored serpent with a poisoned sting. Even so, as he watched the ships of Force Two struggle to withdraw from the enemies that had engaged them from both sides, he almost gave the order to withdraw.

"High Commander," his Ship Commander said, "We are detecting additional vessels moving into engagement range from our flanks. Ship estimates are coming online now."

*Ah,* he thought as he recognized ship classes, *Emperor Romulus IV has committed himself at last.* Even if he had not recognized the energy signature of the infamous battleship *War Shrike*, then he would have recognized the superdreadnought which had been stolen from the shipyards. Now he could commit, confident that the losses he would suffer would be worth the final goal. Now he could destroy this human infestation.

The humans had rallied a number of vessels for their final stand, he saw. A second of their Desperado-class battleships joined the *War Shrike,* along with a battlecruiser, a heavy cruiser, a pair of light cruisers, and at least five destroyers. The squadron of frigates and two squadrons of corvettes completed the force. If High Commander Chxarals could have felt pleasure, he would have for the fact that the enemy had finally come to him and guaranteed their destruction.

"Execute plan *golan*-two, step *jull,*" he said. His ships responded as where the enemy force approached on his flank, the force thickened as cruisers spun to position themselves ideally for the defense, even as his dreadnoughts angled to engage with their full batteries. At the fore of his formation, his dreadnoughts prepared to fire through the gaps in their defenses and clear out the missile salvo, while at his rear, the formation shifted to better engage the enemy from the flank, as the long, armored serpent shifted it's tail to strike.

The enemy was outmatched and outgunned... and Chxarals gave the order to open fire with complete confidence that the enemy would be destroyed.

That was when the universe went mad.

***

Captain Naeveus, gave a hiss of warning as his command squadron swept under the belly of a rock the size of the *War Shrike*. It was not, needless to say, where he had planned to be, but confusion in the bomber squadrons mean he had to reroute some of his other squadrons and he had chosen the most difficult route for himself.

Just as well that he did, for in the tight maneuvers of the Theta Band, he *had* lost some craft to collisions. At least two had collided with debris large enough to damage their craft severely, and one more had struck something hard enough to trigger his antimatter warheads... which had also killed the other five craft in his squadron. *I could have lost half my bombers in a mad chain reaction if it had happened even a few seconds earlier*, he thought.

Yet he hadn't, and the depleted wing of bombers along with his half a wing of Harrassers were coming up on their attack run, along with the six wings of Patriots from Admiral Collae. As far as Naeveus knew, the Patriots had not been retrofitted to carry their antimatter warheads, instead Admiral Collae had fitted them with captured Chxor munitions, sixty megaton fusion warheads built by the Chxor on copied designs from captured Nova Roma missiles. Captain Naeveus fully appreciated the irony of using those to liberate the Nova Roma system.

"All squadrons," Naeveus said as he streamed targeting data to both his fighters and those of Admiral Collae, "engage targets and return to rearm." He felt satisfaction as he saw that wave of missiles go out. It was smaller by a significant margin from the one he had launched earlier... but it was also made up of far more capable missiles, launched at closer range. He saw that Admiral Collae's Patriots had launched on time as well and that they had already maneuvered to return to their carriers. *That's pretty damned scary*, he thought, *Colonial Republic Fleet forces are bad enough with a few squadrons of fighters from one of their small carriers, I would* hate *to face one of his big carriers.*

At least they were on his side in this battle, he thought as his squadrons turned back towards Theta Station and the crews that waited there to reload them.

He didn't know if they would have time to rearm, but the plan called for them to at least try. Naeveus knew that if this salvo went poorly along with the other attacks, the Chxor dreadnoughts would reach Theta Station and Admiral Collae's carriers while his craft were still aboard.

But if the attack *did* succeed, then his fighters would have enough time to reload and come back to finish the bastards off. Naeveus was a strong believer in the power of positive thought, just now. He spun his Harasser away and back along his reverse vector, the agile heavy fighter responding to his touch with the faithfulness of a lover.

His blissful feeling evaporated though as he saw the disarray in some of his bomber squadrons. "Damn you, Bravo Squadron, get your asses back on course..."

***

Admiral Valens Balventia gave a snarl as the enemy formation shifted in front of him. This, he knew, was the most dangerous point, when the firepower of three hundred dreadnoughts would be focused on his ships.

And though he had sworn his oath to Emperor Romulus IV and the Emperor officially commanded the formation... they were still *his* ships and *his* people... just as the plan was one that he and Lucius Giovanni had worked out together.

*It is strange,* he thought, *how easy it is to come to like him.* His father would not have approved. For that matter, Valens wasn't certain he approved of having made peace... yet once it was done, he had felt an enormous relief.

He saw the Chxor formation settle into position, just as the inbound wave of missiles from the joint fighter strike accelerated towards the Chxor formation. On the face of things, with the heavy directed jamming and the screening cruisers, it looked hopeless as Valens tiny force stared down the guns of three hundred dreadnoughts. Yet Valens felt only a sense of tranquility and peace as he saw the Chxor move into position.

There was something very comforting about knowing that Lucius Giovanni was on his side.

"Sir," Ensign Brunetti said from the sensors, "Baron Giovanni sends his respects, he's commencing the attack now."

The Chxor had begun to fire and the *War Shrike*'s bridge shuddered as the battleship took first one hit and then another. Yet the old battleship had yet to fire, they had no targets among the heavy jamming of the Chxor Fleet. "Evasion pattern delta, get us some more space between us!" Valens snapped as he monitored the Fleet's maneuvers. Part of him longed to take control of the ship and direct it, but he had to keep focused on the big picture.

He could see the men under his command dying as the lead ships began to take multiple hits. The small frigates and corvettes couldn't take even a single hit and he winced as he saw two of them vanish in as many seconds. *Lucius,* he thought, *you had better be in position or this was all for naught...*

Valens smiled then as the entire Chxor formation shuddered. Cruisers turned, some attempting to react to orders to shift position while others cut off their jamming as they maneuvered to avoid collisions.

Behind them, he could see the enemy dreadnoughts, the lumbering behemoths tried desperately to turn as something struck them from behind.

Now his ships had targets. "Engage," he said with a snarl.

***

Lucius felt his heart twist a bit as the entire Chxor formation shifted to engage the Nova Roma Imperial Fleet. The tiny force moved forward into the maw of the enemy fleet... all the while they *knew* that they couldn't break that formation on their own... and that they would take the brunt of the enemy firepower.

It was the part of the plan that he and Valens had most discussed, yet they could not avoid the fact that the Chxor had come here to kill the Nova Roma Emperor... and nothing else would force them to commit like the opportunity to kill him.

As the Chxor formation piled up to face not just the inbound missile salvo but also the Nova Roma Fleet, their flank became thinner. Like an armored beast, they could not have thick armor in every direction... that strength had to come from somewhere.

At the rear, outward section of their formation, they were the thinnest. There, only a relative handful of cruisers screened the entire formation's rear arc... and that was where Lucius's forces were positioned to hit them. The problem, though, was that they needed to hit those cruisers hard enough that they couldn't be reinforced or replaced fast enough to close the gap.

"Commodore Pierce, you're up," Lucius said.

The War Dogs' three dreadnoughts opened fire first. The three dreadnoughts had lain quiescent as the Chxor force drew ever closer. Their greatest advantage was not their firepower or their armor... it was the fact that they were so old that the Chxor wouldn't recognize them as a threat. They wouldn't even be in the database.

Those three dreadnoughts opened fire with their railguns at only a thousand kilometers range, close enough that the cruisers never even knew they were under fire before steel penetrators were shattering armor and tearing their ships to pieces.

In that moment, Lucius's Second Fleet brought up their drives. After the engagement with Force Bravo, Lucius had positioned them along the Chxor axis of advance. He had detached the two Archer-class destroyers, since it would take them another hour to reload their external launch racks and they possessed no real armament besides that.

Lucius's force hit while the fighter missile strike was still ten thousand kilometers out from the head of the formation. The human built ships focused on the Chxor vessels closest to them, dealing with threats as they came up, while the *Achilles*, *Hector*, and *Hermes* engaged other targets. He felt the entire ship vibrate as the main battery charged and as it fired, the *Hector* finally seemed to come alive. All three ships had aimed at a single dreadnought, one that they had identified as being the subcommander's flagship for the central section of the Chxor formation.

The *Hector* dumped energy into a quantum matrix which then projected the energy instantly, letting it take form *within* the target, bypassing armor, defense screens, and hitting out to a range of twenty thousand kilometers instantly, with no delay.

The enemy dreadnought died before it knew what had even hit it. For one moment it was there, the next it vanished in thermonuclear fire as all four of its fusion reactors failed critically. *Well,* Lucius thought, *that was a bit of overkill.*

"Yeehaw!" Ensign Forrest Perkins shouted. "Get some!"

Lucius grinned at the other man, "Hardly professional, Ensign, but I'll agree with the sentiment." He updated his target parameters, "Legend squadron, go to dispersal targets." Clearly they had no need to mass their firepower, not with the raw destruction that they had unleashed on just one dreadnought. "War Dogs, you are clear to engage priority alpha. Avenger squadron, take over guidance of the missile flight."

He heard them acknowledge his orders, but his gaze went to the massive missile salvo from the fighters, even as Second Fleet launched some additional missiles of their own.

The enemy formation's head had shifted as Lucius's force hit it. Part had shifted back in an effort to close the wound, but the ships from Second Fleet were already within the enemy formation, while the War Dogs continued to chew their way through any cruiser that tried to close the gap. The big dreadnoughts were killing enemy cruisers fast enough that they had time to shift fire onto the nearest of the Chxor dreadnoughts.

The relatively light railguns couldn't penetrate the heaviest armor of the Chxor vessels, but they *could* shred engine pods, sensor clusters, and even light weapons turrets. The dreadnoughts that they targeted staggered away, blind and slow... easy fodder for Lucius's Second Fleet.

Boris Kaminsky's *Roosevelt Forest* moved among the damaged dreadnoughts like a panther attacking panicked sheep. The battlecruiser's heavy guns ripped through the dreadnoughts' armor at close range and everywhere it went, a trail of debris and gas strung out behind Chxor dreadnoughts, like wounded animals trailing their intestines.

The lighter ships fared almost as well, the savage Kukri-class destroyers had incredibly powerful short range energy weapons and their captains maneuvered almost into contact with the dreadnoughts defense screens before they fired. Lucius saw turrets blasted of the Chxor dreadnoughts from the close range, precise fire.

And then, as the entire Chxor formation shuddered and tried to adjust to this new threat, the missile wave struck.

Lucius's second fleet had taken over control of those missiles, which meant that they weren't blinded by the Chxor jamming. Instead, they swept under and over the formation before they dove down in, directed past the screening cruisers and into the heart of the formation.

It didn't work perfectly. Over seven hundred of the missiles from Admiral Collae's Patriots were too blinded by the Chxor jamming to hear the commands from Lucius's Fleet. Those seven hundred missiles went in against the Chxor screening cruisers and the dreadnoughts that were supposed to protect them.

Yet those dreadnoughts suddenly had two hundred missiles from Admiral Collae's fighters and another five hundred missiles from Captain Naeveus's Harrasser wing and his two wings of Canis bombers on approach from above and below... and ignoring their cruiser screen.

The seven hundred missiles dove in among the Chxor

dreadnoughts. To give them credit, they engaged those missiles with everything they had. The lead squadrons, a total of fifty dreadnoughts, engaged with main and secondary batteries at range and their interceptor laser batteries again as the missiles entered attack range, but they didn't have time to cover both in front as well as above and below.

They killed almost two thirds of those missiles, even so. They killed almost all of Admiral Collae's missiles, either because they had poor guidance or because they didn't have as much maneuverability, Lucius didn't know which. They also killed two hundred and fifty of Liberation Wing's missiles, which still left two hundred and forty of them, spread fairly evenly over the lead fifty dreadnoughts.

The seven hundred missiles from Admiral Collae went in almost entirely unopposed against the Chxor screening cruisers at the fore. More than a third of them were so blinded by the Chxor's firefly systems that they either went past their targets or simply failed to detonate. But, even so, almost four hundred of them detonated among the lead cruisers.

The staggered chain of explosions lasted almost three seconds... and Lucius winced as the glare cleared to show that the entire head of the formation was simply gone. “Adapt to that, you bastard.”

***

## Chapter XVI

Periclum Debris Cloud, Nova Roma System
(Contested)
May 22, 2404

High Commander Chxarals wiped at a smear of green blood that had run down in his eye from where his head had struck one of his monitors. *Perhaps some of the criticisms that stated the monitors should be padded like on human vessels was not entirely out of line,* he noted.

His flagship had taken multiple hits as his formation opened up from behind. He didn't think that the enemy knew his location, else he was certain they would have focused fire to kill him as they had Fleet Commander Fxark, his second in command.

Still, he was still alive, so he should take charge and crush the enemy. Ship Commander Thrxill had confirmed that some of the intercepted communications were from Baron Giovanni, the head of the United Colonies. Chxarals didn't know why the human had sent such a small force, but he was resolved to destroy the human and crush his fleet.

"Forward element, roll formation..." he trailed off as he realized that his forward element was simply gone. A half dozen cruisers near the edges of the fore drifted, battered into wrecks, but the central formation of fifty dreadnoughts and four hundred cruisers had been reduced to clouds of ionized gas. "Rear element," he said, "shift along vector three four seven." That would allow them to flank the force at his rear, though it would cost him firepower that he would rather focus on the Nova Roma forces.

The enemy dreadnoughts to his rear were immaterial, he could see. They must be ancient, possibly hulks that the Nova Romans had retrofitted with some basic weapons. They would take significant firepower to reduce, but they could be ignored until the other threats were dealt with.

"Your priority targets are the *Chinwan* vessels and the enemy battlecruiser," he said. "Engage the enemy light craft after that, and only then the three obsolescent dreadnoughts."

"Acknowledged," Fleet Commander Jxush said. Always a professional, Chxarals thought, even as he turned his attention to his center... and the main body of the Nova Roman Fleet.

His cruiser screen had cracked and the Nova Romans had taken advantage of that. An inbound wave of missiles had centered on the gaps in his formation. "Ships 10997 and 10756, tighten formation." That should, he thought, close off two of the larger sets of gaps.

He was proven wrong a moment later as the *Emperor Romulus* fired through the jamming screen. The huge superdreadnought's main batteries ripped a pair of dreadnoughts apart. A moment later, the other Nova Roma ships fired, and these shots, too penetrated the gaps in his screen to strike deep into his formation. His dreadnoughts had returned fire, but the enemy continued to close, their evasive maneuvers combined with the chaos of the attack at their rear meant many of his ships missed.

His ship lurched again under multiple impacts. *The ambush force is providing them with targeting data to bypass our jamming,* he thought. "Message to all screening cruisers, shift jamming pattern to seven-*jinn*." He waited a moment and noticed an immediate difference as the coordinated shots became far less accurate. *Let us see how well you shoot when you cannot communicate*, he thought.

***

Nova Roma
(Contested)
May 22, 2404

Sub Officer Galt coughed up green blood and leaned against the barricade. Nearby he saw that Hrak and Txinal were down. Both of them were riddled with bullets, their body armor stained green with their blood.

*Yet we have held station command*, he thought absently. He had thought that a team of Chxor were supposed to relieve him, yet he had heard nothing over the net about reinforcements, not since the counterattack.

*Perhaps we have already lost,* he thought with regret. If that were the case, then he wished he had more time to enjoy emotions, particularly humor.

As he thought that, a pair of Chxor in ground force uniforms swept around the barricade. They saw him and froze, yet as he made no move to attack them, they leveled their weapons. "You are a traitor to your kind," the lead one said.

Galt gave a laugh and he could see them both flinch back from the sound. To them, it was alien and wrong, to him, it felt good to finally live openly. If they couldn't see the humor, then the joke was all the funnier. "I am a patriot of our people. Too long we have been slaves to the Benevolence Council. I will die free, slaves."

The one raised his riot gun and Galt closed his eyes.

He heard a pair of shots, yet he felt no pain. He opened his eyes to find a human stood over him, an assault rifle in his hands. "You're Galt?" the human asked, his face filled with distaste.

"I am," Galt said. "Thank you for your timely arrival."

The human shrugged, "I promised Demetrius I'd secure the command section and save any of your team that survived. Trust me, if it was up to me I'd have sat back and watched while some Chxor killed each other."

"Ah, very practical of you," Galt tossed his head back and began to laugh. The human stared at him for a long moment before he began to laugh too.

It was good to share a joke with someone who could recognize it.

***

Periclum Debris Cloud, Nova Roma System
(Contested)
May 22, 2404

Valens grimaced as they lost the targeting data feed from Lucius's ship. A moment later they lost communications with them as the enemy firefly systems shifted to a broad spectrum communications jamming pattern. "Damn it," he snapped, "get me a target!"

*It isn't fair*, he thought, *Lucius is getting to have all the fun.*

He wasn't certain exactly what he had, as the *War Shrike* shuddered from another impact, but he wouldn't exactly call it fun.

"I've got a gap in sector three two," Ensign Brunnetti said quickly. "Data coming up!"

Valens grinned as he saw that data on his screen. The Ensign had dropped a probe in behind the missile flight, with a directional laser link that the enemy *couldn't* jam. "Excellent work," he said, "All elements, new target data coming online, engage!"

The relatively tiny gap was still wide enough for his entire force to fire through, in an inverted cone. The *War Shrike*'s HEP cannons engaged one of the Chxor dreadnoughts through the gap and he growled as he saw the enemy ship's bow shatter. A moment later, his missiles shot through the gap and detonated almost in contact with the dreadnought's hull.

The painful glare cleared a moment later, and Valens could see that the focused fire from the Fleet had ripped a huge hole in the enemy formation. "All elements," he said, "This is Admiral Valens Balventia. Forward into the gap, engage at will."

They were close enough now that his entire formation was able to lunge for the enemy's throat. This was where fast vessels like the *War Shrike* came into their own... and the *Emperor Romulus* was almost as fast, a massive black wedge that drove into the enemy force right behind its smaller brethren.

Yet the fight was not as one-sided as Valens would like. He saw the battlecruiser *Amerigo* shatter as it caught a full broadside from a Chxor dreadnought. The ship, either through direction or happenstance, spun over on a collision course with its killer... and both ships vanished in an eye-searing ball of fusion detonations a moment later.

The *War Shrike* shuddered again, and then a second time as the enemy focused on the old battleship. Alarms wailed and Valens coughed as smoke filled the bridge. He heard Captain Bentucci direct fire on the dreadnought that had hit him, but Valens' focus was on the entire fight and he bit his lip until he tasted blood as he saw the rear element of the formation had shifted. *I should be worried about what will happen to me if this fails,* he thought, *but all I can do is worry about what Lucius will do to me if I let the Chxor destroy his precious* War Shrike.

***

"I won't forgive him if he lets them blow up my ship," Lucius said to himself as he watched the enemy pound the Nova Roma Imperial Fleet in general and one Valens Balventia in particular.

"What's that, sir?" Ensign Miller asked.

Lucius shook his head, the *Hector* fired again at one of the enemy dreadnoughts, and again the destroyer's powerful weapon ripped a dreadnought apart.

Yet the small ship's shield system flared again as an enemy

dreadnought fired on them, and Lucius hadn't missed the destruction of the *Machete* and *Gurkali*, or the numerous damage icons throughout the remainder of Second Fleet. The enemy's rear element was coming into the fight, another hundred and fifty dreadnoughts who had yet to take any damage.

Captain Naeveus and his fighter squadrons should have finished reloading soon, he knew. Yet it would still be several minutes before they would return.

Lucius spared a glance for the larger battle as a whole. The relays from Tommy King showed that the fight with Force Charlie was still under way. The enemy dreadnoughts had begun to withdraw but they left a trail of wrecks and damaged vessels along the way as his light, swift vessels savaged them. He could see that a number of the pirate ships as well as some of the ships from Halcyon were gone, too, though, and it looked as if some of Admiral Collae's ships had taken enough damage to knock them out of the fight.

"Have we got any data on Chxarals' flagship?" Lucius asked.

The destroyer lurched as a dreadnought's secondary battery raked them. For a moment, the shields flared bright enough to overwhelm their sensors. The helmsman sent them on an evasive course even as Lucius queued it up.

"No, sir," Ensign Miller said. "He's using multiple ships as relays, we've taken out about half of them, but we still aren't sure which one is his."

Lucius grimaced at that. He felt certain that the Chxor formation would fall apart without High Commander Chxarals' direction, yet the Chxor commander had dispersed his communications through relay ships, it seemed to prevent against just that.

Lucius brought up a diagram of the enemy ships and he felt the deck shudder under him as they took another set of hits. This one caused the lights to flicker and he absently wondered how much more the destroyer could take.

"Here," he said and highlighted a set of ships at the center of the Chxor formation. He transferred the data to Lieutenant Shaw at the weapons. "These five ships, order the *Achilles* and the *Hermes* to engage these five vessels." It was a hunch, but it looked as if those five vessels were more protected by the other ships of the central formation, almost as if the Chxor had maneuvered to make them safer.

The *Hector* fired and a moment later, so did the *Achilles* and the *Hermes*.

For just an instant, the entire Chxor formation froze, yet the instant passed. A mass of enemy fire seemed to fill the space that the three ships occupied. "Evasive maneuvers!" Lucius barked.

A relay blew out and a jet of flame lanced across the bridge. Lucius heard a garbled, panicked shout from Rory on the ship's intercom, even as the helmsman dove the ship into a cluster of enemy dreadnoughts.

The evasive maneuver took them close enough that Lucius could make out the welding lines on the Chxor hull as they flashed past, yet it shook off the enemy fire for a moment.

The *Hermes* followed them, the cruiser's shields afire with energy. Yet the *Achilles* wasn't so lucky. The destroyer's shield flared bright as a star for a moment before they winked out. The small ship vanished in a heartbeat.

*Damn,* he thought, *Naeveus, where are you?*

***

Captain Naeveus swore as he saw the general confusion that had enveloped the entire central battle. His fighters and bombers had taken longer than he'd planned to rearm as several squadrons had jumped the queue and then landed in the wrong bays. Before he could land to sort it out, they had tried to take off in the middle of his other squadrons landing.

That had taken precious seconds to fix, yet Naeveus now worried that it might have cost them the battle. He brought up the fleet net, "This is Lancer Six, we are in position, what are your orders?" His fighters could volley missiles into that melee, yet it was just as likely that they would hit friend as they would foe.

"This is Admiral Valens Balventia," a confident voice answered. "Engage the central formation, full spread."

"Sir," Naeveus said, "my pilots aren't skilled enough to line up perfect shots and our birds aren't good enough to differentiate between ships in this mess..." In theory the Identify Friend or Foe parameters *should* prevent friendly fire, but with damaged vessels intermixed with the enemy, that was a big risk. To make matters worse, Collae's fighters carried refurbished *Chxor* missiles, which weren't of the best quality in the first place.

"We'll get clear," Admiral Balventia said. "Now launch!"

Captain Naeveus *almost* asked for authorization from Baron Giovanni, yet he had given his oath to the Emperor and he knew that Admiral Balventia was his senior commander. *Maybe I should have stayed with the United Colonies,* he thought, *but I hope the bastard is right.*

"All Liberation elements, engage the enemy, full spread," he snapped. A full spread meant that the squadrons would launch their missiles at everything in the area... and they would rely on the missiles being able to identify their targets.

He heard acknowledgments, and a moment later a wave of missiles swept out from his squadrons, followed by those of Admiral Collae's fighters.

*I hope I didn't just kill a few thousand of our people,* he thought.

***

"Break, break, break," a familiar voice spoke over the fleet net and Lucius's head snapped up as he heard Valens Balventia's tone of command. "All forces, Liberation Wings have launched on full spread, clear the engagement area."

Lucius bit back a curse as he saw just how difficult *that* would be. Both forces were intermixed at this point. "Reverse course," Lucius snapped, "Full acceleration along vector two nine nine, get us the hell out of here."

He saw that of all the fleet, the *Hector* and *Hermes* were the deepest inside the enemy formation. Already, the *Emperor Romulus* had turned hard over and was almost clear, along with the *Peregrine* and most of the other Nova Roma ships... all but the *War Shrike.*

"Valens," Lucius pulled up comms with the battleship, "Why aren't you getting clear?"

"Damaged engines," Admiral Balventia replied. "We're working on it." His voice was tight, yet Lucius could hear shouts in the background. "Get clear, Lucius. We'll be fine."

Lucius didn't exactly consider him a friend, but he knew him well enough to recognize a lie. The *War Shrike* had taken enough damage that its signature wouldn't resemble friend or foe parameters loaded in their missiles. On a full spread, those missiles would track on every target in the engagement area... and Lucius didn't have time to try to take command of that flight. Even if he had, Admiral

Collae's missiles had already proven difficult to control.

*There's only one thing to do,* Lucius thought.

"Adjust course to five seven seven," he said, his voice iron.

The helmsman looked up in shock, but he reacted a moment later. The *Hector* flipped over and accelerated towards the *War Shrike*. Lucius monitored the other ships and saw that most of the others would be well clear. The Chxor had clearly seen the inbound flight of missiles, too, and they seemed focused on forming up to face it rather than trying to engage his ships.

"Lucius, what the hell are you doing?" Admiral Balventia snapped as the *Hector* came in on a direct approach vector.

"Saving your arrogant ass," Lucius said. He tweaked their course and then nodded at Lieutenant Shaw on the weapons, "Prepare to engage in defensive fire."

The destroyer flashed over the remaining thousand kilometers just as the missile flight swept in. On his sensors, he could see the missiles begin to break over the enemy formation behind and above him... and he could also see an even dozen missiles come in towards them.

*I don't believe that we loaded Balor ship parameters into the friend or foe identifications,* he thought absently.

The *Hector* swept in above the *War Shrike* as those missiles came in. He had positioned the destroyer to function much like a Chxor cruiser, to screen the larger ship from direct impact. That, of course, put the *Hector* directly in the path of all twelve missiles.

*It would be very ironic if the two of us died here,* Lucius thought as the missiles closed the last bit of distance. "Engage missile defense pattern delta," he said and the *Hector* opened fire one last time.

***

High Commander Chxarals wiped at the green splatters of blood that stained his monitor. He wasn't certain if it was from Ship Commander Thrxil or one of the other officers killed in the last set of attacks. The important thing, just now, was to see what was happening with the rest of his fleet.

He coughed at the harsh cloud of smoke that filled the bridge and felt something tear in his chest. His injuries were forgotten a moment later, though, as he finally made sense of what he saw.

The enemy fleet had started to withdraw and he saw why almost instantly. Another flight of their damned missiles was inbound. He ordered his own force to reform, but he knew they didn't have time even as he gave the orders.

This missile strike was the deathblow, he knew. Over a hundred of his core dreadnought force of two hundred ships were gone. The rear element, another hundred and fifty dreadnoughts, had intermixed with his central element, and both forces' screening cruisers were scattered, moved out of the way to allow their huge brethren to have clear lines of fire at the smaller, swifter, enemy ships.

*I have lost,* he thought and for the first time in his life, he felt the stirrings of emotion. He felt despair, he realized, for a world in which the power of the Chxor Empire was shattered. His people, his race, had lost... and he knew that with his defeat, with the loss of so many ships, the iron hold of the Benevolence Council would be broken. Even if the humans did not continue their war, his own people would after such a disaster.

That despair was the cruelest twist of all, for it proved to him in his heart of hearts that he had lived a lie all along.

The first missiles began to detonate, a long, continuous stream of detonations that devoured Chxor dreadnoughts like a hungry beast. As the wave drew ever closer, High Commander Chxarals slumped in his command chair, put his head in his hands, and wished that he had never heard the name of Baron Lucius Giovanni.

***

# Chapter XVII

Nova Roma
Nova Roma Empire
May 25, 2404

Emperor Romulus IV stared down at the surface of Nova Roma and felt tears fill his eyes. "I'm sorry," he said softly, "sorry that it has taken me so long, but I am here now."

"You know," his sister's voice said gently, "talking to yourself is generally a sign of insanity."

Emperor Romulus IV turned quickly. He felt some of his tension ease as he saw Lizmadie and her husband and behind them were Admiral Valens Balventia and Baron Lucius Giovanni.

Admiral Balventia looked a bit lopsided with the bandage that covered the left half of his face and his left arm in a sling, but he was at least still alive, thanks almost entirely to Lucius Giovanni's actions. "It is good that you are all here," he said.

"Ready to go down and meet the adoring crowds?" Lizmadie asked cheerfully.

Emperor Romulus IV couldn't quite smile in return. She seemed to realize that her humor wasn't well taken, but it wasn't as if he could criticize her for it. He had fled Nova Roma as a tactical decision, advised to do so by Admiral Mund and other officers. What he had not expected was the reparations that the Chxor had taken as a result... and there was an ugly current within the people of Nova Roma about his departure.

*They thought I was a coward,* he thought darkly, *and they don't care that I did it to rally a force to save them... they only see that I fled.*

It was all the worse for the fact that the same guilt had plagued him for the past year and a half. He *had* run. While his intention had always been to get help and come back, he had lived with the knowledge that many of his people would die under Chxor occupation while he was safe.

*Maybe I should have stayed,* he thought.

"Well," Valens said, "Your Majesty, we should ready ourselves, as the returning heroes." He gestured at the Emperor to board the waiting shuttle, and then the entire group joined him.

It was strange, he thought, to return as the Emperor. It was never a position he had wanted. His father's advisors had groomed his older brother for the job, his father had seemed happy enough to let him dream about service in the Fleet, possibly an eventual command.

*I was just Prince Octavian,* he thought, *until my father and brother were dead.*

As the shuttle landed, though, he straightened his shoulders and stepped out. His Marine detail fanned out around him. They had already secured the Imperial Palace, he knew, and he followed the familiar corridors with an odd feeling of disconnection.

He had already spoken with the leaders of the rebellion, many of whom would be present today, he knew. Demetrius Santi had not been friendly, but he had at least been respectful. Another time, the tone of reverence he used to address Baron Giovanni might have bothered him, but Emperor Romulus IV no longer felt any distrust for the man. *He risked his life to save Admiral Balventia,* he thought, *if there's any sign that he's loyal, or at least harbors no yearning for my throne, that would be it.*

At last, he came to the Imperial Balcony. The platform overlooked the largest square on Nova Roma, where some fifty thousand people could gather. Many of those there today were rebels who had fought in the liberation, some of them shipped in from Nova Umbria but many of them Nova Roma natives.

Emperor Romulus IV took a deep breath and then stepped out on the balcony. He stepped up to the podium with an increasing feeling of disconnection. "My people," he said, "I want to thank all of you..."

He trailed off as the boos and catcalls reached a level that overwhelmed even the speakers. He stepped back with a look of shock and pain on his face, and the crowds seemed to feed on that reaction. They jeered him, their voices filled with loathing and hatred.

Admiral Balventia stepped up to his side, his voice flat, "You owe this man much," he said, "he has earned my respect..."

"Balventia!" A voice shouted, "It's Admiral Balventia, he came back for us, it's true!"

The crowd began to cheer then, though somewhat raggedly. Emperor Romulus IV saw Admiral Balventia's face go hard. Whatever he had expected, he had not expected this sort of praise while his sworn liege was jeered at.

Lucius stepped up next to him then and the crowd went silent. Baron Giovanni leaned over the microphone, "People of Nova Roma," Baron Giovanni said, "You owe this man your respect. No one else has spent as much time and effort in trying to rally Nova Roma's forces. He has worked tirelessly to free you from Chxor occupation..."

"It's the Baron!" a set of voices cried. Lucius Giovanni cocked his head in surprise as the calls went out and he trailed off. A moment later, the crowd surged forward, shouts and cheers loud enough to buffet the Emperor back on his heels.

The crowd began a chant, then, "Lucius! Lucius! LU-CI-US!" Far from losing their momentum, the crowd seemed to only grow louder.

A Marine officer leaned over Emperor Romulus's shoulder, "We should get you to safety, your Majesty."

Yet he couldn't move. His gaze went between the adoring crowd and the shocked expression of Baron Giovanni. The praise, the hero worship, had completely blindsided him... yet it was so obvious now to Emperor Romulus IV.

*I have lost my world,* he thought, *and rightfully so.*

***

"There's nothing for it," Lucius said as the Nova Roma senior officers and the Emperor took their seats. "I'll leave the system immediately. I'm not sure why they focused on me with some sort of hero worship, but–"

"That would be the worst thing you could do," Emperor Romulus IV said.

"What?" Admiral Balventia asked.

"If he goes," Princess Lizmadie said, "It will look as if he was exiled. Half the people out there just finished fighting one bloody revolution, the last thing we need is for them to think they need to fight another."

To Lucius's shock, Emperor Romulus IV nodded. "That is exactly my reasoning." He gave a sigh, "Right now, Baron, the people are unsettled. They lost all trust in the Imperial Family even before the Chxor captured the system. It seems that my... departure, was seen as the final straw for them all. The Chxor branded me as a coward who fled and that, at least, most people believed."

Lucius shook his head, "That is absurd! You had to withdraw. Hell, if you hadn't, none of this would be possible!"

Emperor Romulus IV closed his eyes and Lucius didn't miss the tears in the corners of his eyes when he opened them, "Be that as it may, public perception is that I am a coward. It is mitigated somewhat by the good will towards Admiral Balventia... but the public perception has long been that you were mistreated by the Imperial Family, so anything I do in regards to you will be seen as a continuation of that... even if you leave of your own desire."

"This is absurd," Lucius said. "I'll go in front of them, I'll tell them..."

"What?" Emperor Romulus IV asked gently. "How can you explain it so that it won't sound as if you are making excuses for me? Trust me, I've spent many an hour pondering that myself." He shook his head, "No, Baron, there is only one solution for this."

He paused and took a deep breath, "As of this moment, I formally renounce my authority and abdicate the position of Emperor of Nova Roma. I do so with one condition: Baron Lucius Giovanni will be appointed as the next Emperor of Nova Roma, to be approved by a vote of the surviving nobility and the people of Nova Roma."

Everyone in the room stared at him in shock.

Lucius felt the blood drain from his face. "Your Majesty, you *can't* be serious. I don't want this at all! I don't want to be the leader of the United Colonies, much less any of this!"

"I didn't want it either," he responded. "But it was my duty to take it, just as it is now yours, Baron." The young man smiled, "For the first time in two years, I feel as if I've made good use of my authority and rank."

"Your Majesty," Admiral Balventia began.

"Please," he interrupted, "I think that Prince Octavian will do, Admiral." He shrugged self con-sciously, "Though I'm not sure if I retain that title if I abdicate."

"I think we can operate under that assumption," Lizmadie said dryly.

"Prince Octavian, then," Admiral Balventia said, "You have to reconsider. I've given you my oath. If you think that Lucius, that is Baron Giovanni, or I would not support you..."

"I don't think that at all," Prince Octavian said. "What I am afraid of is what it will do to Nova Roma. They are already unsettled.

We've lost something over six hundred million citizens during Chxor occupation, almost a tenth of our population. There is a great deal of anger, both with the Chxor and also with the leaders who put us in this situation."

He waved a hand, "The *only* thing preventing a fresh start for our people is me. I am the last holdover, the last tie back to the old ways."

"That's absurd!" Lucius said. "You had no say in the policies of your father!" It was as stupid as the blame that had haunted him for the actions of his father. There had to be some way to fix this, Lucius knew, yet he couldn't think, especially not when faced with the crushing weight of responsibility that being the next Emperor would bring.

"Absurd or not," Prince Octavian said, "It *is* true. A clean break is what our people need. They also need a popular monarch, one who will lead them into prosperity... which means you."

Lucius sat back and put his head in his hands, "I can't do this, Your Majesty. I *can't*. For God's sake, my daughter is still missing, the United Colonies is in shambles, and I'm not qualified!" He felt a wave of panic go through him at how his life would change, at the bitter taste of the pressures of dynastic marriage and production of a 'proper' heir.

"You can and you will," Prince Octavian said, his voice iron. "And I've given you no choice in the matter. I said the *only* conditions were that the nobility and people ratify you. How do you think they would react if it became public that you refused the honor?"

Lucius winced. That would crush public morale. They would think that either he thought the situation hopeless or that he hated his homeworld, either would be a disaster for general opinion. "You leave me no choice, then."

"Of course I leave you a choice," he responded, "but you being a good man, you can only choose one option." Prince Octavian sat back. "Now, then, I'll assume that as Emperor you'll petition the United Colonies for annexation?"

"I... suppose," Lucius shook his head. "I hadn't really thought about it."

"Well, you should bring your advisers into this before we go any further," Prince Octavian said. "We'll work out the wrinkles now, before we make the official, public announcement." He looked at Admiral Balventia, "Lord Admiral, I believe you have a list of our remaining nobility, both those who came with me and those who went into exile. I'd like your opinion on who will oppose Baron Giovanni's selection as Emperor."

Lucius sat back. His mind ranged over how the young man had overturned his world in only a few minutes. *He would have made a great Emperor*, Lucius thought with regret, *I will have to do my best to rule as well as I can.*

***

"Did you know?" Lucius asked as Kandergain stepped into his quarters.

She gave him a sad smile, "I suspected. I've been around enough social upheaval in my life to realize that things wouldn't be as smooth as some people expected once you recaptured Nova Roma."

Lucius sighed, "Will this work?"

She shrugged, "I don't know. I can't see the future, Lucius, I just have hints."

"What about what Admiral Dreyfus said, how nine out of ten futures, we fail?" Lucius wondered if the Admiral had seen Lucius as the new Emperor of Nova Roma, if that was why his cabal had fought their return to the system so hard.

Kandergain came over and settled onto the couch next to Lucius. "My love," she said, "the future isn't some percentage game like Rory and Feliks play." Lucius smiled as he thought of Rory and Feliks shouting between them to determine the fate of millions. "There are possibilities, some more likely than others. From what I understand, there are millions or billions of possibilities, many of them fundamentally similar to each other. What we're doing is trying to work our way to the one we want."

"Which is?" Lucius asked.

"Which is the survival of the human race as something other than cattle for the Balor," she replied sharply. "If you think that *I* orchestrated your appointement as Emperor, I'm afraid I don't quite match up to the sinister manipulator role you've cast me in. Actually," she said with teary eyes, "I'm quite a bit hurt."

Lucius bit back a curse. He embraced her, "I didn't mean it that way."

"You *did*," she said. "And trust me, Lucius, it hurts the most because I have done worse... but you have to understand I'm not doing this for me. I'm not even doing it for you or for our daughter. I'm doing it to prevent the extinction of the human race."

"I know," Lucius said, "but sometimes I feel a little overwhelmed."

"Hah," Kandergain let go of the embrace and sat back, "try being me. *You* just have to be the fearless leader, I've got to be the assassin and spy who can't ever fail." She sighed. "Those possibilities that you are afraid of... well, I strongly suspect that Admiral Dreyfus's wife was shown those for a reason."

Lucius's eyes narrowed, "What do you mean?"

Kandergain didn't meet his eyes, "John Mira was known to be... selective about what futures he showed psychics. He was able to block out parts of his mind, futures that he saw, in order to manipulate people. What I'm concerned with is that the futures that Admiral Dreyfus relayed to you were all very similar themes... lost battles and failure. I wonder if John Mira hadn't manipulated him into thinking there wasn't hope, in order to remove him from the picture."

"But, why?" Lucius asked. "He could have killed me. He may have killed our daughter, if he was behind the kidnapping. Hell, he forced us to use a fraction of our forces to fight a desperate battle to liberate Nova Roma..."

"And that all might have been necessary," Kandergain said. "I don't know. I'm just as much a puppet as you. None of this is guaranteed, either, it's all weighted risks, from what I understand. But think on this: If he knew Admiral Dreyfus wasn't mentally flexible enough, that he would lose more battles than he won..."

Lucius shook his head in instant denial… but he couldn't discount the possibility. He felt his heart ache as he saw the level of cold calculation involved in convincing a man to sacrifice everything he knew in order to save humanity... and then to manipulate him into betraying the people who trusted him in order to get him out of the picture.

"I'm not sure how much I can think about that before I start to wonder if we're playing for the wrong team," Lucius said.

"Yeah," Kandergain grimaced, "tell me about it." She sighed, "And stop worrying about our daughter. I told you. I have my very best team on it. They will bring her back." She stood up from the couch, "Which brings me to... us."

"You've got to go, then?" Lucius asked.

"Yes," she said. "and this time I'll be gone for a long time. Decades, probably. Things are heating up with the Shadow Lords and I've a score to settle with Mistress Blanc as well, especially since she's cut ties with Admiral Collae."

Lucius hadn't heard that, but he had noticed the psychic's absense. "Anything I should know about? Any way that I can help?"

For just a moment he saw her hesitate, as if there was something about Mistress Blanc that she wanted to share, but the moment passed. "No, nothing you need to worry about," she said. "Just... don't feel like you need to live a hermit's life, miserable and alone. I want you to be happy, Lucius, so if you find someone..."

"I see," Lucius said. He stood and went to the window and stared out at the city. "I have already found someone, I'm afraid."

"Oh?" He could hear a catch in her voice. "That's good. I mean, that's great. Really, great." Her voice was leached of emotion, though.

"Yeah," Lucius said with a slight smile, "She's intelligent, wise, and she's even got a wicked temper." He turned around, "She's also the most dangerous person I know... and she's got my heart so completely that there could never be anyone else."

Her chocolate brown eyes melted and she stepped forward, "I see." She embraced him again and he felt her heart beat against him. "You're terrible."

"I know." He cleared his throat, "I know you have to be off, save the universe and all that, but do you think we have time to take care of something?"

Kandergain snorted with laughter, "I'll clear my schedule for the rest of the afternoon if you'll do the same, Emperor Giovanni."

Lucius growled at that. "Better make it the whole evening."

***

Tommy King froze as he stepped onto the bridge, shocked by what he saw.

Lauren stood, arms outstretched, at the center of the compartment. The captain's chair was gone along with the other consoles, replaced by an empty platform. She stood at the center of the platform, her head tilted back, eyes open and staring at the ceiling. "Hello, Mason," she said.

"Are you…" He caught himself before he could finish the absurd question. Of course she wasn't "okay." Tommy cleared his throat, "What are you doing?"

"Communicating with the ship," she said, without changing position. "I can *feel* her Mason… and my *God* it feels amazing. Did you know that vacuum has a sound? I can hear it, the void brushing against our skin…" She trailed off. He saw her shudder a bit and then her arms fell to her sides and she straightened and looked him in the eye, "What brings you here?"

"I just talked with our boss," Tommy said with as genuine a grin as he could give. "It seems that Baron Giovanni can sort of accept the idea of Tommy King the privateer… as long as you're around to keep me straight. We're keeping the letter of marque."

"Oh?" For the first time, she gave a smile of her own… though Tommy didn't miss the edge of hunger in that smile. "Who are we going after now?"

Tommy felt his heart leap a bit. It was only a little thing, that smile, but it was a connection they still shared. "Well, that's where it gets fun. It seems that some of the Colonial Republic don't like the United Colonies… we're going to go show them that it is best that they mind their own business…"

***

Lucius took a seat at the table. Around him sat the leaders or representatives of seven other systems, including Harris Penwaithe, Interim President Quzvini, and others.

"Good morning," he said.

"Good morning... Emperor," Harris Penwaithe said with a bit of vitriol in his tone.

Lucius gave the man a level look. The official announcement was still pending, but there was no doubt about it anymore. The surviving Nova Roma nobility had voted almost unanimously for it, while the popular vote had been less so, it looked as if he had carried it by a wide enough margin that no one would oppose it.

*As much as I might wish otherwise,* he thought.

"We are here to settle admissions into the United Colonies," Lucius said. "Now, all of you have worked out the details with

Minister of State Bueller, but I've asked you all here in order to lay all the cards on the table." Lucius brought up the display, "The various concerns that most of you have revolve around being outnumbered and losing local autonomy... along with a healthy dose of fear of being absorbed by a Second Nova Roma Empire."

He saw several of the men and women around the table nod at that. "Now, then," he said, "First off, I want to state that while your individual worlds all have unique cultures and social mores, they all share one thing: all of you have recently thrown off the yoke of tyrants. Whether that be the people of Halcyon throwing out Nova Corp or those of Tehran and Nova Roma ousting the Chxor Empire, all of us have experience with tyranny and all of our people will not forget that. As part of this constitution and as voting blocks, I think we'll see quite a bit of anger any suggestion that some of the voters force others to adjust their behavior. We've also worked some precautions into the systems already, so that we won't get a mob mentality that seizes power later on."

"This sounds acceptable," Interim President Quzvini said. "You have already addressed my general issues. My main question would be about certain rumors we have heard in regards to the Chxor Empire and some of their worlds."

Lucius sighed, "You are speaking of whether or not Chxor worlds have asked to join the United Colonies?"

"I am," he said. Lucius wondered if Quzvini had asked that question in such a neutral fashion to preempt one of the others from doing the same in a less friendly manner.

Either way, Lucius still had an answer. "I have been approached by three Chxor worlds asking to sign on with the United Colonies. Right now we are investigating their systems to verify that they wish to join in good faith and that they will comply with our rules about individual freedoms." He shrugged. "In truth, if they check out, and everything so far suggests that they are willing to play fair, I'm inclined to allow them to join. Those worlds are, by the way, Saragossa, Garan, and Norbar. Saragossa's envoys included both Chxor and Humans."

"I'm not certain I feel safe having Chxor with voting power," Ambassador Matis of Wenceslaus said. The big blonde man shrugged, "We are going to be at war with them, after all."

"We are," Lucius nodded, "Though perhaps not as long as you

may fear." He didn't want to say more, but the Chxor Empire had withdrawn from many human worlds after their defeat at Nova Roma. Some of those worlds they had left as charnal houses, but on others they had abandoned the systems without further atrocities. In some, they had actually formally surrendered to Lucius's forces and asked for asylum.

From what he had heard from Kral, there was a war on between the Benevolence Council and their opponents... and the defeat of Chxarals had been a serious blow for the Benevolence Council's supporters. The time might well come soon when the Chxor Empire was in the hands of allies, rather than enemies. Oddly, much of the hatred to the Chxor had been blunted by the efforts of Kral and his forces to help liberate Nova Roma. There were even some efforts to support "our" Chxor in their fight against the Benevolence Council on both Nova Roma and the United Colonies.

*It is going to be an interesting future,* he thought.

"In any case," Lucius said, "membership by new worlds will need to be ratified by by a vote of congress. Which, if you elect to join, will include representatives from each of your worlds."

"Well, then," Interim President Quzvini said with a smile, "Where do I sign?"

***

Faraday Colony
United Colonies
June 5, 2404

Lucretta Mannetti looked up as someone stopped outside her cell. "Oh," she said dourly, "it's you."

Colonel William Proscia stood there with an implacable look on his face. "You nearly killed the Baron, you know."

She shrugged, "So? Before you lecture me on how important he is... remember, William, I know your secrets." She left it open that she could expose him.

"I'm afraid we're past that point now, my dear," Colonel Proscia said as he stepped up near the bars. He nodded at the security cameras. "I'm not here."

"You're going to help me escape?" Lucretta breathed. She had thought that after her spectacular failure, then surely Marius would let her rot in jail or just have her killed. *Come to think of it...*

"I'm afraid not," Colonel Proscia said. "You're headed to interrogation in five minutes. I'm not going to kill more good Marines just to get your useless carcass free."

"I could ruin you!" Lucretta snapped. "You were my agent, here, I could tell Lucius and..."

He shook his head, "I was never *your* agent. I've always been loyal to the Baron's interests... through his father's efforts, of course. You know that, you've just lost sight of the big picture." Colonel Proscia gave a tight smile, "Then again, you never were good at the big picture."

"What are you going to do?" Lucretta asked. Her mind raced, yet it was a muddled race, she couldn't seem to form any plan. *I've been drugged,* she realized.

"You'll go to interrogation. They'll administer locapan. You'll suffer an allergic reaction, quite a painful death, but it's the least I can do for all of the Marines who died because of you," Colonel Proscia said.

Lucretta sagged back. She tried to speak, but she couldn't seem to form any words.

He leaned close to the bars. His voice was the last thing she heard, a soft, almost loving tone, "Burn in hell, bitch."

***

Tannis System
Independent
June 19, 2404

Reese straightened as Marius Giovanni stepped into the interrogation room. The past few weeks had been a living hell as Marius's agents had grilled him about everything he had done, everything he had seen, and every thought he had during his escape from Halcyon.

They had not resorted to torture, though they had interrupted his sleep and used drugs at least twice from what he could tell about the fuzzy gaps in his memory.

Yet they had ceased their lines of questioning the day before and then they had told him that Marius himself was on his way to meet with him. "Sir," Reese nodded respectfully. He understood why they'd done what they had. Admiral Mannetti had clearly been badly defeated and as the only one to make it out, they were suspicious that he might have had a role in that defeat.

"Hello, Reese," Marius said. He gestured at the chair next to his bunk, "May I?"

"Of course, sir," Reese said. He took a seat on his bunk a moment after Marius sat.

"First off, congratulations, you are the father of a healthy young boy, I understand," Marius said. "I hope that you'll get to meet him, but right now, I'm afraid that you aren't a favorite with my daughter."

"I see," Reese said. "What... what is my son's name?"

"Anthony William Giovanni," Marius said.

Reese felt his eyes tear up a bit. "Anthony, a good name." He respected Anthony Doko, though he disagreed with the dog-like loyalty the other man felt for Lucius Giovanni. *I will break my son away from that bastard before it costs him his life,* Reese thought.

"Now, then," Marius said. "I have some good news for you, Reese. I've had a position open up with my forces, now that Admiral Mannetti is gone."

"She's dead?" Reese asked.

"I'm afraid she died in interrogation," Marius nodded. "An error with the dosage of drugs. My agent wasn't able to facilitate her escape."

Reese just shrugged at that. He didn't much care what had happened to her. Taking her position, though, that meant quite a bit. "I would be your public face, then?"

"Absolutely," Marius said. "My personal agent. I truly appreciate what you were able to recover from the base at Halcyon... and we'll be pouring over the data from the systems for years, I'm certain. Quite a bright future for you with us, Reese... and one day, you'll be reunited properly with your son and my daughter."

Reese nodded at that, "Of course, sir, I'd be honored."

***

Shadow Space
June 19, 2404

Marius Giovanni sighed as he read the news article. It was clear that President Spirodon didn't control things as well as he thought back on Elysium. The latest round of protests showed that, even if the recent assassination of his niece didn't.

He turned at a giggle and saw his granddaughter had pulled herself up on the edge of her crib. "You're a very smart little girl," he said with a smile, "too smart for your own good, I'm afraid."

She blew a raspberry at him for that and lowered herself down. He ignored the disrespect, for now. Soon she would be old enough that he would begin training her in proper behavior. For now, it was important that she bonded with him. She would be more malleable if she felt he had genuine affection for her.

*Which I do*, he thought, *as I also regret the necessity to kidnap my own flesh and blood.* His son had given him no real option, though. He had refused his offered alliance and then had the termidity to declare him an imposter.

Granted, Marius had seen the writing on the wall before that, which was why he'd had his commando team make contact with some unhappy locals and pressed them to take action. Their marginal competence had provided the perfect screen for her abduction and the idiots hadn't even realized which of the children they took was the actual Kaylee Giovanni.

Marius still felt the name was too light. His grandmother's name didn't fit the child, she would be a warrior, he felt, and she should have a warrior's name.

Marius felt a bit of sadness, that she wouldn't get to have much of a childhood, yet that was overrated, anyway. He hadn't had a childhood, after all, there had always been his purpose, his destiny.

Soon his ship would arrive at the Centauri system and his granddaughter would meet her destiny. She would be trained in the various skills she would need, raised as the daughter of nobility as she should be, and indoctrinated into loyalty to President Spirodon.

The shadow space jaunt had taken a few more days than he had planned, mostly because of the need to avoid unrest across human space as dozens of systems broke off from the Colonial Republic and swore on to the United Colonies. *As if they will be trustworthy allies,* he thought, *I offered so much more... a shame he forced me to take what I needed.*

He looked up as he heard a gunshot. His gaze went to the commando on duty. "What was that?"

The officer spoke into his comm. "Reports of shots fired near the bridge, sir," he said a moment later. "My team is en route." He looked up then at a spat of gunfire in the corridor outside. He spun towards the door, "Get to cover, sir!"

The hatch slid open and a huge figure lumbered through. The commando officer fired, but his rounds bounced off his opponent to no effect.

*Powered armor,* Marius thought. Yet the form that came through the hatch wasn't human... its eight limbed figure was clearly Ghornath.

The Ghornath didn't fire, he simply caught up the commando in his armored arms and *squeezed.* Before he dropped the lifeless body, a tall, beautiful blonde woman stepped through the hatch behind him. "Ah, there you are sweetheart," she said as she swept past Marius and picked up Kaylee out of her crib. Her face was filled with warmth and good cheer and Kaylee gave a giggle and tried to pull her blonde hair.

"Excuse me," Marius said as he pulled a grenade out from under his desk. "I have to insist that you set the girl down and step away."

The blonde woman's gaze fell on him and all the warmth in her face vanished. "Really, a grenade?" Her voice sounded exasperated.

"I'd use a pistol," Marius said, "but your big friend would just ignore it."

"So would I," she said. She closed her eyes and a moment later, the grenade was ripped from his hand and she caught it. "Care to try again?" she asked.

Marius felt the blood drain from his face. *Psychic,* he thought, *psychokenetic, probably navigation skills too, which is how they boarded my ship in shadow space.* "This is a diplomatic ship on a diplomatic mission..."

"Oh, please," she said. She looked over at the Ghornath, "I'll finish up here. Take the girl."

She passed the girl over to the Ghornath and the big, armored alien took her gently. He made silly noises at her as he did so and she giggled as he took her out into the hallway.

"Now then," the woman said. "I'm here to pass along a message... the girl is off limits."

"Oh?" Marius felt a bit of relief. It seemed the woman wasn't here on the behalf of the Shadow Lords, after all. If she wanted to send a message, then she would probably want him alive to send it. *More the fool, her*, he thought, *I will hunt her across the stars to recover the girl and the resources she's shown here just means I'll need to be more cautious when I finally strike.*

"Now, then," she said. "My other companions have set your ship to arrive in orbit over Elysia with no other assistance needed, so there's just the exact phrasing of the message to cover.

Marius frowned as he saw something like fire flicker at the back of the woman's eyes... and then he thought he smelled burning hair. "What do you mean by that?"

*What I mean,* she spoke into his mind, *is that I don't like evil bastards who kidnap little girls.*

Marius felt heat wash over his body then, but he didn't have the opportunity to scream before she set him alight with her mind. Marius's last few seconds were filled with overwhelming pain.

When it was done, the woman stepped out into the corridor and then hurried along to where her companion stood with the girl. She took Kaylee up in her arms and gave the girl a smile, "Now then," she said, "let's get you back to your father."

###

*The End*

## Diagrams

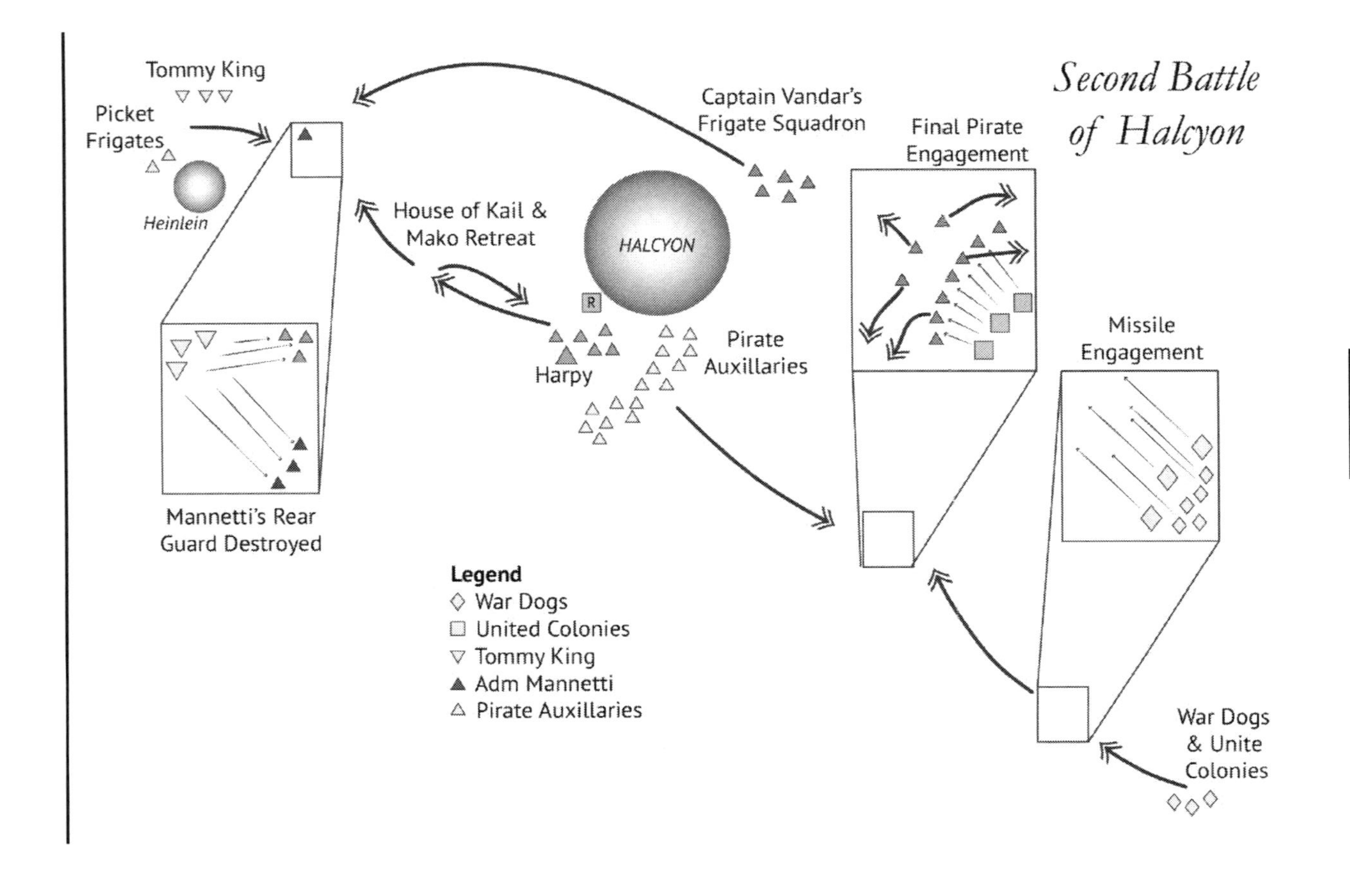
Second Battle
of Halcyon
Tommy King
Picket
Frigates
Heinlein
Mannetti's Rear
Guard Destroyed
House of Kail &
Mako Retreat
HALCYON
R
Harpy
Captain Vandar's
Frigate Squadron
Pirate
Auxillaries
Final Pirate
Engagement
Missile
Engagement
War Dogs
& Unite
Colonies
Legend
War Dogs
United Colonies
Tommy King
Adm Mannetti
Pirate Auxillaries

# *Second Battle of Nova Roma*

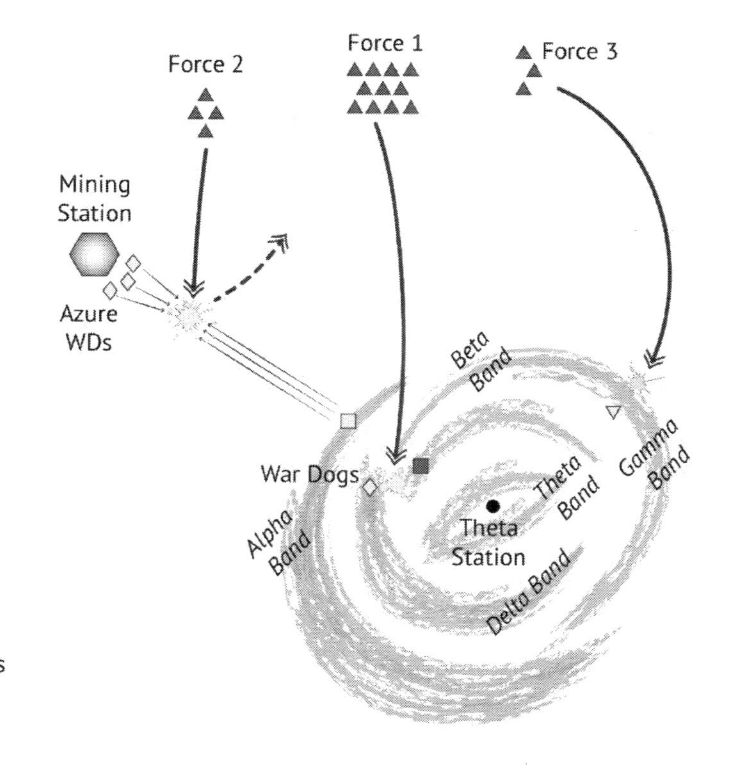

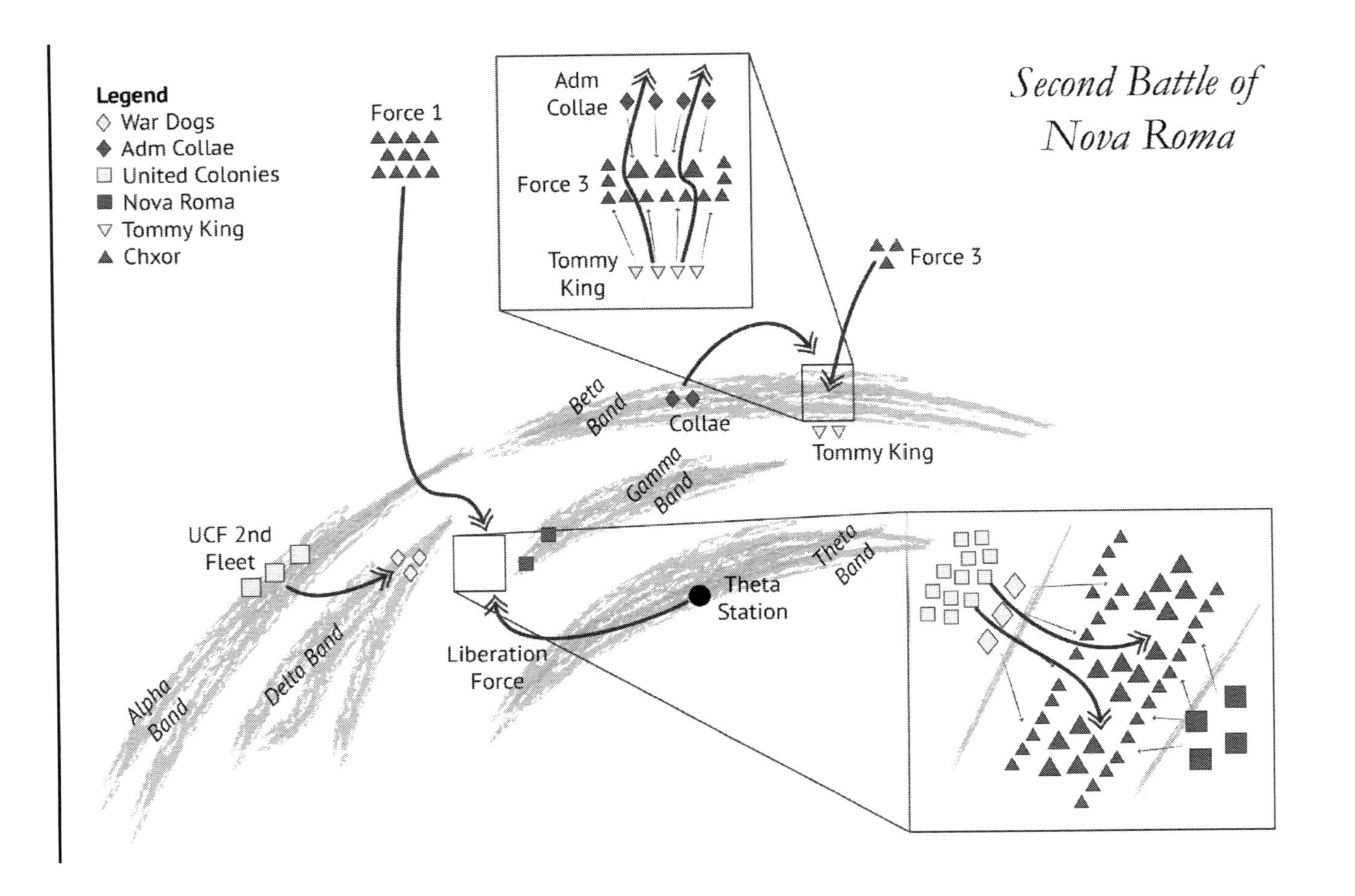

Second Battle of
Nova Roma
Legend
War Dogs
Adm Collae
United Colonies
Nova Roma
Tommy King
Chxor
Force 1
Adm
Collae
Force 3
Tommy
King
Force 3
Beta
Band
Collae
Tommy King
Gamma
Band
UCF 2nd
Fleet
Theta
Band
Theta
Station
Liberation
Force
Alpha
Band
Delta Band

## About the Author

*Kal is science fiction and fantasy author. He's a US Army veteran with deployments to Iraq and Afghanistan as well as an environmental engineer. He lives in Colorado and is married to his wonderful wife (who deserves mention for her patience with his writing). He also shares his home with his infant son, two feline overlords, and a rather put-upon dog. He likes hiking, skiing, and enjoying the outdoors, when he's not hunched over a keyboard writing his next novel.*

Made in the USA
San Bernardino, CA
30 September 2015